THE AUTHORS OF THIS DREAM

THE AUTHORS OF THIS DREAM

EDGE OF THE KNOWN

BOOK ONE

SETH MULLINS

ISBN: 978-1-7352689-7-2 (Paperback)
ISBN: 978-1-7352689-8-9 (eBook)
Library of Congress Control Number: 2020921128

Any references to historical events, real people, or real places are used fictitiously. Names, characters, and places are products of the author's imagination.

Books Fluent
3014 Dauphine Street
New Orleans, LA 70117
booksfluent.com

THE EDGE OF THE PRECIPICE

I suppose you could compare it to driving on a high mountain road. You don't realize how close you are to free fall, or how sheer and far is the plunge, until you go around a bend where one side is exposed to open air, and then there it is—the Abyss.

There's this edge that you can come to—I imagine it's a different place for each of us—and you just know that, once you get swept over it, you won't be coming back. By the time you're close enough to see it, you may already be too late. You could find yourself teetering, suddenly hearing the warnings that life had been giving you all along, knowing that it's become impossible to step back because, by that time, those other forces—the ones pounding like the rapids at your back, always trying to push you towards that edge and then over it—have grown too strong.

Tommy and I first talked about forming a band together before either of us had learned to play an instrument. We both perceived music—particularly its heavy, extreme undersides—as the ideal vehicle for our personal salvation. The first guitar I purchased, a Fender Telecaster that I immediately spray-painted black (to my father's horror), became my refuge. It was my best friend and confidante. It gave me a convenient excuse to avoid social situations that, more often than not, would only remind me of how far off the beaten path I really was—and, oftentimes, would land me in one merciless scrap or another. Instead, I could just sit in my basement room for hours, listening to my various hardcore underground cassettes while trying to trace the riffs I was hearing along the frets of my charcoal-colored axe.

That's how I learned to play so well within just a handful of years. I gave up on the romanticized notion of a normal social life, and focused on practicing and creating. Tommy, meanwhile, picked up the bass. We discovered that we each had halfway decent singing voices as well—at least for the kind of abrasive music we were writing.

If you've followed our band Edge of the Known, even casually via articles and interviews, then you know Tommy's the pontificating and speechifying bass player with the voracious reading habits. Growing up, he read in order to arm himself, like an intellectual duelist. His heroes were the philosophical rebels, the blasphemers and infidels and corruptors of youth, problem children all: Friedrich Nietzsche, Arthur Schopenhauer, Alfred Korzybski, William Burroughs, Arthur Rimbaud, and so on.

Even back in school, he wore his trench coat and black leather cap nearly every day, regardless of the season. He could look imposing in such an outfit, considering that he was over six feet tall by the time he was a sophomore. Oftentimes, he'd tie his long brown hair back. But he didn't advertise his metalhead status as blatantly as I did. Me—I'd deliberately rummage through my dresser to find the T-shirt that was bound to offend the most people that day. Oh, the debates I had with teachers regarding what, exactly, constituted "obscenity"! It's a fine line, I reckon, and one that I was always testing the boundaries of.

When we'd walk side by side through the halls in high school, I felt like I was traveling with a bodyguard. The psychological implications of this grew to be even more significant for me than the physical. Tommy understood my volatility. My perception of the world was unlike that of anyone else I'd ever known; and even if Tommy didn't necessarily share my penchant for seeing and feeling dream phantasms intruding upon the realm of the "real," still he had decided, apparently, to interpret this faculty of mine as a gift rather than a symptom of insanity. I doubt that I ever would have become a musician, or even a relatively stable human being, if not for Tommy's intervention.

He and I couldn't envision ourselves doing anything else with our lives. And this conviction deepened the more we discovered bands that were really baring their souls, defying the veneer of the complacent society all around us and pushing the very contours of rock. Underground music can teach you that there's a place in this world for any possible way of thinking and being, if you're willing to forsake the tried-and-true roads and carve that place out for yourself.

Of course, many of us never felt like we had any other choice. That's why the pantheon of rock 'n' roll is chock-full of misfits. Sure, on the one hand there's the dream. But on the other, there's the persistent thought of "what the hell else am I gonna do?" The true originals could never have fit into society in the first place.

That's what made it such a celebratory experience any time one of us discovered a new and truly great record and brought it home to devour. We were unearthing much more than some tasty riffs and beats and thought-provoking lyrics. The records informed our way of perceiving both the world and our place in it. They lent us new sensations to explore and new dreams to nurture.

Tommy also lived in Sadenport, Oregon, to the south of the Matterpike River, and my house was tucked into a cul-de-sac to the north of it, so St. Christopher's Bridge often served as our meeting place to discuss our visions for our fledgling band and its future. Two years out of high school, we started rehearsing with Tim Peralta on drums. Tim was a heavyset, laid-back, affable dude who always kept his hair in a braid the length of my arm, and sauntered along as if he had all the time in the world to get wherever he was going.

We kept his parents' garage door up so that the rest of his neighborhood could hear our sometimes-aborted efforts to weave our dreams and fantasies into music. Tim's mother, a petite Mexican woman with a warm and ready smile, would bring us coffee and meals of bean and pork burritos with Spanish rice whenever the task of woodshedding new songs led us to neglect lunch or dinner. Since I'd lost my mom just as I'd entered my teen years, I suppose that's why those memories of Mrs. Peralta stick out in my memory so much now.

Tommy had his own personal ideology with regard to the band, and he tried to impress it upon us during nearly every practice session. He was steeped in all kinds of psychological concepts from reading the works of Carl Jung, R.D. Laing, and other writers like that. He'd come to perceive the band as a vehicle through which we could let our "shadow selves" be expressed without inhibition.

He was most especially interested, though, in the myth and lore of the shaman, particularly of Inuit and Native American tribes.

"There's no escaping suffering in our lives," he lectured us. We were jamming on a Saturday, with just a few hours' window before I had to go to work. "That's where so many other philosophies and dogmas get it wrong. In this ephemeral world, we'll grow attached to people and places and experiences that we'll inevitably lose, and it hurts. You have all these religions that try to manage that pain somehow, either promising to make up for it with the rewards of an afterlife, or else telling you to dodge the whole dilemma by becoming egoless, without desires."

"Jesus, Tommy," I moaned. "It's ten in the morning!"

"Don't you even want to know about what makes all the work we're doing worthwhile?" he chided. "The myth of the shaman—well, that and Dionysus— they're the only things I've found that embrace everything instead of trying to deny or control or judge it. Even the pain. Even when it feels unbearable. You work yourself into an ecstatic state—in which everything becomes rapturous."

Tim made a show of good-natured interest. "So how do you get to that state of mind?" He was always a pragmatist at heart. But the initial thought quickly soured for him. "Most bands play sloppy when they're on drugs," he opined. "The sense of timing is all off. It's like they're hearing this music in their heads, and it might sound tremendous, but they don't realize that this isn't what the audience is hearing."

Tim was essentially making the same argument that he would repeat over and over again throughout the months of his tenure with the band: "Why can't we just relax and have fun with it and jam?" He didn't need an underlying philosophy to justify the music. To him, Tommy's interest was tangential and a little obscure. It's obvious, looking back, that the more Tim realized how truly crucial our artistic credo was to us, the more his devotion to the cause wavered.

"It's a perfect fit," Tommy persisted. "These medicine men were the misfits of their time, just like we are, here and now, in America. The vision had to be reached in that way. The shaman separates from the human community for a while, because the healing that he or she is eventually able to offer involves aspects of consciousness that the community lacks—and longs for."

I gave him my best slow and sarcastic drawl. "Alright, why don't you repeat all that...this time in English?"

"The stories of their initiations all follow the same arc," he said. "They usually begin with some circumstance that makes it impossible for the person who would become a shaman to 'lead a normal life'—whatever that might mean in the context of the culture they're living in.

"Alright—plain English. You look at it on the surface and it seems like they were dysfunctional, like they just couldn't fit in. But these people didn't want to fit in. They knew they were in touch with a forward-moving vision, and that's what they'd communicate to the rest of the tribe with their songs and dances and stories: a new vision of reality, one that's potent enough to transform the conditions of life. It's all so close to the ambitions we have for the band."

I'd been aware for a while that we weren't quite mining the gold that Tommy was after, though. During our next rehearsal, he took the opportunity to push me, insisting that I was still "holding back" and disguising my natural voice.

"I'm carrying around some damage, man. Really heavy shit. And I know that you're carrying it too, Brandon. Your old man has been hitting the booze for so long now that he hardly remembers your name, much less when your birthday is. He left you to basically raise yourself and Rachel. That's why you can't leave home and get on with your life; and I know that all the frustration you have around that makes you practically psycho at times. And yet...when you try and write lyrics, you end up with some cartoon Satanism or clichés about corrupt politicians or doomsday.

"Man, you gotta get down to what hits home for you. Right where it hurts. Let your damage out! Put it through your goddamn guitar. Abuse the hell out of that thing if you have to. Find the place inside where something's eating you alive—and then make that your music."

Well, after that sermon I dug down and unearthed the first really great riff I'd ever played. It was mean and primitive, and it succinctly echoed the collective mood in the garage that night. I could tell that the other guys felt it too. Music and dreams can really tear away the fabric that seems to partition off the other worlds from our view. Certain poems and great paintings can do that for me, too. As it was, I'd always had at least one foot in the other world.

There were maybe two or three dozen songs in all creation that could work that alchemy for me, and I held them sacred. Tommy and I aspired to similar heights of inspiration. We never perceived ourselves as mere entertainers.

Tommy sang some snatches of tune over my chord progression. But I was hearing a different melody, one that kept rolling around inside my head as we drove back from that rehearsal. I felt a premonition of words coming to join with the music, and I hoped I'd find some privacy to set them down.

I preferred to be asleep before my father got too heavily into the rum, because by then he usually left me alone. As I came in the door and passed by the kitchen, though, I realized I'd missed my opportunity.

Dad was in his mid-forties by this time. He was an erratic drunk, meaning that he could veer from gregarious and sentimental to vicious and sneering within two or three drinks. Somehow, he'd never learned that when you cross that threshold it isn't artificial bliss anymore. But then, that's the advantage of being the one who is three sheets to the wind: your memories are never clear enough to serve you up the consequences of what you said or did.

I was willing to make myself the target of his abuse if it would deflect it away from my sister, Rachel—or if it meant that I'd be around to steer her out of the room when his rants got off-color and frightening.

I'd tried, countless times, to unearth the reasons behind his quest for oblivion. But the thing is, once you've decided to walk that path, you always find a reason. You drink to celebrate every one of life's victories, and to numb yourself to all of its pains and disappointments just the same. No doubt, this struggle of Dad's worsened after Mom's death. But I can't say for sure that it wouldn't have progressed that way anyway. Ultimately, my old man wanted to live in a numb and insulated space, where there was room for just one person: himself.

Until recently, he hadn't carried much evidence of his self-abuse. His physique had been muscular and toned and his posture had been good, with only the faint suggestion of a paunch showing over his belt. But he softened quickly after a construction accident ruined his back and relegated him, for the most part, to a recliner. That's when he grew more vindictive, too. Feeling useless, he tried to compensate with spite.

That night, luckily, he wasn't in the mood to fight. He was already too far gone. I heard him mumble something about "Devil's music" when he glanced at the T-shirt I was wearing. Then he mustered himself for one coherent half-sentence, "If you'd spent half as much time studying as you did daydreaming about being a goddamn rock star...."

I just sucked it up, silently. If I'd bothered to bleed every time my father's words cut me, I would've died a long time before. Back then, the ambiance was sunnier inside a morgue than it was in any room occupied by the two of us alone. I turned and escaped down the basement stairs.

It always smelled like mildew in my room; it was bred into the hard, green carpet and the rectangular space was as dim as a dungeon even with both lamps turned on. All of this suited me fine, as it meant that I was the only one who ever enjoyed being down there.

I retrieved a battered notebook that had originally been intended for homework and began scrawling lyrics as they came to me. The melody was still humming inside my head. It sounded more poignant now, but I shoved that feeling aside and tried to focus on my anger.

The theme would be a recurring one for me, back then: projection and blame. I aimed my ire at what I thought of as this malignant presence that wanted to hold me back, and keep me from becoming the man that I was desperately fighting to be. It spoke in the voices of teachers, authority figures, television personalities, and politicians from throughout my life—anyone who'd tried to tell me what life was all about, instead of letting me figure it out for myself. I hated that voice, and I set about crucifying it in my new song.

I entitled this crude and rudimentary piece "The Tyrant."

At some point during my creative struggle, I heard the carpet rustle and looked up to see Rachel standing maybe ten feet in front of me. She was barely six years old at the time. Her hair was still reddish and curled, and she had dozens of cinnamon freckles. She was wearing her favorite yellow pajamas, embroidered with a design of two elephants passing a beach ball back and forth with their trunks. I don't know how long she'd been watching me.

"What are you doing up?" I asked her. "It's late." This was more chiding than reprimanding. Rachel received the softest side of me, always.

She shrugged—a touch dramatically. "I couldn't sleep. I saw the lights on down here."

"Did Dad see you?"

"He's sleeping."

Somehow, Rachel already understood that our father was not someone who she could go to, that he was not really available. She always came to me.

She gripped her pajamas and began twisting from side to side like a little gymnast warming up. "What are you doing?" she asked.

I waved the lyric sheet that I'd torn out of my notebook. "Writing a song."

She stopped and straightened, smiling impishly. "Does it go like this?" Then she proceeded with a string of coughing and growling sounds, ending with a high-pitched squeal of delight.

I laughed too. I may be biased, but she was, without a doubt, the most adorable and precocious little girl on Earth. And she'd obviously heard me playing my records a few times. "Something like that. And you sing it better than I do, so maybe I'll have to take you out on the road with me. But right now you should get to bed. It's a school night, you know. Come on—I'll walk you up and tuck you in."

❖

Within our band, we were trying to reject it all, everything that had been instilled in us, so that we could expose our real selves to the world—even the dark, ugly aspects that most people didn't want to admit the existence of. Gradually, the music emerging from our rehearsals grew more and more congruent with the sounds that Tommy and I were hearing in our heads. I gave myself over to the voices inside that were clamoring for release.

In April, a week after my twentieth birthday, the three of us pooled our money and secured ten hours of recording time at Ambergris Studios. We were able to commit all of our songs to a master with almost an hour to spare, so tight and exuberant in our practice we'd become by that point. Tim was doing odd landscaping jobs, Tommy delivered pizza, and I bussed tables at a steakhouse called Jaspar's. But we all devoted whatever time we could spare to shopping our demo around town. By the end of the month, we'd landed our first gig.

For me, music always consisted of more than mere sounds and the images and wild flights that they aroused in my mind—as galvanizing as all of that was. Great music also created this place where freaks could congregate, where taboos could be explored (or, at the very least, dragged into the light and talked about), and where all your mad visions could be channeled into a medium that even our crass materialistic culture knew how to validate and reward.

I figured that a poet in our age didn't need to starve in obscurity, misunderstood and forsaken. He or she could become a rock star: adored, embraced by the world, buffered by money and all other manner of material satisfactions. If one could only manage that ascent to the mountaintop....

Sadenport, Oregon, was an ideal place to abet such fantasies. It had some killer record stores, places where you'd be richly rewarded for your patience. But you had to take your time and sift through everything. The owners and staff didn't always know where to shelve certain bands. Some stores weren't even organized according to category to begin with. You'd walk into a long, dimly lit room with everything asprawl, tables weighed down with vinyl that was stuffed into cardboard boxes or plastic crates. Oftentimes, you'd come across names you didn't recognize, and you'd refer to the cover and the photos of the bands for clues as to what sort of music might lie therein. There were days I'd go in with a list of things in my head to search for, and I'd leave the store with an armload of unexpected finds instead.

This was before the rise of Visionary Chapbook and similar "underground" publications, so you often had to rely upon the word on the streets. I'd stop guys on sidewalks if they were wearing shirts of bands I'd never heard of. I liked a lot of older rock—the darlings of the Baby Boomer generation, for example—and it was easier to learn about those records because they were referred to in prominent magazines. Getting hip to anything current that carried a comparable degree of passion and innovation was more challenging. Most of the popular, heavy-airwaves fare was insipid and vacuous to my ears. The awareness that there was a viable and energetic alternative to all of this awoke in me slowly. I was too young to go out to the local clubs, and few people in my school shared my taste for raucous, anti-establishment sounds.

This is the most significant reason why Tommy and I, from the earliest days of our band's conception, vowed to play as many all-ages shows as we possibly could. We perceived it as one of the chief liabilities of the music scene in general that the largest record-buying demographic is too young to frequent the places where all the struggling bands are playing. It hits upon a conundrum that can drive any creator mad, regardless of his or her medium. Deep down, you just know that there are thousands of people (maybe millions) who crave what it is that you're offering, at least in the privacy of their secret hearts. But you resign yourself to the reality that you don't know how to reach them; and the people you do reach couldn't care less.

So Tommy won over the owner of the Samurai, a tavern near the wharves on the south end, and landed a date at an all-ages show in the warehouse adjacent to it. Two other acts were on the bill, but the owner had been impressed enough by our demo to offer us the coveted closing spot. He was a metalhead from way back.

"It's time we unleashed it," Tommy told Tim and me. "Make 'em exhilarated. Make 'em scared. They might not know why they like us. They may even think that they hate us. But they'll be confronted by something within themselves when they hear our performance. These deeper forces, the stuff that people usually tamp down on…when they're given an outlet, everyone recognizes it in their gut. They see their own reflection swirling around in the dark epicenter of the music. All of the truly great performers have tapped into that. But I think we're taking it farther than anyone's dared to go before."

If you befriended Tommy, then you had to grow accustomed to such speeches. But, at the time, I shared his belief. We'd conjured up some primal and powerful forces within our songs. They were shocking, confrontational, rebellious, frightening…and yet poignant, for all of that. And they had altered us—in ways that we were just beginning to understand.

My father caught wind of our upcoming gig and used it as a fresh excuse to revile me about my choices, my goals, and my whole path in life. He smacked me around a few times when he was drunk and apologized for it later when he was sober, if he remembered.

I just held on to all my frustration, rage, and confusion and then screamed it out through my guitar at our next rehearsal.

The night before our performance, I fell into another one of the black moods that had been hounding me for years. These nihilistic spells had only grown worse since Mom died. Now, I was gripped by the idea that going for broke onstage was my sole alternative to self-destruction. For me, as a teenager and twenty-something, life in this world as we knew it was soul-dead. And life without the soul had always lent a kind of obvious and simple logic to the idea of suicide. If there's no place here for what I feel, perceive, dream of, and long for—then I'm bound to have better luck elsewhere. And I'm sorry that I have to hurt you, precious body, to get there. It's necessary…I don't know any other way. I guess I'll never know what your promise was....

I was fighting a surge of tears, and at the same time trying to drive the memories away. There was always that little voice among the multitudes in those moments, a voice that cannot and will not give up on the promise of life: the beauty, the love, the hope that insists, "Just give me one more moment, and maybe I can show you how it all can be different." That voice would soon find an ally in

15

Saul Mason, the man who would teach me that there is no such thing as a hopeless life situation. For the moment, though, I was alone with the consuming darkness.

When Tommy came to pick me up the following afternoon in the gray van that the three of us had chipped in to buy together, I packed my gear into the back without saying a word. Rachel watched from the window. Sensing her presence just made the emptiness inside me gape even wider.

We'd grown attached to our own equipment and therefore didn't care to use the venue's PA. It takes time to learn how to coax the precise sounds that you want out of the gear you've got, and you don't want to be starting that process from scratch while you're onstage and the audience is watching. We left everything in the van and waited for our hour to come. Our nerves were tuned to a high pitch.

The warehouse was the size of an average school gymnasium, and the sound system couldn't quite fill the space. I doubted that our setup would do much better. There were about thirty people milling about when we arrived, and that number probably doubled by nightfall. Heavy metal kids, punks, middle-aged guys who looked like they'd been frequenting shows since before I was born. We didn't mingle, and I didn't care for either of the bands that went on before us. Their derivative sound reminded me of how hard we'd worked to create something uniquely our own, so I resented how the audience just ate up their pallid imitations.

Disgusted, I went outside to smoke. There were people all around, leaning against their cars, passing around beers and joints. I had to walk for a while to get away from the laughter and the chatter. The moon over the river was no doubt beautiful, but the sight of it didn't touch me. I ambled towards the water anyway.

Then something collided with my side, almost knocking me off balance.

He'd crashed right into me. Whether it'd been deliberate, or whether he'd just been too drunk to notice me coming, I don't know. I was more captivated by the dark landscapes yawning hungrily in my head than I had been by my surroundings.

"Watch it, huh!"

He shoved me with both hands. And this time I did go down, my ass kissing gravel and sand. I glared up at him. He was a thin, wiry guy—no taller than me, though he was probably twice as old. He was dressed in boots, tight and faded jeans, checkered flannel, and a cowboy hat. He muttered some ugly, derisive remark and started stumbling away, lost in a world of his own drunken making. But I didn't let him go.

It amazed me how easily I took him down. He just crumbled like a wilted flower when I laid hands on him. Miraculously, his hat stayed on his head and his bottle of beer remained in his hand. He stared up, not so much at me but more toward the sky. He just looked dimly surprised to find himself on the ground with someone hovering over him.

That's when the madness took hold of me: madness and exhilaration, indistinguishable. I'd been powerless my whole life. Everything was always spinning beyond my control. But not now! I had this bastard in my hands and there wasn't a goddamn thing he could do about it. I landed a few punches to his face, registered his hollow grunts, but that didn't satisfy me. I wrested the beer bottle from his grip and broke it over a rock that lay near where we were struggling.

It came back mean, jagged, and dripping—a V-shaped gash the size of my thumb lending it a sinister crown. Inebriated as he was, this man knew his peril now. He started panting. His fear must have sapped the last vestiges of strength from his muscles, though, because I was able to pin his arms together at the wrists with my left hand. Then I pressed the twin points of the broken bottle against the soft of his neck.

I'll never know how far I planned to go. Had I just intended to scare him, or had I really meant to bring my life's long despair to its logical culmination?

Tommy's voice reached me as if from another world.

"Whoa, Brandon. Hey…easy. Put it down, man."

Tommy, the one guy who could reach me…. He was hovering off somewhere to my right. But he and the man beneath me, they both scarcely existed.

"This isn't what it's about. It's having power over your own life. Not throwing it away—or taking it from somebody else."

I'd begun to shake. I was close to weeping.

"Let him go, Brandon. He ain't the Tyrant."

That word brought me back to my surroundings. It led my memory back to that night months before, when I'd written my first proper song and Rachel had dropped in on me unexpectedly. She'd made me laugh as if nothing else in the world even mattered. I'd experienced so many moments like that with her, and it was as if I was remembering them all for the first time.

"Jesus!" I relinquished my grip, flung the bottle, and stood up. The world lurched sideways like a ship about to capsize. "I'm gonna be sick, man!"

I ran to the water's edge and knelt just in time to empty my stomach. I spat several times, reaching for purgation. Sometime later, I felt Tommy's hand on my shoulder.

"Where is he?" I managed.

"He stumbled off somewheres. My guess is he'll be passed out real quick. He ain't gonna remember. Hell, he hardly seemed to realize what was happening as it was."

Tommy had said enough; but maybe he felt obliged to add more when I didn't reply.

"Look, we both know it wouldn't have gone any farther. You ain't a killer. No one else was close enough to see what went down. And you know nobody's gonna hear anything from me."

I stood up, but had to brace myself with my hands on my knees. I was shaking all over. "I still want to play," I finally muttered.

The way Tommy hesitated told me that he harbored serious doubts about that idea. But I knew that it was the best thing for me to do: keep moving.

"Well, we're on in half an hour or so. We'll have to get set up. Dream Screamers are playing now. They sound like watered-down Makoshark."

I grinned for the first time in days. "Good. Maybe people will be ready for something real by the time we get up on that stage."

TANGLED THREADS

I was too shook up to really pay much attention to what I was doing onstage. I pulled it off simply because we'd practiced those songs so much that they'd become a part of my bodily memory. If not for Tommy's presence, I doubt I could've gone through with it.

The gig was significant, though, despite all its flaws. Not only was it our first performance, it was the first time we appeared under the name that most of the civilized world would come to know: Edge of the Known.

One morning, after I saw Rachel off to the bus, I drove over to Tommy's house. His parents were separated and he stayed with his mom. She worked at home a lot, handling the billing for Cashau Hospital. "Harassing people who'll never be able to settle up no matter how much you threaten them," was how Tommy described her job. But Miss Visconti was always real cool with me. She was fairly attractive, I guess—slim, with curly black hair—but with an all-business demeanor that disguised her native beauty. She also had an annoying habit of asking you questions like how you were doing and then rushing on to something else before you had a chance to respond. This made me feel like she wasn't too concerned one way or the other. But, I have to credit her for tolerating my living at her house more often than at my own.

She rented a condominium in the complex over on Baird Street. It was always hard for me to relax in places so clean. Miss Visconti probably vacuumed that beige carpet, which covered every inch of the floor space save for the kitchen, on a daily basis.

Fortunately, Tommy had done the same as me and claimed the basement for his living space. And he'd made it clear that she didn't ever need to "tidy" it. The walls were covered with silken tapestries, replete with all kinds of medieval imagery, which lit up garishly beneath the black light. Tommy had spent all the money he'd earned, from his first year of being the pizza delivery guy, on his waterbed and the pool table that dominated the center of the room.

It was there that the first conversations occurred, that the first fantasies regarding our intended band were hatched.

"Alright, then—who do you like?"

I reeled off a list of names: Acidhartha, Infidel Tabernacle, Foment Revolt, King Brunette....

We quickly realized that we were dissatisfied with our initial name, Crave Oblivion. It had too narrow of a focus. So that afternoon, a day where neither of us were scheduled to work, Tommy and I revived our discussion about our possible new identity.

I'd always been intrigued by the name of one of my favorite restaurants down by the campus area: The Pioneer. Was this not my most secretly cherished ideal, to become a kind of musical pioneer? And yet I longed to do more than simply invent a new style of music and a fresh lyrical approach.

"I want to use the music to explore the frontiers of consciousness," I told Tommy.

"To break through the artificial barriers that our self-conceptions create, and lay bare that virgin territory of the mind!" he gushed. "Yes! Unearth the untapped potentials that have lain latent within our race for as long as we've walked the Earth!"

I'm not making this up. He really talked like that.

"Yeah," I said. "I'd like for the name to have something of the frontier, the frontiers of consciousness, in it."

"Or maybe 'the edge,' for simplicity's sake," he offered. "Like the edges of madness or breakthrough." This was how we got rolling on a good day.

"The very edge of what is known," I added, "beyond which is the unknown."

I could tell, by the way that Tommy's face lit up, he was excited by this new direction. The guy couldn't fake enthusiasm to save his life.

"What about 'The Spiritual Edge'?"

I wasn't so taken by this. "'Spiritual' is such a loaded word."

"Hmm…'metaphysical' or 'psychic' would carry the same meaning, but those words are even more ponderous," Tommy considered.

We eventually settled on "Edge of the Known." This was a longer name than either of us had wanted, but none of the shorter versions that we came up with conveyed the concept as well. No one else was bound to have that name, anyway, so it worked on a pragmatic level at the least. I imagined that it would look good up on a marquee—a premonition of what the audience was in for: a trip beyond the comfortable confines of their familiar reality where everything unfolded as expected and inevitably resulted in stagnation.

Things would never be stale within our band because we would always be out there on that edge, probing its limits and pushing its boundaries and reflecting what we found there in our music and lyrics, so that the people who listened to us could grow familiar with all of its strange territory.

After that first performance, I met a girl named Kelly. She was wearing a single-piece blue dress, cut low in the back so you could see her swirling trail of butterfly tattoos. She had long auburn hair, and pretty—and mischievous—brown eyes. There's something about a girl who's bold, and yet still a little shy, that really entices me. She told me our band sounded good, but that I looked like I needed to loosen up a little.

"What do you mean by that?" I snapped. Because you get off a stage, man, and you feel like a god—especially if you played well. I wasn't prepared for such a sobering remark.

"Let's go into the bathroom and I'll show ya," she said.

Well, I really had no idea what to expect. Perhaps I was about to get laid? There was nothing to do but follow her, really.

Both of the bathrooms that had been added to the warehouse in order to make it a "suitable performance space" featured single toilet stalls, so we went into the ladies' room. Kelly locked the door. Then she pulled a black film canister out of her purse. Her air of ceremony and expectation told me that there was something more potent than weed inside. Kelly ripped off a bit of paper towel from the dispenser and wiped the rim of the sink dry.

"You ever done coke before?"

I hadn't. But a friend had once described his experience to me: losing sensation in his lips, nostrils, and even parts of his cheeks: numbness. I could use some of that. I shook my head, but moved closer to her to indicate my willingness.

That first snort…man…you tilt your head back and suddenly it feels like a tremendous burden has been lifted from the whole cosmos. This was probably the closest I'd ever come to ecstasy. As if my inner plentitude needed further encouragement, Kelly leaned in for a quick kiss before cutting herself a line.

We were using a cut-off piece of a red cocktail straw that she'd kept in the canister. After the second blast, I felt ready to run around the block several times. Someone rapped hard on the door and we just looked at each other and, after a pause, laughed in unison. I stumbled back against the yellow wall and let out a long, exultant sigh.

Somehow, it all hit me then—the full weight of what had occurred outside. My wall of numbness was ripped away and the reality penetrated my brain like a spear thrust between my eyes. Then my knees lost their battle against gravity, and I crashed down beside the plastic trash receptacle amongst the crumpled balls of paper towel that had missed their target. I hid behind my hands so that Kelly wouldn't witness the contortions of incomprehension and anguish twisting my face.

"I am not a killer!" I ranted, as if contradicting an omniscient judge who was hovering somewhere above me.

"Who said you were?" Kelly's voice was suddenly cold. "God, I wouldn't have given it to you if I knew it was gonna fuck you up like this."

I could tell that she wanted to leave. But some lingering compassion, or maybe guilt, constrained her. So I cut her loose by making a perfunctory wave towards the door, still shielding as much of my face as I could with my other hand. With a huff of disappointment and offended pride, Kelly shot out of the room.

A moment later, a blonde girl rushed in, froze, let out a hiss of alarm at seeing me crumpled on the floor, and darted back out. I couldn't stay here forever, obviously. Finally I thought, to hell with it if I go out there with the telltale marks of wet and reddened eyes. There were worse fates.

Like just having killed a man, and weathering that aftermath.

Deep down, I knew I was in trouble. I wasn't stupid, even back then. All the signs and omens were pointing down a black alley with a precipice at its end. It was as if my life was a river hemmed in on both sides by high granite cliffs, and pulled by gravity so that it had no recourse but to plunge over the falls.

Usually I liked to sort through the tangled threads of extremity when I was alone with my thoughts. Unfortunately, the coke was still working in me throughout the ride home, and that made me unusually talkative. I'd told Tim and Tommy that I was in no shape to drive the van, so Tim had taken the wheel. A silly mood overtook me at first. Probably, it was an instinctive defense against the sense of horror that I had smothered, at least temporarily. Fresh from a good gig, you can feel invincible. The other guys were feeling it, too, which was probably why they didn't get as irritated with me as they might have on other occasions. Both of them were envisioning possibilities now. Our band was no longer an abstract idea in our collective minds consigned to the rehearsal space.

"I can't face my father like this," I blurted suddenly.

My mood swings could be dramatic, even under normal conditions, when they weren't being abetted by a hard drug notorious for provoking that sort of thing. After a moment's silence, the guys each, in turn, offered me a couch to sleep on for the night.

"What about Rachel, though?"

I couldn't disentangle it. It was as if I'd never peered into the fragility, the heart-wrenching hopelessness, of my home life before. I was meandering into a paranoid phase of my high. It snagged all my thoughts between opposing fears: fear of my father, and fear for Rachel alone with no one to look after her except him. I'd been stalemated by this particular psychic tug-of-war before, though, and my concern for my kid sister usually won out in the end.

"Drop me off at home," I insisted to no one in particular. "If he's up, I'll deal with it."

A moment later, Tommy told Tim, "Just take him home," as if he was the final arbitrator. But I bit down on my irritation. After all, this night could've taken a much darker turn if not for Tommy's intervention.

Ahhh…the advent of our first performance, the culmination of so much rehearsing and soul exploration and dreaming, deserved a much more celebratory end than this. But, as we turned into my cul-de-sac, I felt like those dreams had been living inside a gigantic urn that was suddenly turned upside down, pitching them into blackness. The sensation made me itch for another fight.

I paused with my hand on the door handle. "This was just the beginning of things, guys. I've just been finding my feet. I'm gonna take it so much deeper. We all are."

Gregarious Tim just nodded and smiled. But Tommy leveled his censuring eyes on me. "I know you've got it in you, Brandon. But you can't accomplish anything unless you keep yourself alive first, right?"

Everyone knows the simple solutions to problems that are not their own, I thought.

"The music could last forever, Tommy. That's what counts."

I stepped out into the night, staggered by the many emotional blows that had been dealt me, and I braced myself for one more—perhaps the worst of the lot. But grace decided to smile upon me at last. My old man was passed out on the recliner and all the lights were out. I tiptoed by him, heading for the basement. Then an obscure impulse turned me around. I climbed the stairs and crept into Rachel's room.

I wouldn't be able to unwind enough to sleep for a few more hours anyway. And I'd done this before, so I knew she wouldn't be too startled in the morning. I grabbed some of her discarded clothes to make a pillow and stretched out on the carpeted floor beside her bed, right where I could hear her light snoring. She shifted at once, as if some part of her acknowledged my presence.

My imagination drifted back to the fight by the river and the hideous sweep of my own rage. I remembered how my thoughts of Rachel had helped to bring me back to myself. "You don't realize it, kiddo," I whispered, "but you might've saved my life tonight—along with someone else's."

SAUL

My brief flirtation with the occult occurred around this time.

I've mentioned that Tommy and I were united in our philosophy with regard to the band, from the very earliest days of its inception. It was to be an outlet for everything inside of us, particularly those dark and ugly feelings and impulses that society preferred not to see—that it denied the existence of.

But I wasn't satisfied at first. See, when you aren't healed inside, then none of your accomplishments can really touch you deep down where it counts. Nothing is ever enough. So that's when I started wondering whether there were deeper depths to plunge to.

Reality was just not a tolerable place for me. Our songs had helped me to carve out a sanctuary; but that only took me so far. If our music was really going to salvage my life from unending penury, from forever reciting a soulless script within a system that I despised amongst people who could neither understand nor accept me, then it needed to somehow become a much more powerful force. It needed more than what we could lend to it. I really believed that at the time.

One day that June, I was talking to Rachel shortly before her seventh birthday.

"Alright, listen to me: If Dad finds these packages, then I'm really gonna catch hell. And I won't always be around to check for them. Now, you know there's times when he's not paying attention to you, like when you go into the basement to watch TV and he never even realizes you're gone."

I felt guilty about laying this on her; but I didn't have much choice. Facing my old man, trying to explain my interest in books on black magic and an assortment of esoteric items intended for use in conjuration…well, a scenario like that just couldn't lead to any kind of positive outcome.

"Could you do me a favor and just sneak out some of those times when he's not watching, and check the mailbox? Bigger stuff might be on the steps, or leaning against the door, too."

I was still living at home because of her. Sure, I could say I'd spent most of my savings on equipment and the cost of our demo. Truth is, though, I could've easily picked up extra shifts if I'd wanted to earn enough to cover rent and a security deposit for my own place. But what would happen to her? Rachel was thirteen years younger than me. Our mom had died before she was even two and Dad was too drunk, most nights, to ensure that she even brushed her teeth and got into bed. And he was too hung over in the mornings (if he was even conscious) to make her breakfast or see her off to the school bus. I was Rachel's father, basically. If the band ever took off, then I was gonna use the first bit of money we made to fight for custody of her.

I figured the only reason I hadn't been kicked out yet was that my father just didn't possess the presence of mind to conceive of the idea, and hold onto it for long enough to actually follow through. Whenever he said anything along those lines, I just assumed he'd forget about it the next day, which invariably proved true.

Rachel looked a little nervous, but she just nodded her head. "What kind of stuff is it?" she asked. "Why would Daddy get mad?"

"They're books, mostly."

Whenever she grinned, there was a sparkle in her eyes that suggested she understood more than she ever let on to anybody. "Do they have lots of swear words and pictures of naked people?"

Back then, she was the only person in the world who could make me laugh—seriously. I tried my best to compose myself and impress upon her the gravity of the situation, but I about had to bite my tongue off to do it. "Nothing like that.

Just things he doesn't want me learning about. You know how he gets. So…is it a deal?"

Fortunately, most kids possess the innate desire to be in on a conspiracy. After thinking it over a moment longer, Rachel smiled and slapped me five to seal the deal.

❖

Tommy called me later that night. "There's gonna be some changes, Brandon. We can't practice at Tim's anymore. They've been getting too many neighbor complaints about the noise. Besides, he's been itching to find a place to live with his girlfriend."

Tommy knew me well enough to interpret my silence as a sign of distress.

"Anyways," he assured me, "I think I found us another place to rehearse."

He had this gift for making his way in the world and connecting with just the right person at the right time. Without that unerring instinct, I doubt that anyone would've ever heard our music.

"I made a delivery to Townes Street yesterday," he went on. "Towards its far end, where you're getting to Sadenport limits. The guy's name is Saul Mason. I pulled up to his house—looks like a sturdy little shanty from the days of the Gold Rush, seriously—and his yard is littered with scrap iron and car and Jeep parts; just, like, disemboweled and left on the lawn.

"Anyway, I brought him and his wife their pizza and…Saul's like this quietly intense guy. He managed to keep me there a while. Talked just enough to keep me talking, and before I know it, I'm tellin' him about our band. He really liked the name and was asking me what it means to us. He even got me to recite a few lyrics. And then, right there, he offers us the use of his basement any time we want."

"Seriously?" I was incredulous. Surely, he'd change his mind once he actually heard us.

I could sense Tommy's grin over the phone. "He said, and I quote: 'If you guys are trying to sound like yourselves and no one else, then I'm sure I'll like it— no matter what genre tag you may want to slap on it.'"

"Well, hopefully he means it," I said, still feeling only half-convinced.

❖

The first package to arrive at my house included *The Lesser Key of Solomon*, *Goetia*, *Abremalin*, and a couple of tomes that were even more obscure. Rachel found the box first and hid it under my bed for me. Then I drove her to Magpies and rewarded her with a double fudge sundae.

The black mirror and invocation mat that I'd ordered online followed soon after. By the end of the week, I'd collected everything I believed I needed in order to pierce the veil between the worlds and usher in the means of my personal salvation.

I probably would not have pursued my occult studies and practices as far as I did, had I shared my ambitions and secret hopes with anyone else. But I knew that Tommy wouldn't approve. He scarcely condoned supernatural references in our lyrics, and had long tried to steer me away from my interest in the subject.

I just couldn't accept the world as it was. There was too much suffering and confusion—and too little triumph. Futility seemed to define the human race, and this was evidenced by its inability to transcend the weaknesses that had plagued it for as long as it had been on the planet. Some other agency was needed. God? Ha! Churches had been around since the very dawn of our civilization, and what had they ever accomplished? When had their God ever intervened on our behalf? No—if salvation was to be attained, it would be through the aid of those other forces, the ones that humankind shunned and feared.

And if I was going to die, or go mad in my attempts to contact those forces, then so be it.

Beyond the boundaries of this world, that's where the great artists, writers, and musicians—the truly eternal ones—reaped their inspiration. And the powers from beyond also wrought their fame. I was convinced of that. I was willing to forsake reason and safety in order to follow in their footsteps. Physical reality was not enough. There had to be something more to Creation; and I knew of only one way to search for it.

We arrived for our first rehearsal at Saul's house just as the sun was setting behind the bare hills on the edge of his property. His homestead was simple, just as Tommy had described it: a tin roof with a steep pitch set atop a square shanty that was painted mud brown. The barn behind it was nearly as big as the main floor of the house. Tommy had brought along a gift: two boxes full of assorted unsold pizzas. We let Tim, the most affable of us (and the least threatening in appearance), step up to the door and knock.

Saul was a little shy of six feet tall, rugged, with a trim mustache and beard. Jeans and a dark, short-sleeved button shirt clung to his brawny frame. He paid scarce attention to the metal regalia—spiked bracelets, studded leather belts, dangling earrings, and lurid band T-shirts—that Tommy and I wore. He was more intent on making eye contact. When he finally nodded to himself, I felt like I'd passed some sort of initiation.

Introductions were made all around. Then Saul led us out to the barn, which was painted the same muddy color as his house. The coat of paint looked relatively new, though—only a year or two old, I guessed. On the right side of the building, a stone stairwell plunged steep below the ground level.

"The previous owner was really paranoid about Armageddon, apparently," Saul said, "so he had this shelter built down below. The space was packed with canned food, sacks of grain, shotguns, and literally a barrel full of shells. That's how rumor has it, anyway. After he died, his surviving relatives cleaned it out. It was all empty when I bought the place. Like I said, you guys are welcome to play here whenever—so long as it's not real, real late. I have no need for the space."

We all murmured our gratitude as he led us down the steps. The stairs ended at a heavy iron door that was painted red. I felt like we were about to break into an abandoned government facility, maybe experience the aftermath of some chemical or biological experiment gone awry. Saul showed us where the key was hidden behind one loose brick in the stairwell. Then we entered what we came to call "the Catacombs."

The lights scarcely illuminated the space. All of us had to duck to move beneath the ceiling beams. A tiny cubicle with a small window was closed off to the left. I saw that the room had once been utilized for storing coal. A couple inches of it still carpeted the floor. At the end of the space, and to the right, sat an old rusted boiler. The cement floor was uneven and cracked in places.

"Do you mind if we do some things to soundproof it, Saul?" Tommy asked. "Like maybe glue egg cartons to the walls?"

"Knock yourselves out," he said with a smile.

Tim was grinning as he scanned the tight little bunker. "You guys are gonna kill yourselves if you jump around and headbang down here," he said.

"If your drumming doesn't bring the ceiling down on us first," I returned cheekily.

I was already growing acclimated to the place. Sure, we had a lot of work ahead of us to make it soundproof and habitable. But I'd rather put in the grunt work myself—and personalize the space in the process—than rent a rehearsal room in a complex where we'd be hearing other bands to both sides of us. Besides, the atmosphere here seemed more conducive to creativity. I could almost feel the desperation of the man who had lived here before Saul, the vivid visions of catastrophe that must have driven him to build this refuge. Also, there was something about being underground, among the roots of the world and beneath its surface hysterias—the relentless chase after things that can never be captured— that soothed me. I nodded in response to my own monologue.

"Thanks so much, Saul." My voice was just swallowed up by the stone.

We chatted for a few more minutes and then Saul left us alone. We retrieved our gear and set up. For the first hour or so, we ran through our established numbers. Before woodshedding new material, we called break so that Tommy could smoke, Tim could catch his breath, and I could make a trip to the outhouse.

My head was still subsumed in the music, so I nearly ran into Saul on the way over. Something in his expression told me to stop. There wasn't much sunlight left by now, and he seemed larger—ominous, even—in the shadows.

"You guys play and sing like your lives depend on it," he remarked. I detected no condescension whatsoever in his voice. "Any of those songs yours?"

"A few," I said, feeling suddenly grateful for the opportunity to talk about it. "It's kind of a new outlet for me. I'm really just starting to get the hang of writing."

His gaze sharpened, and for the second time that night I got the impression that he was weighing me, somehow.

"Some people—well, a lot of people, really—never own their own pain. Others let it run their whole lives. You're trying to use yours as fuel. I'd say that's the wisest of the three options."

His kindness, his recognition of what I was struggling through, lent me the courage I'd been looking for. "Listen, Saul, I wanted to ask a favor. It's just that…there's times when the other guys can't meet for practice and I still feel like working on music. But it's not the same at home. A rehearsal space…once you play there a while…you generate a certain atmosphere within the place. It's really conducive to songwriting, at least for me. Anyway, would you mind if I came by myself occasionally and jammed in there?"

After his magnanimous display of generosity, I took advantage of him like that. My duplicity sickened me. But I was desperate. The ritual I had in mind was sophisticated and lengthy. Trying to pull it off at home, with the possibility of my father stumbling in at any conceivable stage of stupor, and of Rachel being exposed to it, was out of the question.

Now, more than ever, I felt exposed to Saul's gaze: as if he was capable of stripping my layers off one by one until he uncovered my secret motives. But he just nodded.

"That sounds fine."

I told my father that I was considering moving into a shared rental space on Mercy Street, and that I would be spending the night there to try it out. I told

Tommy not to call me because I was sick. Rachel was the only one who got any semblance of the truth out of me.

"You know the story I read to you one time—Arabian Nights?" I asked her.

I was tucking her into bed—wet, freshly shampooed hair and all. She just watched me, waiting. The trust in her eyes, the unabashed love, made me wish, at least for a flickering moment, that there could be some other answer to the cruel riddle of my existence.

"Well, there are real genies in this world; and if you know how to call them up they really do grant wishes."

Rachel was always quick with pragmatic concerns. "How come I've never seen one?"

"Well, that's why I got those books. It takes a lot of preparation. There's words you've got to know, and you've got to say 'em just right and concentrate real hard. Because they come from another place. They don't live here, usually."

"Are they good?" Another pertinent question.

"I'm willing to bet that they are. And if I get my wishes, then you won't be having to get yourself ready for school anymore when I'm not here. And our dad will get the help he needs. And—" I tapped her nose, "the next time you see me playing guitar it'll be on TV."

She was really tired. "I hope they are good," she murmured. A moment later she was asleep.

My father was unconscious, too, in the recliner downstairs. I had to sneak past him twice in order to get all my paraphernalia into my car, a tiny blue-gray two-door, well beyond its prime. But he snored soundly the whole time.

I studiously obeyed the speed limit all the way to Saul's property, as if I was carrying contraband and didn't want to draw attention. I made my way across his yard by candlelight. Having subsisted on nothing but bread and water for the past few days (a passage I'd read had recommended this as a preparatory ritual), I was weak and shaky. But my will had been sharpened to a perilous edge. My nerves were attuned to vibrations from the other world. I didn't go to the shelter. I felt safer in the barn itself, which I knew was never locked. Saul didn't use it, and the space contained little more than the debris left behind from former wood piles. I stepped inside, unrolled my mat, and set down my mirror, candles, and books with a kind of fatalistic calm.

The incantations are no joke. They really alter your consciousness in a profound way. After I'd repeated a certain passage a few times, my surroundings disappeared. The candles burned inside my mind. The whole universe seemed to exist right there: there was no "outside."

Then I started reading from the Invocations of Aziel, which are expressly forbidden by the very book within which they appear. But these were simple incantations—meaning convenient for me, as no precious metals or virgin's blood was required—and they were intended to evoke a mighty entity that had been worshipped in the days of Sumer's infancy. The circle I drew in white chalk over the dusty floorboards was supposed to protect me from anything that was summoned during the ritual. Aziel would be under my control. But why—I considered this during a moment of madness, it seems—should he submit to my domination? He was native to dimensions that surpassed ours in every realm of endeavor; his was the superior wisdom, knowledge, and might. Better that he seize control of me.

Maybe a part of me hoped that I'd perish in the ritual. It's hard for me to account for my recklessness in any other way. *Take my hands, use my voice—make me your instrument!* This prayer swept through my consciousness like fever. The candles flickered wildly. The atmosphere within the barn had been roused like a disturbed beehive. I felt Armageddon stirring beneath my skin. *Make an end! Make an end!* Glory or annihilation—it no longer mattered which. Egged on by the fanatical bidding of this idea, I rolled out of the circle.

I can recall the sensation of falling, of hearing my own hysterical laughter as if borne on dark wings from the other side of the Abyss. I fixed my gaze on a slit of candle flame, and it continued to widen. Then night closed over me. The embers of my spirit burned on, but in a place that my mental fingers couldn't touch. Later, I opened my eyes and felt myself being hauled over gravel, dirt, and grass. Existing, as I did, in uneasy alliance with my own body, I hardly registered the sensation of my feet dragging. Looking back, I saw the dancing light of flames through one of the barn's windows. I stared up into Saul's eyes for a moment before losing consciousness again.

I awoke on a patch of rough wood floor, inside a down sleeping bag that reeked of campfires. Saul hovered over me. He offered me a steaming mug of coffee.

"I know what you'll say, so just hold your peace until you've finished this," he said. "Nothing's done that can't be undone."

I took a sip, but then, despite his words, I couldn't contain my remorse. "I'm sorry about the fire, and my lying, and…everything, Saul! I'll—"

He waved me down. "I got the fire out before it did much damage. We can talk about reparations later. I've got something to show you first. Finish your coffee."

Then Saul left to fetch something. He returned with a hat—a dark blue prowler's mac, which he instructed me to put on so that it covered my eyes.

"I'll guide you," he said. "This won't have nearly the impact that it needs to if you can see."

I did as he told me. I suppose I could've peered through the hat's thick mesh if I'd wanted to, but I didn't try. Saul helped me to my feet. Along my blind passage, I heard the squeak of a screen door opening. Then I counted six steps down, followed by the sensation of springy grass on a downward slope and then some serpentine progress, which told me that we were meandering around the scrap metal strewn throughout his yard. Then we stopped.

"Kneel down and lean forward," Saul commanded. And in a moment, I was down on all fours, feeling cool mud beneath my knees and palms.

"I'm about to show you the true source of the power and wisdom that you tried to conjure up last night," he said. "This is the place where wishes are formed and granted. Look hard!"

And with that, the veil of woven cotton was pulled from my eyes. I was staring down at still water. My own reflection met my gaze at the edge of his pond. My brow was furrowed with hurt and remorse. My eyes were caught in a battle between hard resolve and the softer empathy that pain brings. I was not as tough as I'd thought. Nor was I as blithely eager to forsake the world. I had inner purposes yet unfinished.

From behind me, Saul continued. "Consider this: You aren't the first person to have heard that nagging voice inside, the one that insists that your true identity is so much greater, so much more potent, than what you grew up believing. There's a wider world beyond the stories of the mind; I'll tell you that for certain."

I burst out laughing. I could've either done that or wept, I suppose. "You're telling me that I'm the source of the demons and the angels?"

"You are so much more," Saul repeated. "You were right about that. But you won't come to the realization of it by annihilating yourself. People throughout history have tried to transform themselves into the 'equal God' without realizing that they were divine to begin with." Then he finished more softly. "Your destiny is yours to shape."

My head sagged, as if from the weight of his revelations. I felt his grip on my shoulder.

"Come on, son. Let's have breakfast. Then we can talk more about all this while we repair the barn!"

❖

"Forgiveness is only really possible when you realize that the other person was never the source of your pain to begin with," Saul began. "And that's where I'm coming from. I'm just saying that so you'll understand why I'm not angry. I'm actually curious." He flashed me a quizzical smile. "Why did I draw someone like yourself to me?"

I was devouring a breakfast sandwich consisting of two scrambled eggs, mushrooms, and cheddar on rye bread. I glanced up. "You're asking me?"

He chuckled. His brown eyes were so intent they made me uneasy. "I must've decided—somewhere inside myself. I must have said…that this is another opportunity for me to share what I know with a suffering soul."

37

"I can get by on my own perseverance, Saul," I replied, staring at my now-empty plate. "Besides, you only have to take a look around to know that everybody suffers. No offense, but nothin' you say is gonna take that away."

"I don't doubt that you chose the path that you're on," Saul came back. "But I think it could help you quite a bit if you could uncover some of the reasons for that choice. Pain is more easily borne when it has meaning for us."

The cynical part of me was thinking, *This guy's even more of a preacher than Tommy! And I'm committed to staying here and spending the afternoon helping him fix his barn?*

Saul stood up and took my plate, stacking it on top of his own. "There's also a time to just not think too much about it all," he said. "We're here to learn from each other, Brandon. I've no doubt about that. But that's not something that we have to get to the bottom of right now."

Impelled by curiosity, I stood up. "What could you possibly have to learn from me?"

Saul shrugged. "You know enough to realize that you'll have to completely trust what's inside of you and move with it if you're going to fulfill the promise of your life. Many people go their whole lives without learning that lesson. A guy like you could burn like a supernova for all to see—if you don't implode first. Don't think I don't admire that kind of courage."

Five minutes later, the rain started, and the pines started swaying. Before we began work on repairs, I met Saul's wife, June. I'd get to know her more throughout the months that Edge of the Known rehearsed in the Catacombs. June seemed shy whenever you passed her by; she'd smile slightly and offer a half-wave. But then, if you asked her a question, she'd speak her mind with startling candor. She had wide eyes big as chestnuts, within which blue-gray waves danced, and light blonde hair, almost white, that fell straight to her shoulders. She and Saul had first met through their work, so I imagine that June had seen her share of people in crisis. If you ever called the popular suicide hotline in the city, chances are you'd end up talking to one of the Masons.

Two people bonding over a common desire to help others heal: what better basis for a relationship could there be than that? It was the kind of thing to give a young man hope.

Saul stood under the eaves of his porch and smoked his pipe, while June and I made small talk. Then I went out and joined him, lighting a cigarette.

Saul glanced at me and said without preamble, "You're going to have to stop thinking of your father always as a drunk."

To my ears, this statement was not only uncalled for, but also absurd. And, of course, I'd always been one to shoot my mouth first and reflect later. "If he ever starts acting like anything other than a drunk, then I'll think differently!"

Then my body tensed up as Saul drew closer to me. "See, that's been your problem all along," he said. "Not just at home, but also with your music and everything you want to achieve with your life. You just exist in reaction to the world, Brandon—or what you perceive the world to be. You aren't acting independently."

I reached for a retort and found only empty space inside: numbness and darkness. It was as if his speech constituted a form of viral attack for which my mind and emotions had no defense. "Do you know what it's like?" I managed.

Saul laid his pipe and lighter on the rail and faced me again. "My father was brooding and vicious when he was into the whiskey," he said. "He got that mean look in his eyes, just squinting with spite and distrust, looking for something or someone to focus that rage on—that rage that was always in him. He wasn't a screamer; no, much the opposite. He'd say something real low, almost in a whisper, and then you knew it was all over."

"So then you oughta know how pointless it is, thinking you can ever change somebody like that," I said, feeling like I'd finally found some ground to stand on.

Saul stared at me for a moment; and I saw that his reply was already there, fully formed in his mind, and that he was just considering how to lay it on me. "What's pointless is wasting our energies on trying to manipulate anything outside of ourselves," he replied finally. "That means any person, any situation in the world. Doing that just feeds the illusion of our own powerlessness. If you can manage to think of your father differently, then maybe, in time, the person you experience will be a different man."

I blinked in disbelief. "Is that what you did?"

"Yes."

This concept baffled everything within my mental arsenal. "And he just…turned himself around?"

"I wish that were so," Saul said. "What happened is he dropped out of my personal experience completely. He left my mother and me, and eventually became a tramp upon the byways of the world. I know this only from rumor. But in any case, the particular threat he'd represented for me disappeared from my life."

Then he shrugged. "I have no idea how it might manifest for you. But when something inside of you shifts like that, then you step right out of one world and into another one. That's how real change always occurs."

See what happens if you hand that kind of advice to your average teacher, preacher, or psychologist, I thought.

Fortunately, the mind is naturally curious. We'd probably never move from our fixed positions if that wasn't the case. Curiosity, pain, and desire are our primary motivators; and the optimist could argue that love underlies them all.

"Long may you philosophize, Saul," I said, "but I'm not sure that I follow."

The rain had stopped. By tacit agreement, we tramped through the mud towards his barn. "The value won't be revealed to you if you just sit around and think about it," Saul said. "And ultimately, there really isn't any middle ground. You either take responsibility—and credit—for your whole life as your personal creation, or you don't."

After that sermon, we talked casually for the rest of the afternoon. I think Saul realized that he'd already told me as much as I was prepared to absorb.

❖

Saul wielded some oblique influence over the future direction of my band even at this early stage. I started reevaluating my conception of art, the artist, and the act of creation—and of what Edge of the Known could possibly accomplish—thanks to the way in which he'd thrown my thoughts into disarray.

Only familiar things can be stuffed into the mental category of the "known" and thereby lose their power to move us. When the mind is caught off guard, when it's confronted by something that it can't label, then there must be an opening onto direct apprehension. New ideas, sensations, and mental landscapes all have a chance to slip through the cracks. Spurred on by this inspiration, I told Tim and Tommy one night during rehearsals that we should have certain songs—or, at least, certain movements within our songs—that we never played the same way twice.

"We'll just create the space for whatever wants to come through in the moment," I said. "And then we've got to run with it—that's the thing, even if it takes us to some scary places."

Tim and I both looked at Tommy, who, like a ship's captain consulting an internal compass, was weighing this information alongside his own guiding philosophy. "Alright," he conceded. "We'll do it with your songs, Brandon. If we land some longer gigs—and I'm hoping that we do here, soon—then we'll need to extend our repertoire anyway."

This was the first time I'd ever really spoken up in an attempt to alter the band's course. Before this time, Tommy and I had always been in silent agreement about our desires. More drastic changes in direction were yet to come; but for the moment, I was content. Something was beginning to stir beneath the surface of our music, something so volatile and potent that, at times, even I felt afraid to approach it. I was glad we were able to provide an opening through which it could emerge and touch us—because then, through us, it could impact all those with the ears to hear it.

CAST ADRIFT

And now: the events that finally precipitated my permanent move away from home....

My father's temper slowly transformed from futile bitterness to more focused hostility. He started hitting me occasionally, even when he was sober. And he did it deliberately, as if it was important to him that I acknowledge his disgust in me as much as I felt the physical blows.

My thread of restraint grew too tenuous. One particularly ugly night in late June, it finally snapped. He had me pressed up against the refrigerator. His face was red, his eyes were bulging; he reminded me, absurdly, of an over-ripe tomato being squeezed.

"You look down on me—you lousy shit—and what are you?! What kind of life have you got?" He sprayed my face with these lacerations. "You think you're the better man to raise my daughter!"

"You're fucking right I do!"

Then I maneuvered my palms against both his shoulders and shoved him with full force. He staggered backwards across the room and slammed against the counter. Given his physical condition, this wasn't hard to do. But my fury was only partially spent; it was yet to sweep me still farther. I twisted to my left and instinctively found the handle of our heavy cast-iron frying pan. I hefted and hurled it.

I'd intended to miss him. I just wanted to shake him up. At least, I'm fairly sure that this was my underlying motive. Heated scenes like this flash across your life quickly, like lightning. All the feelings and thoughts wrapped up within them can be difficult to unravel afterward. At any rate, my father had no way of gauging my intentions. He ducked down almost to the floor when the thing flew, sheltering his head with his arms as the glass of the kitchen window above him exploded.

I heard Rachel cry out from her bedroom upstairs: the single most horrific moment within this entire nightmare. I was breathing hard and trembling, suspended somewhere between disbelief and vindication.

When my father rose, he was no longer cowering. "I'm calling the cops."

And that was it. I resigned myself before he even picked up the phone. Rachel's outcry was still echoing in the empty caverns of my head. What could I do, anyway? My fate had become a sand trap. The more I struggled, the deeper I sank.

The officers arrived within a half hour. One was Hispanic and the other Caucasian. Each wore a different version of the same dour face; but they were fairly polite overall. Maybe that's because I didn't offer them a bit of trouble. In some indefinable way—I swear—I was nearly at peace. I guess that, when you spin so far away from the epicenter of your own life and sanity, you may be inclined to welcome anyone who will step in and take control of the situation, even if such a solution costs you your very freedom. Of course, freedom itself is scary— particularly if you don't trust yourself.

My father was half-crocked that night. But, of course, he managed to appear perfectly lucid and coherent the entire time the police were there. To all appearances, he was a humble and somewhat frail man who was disturbed and shaken by his son's (completely unprovoked) violent outburst. In hindsight, I think he was scared shitless by the presence of the cops, and his fear made him just as meek and docile as many people in authority prefer to see you.

Poor man—he could've used some intervention himself. But on that night, all appearances worked against him.

Then—ah!—being led past Rachel while I was in handcuffs; her standing at the bottom of the stairs in her panda pajamas and dragging her green alligator. I would've rather spent a month in jail than suffer that moment. I chastised myself, *Smile, at least! Reassure her that you're really OK!* But I could scarcely even glance in her direction. I spent the whole ride to the station wondering if she'd ever get back to sleep, and whether I'd ever get the chance to explain this night to her.

Saul had once been hauled to a police station in cuffs—before his "awakening," as he calls it. The way he explained his reaction has always stayed with me. He said that being taken into custody is like the confirmation of all of your darkest suspicions about your own human nature. All your life, you remind yourself in so many subtle ways that you're basically a blight upon the face of the planet. Maybe you call your disease "Original Sin." Or maybe you're more scientifically minded and have accepted the idea that your most intimate thoughts and feelings are basically as meaningless and accidental as (supposedly) the universe itself is. There's a thousand ways to explain and "justify" the notion of tainted humanity. In any case, you walk through those doors and contemplate the iron bars as you look at all those armed men in uniform…and in some way, you just want to nod your head like it was all inevitable. *Yeah—I've been heading this way my whole life.*

As it turned out, I wasn't in the station long. I had to fill out a few papers, and then they took my picture: not a mug shot, but rather a photo to use as evidence that I hadn't been roughed up. "If you got wounds anywhere, now's the time to show 'em off!" one cocky officer said. He probably enjoyed telling that to people who'd just been pepper-sprayed, knowing they felt like they were on fire, but that it wasn't anything that would be caught on camera. I just scowled at him and didn't waste any words.

The station is an existential juncture in the most surreal sense. People get hustled in there knowing that it could mean the utter end of whatever life they'd been leading up until that point. And to the men and women processing paperwork, or enjoying coffee breaks between beats, it's just another night at work. You can get yourself unsettled in the deep regions of your soul if you think too much about it.

A trim and clean-cut young guy who looked fresh out of college came and introduced himself. He was to escort me down to the psychiatric ward. But first, he asked me a bunch of questions and jotted down my replies on a clipboard that he kept referring to. He warned me, with a smile, that I was going to endure many of these same inquiries when I saw the psychiatrist.

❖

I suppose it's never pleasant visiting a psychiatrist—especially when it's against your will—but it feels particularly strange to do so late at night.

Dr. Lisbet was a petite and humorless lady. She was probably forty years old, and looked like her stony face would crack if she ever smiled. The intern gave her the questionnaire he'd filled out and then offered me a pat on the shoulders—as if I needed the reassurance—before walking out.

Dr. Lisbet was, for several minutes at least, much more interested in the papers than she was the actual human being (me) sitting in front of her. Once she finished reading through them, though, she glanced up and addressed me as casually as if we'd been involved in conversation for the last half hour.

"No doubt you're tired by now, Mr. Chane, but it falls on me to make some kind of judgment with regard to your situation, as your father isn't pressing charges. I'm going to have to ask you a few questions. Had you been drinking tonight?"

I decided that I could be a perfunctory robot, too, if that's how this game needed to be played. "I was working at Jaspar's tonight, bussing tables, and hadn't even been home an hour…. No. I had nothing but iced tea all evening."

She raised an eyebrow. "Real brewed tea? You mean caffeinated? Were you planning on being up half the night?"

Play ball, man, or they're not going to let you leave, I cautioned myself. I stuffed my irritation into an inner compartment that I kept empty for occasions like this. "I'm a night owl anyway. And I always work nights, so there's no reason for me to wake up early."

No reason—save for Rachel—but she didn't need to know that.

"What precipitated the fight with your father?" she asked.

46

I hate half-truths almost as much as outright lies. I could tell that this was not going to be a simple round of verbal fencing. "Look, my old man's beat me up more times than I could possibly count. And I've never fought back before tonight. That's gotta count for something," I reasoned.

She scrawled a note on the paper that the intern had given her. I had no idea what it said. Her face betrayed nothing. I admonished myself again. Soften up: look repentant and humble—whatever it takes. Even if it makes you wanna puke.

"So he was abusive tonight?"

"He had me by the collar and I shoved him away. I was honestly just trying to scare him by throwing the pan."

Without warning or transition, she asked, "Have you ever experienced auditory hallucinations—heard voices?"

I'm a songwriter. I wouldn't be much of one if I didn't hear voices! "No ma'am."

That earned me a stony stare. I'd lathered my tone with a bit too much butter.

"Does your family have a history of alcohol or drug abuse?"

"I'm not sure. I don't think so. My father only started drinking heavily after my mom died."

That was only partially true. I think her death had only exacerbated a pattern for him that had already been well established.

"Are you currently using any recreational drugs?"

I really had to bite my tongue this time, as that particular term always gave me visions of playing badminton with syringes. "I tried pot a few times in high school and didn't care for it. It was disorienting. My thoughts seemed to come too fast for me to keep up with them. No...nothing."

"Will you be able to find someplace to stay tonight—preferably somewhere you can live until you find more permanent accommodations?"

"Uh...I don't understand."

"Well, you can't expect to simply go back to your father's house, Mr. Chane. It says here you've been employed at the same restaurant for three years. You have your own transportation. You recently turned twenty. Isn't it time you got your own place, had some space to yourself…to ensure that incidents like this don't occur again?"

Life was in impeccable order within that square room. The plaques on the white walls attested to society's faith in Dr. Lisbet and her ability to dissect your psyche with sober precision. She, no doubt, polished the surface of her dark wooden desk in between clients. If you had any doubt that you were here to be treated as a patient, the pale fluorescent lights, some four feet overhead, served to remind you that this was really a hospital room. Unfortunately, the surgical tools employed here were psychological, not physical—which meant that the incisions they made were much harder to see.

I might have been easy prey. But all those debates with Tommy had prepared me for this strange world that had been invented by those who presume to define sanity for the rest of us. "Most of modern psychology is just the handmaiden of the culture," he'd told me. "Remember that. It doesn't grapple with the real nature of things. Take away the consensus reality, and it doesn't have a stone to stand on."

Nevertheless, I read the look in Dr. Lisbet's eyes and knew that I had no wiggle room.

"Can I get your promise, now, that you'll do this," she said, "so that I don't have to type up a recommendation?"

"Look," I said, forsaking prudence, "my sister lives in that house. She's scarcely seven. She's got to get herself ready for school in the morning because Dad could be passed out until noon. I've basically been taking care of her since Mom died. You don't know what you're asking. I can't just leave her."

"That's an issue for Child Protective Services. You have to realize that it's out of your hands now. Obviously, you aren't doing her a whole lot of good if you're breaking windows in the house, right?"

Battles have to be chosen if, in the long run, one hopes to win the war. I knew enough to realize that this particular battle was a losing one. "Are we in agreement about this?" she persisted.

Though I was raving inside, I somehow managed to nod and look penitent. "Yeah, I'll find someplace else to live. I won't go back there except to fetch my stuff—and to visit, later on, when things have cooled down."

"Is there a place you can stay tonight? Can someone pick you up?"

"I'll call my best friend. I've slept over his house plenty of times anyway. It's cool. His mom and I get along real well."

She made another note on the questionnaire sheet. I noticed, for the first time, that her nails were painted burgundy. Somehow, that little detail reminded me that she was human.

"You'll need to call us a month from now to confirm your new living situation. I'll give you a reminder." She retrieved a personal business card from the stack on her desk, scribbled a date on the top of it, and handed it to me.

"Now, I'm not going to insist upon it this time...but I strongly suggest that you take advantage of the mental health services that we have here. Financial assistance is also available. Right now we have a waiting list; but if you call, we should be able to fit you in so that you can start seeing someone in a month or two."

"Thank you very much," I said, hoping that she'd think I was seriously considering the suggestion. Then we stood up and shook hands.

She wasn't a bad lady, really. I suppose you have to develop a hard shell after years of immersing yourself in human suffering and confusion for a living.

By now the hour was getting late, which meant that I had to wake Miss Visconti up and she, in turn, had to venture down into the basement and rouse Tommy. In a way, I was glad that he was only half-conscious when he answered, because that dulled his reaction to the news of where I was and what had happened.

Tommy arrived to get me with his stoic face on. His presence helped me to ignore all the officers who stared as we walked by. Tommy was at his most pragmatic when situations were dire. "Let's get the hell out of here, first off," he muttered.

We both strove to appear neutral—neither too insolent nor too scared—as we made for the door. The cool night air hit my face and felt like freedom. The temperature must have dropped ten degrees since I'd first been hauled into the station.

"It was time for you to move on anyway, Brandon," Tommy said. "How long were you planning on dragging it out?"

His present self-righteousness was, I suppose, his subtle revenge for having been mustered out of his warm waterbed. "Let's not talk about it right now!" I snapped. "I can't think straight. And you know it's not so simple as all that."

"Fine. You staying at my place, then?"

We reached his car, a compact little black beast that rode low. I paused. A new plan had begun to germinate in my mind. "I'll catch up with you tomorrow," I said. "Why don't you drop me off on College Street?"

We got inside the car and Tommy started her up. She was twelve years old and always sounded like she was coughing sand, but she ran well—except for when the chutzpah sapped right out of her on steep hills. "Haven't you had enough of an adventurous night already?" he asked.

"Look, man—it's gonna be hours before I unwind enough to where I could fall asleep anyway. I might as well walk it off."

This time, he spared a sidewise glance. "I'm just wondering if sleep is even a part of your plan."

I had no answer for that. When you're caught, you're caught, and I had no intention of bullshitting my best friend. Luckily, he didn't pursue it any further, because that's the kind of friend he was. He parked near the top of the long, sloping street that eventually meets with the Matterpike. The neighborhood was the most popular hotspot for students of De Flores College. Plenty of them were parading the streets at one a.m.: Girls in tight jeans who made my pulse quicken and my throat feel tight. Guys in clean jerseys who hovered around them like guard dogs. Their whole world was foreign and impossibly remote from my vantage point, even as they passed by close enough to graze Tommy's car.

"This is really where you want to be, huh?" he asked.

Considering the night ahead of me, I asked if I could borrow a red sweatshirt of his that I noticed in the backseat. "I'll see you tomorrow or the next day. I think you were right: maybe this was for the best. I might end up being grateful for getting this shove out the door."

My bravado was entirely hollow. I hadn't processed any of my recent experiences; they were still too raw and hot. I felt like curling up and weeping in an alley. I shut the door without a backward glance and slipped the sweatshirt on that he'd kindly lent me.

If you hung out anywhere in the park area, particularly at that time of night, then the right people would know you were looking to score something. I was on the hunt for psychedelics—and they were especially easy to find during the summer and fall months. I only had to walk three blocks to reach the green. It was hemmed in by a drugstore, a café, a sub shop, and two bars. I found a place to sit with my back to one of the bars, named Duffy's. Two lovers were in the throes of amour on one of the park benches. On another, an old man in a puffy jacket and knit winter hat slept beneath a bed of newspapers.

Within twenty minutes, I met a twenty-something fellow with a thick beard, wearing a rainbow-colored beanie. We made the exchange—money for mushrooms—right there. It was quiet enough. Not much happened on Monday nights in Sadenport, typically. Neither bar was hosting a band, and last call was fast approaching. I pocketed the bag that he sold me—not stopping to examine it just yet, but opting to trust him—and set out in search of a secluded place where I could munch its contents.

The west side of the college meets with a gradual, grassy slope. A little creek runs along its feet and, at one point, meanders through a tiny patch of woods. Feeling anxious to split reality at the seams and enter into realms where the rules of my accustomed nightmare no longer applied, I made for this shadowy sanctuary.

Yeah, I was in need of a more substantial reprieve than what a simple night's sleep could provide.

Like a phantom, I moved past occasional bands of students. The snatches of conversation that reached my ears—revolving around exams, sex, teacher so-and-so, and so on—existed on the shores of a world that I was about to cast off from. Was I even substantial enough for anyone to see? I shuffled down the moonlit hill and, in another moment, became a creature of the trees.

I ate two caps and twice as many thin stems. But I felt myself slipping into an altered state before the psilocybin even reached my stomach. Everything within me was slowly disengaging from the erratic fits and starts of "normal life" and leaning toward deeper and more subtle pulsations. I was ready for the plunge.

Drugs were practically redundant for me, truth be told. I kept such a tenuous grip on this paradigm that everyone else seemed to be plugged into that all it really took was a gentle tug to pry my fingers off of it entirely. I washed the bitter taste of the mushrooms down with a handful of water from the creek.

Having consumed the blessed sacrament, I relinquished myself to a patch of the slope that was cushioned with thick wheatgrass. A moonbeam beside me seemed to emanate reassurances as I slipped down into a waking dream. This was my first intimation that the world was changing: I realized that I was not alone. The personalities within the grass, the creek, and the pines made themselves known to me. My body sank into the Earth, even as, on a purely physical level, it remained motionless.

Father was drunk in a house with a broken window. Rachel was possibly still awake, not sure about what any of this meant. I wept and howled into my hands.

Afterwards, I drifted through a series of absorbing daydreams. Time could not be measured. A few of my favorite songs drifted through my consciousness, the words assuming new meanings and significances. Are authors and singers even aware of the incantations that they weave?

At some point, I grew restless, and no longer wanted to lie in the Earth's warm cocoon. I crawled to the water's edge and washed my face. Every splash whispered secrets too quick for me to catch. Then, for the first time in days, I smiled. The world was good. Why had I longed to escape it? Magic and love hummed within every portion of it. Feeling eager to explore this place and all of its wonders, I jumped to my feet.

My exuberance carried me to the top of the hill, each step upheld and encouraged by the damp ground that met my boots. I could smell the grass and loam distinctly. Then, when I noticed the kids walking to and fro across the dim campus grounds, I froze.

I blinked, looked again, and beheld an entirely different scene. I saw human beings who were all dependent upon the same life-giving air and sacred ground that I was. My clear senses somehow peeled back their surface layers and revealed the naked reality that they lived within. So many private battles being waged. What "world" was I thinking of being so alienated from? Who had the energy or will to organize a vast conspiracy against my happiness and sense of belonging?

Bullies and friends, monks and hedonists, nobles and peasants—every conceivable form of human endeavor and focus paraded through my mind, mingling and merging, and I could only conclude that there was no sorting it all out and pronouncing a summary answer.

We all have to learn to trust ourselves.

Hadn't Saul said something like that?

No sooner did I think of him than I realized that his house, and his presence, must be the ultimate destination of this holy quest that I had embarked upon. Saul was familiar with the dimensions that I was passing through; somehow, I was certain of that. My trip was peaking and instilling me with a sense of immortality. It required an epiphany, the culmination of all the shadowy hints and whispers that the summer air was carrying. Like a navigator on a space freighter, I set a new course.

A HOSTEL FOR LOST SOULS

Somewhere along the way, I realized that I had just committed to walking roughly ten miles. Although distances meant little to my transcendent form of reckoning, I was still dimly aware of my mortal limits.

I decided to fuel up at my favorite restaurant: the Pioneer. You might recall that this establishment had obliquely provided us with the inspiration for our band's name. It existed within a spacious log cabin where even the tables and chairs looked ancient and roughly hewn. The menu was carved out on a huge slab of maple, probably six feet long, which hung on steel chains screwed into the ceiling. You could sit at the long bar beneath that sign and watch everything that was going on in the kitchen.

The Pioneer was open twenty-four hours a day and served breakfast entrees around the clock. Their jalapenos were the hottest around, and their horseradish cleared your sinuses real good. If you wanted coffee—they ground it fresh. The restaurant made for a somewhat bizarre spectacle even if one was not tripping, flanked as it was by the quaint Rainer Tea Room on one side and a drugstore on the opposite corner. On this particular night, I felt like I was meeting Daniel Boone and Meriwether Lewis for dinner at a trading post.

Tommy and I were the fringe-dwellers of consciousness. I momentarily envisioned new band outfits composed of buckskin leggings with fringe, armbands studded with arrowheads, rawhide belts, and coonskin caps.

The faint sounds of life within the building both drew and repelled me at once. For a few minutes, I lingered on the sidewalk wavering and swaying. I wasn't particularly hungry. Really, I just wanted to know what the hive of human social existence might feel like at that moment. I was curious.

The allure of the unknown pulled me into the Pioneer at last. My first sight was of Shannon, a dark-haired lady probably in her late thirties, flicking on the coffee brewer. She worked weeknights. I'd always liked her. She never sounded condescending, nor had she ever looked askance at my clothing, jewelry, or hair. She had a couple of tattoos herself: a dreamcatcher on her right shoulder and a little leafless tree at the base of her neck. They made me wonder about her musical tastes, but I'd never asked.

The sight of her steadied me. I might've turned back around, otherwise. Far-off echoes of Mom suddenly reached me, evoking cold shudders. This was a mistake. I should have been back beneath the pine trees, curled up in a fetal position and weeping.

"Hi ya Brandon!" Shannon called. She rarely smiled, but just felt kind—if that makes sense. "You here for late dinner? Or early breakfast?"

"I'm not sure." In my current mood, I couldn't give her wry humor the response that it deserved. I pointed to the coffee. "I'll have a cup of that once it's done brewing, though."

I claimed a stool at the left end of the bar. Two heavyset men—in their late forties I guessed—dressed in flannel, corduroys, suspenders, and cowboy hats were sitting to the right of me. One had his nose in a newspaper, and the other was puffing on a cigar, occasionally eyeing Shannon up and down.

She brought me my coffee, having already added the half-and-half because she knew I liked it that way. "How's the band going?"

Something about the way she said it, without a trace of derision, made me smile. I began rambling right away, my thoughts tumbling over one another in my enthusiasm. Somehow, within half a minute or so, I managed to convey to her that I'd begun writing my own songs, that we'd played our first gig a few weeks back, and that this very restaurant had formed part of the inspiration for our new name.

Then something in my manner must've caught her eye. She leaned forward and got a good look at my pupils. "Oh, Christ!" Mario, one of the cooks, called out the order that was in the window. Turns out it was for the cowboys. "Honey, you've got to slow down. Get yourself a girlfriend, find some sanity. And just be careful, alright?" I could tell that she wanted to say more, but there was no time. She left to fetch the plates.

As soon as she was gone, the guy two seats away from me laid down his newspaper, leaned forward, and said, "I can't tell for the life of me whether you're a faggot or just a plain freak!" The one puffing on the cigar let out a full-belly guffaw as if it was the wittiest thing he'd ever heard.

"Fifty bucks for you to find out one way or the other—you fat fuck!" I shot back. "I don't do your kind for free!" Even the psychedelic state of mind, which made the edges of the world blur and melt like clocks in a Salvador Dali painting, couldn't dull my eagerness for a fight. Spiritual epiphanies didn't seem to touch that place. I would've made a lousy hippie.

But my belligerence just set both of the guys to laughing. "You have that much on ya?" the closer one asked his buddy in his heavy Texan accent. He pretended to check his own wallet. The other called over to me.

"Son, I doubt you're worth spare change. Maybe if you paid me the fifty bucks. But I'd have to insist that you shower first—and get a haircut."

I knew I didn't want to cause a scene in front of Shannon right in her workplace. I was already laying my money down on the counter when she arrived with their plates. I tipped her a couple of dollars just for being my one reminder of decent humanity that night. Since I'd left Tommy, anyway.

Two shouts followed me out the door. "Be careful!" That was Shannon. "Goodnight, sweetie!" called one of the Texans.

I'll be giving you a proper goodnight in a minute, I thought.

The parking lot stretched to an embankment that overlooked the Matterpike River, which, in this area, was about fifty feet wide and rushing. There were only three vehicles parked, and the one in the right-hand corner was a bloated white truck with Texas plates.

That had to belong to at least one of them; and since the other cars were a distance away, I was prepared to assume they'd driven there together. The Pioneer was ringed with windows, which carried the risk of discovery but also meant that I could see what was going on inside. And I was clothed in shadows. The one cowboy was still flipping through his newspaper, and his friend was halfway to the restroom. Perfect. I scampered over to the driver's-side door.

I tried the handle, praying that there was no alarm. The door came right open—silently. I glanced back again. The coast was still clear, so I opened the door all the way, stepped up into the opening, and undid my pants.

I hadn't pissed since leaving home. How long ago had that been? At first, I was too stricken with adrenaline to release it. I got anxious and looked back again. But everyone inside was occupied and no eyes were turned my way. Suddenly, I started relieving myself in a steady, acidic stream. I saturated the driver's seat and hit the other one as best I could from a distance. Then I hurried down, zipped and buttoned myself, and secured the door as quietly as I could.

Satisfied that my deed had gone undetected, I found the nearest alleyway. There, I remembered that tonight's epic sojourn must land me at Saul's house. The distance was daunting; but I still felt invincible. I was travelling through a magic kingdom, where concepts of miles and boundaries had long since dissolved. The meandering dirt alley, hemmed in by wooden fences, had become the Bifrost Bridge. And Saul was the great and powerful Odin.

I recalled the night that I'd spent in his barn alone. I'd been convinced that one must take elaborate steps to summon spirits from far-off places. Now, here I was, moving through early summer air thick with spirits of every description. Whispers crowded me. Oh—I had the answer to Dr. Lisbet's question about hearing voices, now! I could have followed a thousand strands of conversation to strange and wondrous realms. Or at least I might have, had I been capable of focus. But my mind was like a sieve—touched by all the waters of life and yet incapable of retaining a single drop.

The air was alive. It stirred and moved in response to some invisible will that lies beyond our ken. Was the force that lent it mobility the same force that kept my feet in motion even when I paid no attention to walking?

Such thoughts gradually led me back to the sacred sense of life that had swept over me earlier. I suddenly regretted what I'd done in the parking lot. The fact that those guys had been complete jackasses did not console me. I told myself that the whole episode had been a dream. This argument was almost plausible. I finally reached Church Street, crossed at the light, and then turned right to begin ascending the long hill.

If I'd followed the road a mile or so in the other direction, I would've reached Samurai Tavern. This conjured up more memories that I wasn't prepared to deal with. I was beginning to understand the inner urgency that drove me towards Saul's house. There were forces inside me that I couldn't handle: they were pushing me towards that perilous edge. I knew Saul was acquainted with self-destructive impulses—and with overcoming them.

Among other things, this trip had revealed to me that I didn't actually want to die.

Effort and result, I discovered, are both mental phenomena. My body seemed to hold the location of Saul's house in its store of fleshy wisdom. In the meantime, I was beginning to perceive signs of mundane reality piercing my waking dream. More constrictive and pessimistic thoughts started asserting themselves. The breath of trees and shrubs was more subtle. Joggers passed me by here and there, warning that dawn was approaching.

My legs began to ache. But I made it to the top of Turnpike Avenue and crossed over into what we referred to as "Old Town." The sky was now dark blue and clear. It promised to be a beautiful day: one that I was going to spend asleep, assuming that I found a place where I could lay my head down.

I finally stumbled across Saul's driveway just as he was warming up his dark blue truck. He noticed me in his mirror and rolled down the window.

"I'm just heading off to work," he said. "What happened to you?"

What could I say? My psyche was swarming with insights and revelations, and I seemed unable to differentiate between what was relevant in the moment and what was not. Maybe all of it was—or none. All my wild epiphanies of the night before failed to come to my rescue. The best I could do was ramble on about how things had come to a head at home with my father and then say, "Can we talk when you get back?"

From his expression, and the way he nodded, I could tell that Saul had guessed the true nature of my condition. He gestured towards his house. "Why don't you go in and get some rest? It's unlocked. June's already gone. She's making a house call. You can sleep on the couch downstairs, get washed up, fix yourself something to eat, whatever. I'll be home this evening."

"Thank you." I slapped his hood for emphasis. "Thank you," I repeated. I watched as he pulled out of the driveway. But Saul seemed preoccupied. He didn't look my way again.

Another level of reality was descending upon my awareness. There was a whole mess that needed taking care of. And the previous night's adventure, for all of its fascinating side excursions, hadn't offered me any answers. Nonetheless, I could postpone that moment of reckoning with sleep. I went inside and found Saul's couch.

I soon discovered that the lingering comedown off my trip lent my imagination a sharp and pristine edge. I could visualize things—especially when I closed my eyes—with utter clarity. Remembering my brief encounter with Shannon, I started fondling and undressing her in my mind's eye. I'd seldom fantasized about someone so much older than me. But she was a good woman, one who treated me with a rare kind of respect, and that counted for something. The whole encounter sprang to vivid life. I knew right away that I was in need of some relief. I ran to the bathroom and returned with a fistful of tissues. Then I returned to my conjured lover. It was the most realistic sexual fantasy I'd ever experienced. I could almost smell her breath, feel the moistness of her vagina. We'd hardly gotten going within this dream consummation before I made a complete mess.

About a half hour later, I finally fell asleep.

❖

Loneliness engulfed me as soon as I woke. I felt forsaken by everyone and everything. It was as if my entire mental existence was a pendulum and so, for every moment of transcendence and liberation I'd enjoyed the night before, I now had to endure an equivalent swing in the opposite direction. Moreover, I was stuck with the bare facts of my situation staring me in the face, with no numinous magic to soften the blow. My attempt at flight had only sharpened my awareness of the gulf that existed between myself and true transcendence.

Facing Saul was not easy in that moment. I heard him moving about in the kitchen. But it was some time before I was able to rise and join him.

No light shone through the windows. I'd slept clear through until evening. Saul was standing by the stove, dressed in his blue bathrobe. His hair was wet, so I assumed that he'd recently showered. I peeked beyond him and saw red potatoes in one pan and asparagus in another. The aroma of some kind of roast wafted over from the oven. All of Saul's various utensils hung from a half-circle of iron that was screwed into the wall. Half of the wooden countertop was occupied by buckets used for compost and recycling.

"I invited you to dinner," Saul cracked, without turning from the stove, "but you don't remember because you were unconscious."

"Where's June?" I asked, stalling.

"She's spending the night at the house of a client, someone who she really feels should not be left alone at the moment."

Rinsing his hands then drying them on a dangling washcloth, he added: "It looks like you let go of the world last night—or, at least, what most people would call the world." Then he faced me. "It can be healthy to let the old stories fall away so that we can write new ones. But we always need some belief system or another. Remember that. You don't want to cut every cord that binds you to your own life. There are gentler ways to awaken."

I tried to smile, to invest my words with some sense of irony, but my voice came out hollow. "I guess that's why I'm in such a shitty state of mind right now."

"You're probably comparing your ordinary state of consciousness—which you're in now—to the much more illuminated state that you visited for a brief while," Saul said. "The disparity that seems to exist between the two worlds can make people feel depressed and frustrated. It's an illusion, but the effects of believing it are real."

His oven timer rang.

"Well, I've got news for you," he added, his eyes sparkling. "I said 'the two worlds,' but there's really no such thing. They're one and the same—and they're here!" He swept a hand to encompass the room. Then he turned, grabbed a potholder and pulled out the sheet pan of pork roast. Saul served everything up with a glass of red wine for each of us.

"You just learned to accept a version of your own identity that's so much smaller than what you really are," he continued. "Don't feel bad—most of us do that. But that's basically what you're fighting against. It isn't anyone or anything out there in the world. And it's what you're rebelling against in your songs, too, I'll bet. Some part of you knows that there is so much more to the human story."

I ate in silence for a few minutes. My rambling thoughts failed to cohere into anything that might contribute to constructive conversation. But I did wonder where Saul had gotten these ideas. "So what, do you have a psychology degree or something? Or did you study anthropology and pick this up from some tribal shaman?"

Saul seemed to find my question amusing. "Psychology? I suppose you're on the mark there. That's what I went to school for, but just so I could jump into the game. I work for a suicide crisis hotline answering the phone all day, and I couldn't hold a job like that if I didn't have some decorations next to my name.

"I hate to come down on it so harshly, but really, psychology as we know it does a lot of harm. Seriously. To the point where most people would be better off just taking their chances in the face of reality. Trusting their instincts. See— psychoanalysis, as it's generally practiced, sets you up to dive into your own psyche in search of monsters. And so then, you create those monsters with your own focus and belief!

"How insane is it to depict the unconscious depths as this whole, chaotic world of violent instincts and shady impulses and repressed emotion; and then to tell someone that the way out of their predicament is to go down there? Why not point out, instead, that this realm is the source of magic that knits our whole universe together with loving intent…that binds us to one another?

"And I don't just mean humanity—though that would be good for a start! I mean the whole of creation. Every living thing. We all cooperate in this living venture. But we've learned to believe, instead, that we have to compete with each other; that we have to fight one another for limited abundance in a dying universe that has no meaning. No wonder people have such a hard time believing that they can find guidance within their dreams! No wonder they go into analysis and immediately run into demons! And then, they're told to experience the horror all over again—to comb through their past with mental searchlights and look for trauma and hardship, rather than being encouraged to believe that they can paint a new picture in their minds, here and now." He chewed a bite of pork and washed it down with wine. "But I doubt very much that the things I'm telling you are taught in any college. One's reason to live is not to be found in a textbook."

I stared down at my plate. The dark fog was still trying to smother me. "I really don't think I'll ever be going to college anyway."

Saul nodded. "Seems unlikely. There isn't a major that covers the path you're on." Then his eyes sparkled again. "Just remember that the journey is only as difficult as we're convinced it has to be. If we don't take responsibility for our own lives—or, maybe I should frame that in a more positive way. If we don't take credit, then our only other options are either to treat everything that happens to us as random accidents, or else believe that some other power 'out there' decides who thrives and who suffers. It doesn't make much difference whether it's a God who plays favorites, a society that's against us, or an aspect of our own psyche that's bent on destroying us. The result is the same: we feel powerless."

He stood up, took our plates, and brought them to the sink. "I think that might be enough for you to mull over for a while," he called back. "Some of these things are fairly easy to comprehend intellectually, and yet they can take a long time to really accept. It sounds like you at least had a moment there where you knew your fate wasn't in anyone else's hands, though. You stopped being afraid."

Then he turned to face me, smiling. "Have I addressed the questions that brought you to my house this morning?"

Saul's ramble resonated so much with my own private, inner experience of reality that I wondered if he was psychic—and how I might go about asking him. I heard the echo of so many of my own deepest convictions in his words.

But I didn't understand how any of this was relevant to the overall hell of my life. Reality was out there, solid and tangible. What did my ideas have to do with it, one way or another? This was the disturbing undercurrent that ultimately sapped the joy out of all my realizations.

I also saw, in a sudden sweep of comprehension, that the vision Tommy and I had crudely outlined for our band had grown stifling for me. We had loosely defined it as a philosophy of "total freedom" and yet, obviously, our mutual biases leaned heavily towards darkness and aggression. I'd experienced a realm of insights, feelings, and sensations the night before that could never find their home within our band as it currently stood. I knew that I was going to have to fight to expand its boundaries.

I just felt overwhelmed by everything I was facing. The mountain of resistance seemed impassable. What's more, I couldn't accept Saul's assertion that I was somehow responsible for it all.

When I failed to respond, he said, "How 'bout we step out on the porch for a bit?"

Once we were out there, I lit up my first cigarette in over twenty-four hours. Listening to the crickets in conversation, I recalled moments from the previous night when everything in creation had seemed to be in its perfectly ordained place.

The tobacco in Saul's pipe smelled faintly of apple. Neither of us spoke for a few minutes. Then Saul made an announcement.

"I've been thinking of pursuing my own practice from home. In the few years that I've been at my current job, I've made strong connections with quite a few of the people I've helped. Many of them have expressed interest in one-on-one consultations. Of course, I'd love to be my own boss and set my own schedule, anyway. All of this means that I'd need my own office space. And along the lines of that, I've been thinking of building an addition coming off of the living room. Would you be willing to help me? It'd mean work for you from now until sometime in autumn."

I was seized by an instant of wild hope and relief. The prospect of working alongside someone who I respected, and who seemed to understand me on certain levels, was appealing.

"You could stay in the loft in the barn, too," Saul said. "There's no heat in there, but that won't be an issue while the weather's good. And you'll be able to use the bathroom and kitchen whenever you want. This is an invitation for you, though; I'm not opening my home up to an ongoing party scene, understand? But your whole world could be centered here for a while—the work you do for money and the creative work with your band."

Life suddenly seemed to be opening its arms. And yet, I still felt uneasy. Saul's philosophy of self-responsibility wasn't something that I wanted to accept. I didn't want to be held accountable by him or anyone else. For a moment, I considered whether "true freedom" might be worth couch-diving or even spending my nights under a bridge somewhere. I'm not sure if Saul noticed my resistance, or guessed the reasons for it.

"It's work until sometime in October," he persisted. "Either we'll have finished the addition by then, or else we'll have to put the project on hold."

My will wavered just a bit longer. Then I considered how a few months' earnings and a rent-free existence could eventually purchase my freedom—and benefit the band. "I really appreciate it, Saul," I said at last. "Seriously—for everything you've done. I hope you're not ready to strangle me by summer's end."

"I guess that remains to be seen," he said with a grin.

❖

I called Tommy and told him about my new plans. His relief was palpable over the phone. We agreed to get back into the habit of rehearsing, starting the following night. I called Jaspar's and told Phil, the manager, that I would only be able to give him a week's notice. The phone call that I really agonized over, of course, was the one to my father. But when I finally lifted that mouthpiece and dialed, I found him calm, responsive, and apparently sober.

"I got a new job and living space," I told him. "That's where I'm calling from now." Then, my nervousness made me rush through the most delicate part of the conversation. "I dunno, maybe this was really the best thing for both of us. I wish it could've happened some other way, but…"

"It wasn't doing you no good being here, Brandon," he said. "And I know what you'd say about Rachel. You're right: I haven't been paying enough attention. I'm gonna slow down—get off the sauce. You know, maybe when we see each other again, a lot will have changed for the both of us."

All of this was a shock to me. Saul's words echoed in my head: *You've got to stop thinking of him always as a drunk.* Then again, I'd heard this spiel before. A moment of sincere remorse could inspire my old man to make all kinds of promises and resolutions that he wasn't capable of following through with. What was the reality, this time?

"I hope so," I said. "Listen, is Rachel there?"

"Yeah, sure. Hold on a minute."

I had to wait a while for her to come to the phone. Finally, I heard her say "hello?" tentatively, as if she had no idea who was on the other end.

"Hey princess! How are things?"

"Good. Misha, Mombo, and Tom-Tom are getting ready to take an air balloon to the—" she groped for the word "arctic. I'm using markers to make a map for them. The red shows the way they have to take. Are you coming home? Why did you break the window? Were you mad?"

Misha, Mombo, and Tom-Tom were her doll, alligator, and jackrabbit, respectively. I'd long suspected that Tommy had been the inspiration for Tom-Tom. "Make sure they dress warm. And Mombo should eat before he goes, so that way he won't want to hunt the penguins."

I was tempted to dodge the question of the window. But I knew she'd keep thinking about it even if she didn't ask again. "That was an accident. I'm not mad.

66

And even if I was, you should know that it would never be about you. Dad and I have talked, and things are OK with us. I ought to be able to visit tomorrow, alright? But…I'm living in a different place now."

"Is it far away?"

"No, not at all. It's in Old Town—you know, near where the closed-down drive-in movie place is."

"Maybe I can see your new house sometime?"

I laughed nervously. "Well, I won't be in this place for too long, and it's only a room up in the loft of a barn. But this is to save up money so I can move to a place that's mine. And you can visit there all you want."

She accepted this casually, to my relief. "OK. I have to go, Brandon, 'cause Daddy says my grilled cheese is ready."

"You go enjoy your lunch, princess. Bye for now."

❖

Edge rehearsed that night—Wednesday—as the other two guys had the night off from work and I'd taken a "mental health day." Tommy cast me a quizzical look after every song. He could tell that my presence was fractured, that I couldn't fully focus on the performance.

I finally realized there was nothing for it but to take the plunge. "I want to change direction a bit," I announced. There was no way to lead into it gently. "This stuff's gotten a little stale for me."

My heart was pounding. I lit a cigarette; and although I did it with an air of bravado, I was really holding on to it for comfort. Tim toweled his face dry, seeming lost in thoughts that had nothing to do with the Catacombs or the rehearsal.

"Well, if you've got some ideas then let's hear 'em," Tommy said. "That's what we're here for."

"It's not the music itself," I explained. "It's our concept. Don't get me wrong—I love the heaviness. But there's a lot more things that can be expressed, and I think we need to make room for those other things.

"Like, this morning I was talking to my little sister. And it got me thinking about the moments in life that can be really special to you, and how easily they can be swept away in the blink of an eye. Are they so precious because you know that they'll inevitably fade—that nothing lasts in this world? See, with the band the way it is, the image that surrounds it now, you couldn't write a song about all that.

"It was supposed to be no rules, right? Total freedom. What's the point of rebelling against repressive restrictions if we just turn around and create a bunch of our own?"

"I'm down with all of that," Tommy said. "But I'm not sure about what you're after. You are being a little vague."

I was. And the reason was that I was acting upon an essentially emotional, rather than intellectual, realization. It was a sense of the possibilities, a hint of direction, and nothing more.

"What are we rebelling against?" I asked. "The hate in the world? Well—are we just gonna add our own hate to the pile, or are we gonna offer up some kind of alternative?"

Tommy raised an eyebrow. "Meaning?"

"Meaning, if this band is to survive, then it's got to find something to love."

Saul and I worked together over the weekends. During the week, he would leave me with notes and instructions for prep work that I could do on my own while he was at his office. The summer was a hot one. I probably sweated ten pounds off of me during all those hours of sawing, hammering, and drilling. When I worked alone, my daydreaming mind would hum with melodies and lyrical ideas. Physical work seemed conducive to that sort of thing.

By mid-September, we were ready to paint the addition. As we toiled, Saul told me a little about the counseling that he did with his high-risk clients. He said that one of the hardest things for people to accept, especially when they're suffering, is the idea that all the answers to their problems lie within themselves.

"People will accept nearly any substitute for that belief you can imagine," he said. "Wonder diets, religions of all kinds, spiritual gurus...and even the so-called authority of therapists like myself!" He laughed. "It's much easier—or at least, it seems to be—to get handed a set of rules and then tell yourself that if you just toe that line then some sort of good outcome is assured. So much easier than saying, 'I see that I created this hell for myself, so, with that same power that is within me, I'll paint a new picture of my life. And I will ascribe my own meaning to it.'"

"So what do you tell people like that?" I asked—just as if I had nothing in common with them.

"A lot of times, I let them use me as a crutch," Saul admitted. "I accept their projection, even play it up a bit, if that allows them to hear things from me that they wouldn't be able to acknowledge from their own intuition. I let them pretend that I'm enlightened for a while until they learn to trust themselves better."

The wry smile he flashed me implied a thousand experiences, both rueful and fulfilling. "You'd better get used to that dynamic, too, if you're gonna be a rock star someday."

I snorted. "I can't imagine anyone looking to me for answers in the first place."

"Why not?"

Urged by the sweep of my imagination, I ignored his question and plowed on. "And even if they did, what harm would it do? Hell, I've endured twenty years of an existence of no consequence. If any groupies and sycophants give me attention, then I'll consider it nothin' but the just compensation for a life of deprivation."

That set him to laughing.

"Be as dubious as you want," he said. "You won't know 'til you get there. And by then, it may be too late for all my well-intended advice to do you any good!"

I grew more and more anxious as fall progressed. Once the painting was completed, the work would be all dried up and, as it turned out, adding two coats to Saul's new office only took us a day and a half.

I knew Jaspar's would probably hire me back. Like most restaurants, the steakhouse saw some high turnover. Phil was usually grateful to anyone who was willing to come in and do the dirty work, even if he rarely showed it after the person was hired. But I'd gotten spoiled by my time with Saul. It'd been a distinct relief to work free of the overarching corporate structure that I could neither comprehend nor respect.

I so badly wanted the band to sustain me! But I wasn't even old enough yet to play in many of the bars—the ones where the owners were sticklers for the rules, anyway. And the band hadn't developed to the point where it could make the live performance impact that we all wanted it to have. Supporting myself through music was out of the question, for the moment. But I honestly didn't think I was good at anything else. Certainly, at least, the passion would be lacking in any other vocation.

One evening, such thoughts made me particularly restless. I ended up at Ashley's Pizzeria, where Lacey's Foxhound was playing.

There's a small stage right to the left as you walk in. The building has a glass front, too, so you can see the performers from outside. When bands play there, they just plug into the house PA. Usually, it's something family-friendly like jazz or the mellow side of Indie rock, but I'd seen punk bands there on Friday nights. I'd pegged Ashley's as a place we should approach for a gig, as our ages wouldn't be a deterrent. And maybe that was the logic that drew me there that night.

I arrived just as Lacey's Foxhound was nearing the end of their first set. I knew the band's guitarist, James Crichton, from high school. He'd graduated a few years before me. Tonight, he was dressed in a Scottish kilt, shiny black shoes, a plain white T-shirt, and green beanie. His deep green eyes were offset by a head of fiery red hair that grew more out than down. All in all, he looked like a mythic figure—some kind of elfish minstrel. The whole band had that old world air about them. At first, I couldn't enjoy the music so much because I was nagged by the thought that Tim would've much preferred playing in this group than ours. But they were employing bongos and toms rather than a proper rock drum kit, anyway. The ensemble was rounded out with a flutist and harp player. It was the singer who played the flute. He'd blow his lines in between verses, like blues singers are wont to do with a harmonica.

Music is difficult to describe unless you can liken it to something else, and Lacey's Foxhound did not invite comparisons. I was palpably excited: here was a group who were breaking into their own imaginative sphere, just like I hoped to do.

When they took their break, James walked right over to talk to me. Our interactions in the past had been sparse but always friendly. He asked me what I was doing with myself, and I mentioned my job at Saul's. I didn't want to reveal how I was basically adrift these days. James was keeping busy himself, working at the Abyssinian Grounds café, going to school for graphic design, and practicing and performing with Lacey's Foxhound during whatever hours were left over.

"Hey, I just remembered that you play guitar and sing yourself," he said. "You should go up there and do a couple songs while we're on break. You could use my acoustic."

"This really doesn't look like my kind of scene, James."

"You know what I do when I feel like that? I just play for myself, man." From the lilt of enthusiasm in his voice, I could tell that he wasn't going to relent. "When the audience isn't into it, the atmosphere feels totally dead...you just jam to get yourself off and nothing else matters."

I did ache to get up on that stage, in a way that would probably be hard for any non-musician to understand. The music that's within you wants to pour out and engulf the world. That's the best way I can think to describe it.

"Alright," I conceded. "Just one song, though."

I said that because there was only one song that I felt like playing: the one that I'd most recently composed. It'd been inspired by my run-in with those two cowboys in the Pioneer. It was humming so loud in my inner ears that I doubted I could've summoned any other tune to memory.

"Awesome!" James smiled. "Well, I'm gonna go get a couple of garlic and artichoke slices and fuel up for the second round. Good luck up there!"

But luck wasn't going to play any part in this. I needed to focus. I covered the distance between the booth and the stage in a trance-like state that was only a few shades lighter than sleepwalking. James had been using a Fender Stratocaster, running it through a pedal to distort the sound that came out of the house PA. But I found his Guild acoustic, replete with a pickup, which was much more suitable for this particular song. I strapped it on and plugged in. Those first couple of experimental chords rang clean. I did all of this quickly, and made no attempt at introductions. I knew I'd probably lose my nerve if I drew too much attention to myself before playing.

I didn't even test the mic beforehand. I took James' advice and just performed my new song for myself.

It's best for both of us if I just walk away
Guess that leaves you free to boast another day
I'm sure you'll make a scene here, once my back is turned
I would have thought, after the last time, you'd a' learned

If you don't watch it, you'll be taught a thing or two
Next time I come along I'll knock you off your stool
readjust your point of view

You don't want this with me
I think that you're barking up the wrong tree
If there's a next time, better be ready to stand your ground
And don't say "hey boy!" when there's no boy around

72

Of course, it wasn't just about those cowboys in The Pioneer. I could apply the song to everyone I'd encountered in life whose heads had swelled too big for their top hats. The thing is, indulging in a bit of lyrical chuckle about the whole thing enabled me to gain some emotional distance; and from that place, I could see how ridiculous it was, really, to become irate over every little pebble of spite slung my way.

> Let's hope there's not another time we're gonna meet
> when I'm bad-tempered and you pass me on the street
> Right now I feel alright and I can let it slide
> But don't think 'cause I walk that means I'm gonna hide

There was even a burst of rhythmic clapping coming from somewhere as I got into the second bridge.

> So if you think it's time to fill your empty cup
> It might be wiser to go ponder what you've said
> once you sober up
>
> 'Cause no one else around here seems to be impressed
> Maybe it's time you knocked that chip off of your shoulder
> and gave your mouth a rest

I got pretty loose towards the end, and suddenly found myself wishing that I was there to play a full gig that night.

> You don't want this with me
> I think that you're barking up the wrong tree
> If there's a next time, better be ready to stand your ground
> And don't say "hey boy!" when there's no boy around

And don't say "hey boy!"
when there's no boy around

All in all, I was grateful for the experience, even if the situation did seem a bit absurd. I received a few compliments before I left that night, too. But the most serendipitous occurrence, in hindsight, was when I spoke to James again after Lacey's Foxhound finished up, and we traded phone numbers. Well, I had to give him Saul's number for the time being, but that was the best I could do.

Earth to Brandon

I wasn't nearly as relaxed when I played the song for my bandmates. I realized, part way through, that this was because I'd forgotten to give them my disclaimer that it wasn't my intention to make this new composition a part of our permanent repertoire. Nor was it even meant to illustrate a hopeful new direction for us. Rather, it was symbolic of our making a break from the stiff mold of our previous philosophy, and creating an environment within which many more forms of expression could be welcome.

The atmosphere in the Catacombs turned icy. I think Tim was just ill at ease, because he picked up on the overall tension. But Tommy....

"I don't know, man. I'm not sayin' it's a bad song..." He drifted off.

"But...?" I pushed.

"It's such a departure. From extreme heaviness and a punk attitude to this satirical little vignette? Don't get me wrong, it's real creative, man—and it's a catchy tune. But a band has got to have a focus of some sort!"

I couldn't argue, because his objections so clearly echoed my own doubts. "Freedom" means that you're obliged to choose from a nearly endless field of possibilities. I was beginning to discover this about our self-appointed mission. There are many edges between the known and the unknown that can be explored—and our mortal lives are measured in years, not eons.

I lit a cigarette. Out of respect for Tim, I almost never smoked down there normally. For a while, I just puffed and stared at the cracks in the cement by my feet.

"We could just leave it open for now," Tim suggested. "Obviously, this band is in some kind of transition. You've been talking a lot about your original concept behind it, how it needs to expand to keep up with your new ideas. Why don't we just give ourselves permission to experiment for a while, explore any direction we want without feeling like we need to define what kind of a band we are?"

I really appreciated his little speech. Sometimes it actually worked to our advantage that Tim was not as committed to the band. This allowed him to be more objective oftentimes—when Tommy and I were too identified with the project to be flexible when change was needed.

I shrugged and glanced at Tommy. "Anything goes—and no rules for a while?"

He nodded slowly. "So long as it's for the sake of evolving and not just spreading ourselves all over the place, OK? Let's hold on to that much of a guideline."

Once the matter had been settled for the time being, I was able to dig deep into the remainder of practice, which consisted of all the older numbers that we still collectively cared about. The more I relaxed, the more I was able to remember why I was so passionate about music in the first place. I suppose it's like sex in that way: the more pressure you put upon yourself to perform well, the less likely you'll be able to actually do it.

Joy and pain, satisfaction and longing—all commingling to form, finally, a sensation that defies categorization. One that both contains and transcends all other emotions. This is the thing I was always seeking when I performed. I could say that the feeling lifted me out of myself; and yet, I was more entirely myself when immersed in it than at any other time.

Afterwards, I stayed up deep into the night. Having little semblance of a structured existence, I was free-floating between the poles of relief and anxiety. I was not a lazy person. But trying to fit myself inside the mold of the world's facts was uncomfortable at best and humiliating—enraging, even—at worst. Being in Saul's employ had offered me a brief but welcome respite. Now, more than ever, I ached to find some way to support myself through the band—the one vehicle that enabled me to find my bearings when I'd lost sight of all shores.

My thoughts kept revolving around this conundrum, persistently raising the questions and then conjuring up all kinds of dire reasons why they could never be answered. No doubt, it was these thoughts that roused me long before I'd had any kind of decent sleep. The sun, in fact, had not even risen by the time I'd dressed. I clambered down the ladder and built a fire in the wood stove that Saul and I had recently installed towards the east-facing side of the barn. The late September mornings were getting chillier. I boiled some water and used it to brew my coffee by hand. While I drank, I listened for sounds of Saul's front door opening.

I caught him as he reached his truck, his own mug of coffee in hand. He gave me a quizzical smile. He was obviously surprised to see me, probably 'cause he knew how much I preferred to sleep late if I had the freedom to do so.

"I was just wonderin', Saul…when you start taking on your private clients, how much are you gonna charge them for sessions?"

"Well, I already have taken on a few. This is my last month at the clinic, as you know…. I'm not sure, Brandon. I take a lot into account. It's a sliding scale—varies from person to person depending on what they're able to pay. I need to make a living, of course, but I'd hate to see anyone go without help that they desperately need just because they can't afford it."

"Well, book me for an hour sometime soon, will you?" I said. "Whenever you have an opening. And charge me whatever you think is fair; it don't matter. I've been savin' up all summer 'til now."

"We'll talk, Brandon," he said. "How's it been, living in the loft?"

"It's great for me," I answered, "except I don't know how long you want me staying there."

He dismissed my concern with a wave of his hand. "There was never a time frame. You needed a place to practice and sleep, and I have a barn that I never use for anything. And also…I recognize that you're in a crucial place along your path. If you get some support now, I really think it could help catapult you towards much larger things down the road."

I thanked him as best I could for all he'd done for me. I was, in turns, effusive and taciturn—and all in all not very eloquent on account of my lack of sleep and the fact that I'd never had much practice with expressing gratitude. Before he left, Saul told me that he looked forward to our first session together; said he liked working with people who continually surprised him.

I climbed back up into the loft and tried to sleep. But it was no use. Although it seemed to me that there wasn't a thing in the world worth doing at the moment, still my mind was ready for action. I decided to go shower up. Later on, I'd sell my balls to the meat market—i.e., ring up Jaspar's and see if Phil would hire me back.

Just as I finished toweling off, I heard the kitchen phone ringing. Normally, I would've ignored it. This was, after all, Saul's house and not my own. But the impulse nagged at me that morning, as if an invisible hand was shoving from behind. When I answered—I couldn't believe it, really—it was James from Lacey's Foxhound.

"Hey, man! How's it goin'?"

"Real good! I—" I wanted to explain how uncanny I found this moment. The one time I answered the phone, it actually was for me. But James was already rushing on.

"So, Lacey's Foxhound—you know, my band—we're going to be playing at the Pumpkin Festival in Jennes. Mid-October. It's on a Saturday. Long story short: my godmother is promoting the whole event, so we got made headliners even though there's probably a dozen other bands that would've loved to do it. Anyway, we get to choose our own opening act. Would you guys be down for it?"

The advent of a gig opening up—particularly when you haven't played in a while—is like the moment when you realize that the girl you want is yours for the having.

"Hell yeah, of course! I can't wait to tell the other guys. Thanks, James!"

"Hey, we of the underground need to look out for one another," he said. Then his voice cooled. "Oh, and Brandon…keep this under your hat, OK? But this is going to be the last Lacey's Foxhound performance."

"Seriously?"

"Yeah, you know—the old 'differences of musical direction.'"

"That's too bad." I felt another inner nudge. *Ask him to join your band!* But this time, I ignored it. "It can be hard to find that right chemistry," I finished lamely.

"For sure. Well, it'll be good to see you guys there. Let's hope it don't rain!"

We hung up. As usually happens after I feel an inner prompt and don't act upon it, I sank into a marginally depressed state. But that only lasted for a few minutes. Then I remembered the upcoming gig and cheered up considerably.

By the time I called Jasper's, I was already loathing my decision. My head was swarming with ideas for music, poetry, pursuing a dramatic life and an even more dramatic end; and here I was, practically begging for the restaurant job that I'd so smugly quit mere months before.

Saul knocked on the barn door as soon as he got home, before even going inside. He told me that something had unexpectedly opened up the following morning. If I was willing to drive out to the clinic on such short notice, then he could see me at ten a.m. I would have met him at four in the morning, truth be told. My parched soul was badly thirsting for any kind of oasis.

His office was arranged much like others I'd seen: A dark cherry desk that was glossy clean. Plaques, proclaiming his education and other achievements, hung on the wall behind. All the prominent names in the field of psychology cluttered his bookcase.

Saul leaned forward and smiled like he harbored a secret. "I'd like to start, Brandon, by assuring you that there's absolutely nothing wrong with you. You have no 'problems' per se. You aren't evil, because there is no such thing. And if you're ignorant, then you are no more so than every other human to ever walk the earth. Now—is any of that reassuring?"

It almost sounded like he was trying to goad me. Yet, his manner and tone implied that he meant every word he said in the most literal sense.

"Of course," he went on, "that's all true only from a perspective that you may have to work hard to arrive at. When you're suffering, it definitely feels like something is wrong with you; and the seeming causes of that suffering are problems. They are the embodiment of evil. And every smiling person you see must be privy to answers that have totally eluded you."

For a couple of minutes, the silence lay heavy in the room. Truth is, I found no underlying thread of hope in his words at first, and that opened the trapdoor beneath my feet to the pit of futility. I didn't like feeling helpless. I'd turn it around to anger whenever I could.

So my frustration frothed over. "You're saying that, once I get a better perspective, I'll what, Saul—learn to like the taste of shit better?"

He was completely unruffled. "What I'm saying is that you'll continue to suffer so long as you believe it's necessary. What we have to uncover are the reasons why you're so convinced of its necessity."

"Well so what? Then I'll know. That doesn't mean that anything's gonna change."

"You'll have to give your mind, your imagination, and your personal will a lot more credit than that," he said, "or this will be very slow going. You can learn to see a different world with the help of self-knowledge and intent. And at that point, you will actually be living in a different world. But we have to start by enlarging your concepts of who you are and what the world is. As things stand, you haven't got a lot of room in which to wiggle."

"So what are your methods, though?" I asked. "How do you get down to what those concepts are and set about changing them? Are you gonna hypnotize me?" I thought about Tommy's books by Jung and Laing. "Interpret my dreams?"

"There's countless ways of getting at your own convictions," Saul said. "And my hope is that you'll get to the point where you can do it for yourself. I won't be out there with you when your band hits the road." He winked. "But really…we can start with practically anything."

The prospect must've scared me, 'cause I half taunted him. "Well go ahead, then!"

"Alright," Saul said with a wry smile. "I'm going to ask you for a memory. Go back as far as you can, to when you were a little kid. Tell me one phrase that you just hated, something that people would say that really provoked you."

The answer came to me immediately: "Earth to Brandon."

"Why? Why did that piss you off so much?"

"Because people act like they're saying that to get your attention, but really it's meant to put you in line. 'Get with the program' expresses the same thing. 'Think like us. Get on board with our agenda. Set your imagination aside and accept what we say is real!'"

"Alright," he said. "And now—who did you hear this from?"

"Teachers, mostly. Sometimes my parents."

Saul stared off into space for a while, his chin resting on both fists. When he finally spoke, he enunciated slowly, as if he were relaying a message that had come from a ways off.

"So we've isolated quite a few things right there, some beliefs that have probably benefitted you a great deal and some others that have, no doubt, been detrimental. And they're all woven together, so it's hard to distinguish one from another."

I gaped in incomprehension and shook my head. "What 'beliefs'?"

"Well, first off, you trusted yourself at a young age," Saul said. "You knew that you were unique, as every person is. You thought of your individuality as something precious that you wanted to preserve and protect. And you believed that it needed protection from the world. That's where we get into the territory of more harmful ideas that were clumped in with the beneficial ones. So tell me this: why wouldn't you want to get on board with whatever their 'program' was?"

I swallowed the bait, launching into an acerbic stream of run-ons that constituted little more than poorly articulated, juvenile frustration.

"Oh, let's see, Saul: They're trashing the planet. They might blow it up with one of their bombs any day now. They lie to justify starting wars. They persecute people because of their skin color. Huh, I wonder. Why wouldn't I want to jump on that chain gang? Beats the hell out of me! Maybe I didn't get the 'program' because they didn't manage to implant one of their computer chips into my fucking brain!"

Saul took this all quite calmly. "OK, that's plenty to work with for now. So you see what we're up against, right? You start out with this strong sense of yourself—this belief in your own insights—and yet, there you were, about to enter into a world that you didn't trust at all. You have been seeing and expecting the worst in humanity; and that put you in a real conundrum, because you're just as much a human being as anyone else. Your own distrust is destined to rebound and bite you. And probably, underneath that, you fear that you'll become like 'them' no matter what you do; that it's inevitable." He screwed his face into an expression of mock brutality. "But you'll resist. You won't give an inch of ground willingly. It's no wonder you're a fighter."

I glared back at him. "So, are you trying to tell me that people don't do these things?"

"I'm pointing out that your idea that people are nothing but shortsighted, greedy, violent cretins has not served you well. The human race commits all kinds of harm through its own lack of consciousness. I'm not denying that. But it has also been responsible for a great many wondrous things—things that you don't focus on nearly so much as you do the negative aspects. You could just as easily admire people for a whole set of different reasons."

I raised a dubious eyebrow.

"Well, you look up to me, don't you?" Saul challenged.

I shrugged. "Yeah. I guess so."

Saul leaned forward as far as he could. His voice dropped to an almost conspiratorial whisper. "Maybe they were scared. Maybe they said 'Earth to Brandon' because they didn't know where you were going, and they weren't sure whether or not it was a safe place. Maybe they wanted you to 'get on board,' to join in the circle, so that they could feel safer. The point is that we're run by any of a million possible motives. You could give people the benefit of the doubt, instead of assuming that every time you get a response from the world, it's coming from somebody who wants nothing more than to blow everything up or turn you into a mental slave."

Saul offered me a bottle of water out of his little cooler. He must have known that I needed a minute to absorb all of this. Fooling around with black magic and dipping into psychology books is nothing alongside the challenge inherent in really looking inward at yourself. I would soon be finding that out. "So you're telling me that no matter how idiotically the human race behaves—I've got to think that it's wise, noble, and full of good intentions? Seriously, Saul?"

"I'm suggesting that there are other aspects to focus on that maybe you've ignored." Saul ran a hand through his hair. Once again, he seemed to be conferring with someone or something far away. "And also, I'm pointing out that what you have focused on has created limitation and pain in your life. It's made things much more difficult than they need to be."

I noticed that my hour was almost up. There was an old clock on the wall between Saul's two plaques. He didn't seem particularly concerned—or even aware—and yet I finished my drink in preparation for leaving.

"Well, I'm not sure what to do with all this," I admitted.

"Maybe it's enough, for now, just to be aware of it," he said. "Just knowing what's there in our own minds can help us to move through it and, hopefully, discard the old junk that doesn't serve us anymore."

Saul ended up only charging me fifty bucks for that session. I told him I'd like to see him again, only I didn't know when. I needed to land on a regular source of income again.

❖

Tommy found an apartment that the two of us were able to move into early in October. It came fairly cheap, due to some recent circumstances. Apparently, the former tenants had been meth-heads who had turned their kitchen into a lab. But this fact was only discovered after their eviction. What happened first was that the couple's rent had been months overdue, and they'd refused to budge from the place even after being served their walking papers. Finally, the police had to be called and they ended up hitting the place with pepper bombs. That finally smoked the couple out of their hole.

When Tommy and I first drove by the place, there were people in full protective suits, gloves, and face masks pulling everything out of the apartment in huge plastic bags. A few days later, the cleaning crew arrived dressed much the same way. Anyway, it was in livable shape by the time we looked at the inside. The carpet was in dire need of a shampoo; there were faint scrawl marks on the walls that couldn't be cleaned off without stripping the paint; and a musty smell clung to everything. The stairs and banister were of dark wood, and would have fit a Victorian home from a century ago. We were warned not to drink the water on account of high sulfur content—the toilet bowl, in fact, always looked like it'd just been urinated in even after a fresh flush. So, I guess what I'm saying is that it was livable by our standards. Sure, we desired much more for ourselves. At the same time, however, we were willing to endure conditions that most people couldn't have tolerated for a single day, for the sake of our band and vision.

Moving into the apartment necessitated a trip back home to collect the rest of my belongings. Dad had left my basement room untouched—almost as if I would be coming back—which choked me up a bit and made the whole ordeal harder to bear. I was grateful to discover that Rachel was gone to a birthday party for the afternoon. I didn't want her to watch me pull my stuff out of the house. I did write a little note, though, and left it on her pillow.

Robert Chane, my father, stood on the lawn with his left hand in his pocket and his right clutching a can of beer as he watched me pack the car, without saying a word. So much for my theory that he was slowing down. I guessed he'd cracked his first beer of the day straight out of bed, by that point.

Robert. I thought of him like that, now. For the first time in my life, I identified him with his first name. It didn't feel like I had a father anymore. Neither did Rachel; and she needed one. *At least you escaped!* I told myself. It was the only consolation I was able to latch onto.

Already, the band had proven itself the vehicle of my liberation, to some extent. There was nothing behind me worth clinging to. Images of Mom, and of

Dad as he once had been, lurked back there. But pain swirled at the core of every memory. I wished that I could just hit the road right then, put some miles between myself and those recollections, let the world completely devour me with the anticipation of its days and the electric restlessness of its nights.

❖

The Pumpkin Festival was held every year at this time on farmland about twenty miles outside the city limits. Whatever acres they were leaving fallow that year were smoothed out with tractors and then made available to the public for five dollars' admission—and whatever else they could squeeze out of you in the various vendor booths. It was basically a giant farmer's market, with meals of fresh organic produce and free-range meat served at the stands along with homemade shirts, jewelry, hats, blankets, belts, posters, and the like.

Tim pulled us up as close as we could get to the action and then we slurped through the mud and grass to finally haul our gear up onto the stage. We crashed into "Half-Remembered Trails," which was mostly Tommy's song, with just a little lyrical help (per the title) from me. The riffs weren't fast. Rather, they crunched like a hot trudge through quicksand, and they got the people closest to the stage bobbing their heads like the freshly roused undead. Some of our sound's intensity dissipated in the open air, failing to produce the ideal sensations of pressure and claustrophobia we preferred, but it carried well enough. Many of the kids were really giving themselves over to their own inner madness. Every time I saw someone thrashing about with abandon, I felt my soul elevated.

Then came the applause—way more than we'd received at the Samurai warehouse. I was a lot looser this time. We all were. Tim hit the skins like he'd just said the absolute final word on the matter. And I watched Tommy at work and thought, *he already has this aura about him of a natural front man.*

We hadn't written a whole lot of songs by that point, so we extended the ones we had with improvisation and, sometimes, sheer controlled feedback. During one of our jams, I even managed to recite some lines of poetry that I'd not yet managed to wed to music. By this time, there must have been a hundred people in the crowd. My belief in the band, in the naïve vision that Tommy and I had first conjured up in his basement, was being justified before my eyes.

Then my eyes caught sight of something else—erratic movement, like a moment of dissonance in an otherwise clean wash of sound. I saw her: she was roughly my age, dressed in overalls like she'd just gotten done cleaning stables, and a green shirt that hugged her tight. The mascara—I could see it from the stage, even—and the dangling emerald earrings she wore somehow complemented her otherwise rustic look. But her obvious Earth Mother beauty was marred by the look of consternation on her face. She jerked again; this time she turned around and cursed. A muscular guy in a crew cut stood close behind her, laughing…taunting. I followed his movement, saw his hands come around and cup both of her breasts at once, and squeeze. She elbowed him. That elicited more laughter from him. He pursed his lips as one hand moved down to clap her ass.

The music squealed to a standstill as I shouted, "You keep that shit up, motherfucker, and you're gonna feel *my* hands!"

The guy flung a string of obscenities my way. I hardly heard any of it. I don't know why I'd bothered to give him a warning when I was already moving. I laid my guitar flat on the stage, dove for the stair, and bounded for the douchebag, the audience parting like the Red Sea around me.

I remember a blur of faces, and then me striking that smug face of his as soon as it was within arm's reach. No sooner did he flinch back from the blow than I charged into his midriff, planting my head against his left side as we toppled over together.

We were fairly well matched in strength, so we rolled around there for a while in the damp grass and mud. I received a cuff to my temple during a moment when he hovered over me, and it made the whole world reel. It sickened my stomach more than my head, but it also lent me the extra bit of motivation that I needed to roll him over and return the favor.

I didn't get the best of him in the end. I couldn't make myself care enough. I didn't want to hurt him—not in that clear, unambiguous way that gives you the edge in a fight. My rage over what I'd witnessed expended itself pretty quickly. I smelled the alcohol on his breath and knew that he'd had a few beers, at least. Maybe that's all it was. Fuck, this just wasn't satisfying.

The drink hadn't made him sluggish or clumsy in any noticeable way. Finally, he landed three good punches to my face in quick succession and I just crumpled. Luckily, he'd had enough by that point, too, or else he really could've done some damage. There somehow just wasn't enough real hatred to carry this fight.

He was breathing hard, his chest and shoulders heaving up and down.... I watched him stagger away. He'd gotten the best of me, but I'd made him suffer for it.

It was a small consolation. The inside of my cranium felt like a hive of buzzing wasps. I noticed Tim kneeling beside me. Tommy leaned down and lent a hand to help me rise. I recovered enough so that the dizziness subsided and only the thick, throbbing ache in my head remained. I braced myself on my knees. Tim was asking me if I was OK. There was no simple answer for that. I'd never been OK, so I couldn't seem to land upon any basis for comparison.

"Well, we were about done anyway," Tommy said.

"No!" I shook my head. I'd just lost a fight. I wasn't about to botch the gig as well. "Let's do a couple more!"

I forced myself to straighten, and shouted to the people milling about, "You wanna hear some more?!"

That elicited enough hooting and clapping to reassure me. I figured that, if I was gonna faint, then I could postpone it for two or three songs. I was forced to limp—I must have twisted my right ankle while we were rolling about—and Tommy let me lean on him for support.

"You'll have a big shiner around your left eye come tomorrow," he told me.

That made me feel queasy all over again. Fortunately, something was readily available that I'd learned, long ago, to rely upon to soothe my pain: the music.

JANIE

All the tension surrounding what had just occurred found its release in the tail end of our performance. I've since met many musicians who feel the need to stop playing if chaos ever ensues. It totally disrupts the inner poise that they believe they need in order to put on a good show. When I'm upset, I ache to play. I turn to my guitar as instinctively as someone else may turn to a lover or trusted friend when they're under duress. I'm not so interested in "putting on a good show"— per se, anyway. So long as the energy and passion are there, there can be catastrophes all over the place for all I care. Music isn't about "getting it right" any more than life is.

Once we finished, though, the undercurrents of sorrow and remorse came welling up fast. I sat down against the backside of my amplifier, out of sight of anyone on the field unless they walked alongside the stage. My head sagged between my knees. I sobbed a little. It was all pointless. After every fucking fight, I swore to myself that I was not a violent person. My heart was sick and twisted.

Most days, I could stash the feeling away and just carry on with the business of living. But my protective walls seemed to have thinned, of late. The lacerations of conscience came through easier—and they hit me harder. Nothing consoled me. Telling myself that the guy had been a pig and a brute scarcely helped.

At some point I saw, through the distortive sparkles caused by the tears in my eyes, shiny black boots splotched with mud a few feet in front of me. I looked up slowly and met the eyes of the young woman who'd been harassed in the audience. Suddenly self-conscious about my condition, I swiped my eyes with my shirt sleeve—a bit too harshly, too, 'cause I grazed over my bruises and felt needles of pain shoot back into my skull.

She looked shy but determined. "Hey, I just wanted to say thank you for standing up for me earlier. He seriously wasn't going to leave me alone. And none of the jerks around me were doing a thing about it." Then she winced. "I'm sorry you're hurt."

I shrugged off her concern, striving to appear casual. Absurdly, I wished I had a towel full of ice laid across my head so that I could feel more like a boxer in the aftermath of a match rather than a derelict who'd just taken a beating.

"I wish I could've done a better job of it," I said. "But that shit just galls me to no end. I don't make music so guys can violate girls to it."

"You're really good," she said. She apparently couldn't help but grin. "I'm not just saying that because you took a few punches for me. I really do like your band." She gestured towards one of the pavilions. "I was working at a jewelry table—some of it's my own stuff—and I got so curious about what I was hearing that I had to come over and watch for a while. You're not pretentious at all up there, like a lot of guitarists and singers I've seen."

"What's the point of that, anyway?" I said. "The music is what's interesting. I don't get up onstage to prove how cool I am. I'm not cool to begin with."

"Well…for whatever it's worth, you seem kinda cool to me."

I slowly grew aware of her peculiar eagerness. It was almost enough to provoke a fresh batch of tears. I drew a deep breath to settle my dread.

"Look, I fight like this—it happens a lot. And sometimes I don't even know why I'm doing it. The band's all I've got. It's my life." Because she didn't seem to comprehend where this was heading, I raised my voice. "I've got problems, alright? You don't want to get tangled up with me."

It was quiet for the space of a few heartbeats. Then I had a moment of weakness—or maybe self-forgiveness. "I have been getting help. Been seeing a guy who seems to know a lot about what can make people—" go over the edge, I wanted to say, but I softened it for her, "act out."

"What kind of therapist is he? A Freudian? Jungian?"

I waved a hand. "Oh, I'll explain it to you another time." Then I flushed with embarrassment, realizing my slip—the assumption that there would be another time.

And I'll be damned if she didn't catch it, too. "Can't make up your mind, huh—whether to scare me away or ask me out?" There was a hint of merriment in her voice that lifted me up. I swear she felt familiar to me in a way that I still can't seem to get to the bottom of.

Then, just as quickly, her voice cooled. "So, if this hadn't happened with me then you might have picked a fight anyway, for some other reason?"

"No, I'm not saying that. Most of the guys I've thrashed deserved it, believe me. I don't go looking for it."

After another space of silence we both burst out laughing.

"I'm Janie."

"Brandon."

She held her hand out, and I took it in mine. I let that moment linger. It was the most human I'd felt in weeks.

"Well, I won't go out with you if you're going to be starting fights," she said. "But if you think you can behave yourself, you can call me."

Some of the guys from Lacey's Foxhound had made their way onto the stage by this point. I could tell that it was getting time for me to move on. I stood up and suddenly felt those cartoon birdies swirling around my head. Janie stepped forward to help steady me.

"My brain's not working too well at the moment." I made an effort to laugh and feared that it might provoke a migraine. "I doubt I'll remember. But if you wanna write your number down on one of our flyers…"

❖

I made another appointment with Saul. It landed on his last day in the clinic. He began by asking me what I'd been up to in the couple of weeks since he'd seen me.

"Let's see…I've been out a couple of times with a girl. I really like her."

Saul smiled. "That's great! What did the two of you do?"

"Well, the first time we made the walk around Regis Pond and then got lunch at the fish 'n' chips place nearby. Oh, that reminds me: Jaspar's hired me back. But they're only putting me on three nights a week for now. I'll still get by, though. Anyway, the second time we did the cliché dinner-and-a-movie thing."

"Did you tell her about your band—about your writing?"

"Yeah, well, we met at the Pumpkin Fest gig, so… And later, we hung out at my apartment a bit and I showed her my lyrics."

"A little window into your soul, huh?" Saul said. "What'd she think?"

"We bond over music quite a bit, actually," I said. "And not just mine. She has good taste. She did say, though, that she thought my words made for better poetry than most of what you find in heavy music. Seriously."

Saul stared at me intently. "And yet you're hesitant."

I laughed nervously. "Is it that obvious?"

He shrugged. "I'm listening to everything you say, and it's almost as if it's framed as a question. Like you expect this whole reality of you and her to just evaporate at any moment, so you want to just soak it up while you can."

I got defensive. "It did seem only right to warn her."

"Of what?"

"Of the fact that I've got issues to work through, Saul!"

His eyes lit up. "Ah! Now we're getting somewhere! Yes—you 'have' issues, much like someone may have pneumonia. And if I tell you that even pneumonia is in the mind then you'll probably call me crazy. But never mind that. What I've tried to impress upon you is that you just believe yourself to be a certain way and believe the world to be a certain way. If you think in terms of issues, though, then your circumstances seem to be bedrock, established facts that you have to do battle with. 'Facts' don't yield easily, because you're convinced of them and you uphold them with your own thoughts. Beliefs, on the other hand, are fluid. Once you identify what your own ideas are, then you can either nurture or discard them. You're whatever you say you are, Brandon. Your suffering only ever has one real cause. Do you know what it is?"

I shook my head.

He pointed towards the window. "Believing that your experience comes to you from out there! When you thank or blame the world for whatever happens to you. When you're ignorant of the fact that it all originated within you—like most people on this planet are, day in and day out."

This was all too abstract for me. I was suddenly agitated. "Alright, Saul, give me one concrete example of what the hell you're talking about."

He didn't have to think about it a moment. "This girl who you've been seeing: do you think your meeting happened by accident?"

"Well, how else would you explain it?"

"I'd say that you crossed paths with her because you were ready to let yourself be cared for. I can see that in you. I hear it in the way that you've been talking all throughout this session. You discovered the intimacy with yourself first, and then the relationship followed."

I had never been confronted by ideas like that before, not even amidst my various readings, and they made me vaguely uneasy. They implied a mountain of responsibilities that I didn't want to shoulder. Any kind of good fortune had to be snatched from the jaws of the world; it wouldn't just materialize for any amount of wishing. Moreover, Saul was giving me credit for things that I didn't even feel capable of in the first place.

When he finally addressed me again, he did so as if he was handling something valuable and delicate. "So you see that we're at an impasse now. No doubt, I'd make a lot more money as a therapist if I peddled miracle cures, if I told people what foods to eat or what gods to worship, but that's not reality to me. I can only try to steer you back to yourself, try to get you to recognize your power to form your own life. But until you can accept what I've told you so far, or at least open your mind to the possibilities, then there may really be no way for us to move forward. That's the prerequisite for everything else."

I shook my head in disbelief. "What do you mean? The therapy is over? Two sessions?"

"What would you be looking to get out of more?" Saul asked. "I can see that you don't buy what I'm telling you."

"Yeah, but Jesus, man—it's a lot to take in!"

"I know. This is where you have to ante up, Brandon. Consider that, just maybe, you're the source of your life experience—both the things that bring you satisfaction and the things that bring you pain. I know that this flies in the face of nearly everything you and I and everyone else learned over the course of growing up. It seems the opposite of common sense. Understand that real change requires a whole new mental orientation. That's what I can try and help you accomplish."

"But if I don't, like, tell you right now that I believe in magic—then you can't work with me?"

"I could continue on, sure," Saul said, "but it'd be a big waste of our time. We'd be rehashing this same argument every week or two."

"You're asking for miracles, man!"

Saul extended his hands in a placating gesture. He gave me a few seconds to settle down. "I ask that, for now, you just open yourself up to the possibility," he said. "Consider that what I'm saying might be true."

And that's where we left it. An hour or so after I got home, Janie phoned and wanted to know how my session had gone. I felt, at once, both embarrassed and surprised. No one sees a therapist in the first place unless they've got weaknesses and problems, right? Hence, my embarrassment. And so, why would anyone want to talk about it? That was my cause for surprise.

Her voice sounded so sincere. I might have brushed her off, otherwise. For a moment, I wandered through dead terrain where I didn't know what I was feeling or thinking. Was it possible that she actually cared?

"Brandon?" she prompted. She sounded a little worried, now.

"Oh, it was alright. Look—I'm not like a crazy basket case or something. It's just that Saul's a really smart man, and I thought—"

"You don't have to be ashamed of it," Janie said. "God, I could use a few therapy sessions myself. Who couldn't? Show me one person who's got this insane world all figured out."

I laughed; and my relief was such that I could literally feel my chest loosening. The idea occurred to me that maybe she really didn't judge me. This insight lent me courage.

"According to what Saul says, we don't have to figure out the world at all," I said. "We just have to know ourselves and look at our lives as being self-created. Then things begin falling into place."

Her tone carried a smile. "Sounds awesome!" She paused before continuing. "Do you want me to come over there, or you could come over here, so we can talk in person?"

My tension returned. We'd hung out briefly in my apartment before. But Tommy had been around, and the mood had been casual. I heard undercurrents of something much more intimate tonight. I'd never had sex with a woman who I liked as much as I did Janie. There was an aspect to my feelings—to their intensity—that frightened me.

"I'd like to, anyway," she offered as the dead air became oppressive.

"Yeah, of course you can come over." I decided to risk the truth. "I'm a little nervous, is all."

"You're thinking about what's bound to happen when we're alone together?"

"Alright: First off, are you a mind reader? And secondly, how come you're so friggin' calm about it?"

"I'm not totally calm…."

Famous musicians probably go through this too, but you don't ever hear about it in their memoirs. I was so tense that I couldn't even go through with it. I'd climb onto her, striving to be impeccably smooth, and suddenly feel like someone had snuffed me out with a fire extinguisher. This happened three times. Janie kept telling me to relax. But trying to relax is like trying to sleep. The more effort you put forth, the more it eludes you.

About an hour later, we made another attempt and my problem reversed itself. I was over-aroused, and spent myself in a minute. I hadn't been with a woman in a while. I hadn't ever been with someone like Janie. I can't explain it. She met me on all levels, and sometimes that scared the hell out of me. That was the truth—and I told her so, that night. Once I'd gotten that off my chest, I was finally able to make love to her properly.

The simplest way to overcome something within yourself is to expose it to the light of day. Things become a much bigger deal when they're allowed to linger in the shadows of our minds, growing distorted in the darkness. Drag them out in the open and they're simply thoughts and feelings with no more life than what we invest in them.

Life seems messy only to the extent to which you hold on to some notion of perfection. Janie and I had talked about that on the phone; and when she came over, she learned beyond a doubt that I was imperfect. But along the way, I discovered that she was kind, patient, and non-judgmental. Once this really sank in, we did have a good—and mutually satisfying—roll around, just for the record.

Sometime during the calm aftermath, she asked me the question that I most dreaded. "What do you plan on doing if you can't ever make a living off of the band?"

"I can't think about it, Janie," I muttered.

She gripped my shoulder. "I'm not saying that I've got any reason to believe you won't make it. I know that you're really gifted. You've got as good a chance as anyone."

Unable to speak, I turned on my side and grasped her tight. She returned my hug tentatively. I think I'd frightened her. I wanted to tell her that the prospect terrified me. That was the barest truth of it. But I worried about driving her away. Our relationship was just opening up. I didn't want to put it to the test so soon.

I got up, mostly undressed, and stretched. Then I paced around my room a bit. Sex had a way of tying my consciousness in a Gordian knot. All my feelings about my own worth, my place in the universe, and the value of being human to begin with got tangled up together. Making love is a way of celebrating something that I'd always felt ambivalent about: being in this world.

"Baby, come back to bed." Janie patted the pillow. "Failure is a shitty thing to dwell on. I'm sorry I brought it up."

This enabled my mind to settle upon something. I looked at her for the first time since I'd arisen. "What do you dream of doing, Janie?"

The curtains were still drawn. The illumination shed by the nearest streetlight was just enough to outline her smile. "I'll kick your ass if you laugh at me!"

I did laugh. "OK! I don't know, though—I've been drinking a lot of protein shakes lately…. No, really, what do you fantasize about?"

Suddenly she was shy. "I want to design a bunch of my own clothing and jewelry. Wiccan and Pagan kinds of stuff. Maybe I'd start out with my own little stand somewhere, be a peddler." She giggled. "But someday, it'd be cool to have my own shop. Like, if some girl wanted to make herself up to be a high priestess, then she could come in and get totally outfitted from head to foot."

I knelt beside the bed, bent down, and kissed her. I had relaxed considerably. Abstractions could give me the cold existential shudders. Clear and concrete details were needed.

"I think it's a beautiful dream," I told her. "And I'm sure you'll make it happen. I had a feeling you must be creative in a way that was off the beaten path, to be drawn to a lunatic like me."

That earned me a pinch in the ribs and another kiss, this one wetter and longer. I love when a woman reveals how she feels about you in the way that she does that. Then you don't even need her to tell you.

All the songs of mine that made it onto our first record were written during those seven months or so when Tommy and I lived in the apartment on Waltham Street. Although we talked for hours whenever we were together, laying our plans for the band and discussing its philosophy, image, lyrical direction, and everything else in minute detail, I always composed alone. That's just the way songs flowed for me. They felt like they were already "there," full cloth. I'd sense the faint outlines, sketch them out with some phrases, or maybe a chord progression to start with. Slowly, all the pieces were laid into a pre-existing groove. It's like learning to read a form of spiritual Braille. Someone else's input would just distract me from feeling my way along, I guess.

My burst of inspiration was probably fueled by my relationships with Saul and Janie, respectively. In vastly different ways, they both laid me bare. Once I became my naked self—at least within those certain sacred sanctuaries in my life—I was able to write in a voice that was mine.

The thing is, if you start out with clear conceptions, then it becomes harder for you to uncover your own uniqueness. Basically, originality entails surprising even yourself, because you're creating something that's never been heard before— even by you.

Despite these fruitful inner changes, facing my father did not get any easier. And I couldn't avoid Robert Chane because I had to go through him in order to preserve my connection with Rachel.

Sometime in early November, about a month after I'd moved into my new place, I showed up at my old house and asked if I could take Rachel out for the day. It was Saturday. I was hoping she didn't have any other plans. I'd figured my best bet would be to spontaneously appear, rather than call ahead and give my father too much time to think it over.

He was sitting in his purgatorial recliner, wearing jeans and a fairly smudged white tank top. It was a warm morning, unusually so for the time of year, and only the screen door was closed. I just let myself in. He was watching wrestling on the television. I don't know if the glass next to him was filled with ice water or liquor. I didn't want to know.

He glanced lazily towards me and mustered the barest nod. If I'd been a thief, I could have cleaned the place out before he managed to rise up from the chair. The stairs were carpeted, so I didn't hear Rachel coming down. Her smile formed slowly; but once full recognition stole over her, she came bounding, squealing, colliding with me and clutched my legs so tight that I nearly toppled backwards. Her exuberance was enough to even make my father chuckle under his breath.

"Brandon!"

"Hey there, princess!"

Struggling for balance, I turned my head in Robert's direction. "I, uh, was wondering," I strove to sound as casual as possible, "could I take her out to Iris Park, then maybe to lunch, have her back here around dinner time?"

He was basically backed into a corner now, and I had to fight to keep my face straight and deny the smug grin wanting to form. Was it my fault that I now "had" to ask right in front of Rachel? And, of course, if he said "no" at that moment, then he'd have a full-fledged tantrum on his hands.

"Sounds OK," he mumbled, squinting towards Rachel for a moment as if she was an unfamiliar sight. She was still dressed in a pair of pajamas: lions and zebras in pink, orange, and black. I noticed that she didn't have any of her little stuffed friends in tow, though.

I smiled down at her. "Then go get dressed. The sooner we leave, the more time we'll have to play." *The sooner you get back down here, the less time I'll have to spend with him.*

And it did feel like an awkward eternity. Not a word was spoken. Dad pretended to be absorbed in the match on TV. I acted nonchalant. When Rachel came back down, my sigh of relief was nearly audible.

Iris Park was only a ten-minute drive away. Rachel and I got some exercise on the monkey bars. She went down the swivel slide several times and then wanted to see how many pull-ups I could do. (I managed eight.)

Then we played chase on the green. At her insistence, I was the Gnome King with the pointy, razor-sharp beard who was always trying to catch the fairy named Ivory Wick (Rachel, of course) and put her in his dungeon with the slimy things that you can't see. If anyone knew how to market Rachel's inventions, he or she could make a fortune.

"Alright," I said, after we were both good and tired out and had relinquished ourselves to the grass. "Should we get lunch at Sandy's Salad Buffet or Miguel's Tacos?"

Both were nearby and had been frequented by us before. It was early afternoon now. The sun was high in the sky and the temperature had to be in the sixties. This was uncanny for the time of year.

"Miguel's has the big sodas!" Rachel gushed.

"Yeah," I smiled. "But you could order a soda at Sandy's and get a refill, so you end up drinking just as much."

My logic didn't seem to take with her. "I like the biiiig drink!" And she indicated a size with her hands that more closely approximated an extra-large tub of popcorn.

I got the chicken enchilada and Spanish rice plate and Rachel got four chicken tacos with tomatoes and sour cream. Eating was more fun for her if she could make a mess and then pick up the little bits that got away. Since there was no talking her out of the ginormous, thirty-two-ounce fountain drink, I insisted that it be our drink. There's only two girls in the world who I'd share a two-straw soda with, and the other was Janie.

"Do you have any secrets, Brandon? Secrets you can't tell nobody?"

"Well, if I did then I couldn't tell you either, could I? And it's 'can't tell anyone'—not 'nobody.'" I had to laugh, then, as I realized she'd probably picked up a lot of her bad grammar from me in the first place.

She ignored my "lesson" anyway. "Who gets to decide what you can tell and what you can't tell?" she asked. "Do I have to keep a promise if I was made to swear?"

It had taken me this long to realize that we were not involved in one of her imaginative flights this time. "OK, Rachel—I can tell that there's something you really want to talk about." I was striving to sound calm, but my heart had begun to race. "My feeling is that it's not fair to have to hold on to secrets if doing that makes you upset, alright? So it's up to you. I'm here to listen if you have something to say."

"Daddy will get mad if you know."

"He doesn't have to find out that we talked. You know that Dad drinks too much sometimes, and says things he doesn't mean."

"Daddy didn't say it, though. It was Auntie Gail…. She said that I might go live with her starting at Christmas time."

I had to enunciate slowly. If Rachel noticed my distress, then that would only feed her own. "So…it may be that Auntie Gail is doing a good thing. She might be able to take better care of you than Daddy can, right now. And Uncle Ernie will be there, too. They're good people; and they love you."

Rachel went back to eating. She was quiet for a while. Maybe my answer satisfied her. Once again, I was struck by the resiliency of youth. I think it has to do with being completely immersed in what's right there in front of you. Me—I felt as empty as a gourd that had been hollowed out to make a rattle.

When I got home, Tommy wanted to bounce some ideas around. I told him that I had to take care of something first. When I explained that it was about Rachel, he let it be.

I phoned the Friedmans. After three or four rings, I heard Ernie's crisp and always down-to-business voice on the other end. "Yes?"

"Hi, Ernie. It's Brandon."

"Hello Brandon. What can I do you for?"

Then at once, the sound was muffled. I knew he'd cupped the receiver with his free hand. For a minute or so, I vaguely heard what sounded like a brisk verbal tennis match between he and his wife. Then she got on the phone.

"Hello Brandon. It's Gail."

She was even more all-business than he was. I figured I had to adopt the same posture, or we'd never advance the conversation.

"Yes. I was out with Rachel today and just wanted to confirm that it was true, what she said."

By her tone, I judged that Aunt Gail was expecting an argument. Full of rectitude, she replied, "You know perfectly well the condition your father is in. It's not a healthy environment for her."

"Yes, I understand that." As if I needed to be told. I'm the one who'd lived with him. Her condescension really rankled me, but I tried to be cool. "It's just the first that I've heard of this."

Again, she made a preemptive strike. "First of all, no one has known how to get ahold of you since you moved out of the house. And secondly, what do you think you can really do for her? I know that you care for your sister, but don't you see that this is out of your hands?"

I let the silence linger too long and compounded the conflict by giving her a further opening. She continued on at me. "It'd be better for you to focus your energies on your own life, don't you think? What have you been doing with yourself since you got out of school? Have you thought about college, or a trade school? I can't imagine that you want to bus tables in a restaurant for the rest of your life—"

I hung up. Then I swayed, suspended, for a few seconds. I knew that I needed a much more visceral release. I lifted the receiver and slammed it down again. That didn't do it either. I yanked the whole thing, phone and cradle, off the wall and onto the floor. Then I pounded the device into a pile of plastic splinters and circuitry with the heel of my boot. The entire destruction consumed a couple of minutes. It felt good. But I remembered that Tommy had bought this phone a couple of weeks before, that he'd thought of it as a kind of housewarming present for the both of us. In actual fact, I used it a lot more often than he did, now that I had Janie in my life. I collapsed to my knees and wept over its remains.

CARLOS

Tommy knelt there beside me for a while without saying anything. Then he scooped up some of the fragments and let them slide off his palm, back onto the floor.

"See? It's just material stuff. Not a tragedy."

My throat was raw. "It was yours, man. I had no right!"

"Yeah, well…I may make you pay for it. We can talk about that later. So what's up? Something happened with Rachel, I take it."

"She may end up living with the Friedmans—my aunt and uncle. Gail is Dad's sister." I wiped my face. I wasn't that embarrassed, as Tommy had seen me cry many times.

"That could be good, though, right?" he asked. "They'll be more responsible than Robert, I'm sure."

I nodded. "It's just everything else around it. I didn't want to believe it was that bad—that it would come to this. It sounds like they're in the midst of a court battle. And I have these really dark thoughts, man—like if Dad loses Rachel then he's going to kill himself. Either drink himself to death or do it deliberately. And there's nothin' I can do about anything. I never have any power. Gail pretty much rubbed that in my face just now."

We were quiet for a few minutes as he sat next to me with his arm slung over my shoulder. Then I said, "Man, I wish we could jam right now."

Tommy stood up and offered me his hand. I gratefully accepted. "At least let's get out for a walk, then," he said.

It'd cooled down considerably; the air outside felt good. Emotional outbursts create a lot of heat inside your body. My heart was still beating faster than usual, but my mind was in the state of quiet clarity that can follow a crying bout.

We followed Waltham Street up the hill to where it meets with Portsmouth, which runs east to west. We crossed there and headed for the dug-up field where several tractors slumbered. The site was intended for a new gas station and convenience store. The construction zone was all fenced in, but we climbed over and tramped about in the overturned dirt

Then Tommy dropped the bomb on me. "Tim called earlier today—called to quit. Said he just wasn't ready to gamble his whole future away on a band. Any band. He didn't want us to think that it was a personal thing."

❖

In light of these events, you can bet I felt almost desperate to reach my next session with Saul. I was to meet with him in his new home office, the one that I'd helped to build, on the following Saturday. He asked me to show up a half hour early, for reasons that he didn't explain. When I pulled up in his driveway that morning, he was smoking on his porch and talking with a Hispanic man who looked to be roughly my age. From his clothes—a red cap set on backwards, tight white thermal shirt streaked with grease stains, and faded jeans similarly marked—I guessed that he worked in an auto shop. He was a head shorter than me, muscular and lean. As I got out, he smiled and nodded towards me as if we already knew each other.

Saul introduced us. "Brandon, this is Carlos Rodriguez. Another seeker after that which already lies inside him." He smiled as if the two of them shared some personal—and recent—association to this remark.

We shook hands. I liked Carlos immediately. He felt real.

"Carlos is in a similar place as you were when you stayed here, Brandon," Saul said. "He's in transition, trying to distance himself from some bad situations and looking for a good place to land. So I've offered him the use of the loft as a base of operations until he can get settled."

"Saul says your band has been practicing in the bomb shelter back there," Carlos said. "Just want you to know that I'm cool with all that. I work a lot and won't be around too often."

There was something peculiarly earnest about the way he talked. He was eager to connect. "You don't need to worry anyway," I said. "The band's in limbo. In fact, I wouldn't be surprised if our former drummer stops by later to pick up his set."

"What happened?" Saul asked.

"He quit. No hard feelings. His interests just lie elsewhere."

Saul smiled. "Well, far be it for me to play matchmaker. But you know—Carlos here is a drummer."

Carlos smiled sheepishly.

"Seriously?"

"I haven't had a set in a while," he said. "I've just been practicing on some pads to keep my timing sharp. But yeah, I've drummed since I was a little kid."

"What kind of music?" I asked.

"Oh, all sorts of stuff, bro. Punk, psychedelic jam, funky grooves, electronic. But what do labels mean, anyway, huh? I always wanted to be in a band that made their own sound."

"That's what we do!" I blurted. I was stunned. It was so perfect; and life had made me skeptical of anything that flowed without a hitch. But I knew that I'd be kicking myself in the ass for a long time to come if I didn't step through this doorway while it was open. "Look, I gotta work tonight, but if you wanna meet here tomorrow, Tommy and I can play what we've written, and you can decide if it's something you're into. I should warn you, though—we're extremely serious about it. If we get the opportunity to record, or tour, then nothing—not girlfriends or jobs, schooling, anything—is gonna get in the way. We put the band first."

Carlos grinned fiercely. "That's the only way to be if you want to make it, no?"

I smiled back. "So what do you say? Tomorrow at eight-ish?"

"Sounds good, bro. I'm a little rusty, like I said, but we'll see how it all goes."

Feeling hopeful for the first time in days, I followed Saul into his office. He fetched us both ginger ales from his cooler, then sat down at his desk.

"Lots of times, things will line up that way when your inner intent is clear," he explained. "You doubt a lot of things about yourself. But you don't doubt your calling as a musician and a writer, and so that part of your reality keeps moving forward."

Which prompted me to think: why does the idea of coincidence feel safer than the idea of an intelligent and responsive reality all around us?

"So…how have the last couple of weeks been?"

I told Saul about Rachel, my conversation with Gail, and how I'd destroyed our phone.

"So you're still struggling with the same things," Saul pointed out. "Do you see that? Giving away your power and then believing that the world has power over you. Your aunt, for example, has no influence over you or your destiny unless you give it to her. What you hear her say is essentially just your own doubts echoing back to you."

"Are you saying that the people we know are all illusions, then? That there's no point in caring about anyone else?"

"I'm saying that there are inner reasons for all of us to have the interactions that we do; and that's the place we've got to work from. If I tell you that you're a sacred and miraculous being, then I would hope you would hold others in the same regard. And as far as that goes—you could focus on the things about your aunt that you admire. She is stepping in to help someone who you deeply care about, right?"

I couldn't answer.

"Do you find that some part of you agrees with what she's saying?" he persisted. "Do you think you ought to be doing more with your life, that you ought to define who you are and where you're going?"

"That doesn't give her any right to—"

"Shed the thoughts," he insisted, "and you might find that you don't hear those words from anyone in your life again."

I knew that I couldn't pursue this direction any further. I decided to change the subject. "What about Rachel, then?"

"If you were to really accept that you're in control of your experience," he said, "then you'd realize that this 'rule'—if we're calling it that—applies just as much to her. Don't let the fact that she's seven years old and seemingly vulnerable fool you. Rachel is every bit as magical as you or I."

He didn't need to tell me that. There'd been times when I felt that I owed my own sanity to Rachel's magic. "Yeah, Saul, but look at what she's up against. She's like a little tugboat out at sea during a monsoon."

"Give her credit for her choices," Saul argued. "She's not growing up with an absent mother and a father who has a drinking problem by accident. There are no accidents."

"So you're saying I should just let it go? Leave it in her hands?"

"Her life is in her hands, whether you let go or not."

That brought me up short. I sank into the couch and tilted my head back until I was staring at the ceiling. "Then it was all pointless," I muttered, as much to myself as to Saul. "My trying to save her, or at least protect her. It was always beyond my control anyway."

"Letting go of the need to play savior might be healthy for you," Saul agreed, "but that doesn't mean that you have to discount the relationship. There are other choices at work here, too."

"Such as?"

"Such as you and her coming into this world as brother and sister. Maybe she was counting on you being there when life got precarious. And maybe her love has really sustained you at times, too. There's nothing wrong with honoring that."

❖

Sunday evening rolled around and Tim had still not picked up his drum kit. I phoned him from Saul's house and asked if he was alright with Carlos playing on it. Tim didn't mind at all. He was, in fact, now planning on selling his set. He couldn't practice at his apartment, anyway, and school plus job plus girlfriend were going to be keeping his life pretty full for the foreseeable future.

Tommy drove us over to the rehearsal in the van—we would now need to pay Tim back for what he'd invested in it—and I introduced him to Carlos.

"It's probably best if we just run through the songs," I suggested, "rather than try to explain our vision for the band or what we're aiming for." I plugged my guitar in and flipped my amp on so that it could warm up. "Jump in whenever you feel like you can follow—or, just listen. Whatever you want."

Carlos got behind the kit and sort of felt it out without actually hitting the drums. He just waved the sticks and moved his eyes back and forth. Then he looked over at Tommy and me. "I was thinking about this before you showed up," he said, "and I decided that I wanted to be forthright with you guys, so you know a little about where I'm coming from." He paused, then went on. "I used drugs pretty heavily for several years. Since I was sixteen or so. It started just with drinking, moved on to coke and painkillers, and then it was crack and meth by the end. I got really sick, physically, and aside from that I just knew I wasn't acting sanely anymore. I had to stop, or else I'd have ended up dead before too long.

"By that time, I was like this: total poverty." He gestured to his grimy clothes. "Any money I got went to the habit. So, I've been getting my life back together, getting healthy. And that's why I've been working with Saul. And I think that getting into drumming would be really good for me. Plus I love it, anyways."

Saul worked with extreme cases. Simple as that, so I wasn't taken off guard by any of Carlos' revelations. I'd already assumed that he'd battled and crawled his way out of some hellhole to get here. I tried to sound reassuring. "You won't have to worry about temptations within this band," I said. "We're pretty straight-edge. That is, if you can ignore my natural state of mind being where most people are when they go off on a psychedelic trip. And as far as that goes, I don't consider psychedelics to be drugs, per se. But anyway, what I'm saying is that we'll totally support your staying straight."

Tommy concurred. "Which is not to suggest that we're a tame band by any stretch," he pointed out. "We just manage to find the divine madness naturally."

Carlos grinned. "I would not describe myself as tame, either. Just seeing life a lot clearer these days, is all."

Tommy and I conferred in low voices and finally settled on beginning the proceedings with a new composition of mine. It was more of a sketch—a poem that I'd set to music—than a full-fledged song (at that point). But I thought it showed promise.

You flee from my reach
On a cool, tropic beach
The spice in the air
The dusk in your hair
And my aching so strong
Headlong...
A maddening fire that
springs from parched desert sands
But you can't be grasped by
fleshy hands
And through my fingers you sift like
Sun and Sea
My sweet and forbidden
Mystery

Mystery. Saul had aroused my curiosity as much as he had often infuriated me. Was it true, as he said, that I existed as more than just a physical being? Was everything I experienced really a product of my mind? A cry of YES burst in my chest every time I was visited by such thoughts. And yet, everything in my environment seemed to contradict that sense of wonder. How could the shit of my life be my own making? And so "To Mystery" was like an internal argument in lyrical form; and I was as liable to take one side as the other whenever I sang it.

I struggled to even concentrate on my vocals that night. The distraction was Carlos' drumming. He was right there, man, in a way that Tim had never been.

Tommy and I could hear the difference right away. You can have two musicians side by side, playing the exact same piece of music note-for-note in sync, but if one of them means it on a deeper and more visceral level, then he or she will make the other rendition seem pallid in a way that's real hard to describe. You would have thought Carlos had written "To Mystery" himself, or lived it.

Tommy and I only needed to confer for about ten minutes, during our first break. I let him do the talking when we went back down into the Catacombs. "This may seem a little abrupt, coming after our very first rehearsal," he told Carlos, "but we're just going to ask you straight out whether or not you're willing to commit to this band."

Carlos shrugged. "I'd jump in now, if I could. But look at me. I'm just starting to get my life back on track. Getting a drum kit is still a ways off."

"Just forget about that for now," Tommy persisted. "The only important thing, in this moment, is whether you want to be a part of this."

Carlos met us each, in turn, square in the eye. "I really like what you guys are doing. This shit is real. I'm in if you want me."

"Then this is how it's gonna be," Tommy said. "You're in. And Brandon and I have talked this over. All the money that we make, whatever doesn't go to basic living expenses, we put towards the band. So we're gonna buy Tim's drums so that you can have them to play on."

The look of gratitude on Carlos' face was well worth the few hundred bucks I ended up shelling out for that drum kit. Backing a group like ours was bound to be fraught with challenges for him—dealing with my temperamental personality being one of the primary ones—so I wanted to start things off in a supportive way.

So that was settled. I was so elated that I actually enjoyed working my shift the following night. I drifted through the restaurant with the reverberation of those songs, righteously torn through by the three of us, ringing up from the deep well of my soul. When I finished at about eleven-thirty, I put in a request to work daytime shifts to free up more evenings for practices.

I had the next day off and really wanted to see Janie. I called her at work and suggested that we take a walk around the nearby docks as soon as she got off. I drove up there and met her at five o'clock. What stands out for me now is that this was the first time we ever walked hand in hand out in public. There were maybe a dozen boats anchored out in the harbor and twice that many people—most of them coupled, like us—walking about. The late autumn air, blown in from over the Pacific, awoke in me those sorts of sensations that probably only the best of poems can evoke.

Of course, before long I got to talking about Edge of the Known. "There's nothin' better," I told her, "than a group of people who are all fully committed and passionate. And that's what we've got now."

"Well then," she replied, with a merry sparkle in her eye, "the next time you're all together I'll have to come by with my camera and do a photo shoot. You guys will need some official band pictures, right?"

We ended up pursuing her idea that very night, before rehearsals commenced. It seemed to me that the timing was perfect: the sun was low, and it left us shadowed and yet still illuminated enough to project our images.

"Now, this is as much an expression of yourselves and your art as your songs are, guys!" Janie said. "Let me see the darkness, the passion…some life!"

The shot she snapped after delivering that motivational speech showed Carlos looking ready to scrap, Tommy glowering like some grim Nordic god, and me baring my teeth as if I was ready to bite the head off a vulture.

Then Carlos glanced over towards me and winked. "I can see why you like her!"

"Yeah, she's a feisty one."

"Alright: let's change up the energy here," Janie said. "Tommy, how 'bout you get on Brandon's shoulders?" We captured a rare moment of Tommy smiling with that one.

"I'll take the best of these and print up a bunch of flyers from them," she said when we finished. "Then you'll have something to use whenever you guys have gigs. When you start playing regularly, you should build up a mailing list, too, and send out newsletters. These images will make people curious about the music."

Perhaps sensing the mood between myself and my girlfriend, the guys then went down into the bomb shelter and started playing around without me.

I took Janie's hand in mine and leaned my head on her shoulder. "I so badly want to be close to you right now that it's hard to break away and go play."

She dug her thumbs playfully into my sides. "Well, you've got a job to do, Mister Music Maker. I'll appreciate it if you hold the thought, though."

"Thanks for comin' out here tonight and doing this," I whispered.

"It's my pleasure. Just wait 'til I have some custom-made accessories to dress you up in."

"Alright," I laughed. "Just for the record, though, I think Tommy would look better in wizard robes than me."

"I'll make something that suits you better than anyone else, then," Janie told me. "Besides, I'm pretty familiar with all your measurements."

"Oh, you're an imp!"

"You bring it out of me, poetry man." She gave me another squeeze. "Alright, go play! You working tomorrow?"

"Yeah. But starting next week my schedule's gonna be similar to yours."

"Awesome! I don't see you nearly as much as I'd like to."

"Me neither."

After a few kisses, I yanked myself away and rejoined my band.

I was pretty reticent, to begin with, the next time I met with Saul. Everything I was thinking and feeling seemed so hard to articulate.

"You're looking like a deer in the headlights today," he said, "so I'll just prompt you with a few questions, alright? How 'bout we start with your relationship? How is that?"

"Pretty good, actually."

Saul grinned. "Do you mean 'so good that it's scaring the shit out of you?'"

"I do feel like sometimes I'm waiting for the bubble to burst, yeah."

"Someday she's going to wake up and realize how 'flawed' you are, and then it will be all over...."

"Something like that."

"You know, you're definitely not the only one to worry about reaching the end of the 'honeymoon period,'" he said. "But I tell ya—that's when you start uncovering the real treasures. You realize that you're both forever learning and growing. And that's the journey. Enter into it together, and you're in the sacred container. And it's not something that becomes stale just because you grow familiar with each other. That's the big myth. If you're honest, then you realize that you've never got the other person pegged. We're unfathomable beings. No one can ever plumb the depths of us."

"I haven't told you how bad it got."

Those words just leapt out. I guess the grief inside me couldn't keep its silence any longer. Realizing that it was too late to change direction now, I forsook restraint.

"I nearly killed a guy."

Then the details tumbled out of me as my heart lurched like the battered prow of a ship in storm and my mind felt glazed over with a protective coat of disbelief. What was real? Tommy had been there; he'd talked me down. Rachel had leapt into my mind, reminding me of humanity. Suddenly I could feel again. In that moment of sanity, I had looked down and sickened at the sight. I don't know—I can never know—if I really would have done it...

Saul's eyes were hard. "What I think it comes down to, for you, is this way that you have of turning your pain inside out so that the world looks like your adversary. You believe that people are out to get you. On top of that, you believe that violence is power. That's a pretty dangerous combination, my friend."

"I know."

"That's the edge we have to work from. You can see yourself, and the world around you, much differently. But if you remain convinced that you're empowered when you throw your fists, then it's going to take some hard work to get there."

Then his voice softened. "Your devotion to your sister's safety and well-being. The pain you feel seeing your father slowly self-destruct. The way that you risk your heart with your girlfriend. Your loyalty to Tommy. The honesty and passion of your songs… All of these things attest to your real strength, the strength of your heart. When you attack someone, for any reason, you give up on all of that and choose, instead, to believe the worst about yourself and everyone else. It's actually a suicidal urge. Do you see that? It's the opposite of power.

"And you're convinced—as so many people are—that life is a struggle. The world is cutthroat, and you can only ever get ahead at someone else's expense. This all comes out of mistaking the outer world for the source. It puts you at the world's mercy. Believe in yourself, and your own creative power, and you'll never have a reason to fight again."

❖

A couple weeks before Christmas, Tommy and I received a small bubble-wrapped package with James Crichton's return address on it. Enclosed was a black leatherbound book and a handwritten note.

Hey guys,

Consider this to be a kind of "passing of the torch." I can't think of anyone else who's doing as much to really push the boundaries of music as you are. Therefore, I have decided to bequeath upon you the infamous Lacey's Foxhound Black Book! Ha ha! I kept this log for the entire three years that our band was in existence. There are almost thirty venues in here, everything from clubs to bakeries to coffee shops.

These are all the places that Lacey's Foxhound played when we toured. Our favorite route took us down through Idaho, Utah, Colorado, New

Mexico, Arizona, up the West Coast to Washington and then back home to Oregon. All the applicable addresses and phone numbers are in here. To the best of my knowledge, all the contact info is up to date.

Hope you can put it to good use when you're ready to take your music out on the road.

Peace,
James

Tommy and I avidly poured over the book for the next few days. I got a map of the states from a tourist booth downtown and played connect-the-dots, tracing a blue marker line over the course that we'd have to take to hit all those venues in a circuit. Once again, our imaginations were brimming with images of life on the road—being beholden to no one, bringing our gospel to the wholly unprepared masses.

But we needed a record to send out to the various club owners, promoters, and the like in order to land any actual out-of-state gigs. The only recordings we had available were those we'd made at Ambergris Studios with Tim—eight months earlier. And we'd become, veritably, a different band since then. The songs on that particular demo were no longer even a part of our repertoire. Our new material constituted a quantum leap in both quality and scope over those earlier compositions.

Our philosophy and lyrical approach had undergone radical transformations as well. We were much more accomplished on our instruments. The Ambergris tape in no way represented the sound and impact of our band in its present incarnation. And yet, if we invested what money we had into making a new studio recording, then we'd be left with nothing with which to finance a road trip to the southernmost states and back.

"A door will open for us, somewhere," Tommy assured me. He sounded half convinced, but leaning towards positivity. "We have this whole book of contacts now. That's no accident. Whatever else we may need to make the tour happen will come our way when the time is ripe."

❖

I fell into one of my bleak moods just as Janie was about to arrive at my apartment. We'd planned to take the van out to the woods and camp out, as we both had the next couple of days off. I shut myself in the bathroom and sat on the floor with my head between my knees.

I heard her knock and, a few seconds later, the sound of her and Tommy talking in the doorway. Tommy was no doubt warning her.

Snap out of it! Snap out of it! This is what criminals and madmen mean when they say they can't stop. You become so convinced of doom that you're helpless to do anything but watch its prophecy unfold. In believing yourself unlovable, you make it impossible for anyone to love you.

I already knew that I was going to drive Janie away, and I hated myself for it. Although I heard both sets of footsteps, I knew it was her hand rapping on the bathroom door.

"Brandon? Hon?"

Anything I might have said was bound to be nasty, so I kept silent. There was nothing but ugliness in me, so how could anything clean come out of my mouth?

"I know you're in there, baby! What's happening?"

Her voice had risen in pitch. The genuine concern that I heard made tears well up. Then the door was pushed open. I caught it with my left foot before it'd even made it six inches, kicked it closed, and held it there. It started rattling.

"Goddamn it! Why are you doing this?"

I found my voice at last. "Just leave me alone, Janie!"

I heard her slide down until she was at the same proximity to the floor as I was.

"Let's go out, baby. You don't even have to talk if you don't want to—or until you're ready to. But let's go have a good time. I can tell you're really down. But...once you get away from everything and you're out there surrounded by trees, and nature, you might feel better."

Maybe there was some fleet of mental viruses within my brain, killing off all of my thoughts as soon as they were hatched before I was able to voice any of them.

"Baby? Have I done something?"

Her refusal to react, to fight me, started to melt some of the ice inside me. I rallied a second time. "No. It's me, Janie. I...this happens to me, sometimes."

She spoke right through the crack between door and hinge. "I'll go, if you really want me to. But it sounds like you're just feeling fucked up at the moment and not knowing how to say where you're at. Am I right?"

I dried my eyes and then chuckled aloud. Her beauty and sincerity astonished me that much. "I don't know how it can be that I deserve you, Janie!"

"Whatever that means." Notes of laughter and derision ran through her voice now. "I wouldn't be with you if I didn't want to be." Then, with even more obvious relief, she said, "Does this mean you're coming, then?"

Even knowing that she couldn't see it, I still smiled for her. "Just give me a few minutes to get myself together, OK?"

"I'll get my stuff and pack it into the van."

I stared at the white linoleum, the faded white walls, and the cobweb in one corner with a few sucked-dry fruit flies dangling in its strands for a bit longer. Then I looked up when I heard the creaking of the door.

Tommy poked his head in. "Hey, man...I'll get your stuff in the van, if you want to chill for a bit longer."

I nodded. "I got it together. It's all in a mound in the middle of my room."

I wished that I could convey my complex gratitude telepathically. "Thanks, Tommy. I'll be out in a few. Janie can get it warmed up if she wants."

I cried some more, and I had to bury my face in my towel to muffle the sound. Once I felt that my outbursts were exhausted, I stood and gave myself a pat down to bring myself around. Then I went outside, found Janie, and asked if she minded driving.

Within fifteen minutes, we were on the interstate and headed out of town. Janie and I were both on weekends-off schedules by this point. The forecast didn't call for rain until late Sunday, and so far, the prediction seemed to be bearing out. The few clouds in the sky were light and puffy as marshmallows.

Winter. I think it's all the evidence of death in the wake of autumn's splendor—the sense that all the surrounding life trusts what is happening and doesn't fear for what it's shedding—that really fires the creative mind. I'd already written three songs since the leaves had first begun to change.

I finally found the courage to speak up. "I'm not sayin' this like it excuses everything, or even explains it," I told Janie, "but my mom would have been forty-five today."

She took her right hand off the wheel and clasped mine. "How long's it been?"

"Little over six years now. She got stomach cancer that came on real fast. By the time people were sure of what was wrong with her, it was already too late to do anything about it.... My mother always seemed like she was Dad's shadow. He could say or do no wrong. I hardly got to know her in all those years, 'cause it was like she was just there to echo him. It's funny to think about that now, because to look at what became of my father after she died—it's like she was his strength, in some strange way."

Janie had the radio tuned to a classic rock station, but the reception was breaking up into static. She reached over and turned it off. "Have the sessions with Saul been helping out at all?"

I didn't like talking about my therapy with her, and she knew it. I had to allow, though, that it was probably inevitable. If we were going to grow closer, then she'd have to learn, sooner or later, what I was working through.

"Mostly it's about how I experience so much conflict because I think I'm at the mercy of the world," I said. "He's trying to get me to understand that I've made my life the way it is, and I have the power to change it."

"So he's kind of a self-empowerment coach?"

118

I smiled and waved at the world outside our windows. "Saul says that we are the authors of this dream."

"Oh, so he's more of a mystic or shaman. Wow. And he works as a therapist?"

I chuckled. "I'm not sure what Saul would call himself. He strikes me as an ancient medicine man somehow transported to the modern world. And I find this ironic, too: everyone who sees him, he tells them to trust themselves and their own inner guidance. I mean, if we all did that, then he'd be out of a job."

About three hours of sunlight remained by the time we arrived. I picked up a trail map and paid for two armloads of wood at the main pavilion. They had a mini-museum set up there that was devoted to the history and natural features of Oregon. The owners were a couple in their fifties who dressed like they were used to living off the land.

Our lean-to commanded a great view of a teepee-shaped butte across the way that was as thickly clothed in pine as our own face of the hillside was. I built a fire in the steel-rimmed pit, and we began unpacking and sorting our gear. We'd brought mostly grill food: hot dogs, burger patties, pickles, and chips. But Janie had insisted on packing salad fixings. She pumped up the air mattress while I toiled over the fire.

It seemed like we so often got to talking about me. I was trying to think of some way to draw her out more about her own life. Then I remembered a sketchbook she'd shown me containing various drawings she'd made of outfits that she wanted to create.

She came and knelt beside me just as I'd gotten a blaze going. We hadn't brought any chairs. "So, I noticed that all of your designs…one way or another, they look like they were inspired by indigenous cultures," I said. "That appeals to you, huh?"

"It's another approach to living, one that's more direct. Like this." Janie waved to encompass the fire, the trees, and the sky. "All sorts of people inevitably got marginalized or absorbed by some more, quote 'civilized cultures.' But then the irony is that civilization keeps going in its direction to such an extreme that people long for the simpler ways. They feel trapped, and they start thinking about how they can break free and start over. Indigenous people remind us of other ways of being in the world. It's a one-to-one relationship: you and the earth; Self and Other. Whereas, in our society, there are always middlemen. But it's like you were talking about earlier—about taking personal responsibility. There's no point in blaming society when society is our creation."

Her words merged with the licks of flame and wove a spell over me. I saw it all: civilizations rising and falling; and always an eternal force pushing through, a light that could never be extinguished.

"That's what music is like, for me," I said. "When I'm in the midst of a song, it's that direct relationship that you're talking about. Me and the universe, back and forth. Like I'm having a conversation with the fire that brought everything into being." That sounded so pretentious to my own ears that I started laughing. "God, don't listen to me! Go on."

"No, that makes perfect sense," Janie said. And the way she looked at me told me that she meant it.

That was as much as I could bear. I stood up, helping her rise with me, and caught her mouth against mine. We started moving at once; almost dancing, her backwards and me forwards. Somehow, we ended up with her back against a pine, bare of limbs for its first ten feet or so, which stood vigil right outside the fire ring.

I started working on the buttons of Janie's black sweater. Words slipped past our kisses and pants. "I'm so fucking crazy about you!" Then, "If you'd rather be in the lean-to, speak now."

"Right here is good, baby." And with that, she started helping me undo her jeans. We were undressed—at least, undressed enough for the task at hand—within another minute or two.

Then we gave each other everything we had, with the flames casting our giant merged shadows over the lean-to, and neither of us giving a damn who might have gone by on the dirt road not twenty yards from our camp. My forearms, even through my sweatshirt, became rubbed raw from shielding her back from the rough bark of the tree. After I spent myself, I swayed for a while, gasping like a marathon runner and grinning with the inane thought that I was never prouder of myself than when I smelled like Janie all over.

We managed a repeat performance a few hours later, this time in our sleeping bag. As drowsiness was tugging me towards that enticing other world, Janie asked, "So, are you glad now that I didn't leave you sitting on the bathroom floor?"

My memory treated me to one of its intimate lacerations. "I'm so grateful that you didn't give up," I said, even as I thought it. "When the band finally takes off, it will all be justified and redeemed. And then I'll be able to treat you like you deserve, too."

I'd been spooning her, but now she wiggled around to face me. "First off," she said, "who says that I'm waiting for some kind of payoff? And secondly, you should know that what you've gone through and experienced has its own value, regardless of whether or not you ever become something 'big' in the eyes of the world. Someday, you're gonna see yourself like I do, Mister Chane—and then you'll never beat yourself up again."

Reticence stole over me again. I stared up at the shadowed pitch of our roof. Janie's voice became even more intent. "Surely you're aware of how many rock stars end up drug-addicted; or commit suicide; or hole up in a mansion somewhere and completely isolate themselves? Fame is not a cure-all. Far from it."

I found my voice again. "It will be for me," I murmured.

At the time, I really believed that.

I'd traveled quite a distance away from my old, nihilistic self. This became obvious to me during one of our rehearsals with Carlos. It was around New Year's, shortly after Rachel moved in with Aunt Gail and Uncle Ernie and all contact with my father effectively ceased.

Carlos was often espousing various philosophies of nonviolence. He admired people like the Dalai Lama, Nelson Mandela, Mohandas Gandhi, and Martin

Luther King, Jr. When he got a TV and DVD player set up in the barn, he began to amass a small library of documentaries. During the few times that I stayed there just to hang out, we watched footage of various famous motivational speeches and nonviolent demonstrations.

I opened up to him on one of these occasions. "You know, Carlos, I have a short fuse at times. I've been in a lot of fights. All through high school, and it even happens occasionally now. I know you don't believe in violence. I don't actually believe in it either. I just lose control. I give in. I feel powerful in that moment when it's happening, and then afterwards it's horrible. Anyway, I just want to be up front and not hide it from you, the fact that I struggle with this. And—" I had to swallow hard before pushing on, "I totally understand if it's something you can't tolerate in a bandmate."

He gave me an inquisitive look. "What kind of things you fight over, bro?"

I shrugged. "Someone disrespecting me, mostly. I got in a scrape over some guy hasslin' Janie, once. Can't say I got the best of that one, but—"

"If you feel secure in yourself," Carlos put in, "then you don't need to care every time someone disrespects you. You see that it's about them, not you. You shrug it off."

"That sounds like something Saul told you!"

"Is that why you started seeing him?" he asked. "So you could learn to manage it better?"

"Well, really it started—try not to laugh, now—but I was foolin' around with black magic. I did a conjuring spell, right in the barn you're living in now, and nearly burned it down."

Carlos laughed. "Black magic, violence, all the same thing. The power of a spell, the power of a fist: all shortcuts, bro."

"I know that. There's just times when I forget that there are other, better ways."

The whole conversation was still weighing heavily on my mind when I met with Saul the following Thursday.

I was trying to quit smoking, mostly due to Janie's urging. It'd been three days, so I was a bit edgy and irritable when I walked into his office. This made me more forthright than I probably would have been otherwise.

"Here's what I don't get. Now, Carlos really looks up to these people who stood for peace. And see, they were surrounded by violence themselves. Look at John Lennon: a peacenik killed by bullets. You keep telling me that we create our experience from the inside out. So how would you account for the fate of those people? If they held to peace in their hearts, then why were they surrounded by violence—or why did they die violent deaths?"

Saul looked thoughtful and distant for a while. Then he met my eyes, seeming to see me clearly for the first time, and suddenly grinned.

"Let me ask you a question," he began. "Now, you've often slammed the modern music scene, saying that most of the bands out there are bland and unimaginative. So why are you, a musical genius—if you'll forgive my saying so— living in the midst of all of that mediocrity?"

"Beats the hell out of me."

"Doesn't it serve as an impetus for you?" Saul asked.

"I don't understand."

"Sixties psychedelia happened in reaction to the commercialism and trite lyrical approach of the earlier era of rock," he went on. "Punk exploded in reaction to the tired and overindulgent seventies hard rock dinosaurs...."

"Alright, I get the point. So... Ah!" I sat back in my seat and let out a breath as the realization stole over me.

"Well? Go on," Saul urged me.

"It's just...I like to think that I always write songs to express myself. But the truth is, I often itch to get onstage just so I can show all the poseurs how it's really done."

From the way Saul nodded, I could tell that I'd gotten the point he'd intended.

"You were born into the particular time and place where your voice would be needed," he said. "Not only that, but the way in which other musicians and writers may fall short of your ideal, your vision of what music should be, only makes you strive harder. It's an incentive. How do you think these 'peaceniks,' as you call them, learned to esteem peace so highly?"

I knew what he was getting at. But I didn't feel like talking, so I just shrugged.

"They saw the consequences of violence all around them. And it sickened their hearts. They shuddered to the depths of their souls. They were so horrified by what they saw that they could only hold themselves erect in the face of it and deny it with their words, deeds, and thoughts.

"Now, I can't claim to know what anyone's soul purposes are. I can maybe make educated guesses with the clients I've worked with for a long time. But I would suggest that the cultural figures you mentioned chose to be born into situations of conflict because they intended to become messengers of peace, love, and understanding. They knew that such adverse conditions would serve as motivation along those lines."

In April, our band's luck started to turn around.

One Thursday night, Tommy came in the apartment carrying a couple paper bags of groceries. "We're gonna make our record! I ran into Chas Gages at the store just now," he explained as I helped him put the stuff away, "Chas of Herring Run. I don't know if you're aware of what happened with them. They got so tired of Pyre-House Records fucking with their sound and image that Chas started his own label to release their records on. He calls it Manhandle—'cause that's exactly what they won't do to any band that he signs, he says."

I'd seen Herring Run twice before. I'd considered their name to be a bit ham-fisted, but I guess it was meant to indicate how they went against the grain of nearly every convention of the music industry. They were punks who weren't afraid to play slow and moody numbers. They'd get up onstage in preppy clothes if they felt like it. And all the members were straight-edged: no alcohol, no drugs. I doubt any of them even smoked.

All their lyrics were about personal empowerment and brotherhood. Their message had provoked a lot of riots in their early days of gigging, when they played in support of much less "uplifting" acts. Over time, though, their refusal to compromise won over a good part of the punk audience. Nowadays, you were as likely to get your ass kicked for saying you didn't like Herring Run as for saying that you did.

"So he's put together his own studio, I take it?"

"Yeah," Tommy said. "Manhandle already has three bands on its roster. We'll have to get their CDs. To hear the production quality, if nothing else. Chas is offering us twenty-five hours of free studio time."

I leapt past the preliminary questions and did some mental math. We'd have a little over two hours to devote to each song that we hoped to lay down. Our band was tight now. We could get a full album recorded to our satisfaction within that time frame, no problem.

Then suspicion finally hit me. "What the hell for?"

Tommy put the dry goods away in the cabinet, grinning the whole time, before answering. "I told him we were itching to do a tour down to the Southwest and then back up the coast."

"And?"

"And Chas is keen to get the word out about Manhandle. The guy's got, like, a messianic vision with regards to everything to do with music. It's all a divine mission to him."

I smirked. Tommy could have been describing himself, there. But I was beginning to feel uneasy. "Are we supposed to get behind the mic at every gig on the tour and say, 'Hey, check out our friend's new record label?'"

"We ain't gotta say nothin'. But we will look like a travelling billboard, assuming we take him up on his offer."

"What offer is that?"

"Manhandle's name and logo will go on our amps as well as all the pressed copies of the record. And it'll be on the van, along with the titles and cover images of the two albums he's just released. A cousin of Chas's—who is, I guess, a killer graffiti artist—will get it all painted over a weekend."

"Christ, we might as well become stock car racers! We're about music. That, and breaking down the barriers in people's minds—including our own. We're not in this to sell or promote anything else."

"We're always selling something," Tommy argued. "You want to collect money at the door for all of these intended gigs, right? You want to sell records." He waved down my budding protest. "I know. This is different. But hell, I can stand behind Chas and his label. It's not like we'll be toting around ads for men's deodorant."

"It's reducing it all to a commercial gimmick," I said. "People will hear 'Edge of the Known' and think, 'Oh, yeah, those guys who work for Manhandle.' We'd practically be corporate employees. It defeats everything that we were supposed to stand for."

"Or, it's a bunch of guys in a tough, cutthroat business helping each other out," Tommy said. "What do we do to finance a record, otherwise? Well, you work a hundred hours cleaning up tables after people eat. I deliver a thousand pizzas. Is that art? Is that freedom of expression? And meanwhile, the tour gets postponed...."

His arguments were beginning to make more sense than my own. "Alright," I said. "I'm thinkin' that selling out means setting a course for something other than your real goal. I guess what this is, is taking a less-than-ideal route to reach our goal. Don't get me wrong: I'm gonna be embarrassed driving around with a logo on our van like we're a fucking cleaning company. But I like Herring Run. I dig Chas's philosophy for his label. And I want to record our songs."

"I've got to give Chas an answer soon," Tommy persisted.

I drew a deep breath, and forced my frustration down to a simmer. "Let's do it!"

The following weekend, we dropped the van off at Chas's cousin's place. Ken was a slim, reticent, and unsmiling character who wore sunglasses. When we drove over to fetch the vehicle that Sunday afternoon, though, we could see that he did put passion into his designs. The Manhandle logo—two hands interlocking as if their fingers were hooks—was rendered in black on both the front doors. The driver's side of the van was emblazoned with the cover of Nocturnia's The Craft album: a cat with four blazing eyes gazing down from a bare tree. This was done with green, red, and brown paint. Underworld Muses had an even more ambitious design for their Light of the Depths album: a party of gnomes who were, apparently, the casualties of an accident involving an overturned mining cart. This was all spray-painted in earthy hues from pale apricot to dark brown, except for their pointy hats, which were vibrant red.

We hoped to earn enough money from the gigs to finance the road trip. And now that we had the opportunity to record our songs for free, it seemed likely that each of us could save up at least a few hundred to throw into the pot. First, we needed copies of the album to send out to our contact list before we could even try to line up those gigs. And I was getting ahead of myself even with that thought. First—we needed to record the album.

Even if all went according to plan, we anticipated being gone for six or seven weeks. This meant, quite possibly, no job or apartment waiting for us when we returned. The details seemed endless. No doubt none of us would've been willing to throw our fates to the wind like that if we hadn't been in such various states of desperation to begin with.

What Casts the Shadow?

It sounds so pretentious, but you really do think in these sorts of terms—like when you write a song, you're doing it so you can set it down for all time or, at least, for as long as the world should endure. Posterity is a sacred notion for many musicians, myself included. You take a piece of your internal world and transform it into something that becomes your contribution to the outside world. You think about the ways that music changed your life forever, and it makes you want to add your own invented myth to that legacy. It's a living myth, a great bubbling cauldron, with every mad artist who ever danced beyond society's proscribed lines coming by to taste what's in the pot and then throw something of his or her own into it.

I was in such a mood when I first walked into Manhandle Studios. The drive over there achieved an air of pilgrimage. I noticed, at once, that the building had a deliberately unfinished look about it. The wood was naked and unpainted. It even smelled of sawdust. It felt like a construction site nearing its final stages, only with all of the actual debris swept away. There was a wide anteroom with a boot mat and a coat rack and windows on both sides, allowing for views of the highway to the left and a wall of pines to the right. At the far end were two doors. One led to the control room and the other to the performance chamber. The windows were wide, so we could see everything inside.

We met with Chas, an energetic and radical character a few years older than us, who was always brimming with so many ideas that sometimes his sentences verged on the incoherent. His enthusiasm was contagious, though. We spent about half an hour getting our levels to where we wanted. Then we recorded late into the night. We tackled a handful of Tommy's compositions first, which gave me the opportunity to ease myself into the whole studio experience without having to worry about vocal duties. There was such a feeling of release of passion and reckless abandon to begin with.

It didn't last long for me, though. Somehow, about halfway through the recording process, I suddenly went cold around the whole thing. I was honestly somewhat averse, even, to performing and singing the remaining songs. I couldn't combat this baffling emotion with reason or willpower. I just felt like I was chasing a delusion. Everything that I'd believed in was hollow. Our band was a pipe dream.

As we made our way to the studio for the fourth time in a little over a week, I suggested that the other guys lay down the drum and bass tracks to a few songs so that I'd have something to follow. We all preferred as much of a "live feel" as possible on the records we listened to, and we hoped to achieve the same thing with our own. It's hard to try and generate the energy and vibe of an entire song when you're alone in a little booth. Chas, though, had insisted that he just wasn't set up to record us as a group and really capture the presence of the individual instruments.

But the truth is, I really wanted the others to play their parts because I knew that nothing I managed to set down on tape would be worth preserving. There's a whole spectrum of feelings that you may want to capture on record, but ambivalence ain't one of them.

Tommy, of course, intuited my underlying unease. "You're too hard on yourself," he said. "I know this is gonna sound like totally heresy; but really, it's just a record."

Carlos, who lacked a license, was taking his turn in the back. I was in the passenger seat. "Yeah," I said, "but who knows when we'll ever have this chance again? It's gotta be everything that we're capable of. And I'm just not feeling the passion for it. I don't know what the hell is going on. It's gone cold."

Carlos leaned forward, grinning. "The Muse, you know, she don't take too kindly to whippings, bro. She's playful."

130

I smiled. But somehow his words, the simple humanity behind them, just made me feel sadder about everything. Luckily, they were able to lay down backing tracks to our remaining four songs—within our allotted time, without my help. I sat and watched the empty vocal booth, remembering the easy rapture that had filled me when I'd last been in there singing. Where had it gone?

All this internal turmoil had set me to smoking again after a few weeks' hiatus. I nursed a cigarette out on Saul's lawn the following morning before I went in for session. I didn't want to attack him out of my own sense of frustration. I shuffled into his office, barely nodded, and then tried, in a stumbling manner, to describe the bleak state of emptiness that had overtaken me.

Saul nodded, almost as if he'd been expecting this. "You know, there's a part of you that doesn't want to make a great record," he said. "It doesn't want Janie to love you, Tommy and Carlos to stand by you, Rachel to look up to you, none of that. You're surrounded by a responsive universe that intends to love you, to support your unfolding, and that part of you says, 'No!' This is where the nihilism comes from."

"Why would I not want to make a great record when I've been focusing all my energies, and practicing and writing all this time, just to get to this point?" I asked. Ten minutes into the session and I was already in danger of losing my temper.

"Here are a few ideas I have," Saul started, "based upon what I've learned about you so far. Perhaps you'd sabotage it because you're not worth it? Or the world is against you, so therefore it doesn't deserve your words and music? No one will understand it, so what's the point? Those are a few of the hidden assumptions that could be undermining what you so consciously long for."

I sat up straighter while he was talking, feeling suddenly more alert. Saul noticed. "What?"

"Oh, it's just that you reminded me of something that I've been giving a lot of thought to lately. Like, who is our audience?"

He nodded, looking as eager as I felt. "Go on."

"Well, like, we've only played a few gigs in the city, and I've never heard much feedback. Except from Janie—and she could be biased. I fought at two of those gigs, too, so that kinda overshadowed my perception of how we were being received. I don't know. I guess if you're making music without the intention of reaching anybody then it's just masturbation."

Saul nodded. "And yet…" he prompted me.

I was confused. "And yet what?"

"What do you feel when you think about reaching your audience?"

On some other occasion, I might have brushed him off with a caustic remark. But my emotions were too raw in that moment to be dismissed. "Scared," I admitted.

Saul stood up and moved closer to me. My whole body tensed. "Now we're getting somewhere," he said. "Tell me: what might you risk by trying to reach people?"

I didn't want him to get any nearer, so I answered quickly. "If we don't try, then it doesn't matter if people don't care. We won't make asses of ourselves."

"Right!" Saul snapped his fingers. "Easier to pretend not to give a shit. That's the posture of many a hard-rocking band, as you know. But you never really wanted to be in that sort of a band, did you?"

"No. But this is a cynical age we're living in, Saul."

"And since when do you care about the spirit of the age?" he challenged me. "Aren't you guys the band that bucks every trend and disregards all conventions? Haven't you put your finger on it yet, what you've been seeking ever since you jettisoned all your old songs and started reinventing yourself?"

"I wanted the music to be an outlet for everything that we feel," I said, "not just the anger and aggression."

"Yes! And a big part of that, I'm willing to bet anything, is that you've been looking for an outlet for your idealism. Yes, being cynical and jaded is the order of business in the modern world. And you listen to a lot of cynical bands, too. But there's that part of you that wants to say, 'Screw it—I believe in humanity, and I

132

believe in myself.' Even if it means that you won't look so tough in the arena of hard rock swagger and insouciance."

Saul had a way of pointing out things that seemed so obvious after he said them. It was true: I'd grown tired of the posture that had helped carry me through high school and the years since. Maybe it had been necessary during that period of time; but now it was keeping my soul in a straitjacket.

❖

Our next recording session was slated for the following evening. Business was slow at the restaurant, so me and Rex, my favorite co-worker, had to rock-paper-scissors to see which one of us would go home. I won two out of three, so it was my choice. I realized, suddenly, that as much as the extra cash would be welcome, it was early enough for me to catch Rachel out at recess.

"You mind staying?" I asked Rex. "I wanna drop by and visit my little sister."

"Hey, more money for me." His spirit was unsinkable; and his apparent ability to be happy all the time confounded me.

I drove to Siddens Elementary within ten minutes. I found a place to park out on the street and crossed over to the playground fence. Easily thirty kids must have been running around in there. But I could spot Rachel from inside a crowd of any size. Her posture was unusually straight, she deliberately shook her head from side to side when she moved, and she clenched her fists tight whenever she ran or raised her voice. I could probably sense her presence with my eyes closed, anyhow. At the moment, she was involved in a game with several other boys and girls. I felt relieved to see her mingling.

"Princess!" I called out. And I realized, for the first time, the irony of that nickname. I'd just been thinking about all of her tomboy traits….

"Brandon! What are you doing?" Rachel didn't give me a chance to answer. Once she reached the fence, she gave it a shake with her free hand. Then she opened the other to reveal the pretty orange agate she was holding. "We just snuck into the trolls' cave and stole some of their treasure, but it's OK 'cause the treasure wasn't really theirs. The boys are trolls. Well, they're not really trolls; we're playing a game."

"That's a nice treasure," I told her. "I hope they all turn to stone and then you can get rich off of their hoarded gold. Hey, can I touch it for luck?"

She held it out. "It grants wishes."

Her remark reminded me of the night when, deluded by fantasies of occult power, I'd promised her that the painful conditions of our lives were about to be transformed forever. I was in need of a different sort of magic today.

I reached my forefinger through the fence and tapped the stone. Excited screams issued from back at the stone igloo, a favorite fixture of the playground.

"I have to go!" Rachel said in a huff. "Marla and Zoe are getting captured!"

"Hey, I'll call you soon. Thanks for the good luck, kiddo!"

Because I'd let Carlos and Tommy record without me during the previous session, the lion's share of the work fell upon me that night. I was so pumped with adrenaline that I laid down my guitar tracks in a take or two. The visitation of energy—that fire that carries the motive force of a song and vibrates out to all receptive ears—was much more important to me than a rendition free of errors. It's best to capture it while the music still excites you, and before you have a chance to overthink things. Once we listened to the playback and were satisfied with the sound, I announced to everyone that I wanted to record my vocals naked.

"If you can't handle the sight, then maybe you wanna wait outside," I said. This was half jest and half challenge.

"Through the booth window, we can only see you from the chest up, anyway," Chas pointed out.

"Now, if you perform a gig naked," Carlos inserted, "I will be impressed!"

I laughed, a bit nervously. "I just want to feel natural when I'm in there. That's what I want people to hear when they listen to my vocal: a naked person."

134

I entered the booth, stripped down, and left my jeans, underclothes, and black thermal shirt in a heap in the corner. I felt like climbing the tan wood walls, just clawing my way up by my fingernails. The songs were clamoring for release. After Chas and I did a couple of mic checks, I made a spirited but imperfect run through of "Sea Breakers." Then I nailed it on the second take.

Yours are not the only hands on the wheel
Other fingers rise up from within
And wonders are wrought when we
turn a blind eye to the spin

What do you really want?
What fleeting dream sees you through?
You're chasing after a ray of light that
never left you

Night closes over the heart
Or so you believe
Hard to distinguish its voice from
the distorted echo your ears receive

Union for pleasure breaks on
the rocks like a wave
In the fear of the plunge, what
fragile hope can you save?

What do you really want?
What fleeting dream sees you through?
You're chasing after a ray of light that
never left you

Far beyond the microphone, the booth, and the window to the outside world, I felt this song stretching out its invisible hands, seeding the entire landscape of my life with new possibilities. The melody imbued it all with light, making those vistas expand and grow. The apt word for this sensation can never be found. But the feeling, if ever it's touched you, is unmistakable.

I rode the gale winds of inspiration for two more songs. I was so elated after hearing the last playback that I forgot to put my clothes back on before rushing out to rejoin the guys. We all had a good laugh about that.

A lot of musicians can't be bothered with the final mixdown. They leave that, the culmination of the music that they worked so hard to create and capture, in their producer's hands. Well, I was probably present more than Chas even liked, and I wasn't about to let a single note be burned to CD before it'd passed through my ears. Chas didn't need much coaching, though. He had a good sense of what we were about and what we sounded like, live and natural in a room.

The music was raw and yet crisp. It was both abrasive and articulate. It sounded, by turns, mournful, angry, rebellious, vulnerable, poignant, and tender. We no longer feared venturing into whatever emotional territory might rear up before us. I was as proud of the finished recording as I'd ever been of anything I'd accomplished in my life.

About a week later, after Chas had finished all his last-minute computer tweaking and we'd settled on a running order for the tracks, I joined Tommy and Carlos for our first rehearsal since wrapping up the recording. I made my pitch during our mid-set break, suggesting that we call the album *What Casts the Shadow?* and use, for cover illustration, a photo that Janie had taken of our three silhouettes.

It was, simply put, a question that I really wanted answered. I knew that every human being who walked this Earth had the immense capacity to express love and usher in light. Yet, this potential was so rarely realized.

We are capable of such greatness. Nevertheless, falling short of that capacity is the norm. It's practically expected. It's what people are referring to when they say that we're "only human." But this is not the summation of what is human. It barely hints at the true scope of what we can achieve—mentally, emotionally, and spiritually.

And so, what is it that makes us fall short of this ideal, time and again, all throughout our history? What casts the shadow upon our race? Why do we destroy, when it is our true impulse to create? Why are we so prone to hate when it's in our nature to love?

I posed the idea to the guys much as I've tried to explain it. It's the kind of evocative phrase that everyone is bound to have their own associations to, which I liked. Also, you can think of anyone you're close to in your life and see how the shadow manifests in a way that's unique to them. My father was drinking himself to death. I would lose control and hurt people. There you have two distinct faces of the shadow. But the underlying failure to love is the same.

I also believed that many people had settled for overly simplistic answers to this question. They may not even give the matter any real thought anymore. What casts the shadow? Oh—Satan, the Republicans, pornography, Capitalism, food additives, Original Sin, the ego, heavy metal. Once you settle upon a scapegoat, it becomes an escape from the paradox of knowing that we're capable of so much more, and not knowing why we so rarely achieve that potential.

But I have to confess that the way this phrase resonates with wider universal truths was really a happy accident. I wasn't trying to pose a question for humanity, initially. I was asking it for myself. I wanted to know what spurred me to act contrary to my heart, to destroy the things I cherished, to drive away the people I loved. All of this had been stirred up for me the last time I'd seen Janie.

We'd just been hanging out at her apartment. She lived in a tiny studio that a former tenant had painted with floral designs and hippie slogans. Our date night soured pretty quickly. After we ate some Chinese takeout (washed down with orange juice), we started talking about the tour that Edge of the Known was planning.

"I'm gonna miss you when you're gone," she said. "You gonna miss me?"

"Christ, it's just gonna be, like, six or seven weeks!" I snapped.

I cringe now, when I think of her playful smile, so undeserving of my reaction. What summoned that deep frost? A glacier would grind across my inner world, freezing the ground and blotting out the sun.

I know that she was stung, but I can only see it now in hindsight. When this mood came over me there wasn't room for anyone else's emotions. I may as well have been the only person alive in the world. If you could call it living.

"I know, but…" Janie looked away, and kind of waved her hand abjectly.

I had no footing. There was no mental space, no pause in the onrush, to even think. I was just lashing out and it had nothing to do with her. I needed to apologize. And then, just get away if I couldn't keep it in. Instead, I rose from the carpet floor where we'd been sitting together cross-legged, muttered "Jesus!" under my breath, and stalked out of her apartment.

I drove around for an hour or two afterwards, aimlessly. I was split in two. Half of me couldn't believe that the incident had actually happened, and the other half wanted to weep on the dashboard. I was too humiliated to go back there and too wound up to return home and try and forget.

I found myself stumbling into Saul's office like a sleepwalker the following Wednesday. He delicately probed me. He could see that I was distraught. I told him that I'd been deeply insensitive towards Janie and, for all I knew, had ruined the relationship.

He was quiet for a long time. I felt no agitation. My belligerence was spent.

"It's not so much that your perceptions of things are wrong," Saul said at last, "but just that you need to arrive at some kind of balance, a more complete picture of reality. I know that your ambitions with regard to your band mean a lot to you. And I'm sure that holding to a very single-minded focus around that was probably necessary, at one point in time. But I wonder if that focus has grown so exaggerated now that the rest of your life is suffering as a result.

"Has it gotten to the point, I wonder, where you view all of your reality from the standpoint of being the 'wounded and gifted' artist? Are you stressing everything that sets you apart from others—and turning a blind eye to all that you have in common with them?"

He was moving in a direction that felt really threatening, for reasons that I couldn't identify. "I don't see what the hell this has to do with Janie!"

"If you're the misanthrope," Saul explained, "if you're the visionary who is set apart from humanity, who is on a special spiritual mission, then it would naturally follow, from that idea, that no one could ever really understand you. That includes your family, me—your counselor—your bandmates, and even your girlfriend. So then you'd better drive her away before she rejects you, right? Before she realizes that you're this 'alien being' who has no real place in the world."

I rarely cried in front of Saul. I don't know if it was a matter of too much pride or too little courage. But that night, the tears came streaming down as soon as I made it out to his driveway. Of course, it would be just my luck that June would come home right at that moment and catch my wet and reddened face in her headlights. I spent several minutes out there, just swaying in her embrace.

Then I spent the whole drive home praying that it wasn't too late. I raced from the door to the phone. Janie answered on the third ring, and I plunged right in for fear that she'd hang up before I said what I needed to.

"I'm screwed up, Janie. And I've been carrying on with you for all this time like I'm hoping you'll never find out. There's no point in me hiding it; and I'm sure you were never fooled anyway. I guess I can't really promise anything. But I am trying to heal from this. I've got my work with Saul; and I've found a healthy outlet in my band. And I've got you. Or I had you, anyway. I understand if I blew it, if you've had enough. I don't know if I'd put up with me either. But I do love you, you know. And I'm so sorry."

She sighed in a way that sounded like relief—and forgiveness.

"The way you left: that was the worst thing," she said.

"I'm sorry," I repeated. "I wanna be there for you, better than I have been."

"Well, I'm still here."

Those were among the sweetest words anyone had ever told me. I hung on the phone a moment while they sank in. It wasn't too late. "Listen, there's something I wanna do to make this up to you," I said.

"What's that?"

"You've mentioned it a few times, how it can drive you crazy having grown up here and never getting the chance to get out. And we had that one conversation about how you like the handmade jewelry that comes out of the Southwest and hoped to see it firsthand someday. Well, if we get this tour lined up, we're hoping to make a loop down to the southern states and back up the coast. New Mexico will be our midway point, more or less. If I get you the ticket, would you want to fly out to Albuquerque and hang out with me for the few days that we're there?"

Her indrawn breath was all the appreciation I could have asked for. "Seriously? You can afford that?"

"I'm pretty sure…but hell, I'll sell my car if I have to. I just really want you to be there."

No one had ever touched me like she had, and that scared me. I told myself that I'd come through this fear, just as if I was walking out of a fog. It can feel endless; but that's an illusion.

❖

Once we had our CDs, Tommy drafted up a letter to send out to every establishment on our contact list. We were ready to put James' black book to use.

Because we were a completely unknown band, we used our cover letter to emphasize both our originality and our extreme dedication. We were confident that the music would speak for itself—provided that people actually gave it a listen. There really isn't much you can say about music when you come right down to it. You write songs that touch upon experiences that are hard to talk about in the first place.

After mailing our packages out—each containing a CD, a cover letter, and a photocopied band portrait—we had little else to do but rehearse, work, put away as much money as we could, and wait. Carlos managed to give our van a discreet tune-up at the body shop he worked at.

I was aching for the sensation of movement. Nothing fires the creative imagination quite like the spectacle of new environs emerging and then vanishing behind: the constant plunge towards the novel moment. Whoever could decipher the pulse of life out there and set it down would be the true poet. It's not a matter of trying to see the future, of attempting to fix in place what must always be in flux. To the visionary, there is no future to foresee. There is a "now" of infinite possibilities, and the trick is to be awake for it.

We were just brimming with too much raw energy, enthusiasm, and reckless spontaneity to be still any longer. We'd given birth to our songs; now those songs needed to breathe under wider skies. All my being was focused upon arriving onstage, in some strange town, and letting the genie out of the bottle. New landscapes, shattered taboos, confrontations with proscribed limits, and morality, and law…goddamn it, the status quo had always been just too suffocating for me. And now I saw a way to forge my own raw life on my own terms. Our tour meant total freedom to me. It had to materialize.

Routes and map lines inscribed themselves upon my mind. Lists cluttered my consciousness: clubs, interstates, motels, rest stops, last-minute obligations to attend to. Details are drudgery when they're part of an existence devoid of flow, but these tasks were like the final shoves one gives a canoe before jumping in and letting the current take it.

During the early days of June, Tommy made follow-up phone calls to the people he'd written to. His calmly persuasive personality made him better suited for such tasks than me. He laid the chumming on so thick that I figure some of those club owners felt privileged to have us by the time he was done.

We managed to spread twenty-three gigs over a period of seven weeks. Tommy and Carlos were amenable to leaving a gap of open days in the middle when we'd be in New Mexico. I wanted Janie to have time to immerse herself in an exotic departure from the trees and rain that she was so accustomed to. I fantasized about us spending a night alone together somewhere out in the desert, just communing with the universe and with each other.

What the Good Poets Do

The prospect of leaving my familiar surroundings for a while made me acutely conscious of the things that held the most sentimental value for me. I ended up bringing an old pirate chest with me, about the size of a portable stereo. Inside it were all my earthly treasures: two watercolors that Rachel had given me as gifts, a cherry pipe that'd been a present from my father, a well-worn book of Rimbaud's poems, a black-and-white picture of my mother in a standing frame, a postcard from a high school art teacher who'd been the object of some of my earliest sexual yearnings, and a local newspaper clipping that made passing reference to our performance at our first gig at the Samurai warehouse.

The skeletal structure of my new, emerging existence was also stuffed into the van: amplifiers, my black Telecaster, and sheets of handwritten lyrics stuffed into my guitar case. I'd made copies of these and entrusted them to Janie in the event the originals got lost or destroyed. Of course, I knew them all by heart anyway.

We began our pilgrimage right there in town, on a Thursday night, playing at The Sparrow Sings. All through the first song I thought about Janie, how I'd spent the previous night at her place and scarcely gotten any sleep because I'd wanted to soak up every possible emanation of her presence before I left. I poured that heart-soreness into every chord I struck.

We probably drew in another fifty people that night. They started sliding tables off to the side so that they'd have more room to move about. Exuberant shoving and slam-dancing emerged here or there. The loud volume extinguished all the voices of destruction in my head. In those moments, you cease to even think in terms of good and evil anymore. It's all some manifestation of ecstasy, and even

143

pain has its sweetness. Damn—we played good. It surpassed anything that our rehearsals had even hinted at. We'd needed the response of our surrounding environment, the energy of the crowd, to really come into our own. They drew in closer, secretly assenting to the laws of our sacred tribe, and by the end of our set I felt like I'd known them all for a hundred years.

Our take for the gig was $150. That was split three ways; but of course, you don't think that way on the road. If you do, then you're not bound to last long. The man who's out for himself will be the first one to go down. Our fates were bound. So the gig money purchased us premade sandwiches, burritos, and juice to fill the cooler with, a full tank of gas, cold double-shot espresso drinks, and cigarettes. Whatever money was left over we relegated to the "security fund." I turned and bowed to the store as we were leaving: my way of acknowledging that this was the last place on our home turf that we'd be giving our patronage to for a while. I was bidding farewell to Sadenport, and perhaps hoping that it would wish me luck.

Tommy volunteered to drive us to Eugene. Once we were on the interstate, he launched into one of his feverish raps, obviously digesting our experience at The Sparrow Sings. "Brandon here was reading all our futures tonight, all the while thinking he was doing nothing but consoling himself. It's that visitation in the moment when one least expects it, altering everything all down the line.

"Now, you both know all about my lifelong love of history. Wrapped within that love is an even stronger thirst for origins. Sure, any ancient civilization wields its fascination; but I want to peel back even that veneer, dig deeper and deeper in the hopes of uncovering the one who first called Marduk by name, or dreamed of Tiamat in her dragon form. What sparked the whole thing? It's got to be catalyzed by someone's primary inspiration, Alexander or Napoleon studying their maps before a single piece is laid on the board....

"And now, here I am, bearing witness to song in its most untouched, primal form. This is a historical point of origin opening up before my very eyes..."

I turned towards Carlos, who was sitting in the back, and we shared a knowing smile. Tommy's praise of me was pretty embarrassing. His enthusiasm, though, seemed to set just the right tone for the sacred quest that we were embarking upon.

"Who knows how far the ripples of it may travel?" he went on. "Humanity has made the world the way it is through language. Our names and labels for things define—limit—how we're able to perceive them. And so now our band comes along to offer people a new language. Well, that might be a bit of a stretch. But I like to think that we're at least introducing some new words into the vocabulary."

"Sounds like the caffeine is working, bro!" Carlos remarked.

We camped out on a butte in Eugene, Oregon, that night, using a three-man tent that June had lent us. I hadn't slept decently in a couple days, so I went down hard—at least for a few hours. Even Carlos' snoring didn't disturb me.

I felt even looser when we played Rudy's than I had at The Sparrow Sings. It seemed like the couple dozen people cavorting about in the cleared space in front of the stage were already familiar with our band, though of course I knew that was impossible. Sometimes the atmosphere resembles the electrical activity preceding a storm, though. The message that you bring, and the mood of the moment, collide and then mesh—and you can tell that things are going to heat up quickly.

I probably looked like I was fighting a stiff wind when I was up onstage. That's how it felt to me, anyway. One leg is always trying to lurch forward, the other one catches me as I fall back, and somehow those motions manage to balance each other and keep my face poised anywhere from three inches to a foot away from the mic at all times. I let my hair fall over my face when I wasn't singing so that I didn't have to look at anything, and could just let the music paint its own landscapes.

Tommy actually moved the most during the slow, lumbering numbers. His head would fall down and then bob a few times each measure, like a hammer coming down and bouncing off of an anvil. When the rhythm quickened, he'd straighten out until he was completely rigid, even tilting his head back a bit. I've seen him go up on his toes in a way that makes him look like he's about to levitate. He was an undertaker with a bass guitar instead of a shovel. The heavy trench coat was not just for looks.

Tim had always sat up straight and bounced his head from side to side as he played. Carlos was even more animated. You'd think he was trying to catch mice that were scampering all over his kit, the way he concentrated on those drums while paddling frantically, somehow creating such powerful reverberations without ever lifting his hand that high above the skins.

That night we ended with one of my newer songs: "Awaken to Spring Grass." The old incarnation of our band would never have tolerated the unabashed hope and idealism of its lyrics.

Smashing mirrors to dispel the truth
of what those reflections showed
But without that angst
I might have chosen another road
Conceived in love, entrusting to hate
Born with the yearning to run and
consigned to a limping gait
But from those missteps
To come to know
The beauty of gardens where
some things can never grow

What will you call yourself when
your worldly clothes are shed?
When every vestige of rage just
binds you more closely to the dead?

Have you forgotten the living light that

brought you here?
Is there comfort in the shadows of
familiar fear?

These are self-chosen pains
Scars born of fictitious strife
And my feet are awakening to
sensations of the spring grass I've been
running over my whole life

Sensations of the spring grass I've been
running over my whole life

The words represented my attempt to relinquish my caustic, protective shell and let myself be seen—inadequacies, frailties, and all.

It felt good. The applause, the way so many people made eye contact with me when I looked out into that crowd. I'd noticed that, during the last half hour or so of the set, they had to shoulder through the roiling mass to get to the restrooms. Our music seemed to be finding its home in the world at last. I felt like I finally understood why we'd formed this damn band in the first place.

After I'd perform, it always took some time before I could settle back into the ebb and flow of normal life and conversation. Of course, I wasn't the most earthly creature or adept conversationalist even at the best of times. I just sat behind Tommy's bass amp sipping a beer. Then I went out for a cigarette. The bar wasn't closing for another hour. The majority of people had stayed; and from the way some of them looked and cast compliments my way, I could tell that they wanted to engage. But I just didn't have anything to say at the moment. I'd said it all onstage.

Tommy found me out there on the sidewalk, just as I was finishing my smoke. "We met a couple girls who live in a quad over at the U of O campus," he said. "They've invited us over, if we want to hang out tonight."

Underneath my sense of exhilaration, I was tired. Anticipating the tour had disrupted my sleep for days on end. I could have used a night in a motel already, but I told myself not to be a pussy. "Why don't you go on ahead," I suggested. "I'll crash in the van."

"We're not due in Boise until Monday night," Tommy argued. "And besides, this could be an opportunity for us all to get showers." He grinned. "I already asked them about that, actually."

I smiled back, a bit ruefully. That was one flaw in our "roughing it in the van" plan that I'd never considered. You're apt to smell as ripe after a two-hour gig—especially on a night when you've played righteously furious—as you would be after an eight-hour day of construction.

"They seem psycho at all to you?" I asked. Sometimes one must focus on pragmatic concerns.

"Carlos apparently knows one of them, at least casually." Tommy shrugged. "They seem alright to me."

So I went back inside to meet the ladies. Both were seated at the bar, leaning in close to one another, while Carlos stood on the periphery, smiling in a bemused way.

Evelyn was short and curvy, dressed in faded jeans and a white sweatshirt—both of which hugged her pretty close—and her hair, though only shoulder-length to begin with, was tied back with a blue scarf. Mandy was slim and tall, with long raven-black hair, glasses, and a look of shrewd intelligence in her eyes. She was dressed in a single-piece black sleeveless skirt. I guessed that both of them were probably a couple years older than me.

Well, we talked, and I concluded that they were down-to-earth and sincere. For one thing, they made a few flattering remarks about our performance without ever sounding like sycophants. After they finished their drinks, we milled about in front of Rudy's for a while in the lingering heat. The air sinks down into Eugene's valley and then refuses to move. You can scream all you want for a bit of breeze, to no avail. The ladies graciously helped us load up the van. Then we followed them up to the campus.

They shared the bathroom and kitchen area with the occupants of two other units. Apparently it was all cool, though, because everyone hung out regularly. Neither of our new friends had beds, just padding and blankets set down with the middle space of the bedroom floor between them. Evelyn had some framed Van Gogh prints on her side—one of sunflowers and the other a predominantly blue self-portrait—and Mandy had covered most of her wall with a diamond of purple fabric.

I was still feeling stiff and socially inept, so when Mandy offered us beer, I gratefully accepted one and drank it down fast. She watched and then asked, rather pointedly, what I thought about when I wrote my lyrics.

I stumbled along in the face of the essentially unexplainable. "Oh, see—I don't try to make statements. There's definitely not a moral anywhere in there, if that's what you mean. I don't know…it may sound pretentious, but I'm more interested in how an arrangement of words makes me feel than what those words actually mean. Words mean different things to each person anyway."

She was persistent. "So what kind of feeling do you search for, then?"

I shrugged, trying to look humble when in fact I was secretly flattered. "Release. That sense, like maybe you thought existence was a dead end and then all these other avenues, possibilities, make themselves known and your world is painted new."

She smiled. "Sounds like what the good poets do. You ever read Whitman? Baudelaire?"

My throat suddenly felt dry. This conversation was going a little too smoothly for my comfort. I quaffed the last of my beer. "Uh, I have, actually. But I don't really read much. I mean, I'm not voracious like Tommy is. But yeah, I have respect for those guys. Basically, I read when I want to remind myself that I'm not crazy—or, at least, that I'm not alone in my perceptions." I ended off with an awkward shrug.

She looked down at my empty bottle. "You want another?"

"Sure."

When she went to the fridge, I sought out the other guys. I didn't want to be caught alone again. A couple other girls had shown up. Tommy was engaged with both of them, waxing philosophical in his deadpan manner, while Carlos was apparently playing catch-up with Evelyn. I interrupted quickly to ask her if she minded if I showered.

"No problem," she said with a nod and a smile. But I hadn't moved swiftly enough. Mandy found me then and proffered a new, opened bottle of beer. She'd heard the exchange.

"Come here, I'll show you," she said. I accepted the beer as gracefully as possible and tried to hide my chagrin. On the other side of the living room was a door that let us into a middle hall. Off to the left was a dimly-lit room that I assumed was the kitchen. I noticed a deep steel sink, the kind you find in restaurant dish pits, filled with pots and plates. The door in front of us opened into a tiny space just big enough to house its toilet and shower.

"The knobs are the opposite of what they're marked," Mandy explained. "I'll go get my towel and throw it in for ya. Be back in a minute."

I undressed hurriedly, intending to be behind the cloudy blue plastic curtain before she returned. I left my beer beside my clothes. Of course, in my generally flustered state I'd forgotten to fetch a clean outfit to change into. I got the water started. It took forever to warm up. But I was grateful for the feel of it after a couple days of deprivation. I lathered myself up with the thick green bar of soap that was there, muttering my thanks to whoever it belonged to.

It suddenly occurred to me that a goodly amount of sexual warmth is exchanged when a woman offers you her own personal (and probably used) towel to dry your body off with. Unfortunately, this insight didn't warn me in time. The door opened; and then, within the space of three heartbeats, the shower curtain was swept aside. There was Mandy in her pale, slim, and shapely birthday suit, smiling and bold. I scarcely had time to inhale sharply before she slipped inside and pressed up against me, her fingertips kneading my temples. Then she leaned forward to kiss me.

"What the hell? Stop!"

I didn't mean to shove her at all. I was only trying to create some space between us—it was instinctive, and there was no room behind me. But of course, congruent with the way that my luck tended to run, she not only lost balance momentarily but then caught her ankle on the edge of the shower stall and toppled out, backwards, to slam her hip against the toilet seat before hitting the floor.

"Oww! Jesus, fucker!"

I think the last time I'd ever hurt a girl—and it was inadvertent—had been in grade school. My humiliation drove me right out of the apartment. I knew that Mandy wasn't injured, anyway, but only startled and maybe insulted. I felt the shocked and confused stares that followed me as I ran through the living room, naked and dripping and cupping my crotch. I felt it all; but I saw only the door. In a moment the warm air—nonetheless cool on my wet skin—hit me. A couple were on the balcony, smoking and talking in confidential voices. The woman gasped when she saw me. I ignored her. I nearly tumbled down the flight of wooden stairs in my haste to get to the van.

Once I was inside, I scrambled around for some clothes. Everything clung to me. There was nothing to be done about footwear as my boots were still in the quad, taken off by the door as a courtesy. I pocketed my cigarettes and lighter and set off, barefoot, down the road.

By now, I'd cooled down enough to realize that I didn't know Eugene very well and therefore didn't want to wander far and get lost. I stopped in the parking lot of a pizza joint across the street, now closed, and smoked. I was halfway through when I noticed Carlos coming across towards me.

I can only assume that the pain and distress showed on my face, because he started reassuring me as soon as he drew close. "It's OK bro. She's not hurt or nothin'. Was all just a misunderstanding. Tommy was in there talking with her when I left. You should come back. It's all cool now. We're just hanging out."

I was still so worked up that my hands were shaking. "I don't know what it is with me, man," I said. "Why I gotta react to everything so dramatically." I took another pull off my cigarette. "I don't know a calm approach to dealing with fucking anything!"

Carlos smiled and shrugged. His accent made him sound sharp-witted even when he was saying mundane things; and this time, his words gave me pause. "Probably that's part of what makes you a great songwriter and singer."

I laughed, just because his buoyancy was so infectious. "Well thanks. But I sure as hell wish there were easier ways."

I finished my cigarette, ground it out by hand, and said, "Alright. But I just can't go back in, Carlos. I'll hang out in the van and write or something. It's too humiliating, walking back in there right now."

But Mandy intercepted me before we'd even made it as far as the van. For a few minutes, the two of us nearly fell over ourselves in our breathless and desperate attempts to somehow heal the breach between us. Mandy started in first.

"I had no idea you had a girlfriend. Tommy told me just now. Obviously, I really should have asked you about that first before, just like, throwing myself at you. I'm real sorry!"

"I overreacted," I said. "I'm sorry. You just caught me off guard. You're really cool. I mean, if things were different…but no, I don't even wanna talk like that. Aww, come here!"

We shared a warm, peacemaking hug. And just like that, the distance was bridged and the frigidity melted. I went back inside and all seven of us partied into the wee hours, laughing and talking. Even Carlos, who's usually wary around that sort of revelry because of his history, loosened up for the occasion. He just incanted, "Everything in moderation—including moderation!" every time he cracked open another cold one.

Mandy and Evelyn both had weekend jobs, so they woke us up in the early afternoon to say goodbye. This was my first taste of the twist of nostalgia and heart pangs that the road can serve you up. The rhythm of their lives, safely grounded in work and classes and clock time, made my own existence feel somehow less tangible, an experience composed of poetry and myth rather than of physical substance. I hugged those ladies hard, as if I was losing another beachhead to the hungry sea that was my Muse. I also knew that, under other circumstances, there could have been an opportunity for real intimacy between Mandy and me. That was an awkward realization to carry away with me.

It all made me anxious to be off. I longed for a sense of movement and momentum, and we hadn't gotten out of our home state yet. I voted for us to drive out to Idaho that night. As it turned out, the others were of like mind.

We hiked the butte again that afternoon to retrieve June's tent. Tommy delivered a sermon the whole way up. Even the rigors of the trail, though they stole the breath out of his smoker's lungs, still couldn't quell his mouth, apparently.

"The sixties were just about pulling back the shades and seeing the first rays of light. People still talk about that time because they remember that there were ideals. There were principles that people tried to live by that ran contrary to nearly everything that this culture tries to ram down our throats.

"Now, you can argue that it's naïve to believe that music can change the world. But what you can't deny is that there were musicians during that time who were fully convinced of that, and the power of their music attests to the power of that belief. That's why some of those songs still hold up and sound revolutionary today.

"Problem is, a lot of people could only hold on to that belief when their consciousness was altered by the drugs. And you just can't keep taking LSD forever. But if you accept that we're multidimensional beings, that we're a manifestation of what the soul is, then you don't need anything but the music— or whatever it is that you're creating—to serve as your illumination. You can live in that expanded state of consciousness.

"We may not have nearly the best equipment. And there are bands that are far superior, technically speaking, to us. We ain't veterans of the road, by far. And maybe even our songwriting could stand some improvement. But from what I've seen, it doesn't seem like anyone else out there has more raw belief in the music, and what it can do, than we do. And that's what's gonna see us through."

And on and on it went. Turns out part of the reason Tommy was so effervescent that afternoon was because he'd gotten Kimbra's number the night before. By sweet serendipity, she'd happened to mention the philosophy class she was taking—which of course had initiated a conversation revolving around Nietzsche and Schopenhauer that'd lasted into the wee hours.

A Band to Justify My Existence

We bid farewell to Eugene at about ten o'clock that night. We gassed up and bought some coffees for the road at a station across the street from an art house movie theatre. Then we turned on to US 20. Restored by all the sleep I'd gotten in the quad, albeit slightly hungover (I hardly ever drank), I took the wheel for the eastward stretch to Idaho. I hit a patch of construction at about two a.m. They'd formed an artificial lane that consisted of the right half of the lane proper and the shoulder, so that you were riding with the edge of the highway between your wheels the whole time.

The border of this makeshift "lane" was demarked by a seemingly infinite line of white reflectors that hypnotized me real quick if I stared at them. Anywhere you look on the highway, you're bound to see the same visual input announcing itself, like a metronome for the eyes, and this has the tendency to flip me into a right-brained trance. To make matters worse, Tommy was uncharacteristically quiet, and Carlos, who'd done more fooling around with Evelyn than sleeping, was snoring away in the back. I asked Tommy to root around for the heaviest metal he could find to put into the player, and I crooned along to keep myself from nodding off as the van devoured the miles.

Because the drive ended up being so unexpectedly taxing, I suggested we find a motel. Dawn arose with a pleasant, filtered light, and I was filled with a feeling of peace suddenly. We were out of our home state: I now felt justified in saying that the tour was underway. I took the first exit that I found after sunup, as the sign indicated that the next one wasn't going to come along for another thirty miles.

It was a local motel, not one of the chains. The lady at the desk informed us that they only had a single bed available. We didn't mind. I'd already woken up with my head beneath Carlos' armpit once during this trip. Any motel room was bound to feel luxurious. Plus, it was relatively cheap.

We finished off the food in our cooler and then stocked up on more sandwiches, burritos, and juice bottles in the early evening. It was beginning to get dark. The steady to-and-fro of headlights on the main street, of people locked into a grid that scarcely acknowledged our existence, dominated the view from the motel parking lot. The feeling that accompanies a rootless existence somehow mingles liberation and poignancy. You are caught constantly in the onrush of new sensations. But each new movement displaces an old one, of course, and so the sense of loss is likewise enduring and without answer.

I didn't go inside right away. Instead I borrowed Carlos' cell phone so I could call Janie.

Technology conveyed the warmth of her over those few hundred miles and left me almost too choked up to speak. I feared I'd overwhelm her if I let my heart rush through my words, so I tried to ground myself in the details of our gigs and travels. I was irrationally gripped by the notion that I could lose her, that the accumulating physical distance could somehow render our connection tenuous. I don't know what provoked this mood. Her voice, her words, did nothing to confirm my fears.

"I can't wait until we meet up in Albuquerque," I said. "We'll talk when it gets closer to the time and make more solid plans. But don't worry—the gray van and its band of ne'er-do-wells will be there to greet you at the airport!"

Sometimes I could tell she was smiling just by the way she spoke. "I can't wait, either."

After we hung up, I lit a cigarette and watched the traffic for a while longer. There wasn't much besides that and cable TV to occupy any of us until it was time to leave. Boise wasn't far, and we had until nine. The myth of the road makes little mention of the fact that sometimes your chief enemies are boredom and an overabundance of time in which to think.

❖

I wouldn't say that our gig in Boise was a disaster, but it was definitely a sore disappointment. The Camel's Romp was a small bar in a poorer section of town. Oftentimes you can sense the collective vibe as soon as you walk into a place. These people were there to drink, not listen to us. The small stage was set against the wall that faced the street, which meant that passersby could see Carlos' back, and his wall of drums, through the tall windows. The bar was opposite us, with tables strewn between. So, basically, the patrons had no choice but to watch us, whether they wanted to or not. I'm sure a good percentage of them would have sooner chosen a game on the television.

On a good night, our music was powerful enough to transform even a demoralizing ambiance such as this. But our performance—though it was, strictly speaking, "good" in the sense that it lacked mistakes—didn't carry our definitive sparks of passion and exhilaration. It was almost perfunctory. As much as I hate to point the finger, it really did come down to Carlos scoring some cocaine and snorting it in the bathroom before going onstage.

It's always astounded me, how those who've been immersed in the drug world can, forever thereafter, sniff out the substances that they crave within practically any environment. Carlos didn't know a soul in the city and yet, within an hour of our arrival there, he'd scored. This in itself put me on edge. After all, I knew how much sobriety meant to him. This concession seemed to betray his integrity, willpower, and honesty all at once—on a whim. I hit an emotional snag, there, which kept me from focusing on the performance like I wanted to. And things got worse once Carlos actually started to play.

Usually his drumming complemented the songs so well, which was something I'd appreciated about him ever since our first rehearsal. You could hear respect in the very way that his beats landed. I'd sing a line and then feel like Carlos paid homage to it with the roll that followed. Well, that night in Boise, I heard attitude. Everything was a bit too loud and obtrusive, as if he wanted to distinguish his drum parts from the rest of the band. This is the musical equivalent of stepping on everyone's toes when you're dancing.

He was just simultaneously pumped up and numbed by the coke to such an extent that he lost the sensitivity, to both rhythm and subtlety, which normally made him such a tactful drummer. Sure, he still hit the skins hard like he meant it. But I much prefer focused vehemence to the attack of a sledgehammer.

Tommy and I just soldiered through it, and the audience was surprisingly receptive throughout. But I'd never wanted to be off a stage so badly before in my life.

I asked Carlos to take a walk with me after he'd packed up his kit. No doubt he knew what was coming down the pike. The effects of the couple lines he'd snorted in the restroom were wearing off, and I was wary of the mean-tempered edge that people tend to get during the comedown. But wariness is not the same thing as restraint.

"You know, we're all dependent upon one another out here," I said. "One of us fucks up and we all go down. Now, I ain't perfect, and I would never skewer anybody for making an honest mistake. But this was a choice, Carlos."

He was thoroughly repentant. The chemically-induced belligerence that I'd feared was nowhere in evidence. "I'm real sorry, bro," he said. "It started for me in Eugene, you know? We partied there and I got a little taste of it…enough to make me want more. I should've known it was going to lead me in a bad direction."

"Alright," I acknowledged, realizing in that moment that I was complicit to some extent. "I screwed up there, too. We were drinking to excess right there in front of you, when I'd assured you that you wouldn't have to worry about being openly tempted in this band." Then I started grasping, trying to be helpful. "Is it being on the road like this? Is it stressful?"

"Nah. It's life. You can always find a reason to want to get high if you let yourself go down that road. Who doesn't ever long for some of the medicine?"

My ire was leaching away, thanks to his humility and his refusal to fight with me. "Well, I definitely understand that," I said. "Hell, I'd probably be an addict myself if I'd ever found a drug that actually worked for me. Honestly, my normal state of mind is like being high, and there's moments when it's a bad trip. You know how sometimes you've had enough, and you just want to come down, see and feel things in some normal way for a while? Me, I can't come down."

We stayed on Main Street so that we wouldn't have to keep track of landmarks and turns. It was a warm and still night. I hardly felt the air at all; it seemed to be the exact temperature of my skin. The beautiful, starry arch of sky overhead was no doubt something I would have enjoyed on some other occasion.

"And I'm assuming you dipped into band funds to buy the stuff?"

There was no avoiding that particular confrontation. My tone was not nearly as sharp as my words, but Carlos still got defensive.

"I brought some of my own money, bro, and that's what I used to pay for it."

"Alright. And yet, here we're supposed to be pooling everything. I hate to repeat myself, but we sink or swim together, man. Have you forgotten how you got your drum set? But see, this is the trap, right here. We start picking at each other over trivial shit and before long the whole tour comes undone, because the people who're supposed to be relying upon each other the most can't stand to be in each other's presence anymore. That's weak, man—and it's beneath us!"

We walked for several paces in silence. Carlos looked thoughtful. The brief hints of anger were gone again.

"So I'll tell you what the issue is for me," I said last. "It's not the money, or that you fell back on a promise that you made to yourself—and to us, by extension. That part isn't really my business. You don't owe me promises. But the real crime that occurred here tonight, Carlos, is we played a lousy show. Mistakes don't mean nothin' to me, man. For me, it's lack of passion that's the one unforgivable sin. Tonight, all three of us failed to play like we really cared. We cheated everyone who stayed to watch us at the Camel's Romp, and we shortchanged ourselves. Now, if you could pour all your heart and soul into your playing while you were coked up, then I wouldn't care. I wouldn't enjoy seeing it, but I wouldn't take issue; even if you did it every damn day.

"Harsh as it may sound, the music's more important to me than longevity. It's not the length of life but what you make of the time that matters. So if you start making choices that steer you away from the passion that we're trying to create together, then I have to ask myself if you're really right for this band."

"It won't happen again," Carlos assured me at once, just as if he'd spent all day deliberating over the issue. "It wasn't worth it to me anyway. I hardly enjoyed it. All those nights I've played with you guys sober were better highs."

I stopped right there, before we crossed the next intersection. "Let's go join up with Tommy and decide what we're gonna do tonight. And we'll make up for this lapse in Salt Lake. Let's shake on that right now."

And we did shake on it. But Salt Lake City, as it turned out, began with an even worse disaster.

We rolled into town the following evening with scarcely enough time left over to get to the gig. We parked on the street in front of Marshall's Bar and Grill. As soon as we stepped out into the noisome night, I knew something was amiss. We heard music, loud and imminent—in other words, not from a sound system but from a live band. Marshall's was a squat wooden building and its windows were dark. But we gazed up at the marquee and saw "Elena's Revenge" written out in black block letters.

"Fuckin' Christ!" Tommy fumed. "Another band is up on their goddamn stage!"

We decided to leave our gear in the van and check things out, as if somehow that would dispel the farce and restore our fantasy of actually playing that night. As I swung open the heavy wooden door, my ears were assailed by a sort of country fried boogie-rock, with a woman's woeful vocals riding over the top of it. The bar, lined with people mostly middle-aged and with faces as lived in as their clothes, was to our right. A wall separated us from the stage. We all stood for a moment, completely at a loss.

Then Carlos noticed our flyer stapled to one of the hall's thick wooden pillars. The scrawl at the bottom of it, inscribed in black marker, proclaimed that we would be performing the following Tuesday.

I saw myself grabbing one of those wooden stools by its bottom legs and swinging it like a pickaxe, demolishing the band's mic stand and drum set. But then the sting of remorse held me. This wasn't their fault, after all: it was the fault of whoever had booked them. My eyes alighted upon a two-top table that stood on one thick oval leg of steel. I'd carried plenty of similar tables at work, setting them to lengthen banquet tables and then removing them once the party left. No doubt I was strong enough to hurl that one through a window....

Now that would get us some publicity. Sure, I'd go to jail, but the story would mention "Brandon of Edge of the Known." That kind of exposure was worth a lot more than a gig.

I made the first couple of steps unconsciously. Then Tommy was in front of me, grasping my shoulders. "You do not want to lose your shit right here in the middle of Mormon country, four dates into the tour!" he hissed. "Just go chill out in the van while we try to get this sorted. I figure they gotta at least pay us for their mistake."

At the moment, that didn't seem nearly as satisfying as the prospect of a shattered window. My body was doped up on outrage and humiliation. I'd never understood any outlet for such feelings aside from destruction.

Tommy was still holding me. Of course he was. Most of my weight was still aimed in the direction of that table. "We've got nineteen more shows to play," he said. "Remember how good the first two were? This is just one stop along the way."

For his sake, and for Carlos's, I relented. As the singer bemoaned her heartache in the wake of another "lyin', cheatin' man," I stomped out of the bar with my fists clenched. My entire being was poised to play—and there would be no performance. I stared at the Manhandle Records logo and album design emblazoned across the side of the van. For a moment, I considered taking my hunting knife and defacing it beyond all recognition. Then I was seized by another idea.

I climbed into the back of the van, knelt beside our gear, and rummaged through one of my knapsacks for the blade. Then I gripped a fistful of my hair—about six inches worth—and started sawing through it. If you've never tried this, I can assure you it requires exertion and exacts pain. You don't end up with anything resembling a haircut, either. I was in no mood to be delicate and precise, though. I hacked and rent, wreaking jagged abuse upon a head of hair nearly as black as India ink that had grown free and unmolested for over two years.

I'd resembled a Plains warrior before. My hair had somehow accentuated the Cherokee in me, from my father's side. It showed in my complexion and bold jut of a nose, too; and in the natural swagger of my gait, which many people over the years had mistaken for insolence. But now, at least one aspect of my "warriorhood" was being scraped off, in gnarled and mangled clumps. Every sawing motion hurt, pulling at the roots, but the pain was a form of relief for me. It accomplished much the same cathartic effect as breaking glass did. It was the same violence, directed at myself instead of someone or something else, but I tried not to think of it in those terms.

I let it all fall onto the foam pad, the remnants of an old self that I'd scarcely known—and that I wasn't sure whether or not I'd miss.

Carlos caught me in there with tears streaming down my face. But I didn't care. You learn to let go of trivial concerns, such as your own pride, with the people you wake up to every day. Besides, the living sculpture that I'd carved out with my hunting knife dominated his attention. I was able to run my fingers through all of my remaining hair in one motion. Carlos remembered my dignity though—such as remained to me—and didn't stare for long.

"Hey, they're going to let us close out the night if we want to." His voice was careful and low. "It'll be from eleven to midnight. And he will pay us either way. The guy who's bartending tonight is the one who Tommy talked to when he booked this gig. He's real apologetic." Carlos grinned. "Too many trips to the nitrous tent, I think."

I tried to smile. "That's cool. Fuck it—let's do it. How much time 'til we go on, then?"

"Oh, about an hour. It's almost ten."

"Hey, can I borrow your cell so that I can call Saul, then?"

Carlos nodded. "Lucky for you I charged it in that motel in Idaho."

He left me alone without another word. I knew Saul's number by heart because I'd given it out as my own number for a period of time. He answered within one ring, catching me off guard.

"Saul? It's Brandon. I'm sorry—I know we don't have an appointment or nothin'. Do you have a minute, though?"

"I just finished with my last client. I was about to turn in," he admitted. "But don't even worry about it. I can hear that you're distressed. I'm here."

I just hung on the ensuing silence, suddenly feeling at a loss for words.

"Look," Saul said, "we can just have a session right now and then worry about you settling up for it later, if that's your concern."

"OK," I said. Then, because I knew I had to give him something to go on, I added, "I just chopped most of my hair off."

"So what's up?"

"Well, I dunno. We showed up at this bar in Salt Lake City and there was another band up onstage, already playing. The guy had double booked."

"Ah, I see," he said.

"You see what?" I demanded, suddenly bristling at his self-assured tone. "Like that alone summarizes everything?"

"In a way, it does," Saul said, "seeing as it's happened to someone who equates his whole sense of worth with his accomplishments as a musician, who writes songs as if to justify his existence through them. To suddenly be denied the opportunity to perform, an opportunity that you'd been promised…yeah, I bet you're feeling like burning the place down right about now."

"I was about to smash a window, before Tommy talked me down," I admitted.

The reception frayed for a moment. I clutched the phone with both hands, as if I believed the extremity of my own need could keep the channel open. Saul's voice came through clear a moment later. "I want you to imagine a spring flower— bluebells, say. Think of what a delicate form of life that is, and yet it thrusts up every year and unfolds its color and fragrance at the appointed time, without fail. Now, do you imagine that our flower is thinking that it must struggle and win out against all odds in order to realize its nature?"

"No," I said, "it probably doesn't think at all. It just does. But what in the hell—"

"Do you think that your ability to compose music, or to distill the essence of your experience into songs, is essentially any different from that plant's capacity to grow flowers?" he persisted.

The feelings that his words stirred up in me made me restless. I stepped out onto the sidewalk, hoping, at the same time, for better reception. Unfortunately, I now had to contest with the sounds of traffic—and of Elena's Revenge.

"I would ask you to consider the possibility," Saul went on, "that your gifts are given you for a reason; that they exist because there's already a space laid out for them in this world, just as every creature has its place in the ecosystem and every flower arises in its ideal habitat. You weren't accidentally born onto the wrong planet, Brandon. And your abilities aren't aberrant. They have their integral place alongside everything else. Why, then, are you so convinced that you have to wage war in order to carve out a place for them?"

"Because that's what my life has always been, Saul—a war!"

He sighed, heavily enough so that I could hear it over the line. "That's what you've always believed your life to be. And that belief probably served a purpose at one time. But is it serving you now? You could let it go. Ah, but would you still be a man? Because a man fights, right? And would you still be an artist? Because an artist, of course, is supposed to suffer. See, we need to get to the bottom of this, to the reasons why you're convinced that you have to take this stance. Because as soon as you understand how needless it is, then the obstacles that seem to stand in your way now will disappear."

I never understood how he did it. But after listening to him talk, even for ten minutes, I seemed to perceive the whole world differently. Suddenly, there were avenues where I thought only walls and fences existed. There were high peaks, waiting to be ascended, where I thought there were only valleys. Somehow Saul was able to paint reality in completely new colors for me.

But I also understood—for the first time, really—how challenging it could prove trying to reach those lofty peaks. My conceptions would be hard to relinquish, to let die. They'd helped me build up my sense of identity, particularly since adolescence. They'd lent me the courage to forsake all pretense of a "normal life" in order to pursue a path that no one around me—with the possible exception of Tommy—had seemed to understand.

"And that's a piece of work that you'll have to accomplish alone," Saul said, as if in response to my internal monologue. "No one can change your convictions for you. I can help you to identify what they are, but then you have to realize the necessity of letting them go for yourself."

"I get that," I said. And I really meant it. "I guess that's enough for me to work with for now, Saul. Maybe I didn't realize…."

"What?" Saul said. "That the work we're doing would force you to search for a new vision of yourself and what your life means? Well, you're ahead of the game in that regard, so you can take some comfort in that. If humanity is going to pull through its present impasse, then a lot of people are going to have to weather some birthing pains."

I scanned Main Street up and down, taking in the lines of convenience stores and shops, the traffic flowing to the arbitrary rhythm of streetlights, and pedestrians moving in all directions searching for satisfaction, respite, or salvation, perhaps. I was hundreds of miles from home, and the reasons for which I'd travelled this far were being redefined in ways that I didn't yet understand. I was certain of only one thing: the scope of the quest was much vaster than I'd assumed.

"Well, we're going to be going on in a little bit," I told Saul. "Turns out we get to play after the other band, for an hour or so, to close out the night. Hey, if I don't talk to you before then…I'll see you when we get home."

"You keep bearing your torch into the world's dark places, Brandon. We'll toast some champagne together on your return."

Then Saul hung up.

TUMBLEWEEDS

We delivered the sonic equivalent of shock treatment to that crowd, after their two-hour dose of melodrama and the pathos of steel guitar. Checking in with Saul, the medicine man of my personal mythos, had restored me to a sense of lightness and play. I performed for myself, and for my love of the other guys and what we'd set out to accomplish together. The entire set was spontaneous. We'd finish a number and then debate what to play next, sometimes over a shared cigarette (we always offered it to Carlos, despite his repeated refusals). Miraculously, in light of the events of the evening, we left Marshall's in good spirits.

We did one more gig in Salt Lake, at the Cat's Eyes Bagel Shop. There was no stage. We just set up on the marble floor at eye level with everyone. Most of the patrons seemed indifferent, and few stayed for the entire performance. We used our earnings to fill the tank and buy ourselves dinner (on our schedule, I suppose this was technically lunch) at a diner where the waitress—a gaunt blonde, probably in her mid-thirties—gave us all the distinct impression that she'd go home with whichever one of us hit on her first. I ordered the chef's omelet with sausage, spinach, and peppers. I loved breakfast food and always appreciated it when I found a place that served it all hours. Maybe I was compensating for all those years of skimping on the first meal of the day in my haste to get Rachel and myself ready and out the door before Dad got up.

It didn't occur to me that I was eating a "morning meal" anyway. Time had grown very elastic and malleable. Moments can stretch or contract; it's all a matter of awareness and focus. I liked existing in a timeless space because I had this theory—and Tommy concurred—that many of the beliefs that create our cultural hang-ups are tied in with notions of consecutive time. Reward and punishment, cause and effect, Heaven and Hell…these are all human value judgments that grow out of a misunderstanding of the moment.

I took my turn behind the wheel that night and drove through what turned out to be one of my favorite episodes of the entire road trip. Few sights can compare with that of a sunrise over a barren stretch of road in Utah. Spines of topaz rock, devoid of any shred of green life, rose to our left, and the world seemed to end beyond their stark ridges. They had cut out, from the heavens, the deepest, clearest blue sky I'd ever beheld. For a moment, I wondered whether the Abyss itself might be azure rather than black, after all. The van's engine rumbled along, racing the Apocalypse. It could only be the culmination of all things, ahead.

The dawn's breathtaking revelation had come upon the heels of a night spent on a high mountain road that would suddenly open upon manmade mining canyons illuminated by garish beams of alien light. The buildings were spider-like, with their great oval bellies and myriad iron pipes, jointed in the middle so that they resembled legs. It would not have surprised me to see engines ignite and lift the entire extraterrestrial craft off of its stone nest and thrust it out into space. None of us knew what the mines were for (copper, turns out), and the mystery just added to their allure.

We didn't speak as the first rays of light crept over the plain. The same sense of awe mastered us all. Once the initial enchantment wore off, we addressed the fact that we were dead tired. We decided to find another motel—the rationale, this time, being that camping grounds would be plentiful in Colorado.

The next exit wasn't for nearly twenty miles, though, so I had to push myself. I decided to engage Tommy, hoping that conversation could keep me alert a while longer.

"Have you ever wondered if you chose the best possible road?" I asked. "I mean, you…you've got the academic intelligence; you took college-prep classes. You probably could have made yourself a success without this band."

"It depends on how you want to define success," Tommy said. "Look at us now: seeing a new face of the world every day, answering to no one, expressing the deepest movements of our souls in our music night after night. Those are rare freedoms, man. We've got an opportunity here to create our own reality, to abide completely on our own terms. If it comes at the risk of a gig falling through and us having to miss a couple meals as consequence, or the van breaking down somewhere in the middle of East Bumfuck…well, those are small prices to pay.

"I've mentioned this enough times, man. You know me. The artists that I've always gravitated towards are the hypersensitive ones, those who drink deeply from the well of life, feeling too much of it too often. That fairly describes most of the creative people who've ever fascinated me. The wounded but gifted.

"You remember when the grunge scene broke, and it made us both that much more eager to make music our lives? It was easy to explain away my fascination with the movement. I told myself I was curious about how these artists had 'made it.' I've only recently become aware that there was another motivation at work. I'm hypersensitive myself. I feel too much, too often. I've spent all this time desperately searching for a way to cope with my own sensitivity."

I gazed out over that baked expanse of tan flats and ridges and felt an echo of all the empty spaces, both in the world and between people. It was desolate and bewitching. Under the spell of his voice, I once again felt myself embarked upon a sacred pilgrimage. Only, in our case, there was no destination, no single holy land. Our quest was to evoke and feel the sacred dimension within every part of the world, every part that touched us and spoke to us. This was the closest I'd ever come to defining my own spirituality. It was something the music had given me—a gift that I sought to repay every time I played.

"The fact that many of these visionaries hadn't managed to carry the vision for very long only made the ones who did survive all the more intriguing," Tommy went on. "What did they find? What answer did they cling to in the chill wind of hypersensitivity? Or was there no answer? Was their survival just a matter of sheer grit and endurance? What do you do when your sense of reality is not supported—or even recognized—by the status quo? Is solitude your only recourse when walking such a path?

"It's a hell of a thing to carry with you into adolescence, this idea that your course is set towards a desert of isolation and mad longings that only the heights of inspiration can satisfy for you. Provided you can ever reach them in the first place. But hey, that's the price you pay if you want to live outside this spoon-fed mass reality, I'd tell myself. Most guys my age were fantasizing about licenses and their first cars, about girls, and about when it might finally happen that they'd get that physical relief their bodies screamed for. I had those desires too, man. But somehow, I already understood that, even if I managed to satisfy them, it would never be enough. I wanted something more. And I read on and on in the search to discover what, exactly, it was.

"Christianity assures us of the possibility of some kind of eternal rest in Heaven. Eastern philosophies entice you with the peace of Nirvana. Materialism holds out an array of incentives: stimulation, excitement, ease, comfort, sex, what have you. What was the preferred reward for the path that I was on at sixteen? Not a lot of goodies in the bag to motivate the seeker along the Way, my friend. I got afraid that those who walked it only did so only because the fever in their minds and the thirst in their souls left them with no other choice."

Tommy turned towards me and offered one of his rare smiles. "Then music hit me."

I just nodded along to the cadences of his inspired stream. This was one of those occasions when Tommy's thoughts so clearly echoed my own that I didn't feel the urge to speak my mind. "I could probably exist like this to the end of my life," was all I could think to add.

Suddenly, we were among mountains and a profusion of green. The air smelled like the breath of trees. We had four engagements to play in Colorado: two in Denver and two in Boulder. Lacey's Foxhound had apparently been well-liked here. I was anxious to bring these people our distinctive brand of Dionysian frenzy and make up for our lull in Utah.

The Boulder crowds were predominantly close to our age. Maybe that was due to the proximity of the college. Energy, intent, and deeper magic were all really beginning to mesh by this point. The raw power and promise that we'd evinced in the Catacombs had been honed by the time spent travelling and gigging. And the crisis we weathered with Carlos had drawn him more fully into the fold. In the van, or in a hotel room or tent, we could at times be petty, irritable, petulant, or withdrawn from each other. But when we hit the stage we functioned as one mind manifesting through three monstrous voices. I doubt there was a soul in the audience, at either of the venues we played in Boulder, who wasn't converted by the end of our sets.

Nothing was going to stop us. I was convinced that we would ride this momentum straight into the public consciousness. You feel that way after a few triumphant performances. That euphoria is like the hand of a more transcendent destiny, lifting you above your misfortunes and limitations and setting you on a higher plane. Middle ground is vanquished: you've landed in the arena of victory or death. My life had never before held out to me any opportunities for glory. The music—and the two soul brothers I had the tremendous fortune to be playing alongside—had given me that.

Offers of drugs were plentiful on both nights. The mushrooms were tempting. We'd already created a communal experience, touching upon the collective unconscious and its store of dreams and fears. How enticing it seemed to extend that visitation; to follow that energy, as if one was chasing a thought to the place it disappears to after being conceived.

I remarked to the guys that I felt hypocritical even considering the idea after having verbally pummeled Carlos for his indulgence the previous week.

"Then let's consider it in its proper context," Tommy suggested. "These are psychedelic mushrooms we're talking about. That's not a drug; it's a sacrament. We aren't partying. We're embarking upon a vision quest—into the mountains, tonight, following a great performance."

"Well, since you put it that way...."

A psychedelic trip didn't alter my thoughts and behavior as much as it apparently did other people's. My normal waking consciousness already lay pretty close to such a state. Sometimes, I felt like the dream world was dripping right through the fabric of my daylight world. Many people experience a lot of fear, or neurotic states of confusion, when they're called upon to let go and flow into other levels of awareness. I didn't get that either. For me, the onset of the psychedelic state felt like going sane.

As soon as we got out of the van, I could feel the precipitation brewing. This was similar to the direct apprehension involved in walking into a roomful of people and reading the collective mood. I was suddenly certain that some connection exists between human emotion and the movements of the weather. My black tank top and jeans sufficed to keep me warm. I did wish that I was dressed in something with more visual interest, though. Every trip I've ever taken, then and since, has made me instantly aware of where hippie fashion sense comes from. But, no matter—there would be trees and blooms and the breath of the Earth to perceive, rejoice in, and merge with. I didn't need to be looking at myself.

"Anybody grab the flashlight?" Carlos called out.

I had the uncanny sense that, if I focused, I could see perfectly in the darkness like a cat.

"Got it," Tommy said. He sounded altogether too coherent. I found it vaguely irritating.

He and Carlos took the lead, starting up a steep and wet path that was just wide enough to admit us, with the weeds and grasses lapping against our sides as if in greeting. I lagged behind because I disliked the sensation of anyone following me. I had the somewhat comical insight that this was my role in the band as well. Tommy ploughed our course and I guarded the rear, ready to take out anyone who might try and ambush us.

Now it was all deepening. We merged with a river born of magic, myth, and the dreams of all those who'd gone before us. I turned to my right and saw some violets casting off glints of tiny light like flecks of stardust. All at once, everything in existence was being created in every moment.

"It's the light that can't be extinguished!" I shouted. "I understand now!"

It's easy to say such things when you feel all of creation communing with you; easy, too, to assume that the other people around you will understand your sense of euphoria. And yet, in actual fact, Tommy did shout "Yes!" from his place at the vanguard as if he knew exactly what I was talking about.

And just like that, our whole holy pilgrimage south flashed across my inner eyes: the distances, the pockets of heart warmth and of emptiness, the strangers met, and the intimacy of the music we'd ushered into their stomping grounds. My imagination deified our trusty travelling van, transforming it into an ancient Egyptian solar boat that had borne us across the heavens of vision so that we could spread our gospel of every human being's divinity.

"It's all familiar!" Carlos gasped. "I go to this world every night when I dream. Dig that, brothers and sisters!"

"It's all a story that we authored ourselves!" I blurted. "That's the thing that Saul's been trying to get through my head!"

I spread my arms out and allowed the living air to weave its loving caresses through my fingers. "Feel it, man! It's our notions of good and evil that keep us from living like this all the time. This is the Garden. It doesn't lie in any ancient historical past. We're surrounded by it right now!"

The drizzle started pelting us at that moment. We followed the now-dim beacon that was Tommy's flashlight. "It's alright!" he announced. And now he had his arms outstretched, same as me, to embrace the rain. "We arose from water along with the rest of primordial life! And to the sea we shall all, one day, return!"

Returning from our magical sojourn in the mountains, all I really wanted to do was daydream about Janie. I could see her vividly in my mind's eye, and the knowledge that she was due to arrive in Albuquerque, New Mexico, shortly after us felt momentous, like Tchaikovsky's musical fireworks to my psilocybin-besotted mind.

❖

We got on the road at about six p.m. the following day. By the time darkness descended, we were gliding down into New Mexico, the fourth state out of eight that we would visit before this adventure was over. My thoughts, however, were all directed north towards Janie. She'd never been out of Oregon. Her father had left her, her older brother, and her mom when Janie was nine—ran off with his secretary, the clichéd bastard. It was well within his means to support them all, from the sound of things, but he was miserly with his money and griped every inch of the way. Vacations had just not been an option for her family.

I wanted to show her the colors of the desert, and the high, flat mesas and the dozen hues of the Santa Fe sunset that I'd been hearing about. Carlos had lived down this way for a couple of years. It'd be my first time witnessing any of these things, but I wanted Janie's wonder and excitement to be a part of that initial experience.

Miles rolled by to the sounds of heavy metal, Tommy's sermons, and the roll call of my thoughts. Taos, Santa Fe, Albuquerque: three performances with Janie out there in the audience. If Rachel could've been perched on her shoulders, then my happiness would have been utterly complete.

I'd requested that we set the dates up that way—in reverse of their logical order—so that I could see Janie off at the airport after our last performance in New Mexico.

Maybe this was only wild fancy, a product of my readings about the region and the many times we'd all discussed it during the long drive south, but in every part of the vast sandy flats—barely discernible through the darkened van windows—I felt the spirits of the land's natives. They hovered overhead, infusing the very air like the ubiquitous scent of sage. The ground sent up a low ceremonial chant that was nearly deciphered by my inner ears. Tommy's mythology about the shaman came alive for me, and I realized that this was one of the precious miracles of music. It could travel everywhere. It could endure in the hearts and minds of those who'd partaken in it long after the performers were gone.

I wished we had a generator with us so that we could set up somewhere out in the desert, far from everyone, and try to capture the mystic, smoking magic that we were talking about. Many of a band's best moments never make it onto record; and some never even get a chance to emerge from the musicians' heads.

Because the terrain there was so level, we could see approaching cities from scores of miles away. It lends the drive a feeling like the aftermath of the Apocalypse, as you quest after the sole remaining bastion of human warmth and light on the distant horizon. You go down a dip here or there, and your glowing oasis vanishes; but then, around another bend, its promise appears again, and hope is rekindled. Albuquerque is not a major city by any stretch. But on this night, it seemed to me an immense sea of lights stretching eternally.

We found a rest area where we could park the van and get some sleep. There seemed little point in driving into the city at dawn. I actually had to put batteries into my tiny alarm clock and set it, for the first time on the trip, because Janie's flight was arriving at two-thirty in the afternoon and the three of us weren't used to being up and around much before then anymore. Neither of the guys muttered complaints about being deprived of a bit of sleep on account of it, though. As for myself, I was so excited about the prospect of seeing her in this strange new world I'd happened upon, that I wondered whether I'd be able to sleep at all.

I got out of the van and stretched my legs on the paved parking area. Then I lit a cigarette and watched the first lambent promises of dawn emerging across the horizon. I swear I even saw green and purple in that sunrise.

The road teaches you that all of reality is a matter of perception. For me, the dawn was a welcome and a promise. And a challenge, too. It dared me to haul my old mindset into this land where cultures met and sometimes merged in a way that was not to be duplicated anywhere else on Earth. "Respect the enigma," the rising sun seemed to proclaim, "and it will treat you kindly."

I told myself to file that thought away for a possible future lyric....

❖

Maybe it was the ancient alchemy of the desert that pulled me down into heavy slumber and dreams after all. I awoke before the alarm and hurriedly dressed, feeling anxious to see this exotic world under daylight.

First, I walked to the restroom and attended to my hygiene, as best I could in the public sink. I hadn't showered in a couple days and loathed the thought of greeting Janie in such a state. I looked at my wet and whiskered face in the mirror and recoiled. I'd forgotten to warn her, when last we'd talked, that I'd chopped my hair off! I was still unused to the look myself; the new image that greeted me seemed to reveal facets of emerging personality that I wasn't ready to comprehend. Long hair isn't just for flailing around when you headbang. You can also hide behind it.

❖

Albuquerque wasn't nearly as gigantic as it'd appeared to me at night—then an interminable river of lights. Going up Central Avenue, we passed Toad's Watering Hole, the bar we were scheduled to play at in a week's time.

We arrived at the airport with half an hour to spare. Now we were, in a sense, amongst people who shared a similar existential stance—transients, neither here nor there, consumed with thoughts of where they were heading and, perhaps, not realizing that here, in this moment, nothing could claim them. They were free. I loved living outside the rhythms of consensus reality, and felt like I never wanted our tour to end. I watched all the weary and excited travelers passing back and forth with a slight smile on my face and the thrum of anticipation in my veins.

Tommy was scanning our surroundings. "Everywhere you look," he observed, "they're trying to remind you of the worldview that you're supposed to be plugged in to. The dire news on every television set. The magazine racks. The poster ads."

Flight number 1489 came in right on time. I stared at the floor and feigned being lost in daydreams because I didn't want the guys to notice how nervous I felt. I'm sure my mask didn't fool them.

When the moment came, it was like it is so often when I'm up onstage. I may be introverted and withdrawn beforehand, detached from the outer world and not wanting to engage with it, but then I start playing and suddenly I rejoin that pulsing magnetic field of interrelatedness. The dam bursts, and everything that had been simmering beneath the surface pours out to the audience. Passion surges forth, evaporating all the fear at its perimeter.

That's how it was when I lifted my head and saw Janie coming my way, her in a black leather skirt and dark stockings, a sturdy tan and fringed blouse that Pocahontas could have worn—and which Janie had probably made herself—her flaxen hair bound back and just a hint of gray-blue makeup on her eyelids to accentuate the gorgeous green of her eyes.

Everyone else in that airport disappeared for me, and I was running. Sheer instinct guided me through the intervening distance and all the other figures around us. I saw her smirk in response to my enthusiasm and drop her bags. Then I swept her up in my arms and let out a deep groan of happiness.

Back in Oregon, she'd always looked beautiful to me. Now she looked dear. That's all that I really wanted to tell her; and there seemed to be no way of accomplishing that, so I ended up pelting her with a barrage of questions about her trip and all that she'd been up to over the last few weeks. She never had the chance to answer any of this, either, because by then Tommy and Carlos had caught up with us and more warm greetings had to be made.

Janie was hungry, so I bought her a veggie sandwich and a blueberry yogurt smoothie. "That's healthier than any meal the three of us have had since we left Sadenport," I told her as we all sat down at a table in the middle of the food court.

"I'll bet," she said with a wink. "It's a wonder you've survived this long." Then she glanced at Tommy and nodded in my direction. "He been behaving on the tour?"

Tommy shrugged. "Remember that we live at the edge of madness or breakthrough, always. That said…there hasn't been a fight yet. We may be looking at a changed man."

Janie squeezed my shoulder. "It's just because I want to see you stick around, babe—that's why I say things like that." Then she pitched her voice for my ears alone. "And it's nice to see more of your face."

I was immensely relived by her reaction to my "haircut." And I experienced, simultaneously, the full rawness of my own love and need in that moment. No doubt, it was the combination of these factors that made my reply so intense and earnest.

"People like you in my life," I swept my gaze across the three of them, "make me feel like I want to be here. God, I'm still getting used to that feeling. Before we got into town today, I was looking at the tumbleweeds that occasionally roll across the desert out here, thinking that that's what my life has so often felt like: just a long rootless tumble."

The loneliness of my particular corner of the universe caught me in its full, cold sweep. I was almost overwhelmed by the sensation. Carlos, in a moment of intuition that approached ESP, came to my rescue. "I think our friend here is road-weary. The thing to do, of course, is for you and me, Tommy, to explore this town on foot for a while and let him and his girlfriend have the van so they can, uh, catch up on sleep."

"That sounds reasonable," Tommy said in his driest tone. "The van does exert a powerful recuperative effect upon all who enter."

We ended up parking beside a relatively quiet recreation field near Old Town. Carlos and Tommy left us alone there, and Janie and I didn't waste a moment. I was aching for her in ways I can't even describe. We were fully united for that half hour or so, moving and responding almost as a singular organism, our agreement upon our most pressing desires and needs so clearly understood that there was scarcely any need for speech.

Afterwards, the coldness tried to claim me again. But I realized that I was armed with tools, weapons of self-understanding with which to combat it. The frigidity came from me in the first place, after all, so how could I truly be at its mercy? Obviously, I did believe, at least to some extent, in my own inadequacy. I believed I was undeserving of love; that I was too crazy to share my innermost self with someone like Janie. But these ideas were mine. Why should I quail before them? They belonged to me; I didn't belong to them.

"I've been thinking about your trip out here ever since I left," I said, lying there naked, spooning her. "On Monday—oh, that's tomorrow, isn't it?—we've got a gig to play in Taos. Then we come down to Santa Fe two days later and end up back here in Albuquerque the night before you leave. But when we're not playing or traveling, I'd really like to be showing you the desert, the hot springs, the galleries…whatever you want."

Janie smiled. "I definitely want to spend some time in the Santa Fe Plaza, see the jewelry. "But—" she wagged a finger, "no buying me any of it, hon. I know how you think. You're still on the road for a few weeks and you need to eat. Maybe I'll pick something up for myself, or maybe I'll just look and gather ideas."

"Well, I make no promises," I said, "so you better not let on that you like any of it—leastways, not in front of me."

When the others returned, maybe two hours later, they were laden with Mexican takeout: enchiladas, soft tacos, Spanish rice, refried beans, and tortilla chips. "You gotta try this green chili sauce, bro!" Carlos insisted. "It's the best!"

We all ate our fill, feeling grateful for the break from gas station fare. This was definitely better Mexican food than anything you could get at Miguel's stand—no offense, Miguel. Anyway, when we finished, we decided to drive on to Taos straightaway. Tommy offered to take the wheel so that Janie and I could lie in the back, amidst the gear and the piles of clothes and personal mementos, and enjoy some relative privacy. I felt the vibrations of the road beneath my side, met the honest eyes of the woman I loved, and felt like nearly everything I needed for happiness in this world was right there in front of me.

MY ANSWER TO EVERYTHING

There was so much I wanted to say to her that I couldn't find the words for. I tried in vain to sort through my logjammed thoughts. I had changed in ways that I didn't know how to articulate yet. It's one thing to make resolutions, and embark upon a new path in your life, and quite another to realize that everything you'd built on that old way of being has been shaken to its foundations. You wonder if the whole structure could come crashing down upon your head.

At one point I asked her, only half-joking, "Would you still find me as interesting if I became a lot more settled inside—if I took a few steps away from the edge?"

Janie shook her head, smiled, then cast me a look of mock exasperation. "You're the one who thinks instability and brilliance go hand in hand," she said. "I look at you and see a caring and gifted person. The other stuff just seems to come out of not having ever learned to live with that in a comfortable way. No one ever affirmed it for you. So, you feel more than you know how to deal with. I get that. But, as far as self-destruction goes, I'll put up with it, where you're concerned. And all the while I'll be hoping that you rise above it. But it's not a turn-on for me, if that's what you're asking."

Her answer soothed me. I leaned forward and cupped her chin, and kissed her forehead. I found the courage at least to add, "There's some other things I want to tell you about, but I can't seem to find the words right now. Just ways that I've been rethinking my life and where it's heading."

"Well, I look forward to you finding those words, my death rocker with the soul of a poet," she said, with a mischievous gleam in her emerald eyes. That earned her another kiss, this time on the lips.

Taos felt like the very roof of the world to me. We found a secluded area to park the van, and I swore the temperature dropped thirty degrees after the sun went down. There was nothing beyond or above us save for the remote stars. Carlos said that we were all gonna trip out when we explored the town itself. "I don't know that anyone here's got a regular job, bro. They're all crystal healers, Tarot or aura readers; or they're psychic…I don't know what all. Maybe Sedona, Arizona is the New Age capital of the world, but I'd say Taos comes in close second."

"We should really play up on our name then," Tommy opined.

"Maybe that's why these people offered us the gig," Carlos said with a wink.

The gig was at a café that served breakfast burritos all day and looked just like a log cabin from the outside: Amalia's Tea Room. They were only open until eight p.m., so we needed to go on by six in order to perform our (slightly subdued, for this occasion) set. We were offered a free meal for our efforts, and the owner promised to pass around a basket for donations. Lacey's Foxhound had gone there a few times simply because they'd wanted an excuse to visit Taos.

There wasn't a stage. We went through the door and set up in a space immediately to the right, which had been cleared for us. We were snug. Sometimes Carlos would hit a cymbal and the vibrations would scamper right up my spine. The place looked like a Native American lodge—a long hall with a high, pitched roof, and dream catchers hanging from the walls in various places. All was bare wood. Nothing had been painted. People came and went. Some were absorbed in the spectacle of Edge of the Known, others were mildly interested, and still others hardly glanced our way. I was almost disappointed that our penchant for drama didn't seem to frighten anyone. They were a hip crowd.

It wasn't a particularly awe-inspiring performance, I was too acutely aware of Janie's presence, of the way that I was exposing myself to her in the songs and not just to an anonymous "crowd." I experienced brief spasms of hesitance before each sung line and chord change. I couldn't get loose. We probably went over fine, and yet I was so much in the grip of personal tension that it sounded stiff to my ears. Music should never be about repeating things by rote, and that's what I felt like I was doing at Amalia's.

Over dinner, we all decided to head off to Santa Fe immediately and find a motel. We were in dire need of showers, for one thing. It's a lot harder to bathe in a river in New Mexico than it is in the other states we'd passed through. Besides, the patrons had been generous with their donations to the band. Anyway, I liked the idea of waking up and being able to explore the town with Janie straightaway. The guys even suggested we get our own room—an idea that we were, of course, not opposed to.

So we bid farewell to this chilly pinnacle of the Southwest, with its airy spirits whispering their secrets in our ears in the late evening. You must learn not to grow attached to places and things if you want to survive a tour. But I could tell, already, that New Mexico was going to occupy a special place amongst my memories forevermore.

Janie could read the tension in me when we got to our room in the motel, even after we'd made love and then washed up and relinquished ourselves to the bed. She asked me what was happening. This time I didn't feel so threatened, though, because I'd begun to formulate an answer to my underlying malaise—one that actually made some kind of sense.

"I guess it's a feeling of anticlimax," I told her. "I mean, you pour so much of yourself into your songs, and then you bring those songs to the people…I guess I'd assumed that somewhere along the line I'd feel like I'd arrived, like I'd done it. But really, it's just that people are entertained for a while and then they get on with the rest of life."

"But you don't know what they're taking away from it," Janie argued. "Some things really do change our lives, you know. Songs, books, poems—even a conversation you have with someone; it can turn you in a different direction."

"Yeah, I know," I conceded. Then I laughed as the inspiration hit me. "It's like the lottery! Hah! Is that not the definitive invention of modern civilization?"

Janie flashed me the impish smile that I'd grown to know and adore. "Oh, do go on, Mister Chane!"

"So many things revolve around that goddamn notion: heaven, celebrity, nirvana—winning on a scratch-off ticket. You wonder why people hustle about looking distracted all the time. They're chasing the illusory moment that these cultural stories promise us, the moment when we've made it. All questions are settled; and all growth is accomplished. It's the myth of perfection. It would mean death, really, if one could ever attain such a thing. And yet, people keep chasing it."

Janie looked into my eyes for a long moment, as if she was trying to catch a glimpse of something before it scampered away.

"Then just keep playing for the love of it, and don't worry about 'making it,'" she said. "If perfection is a myth, like you say, then we've already arrived."

I loosened up a lot more when we played Guillermo's bar a couple nights later. Janie and I stole a few hours beforehand to wander the plaza and the surrounding area once more. Tommy had often described our tour as a kind of vision quest. In the Southwest, this description gripped my imagination most powerfully. There was a sense of remoteness in the air that, for me, deepened the feeling of being in communion with primal forces.

Of course, all of this gets pulled down to a much more banal level when it comes time to drag your gear into a tiny bar and set up in front of a mixed group of people who may or may not have any interest in you and/or the musical message that you bear. But it is at this point that you have to call upon your artistry and internal belief and create your own scene. I'd experienced the way that music could completely transform the ambiance of a place. It's one of the wonders of the line of work that I'd chosen. And this is what Edge of the Known accomplished at Guillermo's.

The place almost looked like a tunnel from the vantage point of the stage. It was three times as long as it was wide, and the ceiling was low. There wasn't even room for a pool table. The long bar was to our left and the line of tables to our right. We were set in the back, as far as you could get from the front door. Tommy said he felt like we were playing inside a mountain hall tunneled out by dwarfs.

Ah, but there's no doubt that this place saw the best action in Santa Fe that night. Another great thing about this town was the way that sound carried throughout its downtown vicinity. We continually pulled people in from the streets. You could tell that the music had drawn them, from the way they looked to the stage as soon as they came through the door.

A few days later, we topped this with our performance at Toad's Watering Hole in Albuquerque, with its garish sign that looked like Mr. Toad from *Wind in the Willows* sipping on a martini. I was revitalized from my previous day out with Janie. We'd driven to the Jemez hot springs for the afternoon, feasted on giant green chili burgers at a nearby restaurant, and then slept beneath the stars amidst the many-colored sands and the faint scent of sage.

Toad's, which sat alongside Central Avenue right before you hit downtown proper, was a hotspot anyway on account of its being located almost directly across from the UNM campus. But what bewildered me, initially, as I was hauling my amp into the bar, was the sight of a few familiar faces at the tables.

While Tommy positioned one of the mic stands, I saddled alongside him and whispered, "Hey, do you recognize anyone who's in here right now?"

He glanced up and scanned the area. This was one of the larger venues we'd played. The tall windows to our right offered a clear view of the street and the illuminated sidewalk. Nearly every table between us and the far wall was occupied. Tommy pointed to a couple of them.

"Yeah," he said, "I think all those guys caught our gig at Guillermo's. They must've driven down from Santa Fe."

I shook my head. "What the hell?"

Tommy favored me with a satisfied smile. "This phenomenon, my friend, is what is known as building a following."

I was grinning to myself as I plugged in and strummed a few chords to test the volume. Applause after a performance was one thing. People being willing to drive a hundred miles in order to hear you again was quite another level of affirmation.

Tommy didn't do his usual greeting but instead plunged right into his "Parched Landscapes." This song begins with a fast, rousing progression and then settles into a much moodier astral movement in the middle, which nearly disengages itself from all sense of time and causality. It makes for a good introduction, as it warns the audience that we intend to take them someplace they've never been to before. Electric fingers seemed to graze along my scalp as Tommy sang.

Until these last few weeks, the idea of "bringing our vision to the world" had really been an abstract concept. But I'd slowly begun to realize that no one can calculate the implications of any creative act. Mainstream music, in my opinion, basically told people what they already believed. Listening to it was like breathing your own breath. We were about shattering all the windows and airing out all the closets, attics, and dungeons of the mind.

Nothing disturbed the flow of it that night. The audience was with us, we were with them, and together we generated a kind of centrifugal force that was greater than all of us combined. At Toad's, we all climbed aboard the Solar Boat and left this world for a while. For an hour or so we slammed the club hard, each number hot on the heels of the last. Then we looked at each other and, with our group telepathy in full force, collectively decided to pause for a breather.

I wish I could recall all the buoyant words of approval, praise, and even awe that wafted over to us from the waiting audience. It made us all eager to continue. We nodded to each other, after sharing a quick cigarette, and meandered over to our respective places on the stage. I was shirtless, by this point, and still dripping hot.

The next song, "Dreaming Mind's Back Door," was my composition and therefore my vocal duty. But as I leaned towards the mic, I realized that I was doing so to speak, not to sing. It wasn't premeditated. I can only suppose that certain thoughts had been percolating inside me for a long time and they wouldn't be denied any longer. I'd thought about sharing all of this with Janie, during a quiet and private moment. But I'd never envisioned baring myself like this in front of a bar full of people. And yet, the vibe in the place was such that I knew that honesty—any piece of reality—would be welcome. I decided to just place my trust in that and take the plunge.

The sound of my voice, unaccompanied, both daunted and elevated me. I'd never spoken into a mic at all except to do sound checks. Tommy had always introduced the songs.

"A couple of weeks ago," I began, "I chastised our drummer Carlos here for getting high before a gig in Idaho and then playing sloppy through the set. On the one hand that's understandable, you know. You wanna put everything you have into a performance; you wanna satisfy yourself and also all the people who were cool enough to come out and see you. So I'm not saying that I was totally out of line. But I definitely overreacted. See, if we botched a gig then I felt like my life was over, basically. That's how overly dramatic I could get about the whole thing."

My throat started going dry, and it seemed to have a lock mechanism that wanted to snap shut. But at that point, I was encouraged by the silence in the bar. These people were listening and hanging on my every word. A few of them had even moved closer to the stage to hear me better.

"So I guess I realized that I'd burdened the band with the responsibility of having to be my answer to everything," I went on. "Like, the music had to somehow justify the suffering and all the struggles that I've ever gone through. And I tell you what: it hasn't been easy to let that go, man. Because maybe you've experienced it for yourselves, how when an illusion gets stripped away you suddenly see all kinds of things that you didn't want to look at before.

"So as we're driving over here, on the night before my girlfriend has to fly back home, I'm wondering what the point of all this is. 'Cause I realized that, no matter how good we performed tonight, and whether or not you guys loved us or hated us—no matter how well the rest of our tour goes—I'll still end up going home to the reality of my dad drinking himself to death. My younger sister—I love her more than life, man—she'll still be living with a woman who considers me a freak, basically. And my mom will still be seven years in her grave."

I heard sporadic calls from the audience at that point, but I couldn't make out any actual words. I was swept on by the momentum of this story, and I knew that I couldn't land upon any internal peace until I'd delivered it right there and then.

"But I guess one point to it all is I've learned to trust myself since we've been out on the road. Maybe I've been learning that for as long as we've been making music. And don't worry, I'll shut up in a minute here; but I just want to say first that there are forces at work in our lives that run deeper than any of us know. Maybe we get it rammed down our throats in school, or at home, that our life is meaningless. But when the music takes a hold of you, then you know what a fucking bunch of nonsense that is, because you feel it right here," I pounded my chest with a fist, "and the heart feels the real worth of everything and everyone in a way that the mind can only keep racing to try and catch up with.

"So yeah, maybe my drunk father wishes that I'd never been born. And maybe to my aunt, the one who's raising my sister now, I'm a loser who'll never amount to anything. But that don't mean that I've gotta take all that on and believe it. And I've noticed how the more I refuse to listen to those voices, the more the world starts singing me a different tune. Have some faith in yourself and all of a sudden the universe starts showing faith in you too."

I felt the backlash of embarrassment from this sentiment, so I reacted in the only way I'd ever understood: I confronted it head-on. "I know it can sound trite, man—oh, 'believe in yourself.' You hear that all the time. And taking personal responsibility sounds like a penance. But if you can really step back from your life, just look at it and say, 'Yeah, I see how I set it all up this way,' then the power to make changes is back in your hands.

"It's like your whole existence is this structure that you built up with kids' blocks—the blocks being, like, your own ideas about who you are and what reality is. You don't like the way the building looks? Fucking knock it down and start over! It's within your power. Yours, mine....

"There's this medicine man of a counselor who I've been seeing back in Oregon, where I live. He's been trying to get this through my head for a year now. But I guess it's one of those truths that you've gotta wake up to in your own way—and at your own pace.

"Alright, I'll shut up now," I finished.

And I'd intended to plunge into the opening chords of the next song. But I didn't get very far. Janie suddenly crashed right into me, nearly toppling me over. She cupped my face in her hands, and then her lips locked onto mine. On some dim periphery of my awareness I could hear the audience hollering and applauding just as loud in response to the sight of that as they had for all the songs that we'd performed thus far.

She was grinning with fierce pride when she finally released me. "You're getting no mercy from me when I get you back to the motel, poetry man!" she breathed.

After she left, it took me a few days to recapture my zest for touring. I recalled something that Saul had said a while back: "When you start thinking that your happiness depends upon someone else, then you've already landed in a patch of trouble." I reminded myself of this, many times. We must "kiss the winged joy as it flies," as William Blake bids us. The road can teach you that lesson, too.

DIAMOND MAELSTROM

Unfortunately, love was the most ruthless force in our universe. That's what I believed at the juncture soon to follow—that I'd sooner endure the ravages of hate any day. Hate wielded the honest pungency of a fist full to your face. Love eviscerated you where you stood and yet still left you standing.

I remember the moonlight on the little window box balcony. Janie was so nervous that she'd stolen occasional drags off of my cigarette. This had been her idea in the first place: the two of us "getting away," booking this room in the Latore Motel.

"I guess maybe I thought I was more adventurous than I actually am," she told me.

The idea—insofar as I believed I'd understood it—had been to pretend we were on vacation, perhaps try and resuscitate the amorous mood that had characterized our rendezvous in New Mexico months before, when everything had seemed to open up and flow. I stared back into the motel living room, which bore witness to the scalds and the warm patches of love's dying embers, as if its solidity could somehow refute what was happening, what could not be happening.

I'd played deaf amidst all of the whispered warnings.

Janie moved to catch me in a hard embrace then. There was tenderness in her clasp; but I see it now, that it was tenderness provoked by remorse, by loyalty to what had been, rather than by any enduring passion. With her lips, her fingers, and all the womanly fire that her body could convey, Janie was saying goodbye. With all the unsinkable generosity of her heart, she gave me a hero's send-off.

"Rachel is the luckiest girl in the world, to have you for a big brother," she said. "Tommy and Carlos…me, too. I've never met anyone like you before. You've opened me up to so much that I was never even aware of. You do that sometimes just with your presence."

Stalling, postponing the inevitable dive into blackness, she took another drag. My tears were subsumed, inhibited by anger because anger was what I clung to in order to see me through this. But I never railed at her that night. I watched her retreat as if I was an impotent mute.

"But I feel as if I don't even know where you're at half the time," she explained. "The way your mind works…it, like, never sits still; it's like this madly spinning gyre. And I try to keep up with it all, but it's like you go around a bend, every time, and I've lost you again."

My entire survival strategy had been contingent upon viewing my tendencies towards mental and emotional extremity as a gift rather than a curse. Of course, this had also rendered me reliant upon the presences of people in my life who could always forgive me for my excesses. Maybe Tommy's rare loyalty had spoiled me. Maybe I had let my Muse lure me into a deluded world where it seemed justifiable to sacrifice anything on the altar of vision.

I gazed down at the street below and felt the whole spinning and sickening free fall that could bring me to kiss that pavement. A couple walked by, hand in hand, oblivious to the clamor of Armageddon.

Her heart was turning away—shining its light elsewhere? I was never going to touch her again? Suddenly, the fall from the balcony seemed the much kinder terror.

"You need someone who can really meet you in those places. And I—"

"Don't!" I managed. "Don't fucking act like you're doing this for my sake. I can decide what's good for me!"

"Fair enough." Her voice was wispy, insubstantial: an echo of the distance that had already claimed us. "I need to feel like I can keep up. It's like…you're living in this world that's being totally reinvented every day. And I'm sort of stumbling along trying to figure out what the rules are."

"There aren't any rules!" I protested. "Just be with me, and—"

"I can't." Janie bit her lip. One fat tear slid down her cheek. I doubt she'd wanted to say it so bluntly. But what gentle way is there?

This can't be happening!

I'd once told her that if it ever came to this, I would understand. I'd been a goddamn liar. The death of something so beautiful and divinely inevitable could never be understood; it was incomprehensible.

Janie reached over and squeezed my arm. "Hey. I do treasure what we've shared."

"Then don't turn your back on it and let it die!" I growled. I could feel my face curling into a snarl. I couldn't stop it. Janie withdrew.

"I really tried, Brandon."

It was that voice, both forlorn and resolute, and every man hears his end in it. The chasm gaped even wider below me. Above me were only stars, beyond reproach or appeal. "You'd better just leave, then, if that's what you've decided to do."

Everything within me prayed that I was calling her bluff. But the deeper, wiser part of me knew that this horrifying rift was an already-accomplished fact. Her voice had diminished almost beyond hearing. "OK."

For a long time, I wavered on that balcony and tried to tell myself that I'd find her when I went back inside, her heart and mind reconsidered. The roiling grief didn't fully announce itself until the receding sound of her engine merged with the rest of the street noise.

I thrust down the fierce impulse to dive down to the pavement, my salvation. Sometime later, I fished out my cellphone and rang Carlos.

"Hullo?" His voice seemed to emerge from inside a bundle of cotton. I'd obviously woken him up.

"Hey, can we talk? I'm sorry. You know I wouldn't call at this hour if it wasn't serious."

He collected his wits pretty quick. "I thought you were spending the night at the Latore Motel."

"I'm still here."

"Then you've got someone to talk to, haven't you? Or what, you're alone? What gives, bro?"

"Look, it's over. Janie broke it off just now. She's gone." Part of me couldn't believe any of the words I was uttering, or fathom the ocean of woe that churned beneath them. "Let's go get a beer somewhere, alright?"

"Shit, bro. It's like, one o'clock or damn near!"

"Please, Carlos."

I was flailing for anything in the manifest world that might ward off the encroaching blackness. The reality of what had just happened was threatening to penetrate my brain, tear through the last thin sheets of illusion and doubt, and make itself known in indisputable searing pain.

We met up at Charlie's Pub on Lincoln Avenue just in time for last call. I asked for a double shot of whiskey and a glass of lemon water to chase it down with. I had no patience for beer tonight. I needed something that was going to hit my bloodstream and brain quick.

Carlos had grown up in Mexico City and, later on in his teens, moved to New Mexico in search of work. He'd subsisted for years on minimum wage or sometimes even less, resorting at times to dealing drugs. Like me, he was acquainted with extremity and desperation. This, alongside our passion for music and self-expression, formed the major pillars of our growing camaraderie.

"So why didn't you call Tommy?" he asked.

I nodded my thanks to the bartender when the drinks arrived and then gulped the stinging liquor down. I needed that moment to compose my answer. "I just feel like he'd want to answer this whole twisted conundrum for me, you know? Provide some summary statement that would explain the significance of it all and the lesson that I'm s'posed to take from it. I don't wanna hear about how the pain

194

will subside in time, or that when one door closes another opens, or that it was better to find out sooner rather than later."

"A raw wound is not to be reasoned with," Carlos concurred.

I nodded. "I don't mean to judge a friend. He'd probably show more tact and sensitivity than I'm giving him credit for, really. But I just feel too vulnerable and I don't want to chance it."

"So what did Janie tell you?"

I noticed the bartender out of the corner of my eye. We shared a wordless exchange, and he offered a conciliatory nod. When he refilled my shot glass, I conveyed my sore gratitude as best I could. Then I turned back to Carlos. "She said that I'm constantly going to places where she doesn't know how to follow me to. You know, in my mind."

My thoughts and I were still both involved in the delicate game of relaying the bare facts of the story without (for the moment, at least) believing any of it.

"But that's not the real reason at all," I said. This remark slipped past my guard. It surprised even me. I was now embarked upon a frightening plunge into the unknown.

"Well, so what is?" Carlos prompted me.

It must be that my fresh wound had temporarily numbed me, like a clean cut or sudden burn that you don't feel yet because the surface nerves are dead. I spoke with the detachment of a sleepwalker. "It was about a month ago. I told Janie about something that'd happened to me, something I'd done. This was right before the first gig we'd ever played, Tommy and me with Tim. I was in a fight. Some drunk—he was probably twice my age—he pushed me down. So I took him down. It ended up where I was about an inch away from opening up his jugular with the jagged end of a broken beer bottle. Who knows if I might not have done it, too, if Tommy hadn't a' stopped me."

"Damn, bro," Carlos breathed. "I had no idea."

I shrugged. "That's because I never had the guts to tell you before. Tommy was there, like I said. Besides him, the only one who knew about it was Saul."

Carlos stared at me for a while with such a look of repugnance that I finally erupted.

"Look, man, you nearly destroyed yourself with meth!"

He was immediately repentant. "Sorry, bro. I didn't mean to get judgmental. You scared me, I guess. You just told me something pretty intense, right there."

I waved down his apology. "Yeah, it is. I don't blame you."

"So you think that's what made Janie want to run?"

"Everything changed after I told her about that. The way she'd look at me, touch me…it was all so tentative. Unsure. I think I freaked her out. I'm sure of it, actually. It had nothing to do with the explanation she gave me."

❖

I didn't have the luxury of sleeping late the next morning, even though it was Saturday and I didn't have to work.

Shortly after we'd returned from our tour down to New Mexico and then up the West Coast, our band had formally signed to Manhandle Records. Chas had been impressed by our ability to sell several hundred copies of our CD to people who'd never heard of us before. He was now speculating about somehow sending us off on a tour of the East Coast, where we would find ourselves, once again, playing in front of completely virgin audiences. He also wanted to get us back into his studio to record a second album. In the meantime, he'd arranged for the three of us to be interviewed by Pat Stavons at the highly-respected underground publication Visionary Chapbook. That was happening this very morning.

I scarcely felt capable of saying hello to anyone without snarling, much less rambling on about my music, my band, and what all of it meant to me. An odd sort of tactful silence prevailed in the van during our drive over to Visionary's offices. I hadn't had a chance to explain the reasons for my nihilistic mood to Tommy, but now I suspected that Carlos had already given him the heads-up.

The low brick building resembled an old fashioned bank or social security office, though its entryway was as plastered with flyers and announcements—the overflow of exuberant grassroots creativity—as any aged nightclub. I felt altogether too disreputable to be passing through those clean glass doors and over the immaculate green carpet. Shouldn't a paper that is devoted to underground music nest in a place more closely resembling a dank basement? For all of its do-it-yourself artistic ethic, the headquarters for Visionary Chapbook certainly didn't look very punk rock.

We met Pat. He was even slightly taller than Tommy—a few inches shy of seven feet, I guessed—and similarly gaunt. He was dressed in blue jeans and a dark corduroy shirt covered by a furry vest of gray and black. His eyebrows were bushy charcoal and scant hair remained on his head. Bristling with energy, he fetched us all coffees from the ceramic spigot and got us settled on the brown leather couch. His office space was wallpapered with old musical headlines. I saw a photo of one of my favorite bands, Foment Revolt, performing at a gig right there in Sadenport about five years before.

I liked Pat, with his buoyant, easy laugh and his obvious love for the music that his magazine was championing. And I think I can speak for the others on that count. I wished I had something else to offer him that day besides my poisoned thoughts and seared heart.

"So I've listened to your record, What Casts the Shadow," he began, "and I was immediately struck by the conviction of your performances. The songs are killer, and you guys play 'em like Hell's pit fiends are flailing fiery whips at your backs the whole time."

His exuberance made me wince. Once—in another life, it seemed—Saul had described our band in a similar way: performing as if our lives depended on it. Which, in fact, they did. And this had been before Carlos joined, transforming us into an even more potent force.

"I may give the album a review in an upcoming issue," Pat went on. "So how 'bout you begin by sharing some of your memories of the whole process of recording it."

Tommy, our self-appointed diplomat, burst right out of the gate. "That was a good moment in time for us to capture. We'd been rehearsing like maniacs, and yet most of the songs were just a few months old and so they were still fresh and vital for us. We were also anticipating taking them out on the road, so that enthusiasm translated into what we laid down in the studio, too."

"And Brandon had a bit of a crisis of faith mid-way," Carlos good naturedly put in.

"Oh?" Pat prompted, staring at me.

"My little sister brought me around," was all I could say.

Silence. I happened to glance in Tommy's direction, and I witnessed within him both the desire to speak and the firm decision to withhold himself and give me whatever space I needed.

"OK," Pat said tentatively.

"I visited her before I went to the studio, on one of our last nights of recording," I elaborated. "See, I didn't know who I was performing these songs for. They'd emerged from such a private part of me. Who else could possibly relate to them, you know? Was I really an alien in this world, or was there a place for me, somewhere?

"I guess you can get to that point where you realize that you could debate and question things forever; but if you're honest with yourself, then you realize that your own truth is all that you've ever got. I just had to hope that it would ring true for other people, too. So, I go see Rachel at recess and she's playing this game where they stole treasure from a troll's cave. This was, like, an echo of my own struggle somehow. I was trying to uncover my own voice—that was the treasure. And all the voices of self-doubt and despair inside, they were the trolls."

Realizing that for the moment this was all I had to offer Pat, Visionary Chapbook, Tommy and Carlos—as well as whatever fans we might have out there—I relinquished the struggle for coherence. How could I even speak when I wanted nothing but to scream? I held on to the remembered moment, the one moment that resembled an oasis of peace, and continued to mine it.

"Rachel was holding this agate about the size of a chestnut. Like a quartz with a little apricot for a heart. See, some people associate stones with that inviolate part of ourselves, this kind of sanctuary where our essence lives and can never be destroyed. My relationship with Rachel has always been like that, an invulnerable place. Tommy and I were butting heads a lot back then. I was constantly challenging the therapist I was seeing at the time. I put a lot of strain on—" I nearly choked, "my relationship with my girlfriend. But all that negativity somehow never intruded when I was with my little sis.

"So it was fitting that she'd be the one with the stone, holding it out and telling me that it granted wishes. It's like she was really saying that she'd been holding that sacred space for me, just waiting until I was ready to carry it for myself."

That was as far as I could go. I stood up, feeling the warmth of tears streaking my cheeks.

"You're a good guy, Pat. I'm sorry. I can't…I just lost my love. She's fucking gone. I hardly care about the music, what the lyrics mean; nothing matters anymore. What can you really even say about music anyway? I guess I've just always been searching for anything that could serve as a mirror for me. I can't do this today. I'm sorry."

A moment later, I was out on the sidewalk. It was damp from a brief morning shower, the kind of flashing spill that our part of Oregon was known for in April. Someone passed me on her way to the door, me with my hands braced on my knees and tears spattering the concrete. Interviews, records, songs, careers, fate…what did any of it mean to a man already dead?

I shuffled towards the van. I was lying in the back, left arm slung over my eyes, when the other guys finally came in. Tommy climbed into the driver's seat and began speaking at once. "He's gonna call and see if we wanna reschedule the interview. Carlos and I talked a bit more, but of course we didn't want to do it without you. It probably won't make it into the next issue now, one way or the other. But, maybe the one after that."

My soul was so raw that Carlos' voice wafted over to me soothing as a lullaby. "Hey, just take it easy, eh? You're in a lot of pain now, I know. It feels like a piece has been ripped right out of you, don't it? It'll take a while to move through it, bro. But you're going to."

In order to "move through," though, I had to find some way to even move. As it was, I was a slug turning over and over on a bed of salt. My mental hands were flailing for answers, insights, as Tommy started up the van.

Following that trek down to the Southwest and then north all the way to Washington, our vehicle had become the veritable fourth member of the band. We'd even given her a new black paint job. Had to treat her right, you know? After all, she could be serving as a home for us again, one of these days....

I immediately shut myself in my room when we got back. The three of us shared an apartment—actually, one half of a duplex—on Baird Street, not too far from Siddens Elementary where Rachel went to school. The epicenter of my creative life lay right there on that brown carpeted floor: my miniature practice amp, which gave me a warm distorted sound even at low volume; my one guitar, spray-painted a charcoal ebony, which had been with me since those beginning days of my first open G chord; and a notebook that still contained even my earliest lyrical ventures, often in the form of frantic scribbles. None of my contributions to Edge of the Known's first record had been created without these rudimentary but essential tools.

Lately, I'd been playing around with a poignant riff, ethereal as a wisp of cloud, and had managed to draw it out further with a haunting chord progression. This, in turn, had evoked a melody line that made the whole piece ache even more keenly. Thus far, I'd failed to compose even a single lyric to marry to all the music. But I felt the words coming now. For a couple hours, I alternately riffed and paused to scrawl down a line or two. I addressed it all to some imagined witness to my pain and abjection—an angel of mercy, perhaps. Maybe my salvation came in the form of the song itself. It wouldn't have been the first time.

> Every word trusts the
> tongue that speaks
> but plays dumb to lend daring
> its weight
> The drama unfolds in

every which way

whether we may jump or

hesitate

Thus begins "Diamond Maelstrom," which became one of my favorite pieces over time largely because I could never pin its meaning down to one logical explanation. The evocative power of poetry thrives upon certain aspects of mystery, I think.

Reckless is the path to

faith

Fallow fields bear fruit on

the Other Side

Who seeks to lengthen his

life in Eternity?

Or cloak his wildness with

a dead bear's hide?

Saul said if there was no inner self, then none of us could hope to hold onto any form of sanity. Our only recourse would be to orient ourselves around the world, and the modern world believed that it had no soul or purpose.

Word made flesh, in

the Maelstrom of thought

remind me of why

I came

Through quiet births, and

bathed in trust,

to be a guest in

your house of flames

And then I scrawled a bit of poetry that the melody had no room for.

Fulfillment is a finite space where the
dreaming mind's back door is left
wide open

After finishing the song, and playing it over again enough times so that I knew I'd never forget it, I curled up in my quilt—a tattered patchwork affair of earthy hues that was one of the last vestiges of my mother's life I possessed. I tried to sleep through the afternoon sun and engine bustle. Life had no more demands for me until we would rehearse that night. In the meantime, unconsciousness was my salvation. My bed was a pyre. I was burning, just like my new song said. This nest of flames was my home.

How was I going to survive this? Or—and this was the more frightening admission—why was I trying to?

I didn't have enough skin for the world. That was it. That had always been my problem. My hide wasn't thick enough for reality. I was a worm turning in the salt.

WHICH VERSION OF THE TRUTH?

At one time, rehearsing in the Catacombs had elevated the quest to create music to a heroic (even mythic) dimension for me. I felt as if I was grasping the raw despair with which the bunker had been built, and transmuting it into defiance, affirmation, and love: the declaration of belief, cast by an unsinkable spirit against an ocean of darkness. But now, all answers and purposes seemed to have fled.

Then I recalled a phrase that Tommy was fond of repeating, no doubt culled from his extensive readings in Depth psychology and related subjects: "The only way out is through." Salvation was not to be found in any kind of flight from my pain. Rather, I needed to embrace that pain as fully as possible, let it fuel every chord that I struck with my hands and every note that I belted from the bottom of my lungs.

I got halfway through the first verse of my new song and could already feel the medicine going to work. There's an effect that words can exercise upon your consciousness that is not dependent upon their logical meaning, or even upon your understanding. There is also a magical aspect to music that has nothing to do with our conceptions of pitch, timbre, and decibels.

Carlos seemed to understand the statement that was being made, and where it all must inevitably lead. He captured and amplified the rhythm and attitude before I even reached the first instrumental break, punctuating my personal catharsis with his own need for transcendence. Tommy was not far behind him. There is something about bereavement that marries so readily with the human voice. All of us understand the language of the wail. For all my emotional extravagance, I kept my voice under control, held its focus.

When I say that music transported me to a wholly different world, I'm not trying to express any sort of disdain for our physical surroundings. It just comforted me to know—to feel—that this dimension that we label "the real" actually exists in relation to so much else. Infinite "something elses," really. My sore suffering in the moment was truth. But it was, at the same time, a story—one version of the truth. I existed on many planes aside from just that one, and the life surrounding me was not confined to the picture that my five senses painted.

Tommy was clutching his bass around its neck and staring at me as I finished. "Jesus!" he breathed. "That's the most shamanic thing you've done in a long time—and that takes some doing."

I couldn't wait to perform the song live. We'd only done a handful of gigs in the city since returning from our low-budget road tour the previous summer. We'd had a lot to attend to upon our return. I was the only one able to slide back into my previous employment, bussing tables at Jaspar's steakhouse. Tommy had been replaced at the pizza place, and he was eventually hired to work weekdays at the local library. That was fitting. He was bound to spend his life surrounded by books one way or the other (and maybe the librarian who hired him had recognized this). Carlos had soldiered through various backbreaking temp jobs until the auto shop had offered him his old position back.

"Chas has been following through on all his connections," Tommy said, "and calling in every favor, just trying to land us a steady gig somewhere. He believes that we'll make our biggest impact if we really dig our heels in and become a fixture at one establishment."

We continued on into the night, dipping into the dozen songs that comprised What Casts the Shadow? as well as a couple of songs that Tommy had written since that summer. This is overly generalized, no doubt, but basically one could say that with Tommy alone you'd end up with a musical structure that, while brilliant, somehow couldn't come across on a street level; and with me you'd end up with a raging fire that had no container. We continually managed to balance one another's tendencies in a way that was really difficult to define.

I was worried about encountering Saul that night, and so I hurried to the van after we finished playing. I hadn't seen him since about a week before Janie had torn my fantasy of requited love to shreds. I was afraid that I'd be transparent to Saul's eyes, that he'd gather all the evidence of my internal distress with a glance. I wasn't ready to endure that level of vulnerability. Fortunately, he was rarely up at this hour. The lights in his house were all out as we made ready to drive away. I felt closer to my band than I had in a long time, at least. This lent me a degree of emotional equilibrium.

I could tell that the fever was going to start raging inside me again. Although I rarely drank, I picked up a six-pack of strong microbrew in anticipation of my night's battle. I downed a couple of the beers quickly and then tramped off to bed. Even if sleep were to elude me, I could still have darkness. *Janie!* Goddamn it, her shade sliced right through me like one of those fabled Oriental blades. How could I banish it? The alcohol somehow only muddled my thinking; it failed to dull my emotional pain in any noticeable way.

Weariness won out over bereavement after an hour or so. It was but a flashing respite, though. I found myself upright, heart pounding, staring dumbly at the white curtain that was outlined with the pale glow of a streetlight in an otherwise pitch-dark room.

I could still hear my father's muffled wail of anguish and despair, almost as if it was still happening in the waking world of clock time. I tried to backtrack from there, to reconstruct the harrowing dream, but could grasp nothing else. Then I had a vision of the house that he lived in, the house I'd grown up in. Every room was dark. This was something more than mere absence of light, though. The darkness was, itself, a presence—a presence that had infiltrated all the spaces that had never really known the touch of light and love. The whole place reeked of death and the Void. My father was in its belly, swallowed whole.

I'd endured plenty of nightmares before, but I was awake now—had been for several minutes—and still the sense of dread clutched me as tangibly as it had within the dream state. Somehow, I knew that the danger was legitimate; real in the waking world of "fact."

I leaped out of bed and began dressing before I'd even reasoned through what I was doing—or what I planned to do. Half of my consciousness still lingered within the stark dream and the other half was nearly unhinged with unreasoning panic. I didn't trust myself to drive. Nevertheless, I had to go to him at once. I'd have to walk—run, rather. I'd made that trip in twenty minutes before. I could do it in ten, or less, tonight.

Within another minute, I had my red sweatshirt on, had pulled the hood over my head, and stepped out into the spring night. The brisk air and the rigor of my exertions ushered lucidity. I realized the absurdity of what I was doing. No dream had ever before set me to roaming Sadenport's streets in the middle of the night. But I was committed now, and by the time I seriously began to question the sanity behind this whole venture, I was closer to my father's home than I was to my own.

What had my dad ever done to earn my panic? It seemed that with every step I recalled another stinging blow to the face, a fresh burst of humiliation, another remark full of dismissal and spite.

The sounds of barking dogs drew me back into the present. I left St. Christopher's Bridge and slipped onto Farrell Street. A few blocks down, it branched off into the cul-de-sac where Robert Chane lived alone. Until about two years ago, I'd called the place home too. I'd spent the better part of my teen years devising ways to stay away from it as long as possible. Only…someone had needed to be around to see that Rachel ate breakfast and caught the bus; that she did her homework and brushed her teeth; that she wasn't so scared that she couldn't sleep at night on account of being effectively left alone at the age of five, six….

Goddamn it! Why was I doing this? *Just go ahead and die, fucker! What the hell do I care?*

But I did care. My love for the man, the man who still lived (I was sure of it) beneath the inebriation and the rages and the projected disgust, was unextinguished. That love was, in fact, one of the sorest sources of grief in my entire existence.

I stopped at the opening of the cul-de-sac. My old two story, three-bedroom home, with its dirty white walls and green trim, hovered at the very rear—perched upon a rise where the stone bared itself, like giant mangled teeth, at various points along the low hill. For a dead-end life: a road with no outlet. It was utterly fitting.

There was only one light on inside the house, and I couldn't guess its source at this distance. Now that I'd come this far, there was nothing for it but to enter—now, in the dead of night, even knowing that I might be doing so at the bidding of a fantastical dream that bore no relation to waking reality. This whole trek could have been naught but the irrational byproduct of fear. The odds spoke in favor of that notion. Hell, he could mistake me for a prowler and bash my head in as soon as I got through the door. He could call the cops on me, as he'd done once before. Or…

Or my dream premonition could be tangible, true, and already have come to fruition. I might encounter nothing in there but his corpse.

I stalked up the stone steps. Those steps that had, a thousand times before, met my booted feet in their haste to carry me away from this place. My sorrow, Rachel's confusion, Ma's ghost…all was encased in that cold stone. I allowed myself no time to consider what I was doing, but pushed on the front door as soon as I reached it. Unlocked, it gave way.

Immediately I was confronted by the sickly sounds of coughing. They were too weak and wretched to have come from any human body that was determined to live. I now knew that my father was upstairs; in the bathroom, no doubt. There was no other logical place for him to be, unless he meant to stare into the vacant room where his daughter had once lived until his heart ruptured in his ribcage. I raced through the tiny kitchen and then up the carpeted stairs.

Time fluctuated to the rhythm of a pendulum, one moment lulled to weary somnolence and the next thick with urgency. Perhaps this was a reflection of my alternating states of panic and disbelief.

Robert Chane was in the bathtub. On the linoleum floor, an empty bottle of bourbon lay on its side beside the blue bathmat and his discarded clothes. A slash of blood, keen as a shriek, covered perhaps a two-foot stretch of the tiles. Robert's head was bowed and shrouded in shadow.

"Dad!"

No answer. I reached in and pulled the drain plug. I grabbed him by his wet shoulders, tugged, and it was then that I discovered that both his wrists were opened. The scent of life's seepage hit me, provoking nausea. I ignored the deep discoloration of the water, the massive blood loss that it implied, and told myself that the only essential thing was to get his arms out now. I maneuvered my forearms under his armpits and heaved him towards the side of the tub.

That provoked the animal instinct in him, the instinct that had been perverted by its long acquaintance with despair. The dream of self-preservation somehow exists even within the longing for death, apparently. Eyes still closed, my father growled and resisted. I was a lot stronger…and it may be that some part of his inner being joined with my efforts, in defiance of his conscious intent. My second expense of strength carried him over the edge and onto the floor.

"Goddamn it, leave me!" This protest escaped him before he'd even had time to figure out who I was. And his drunkenness delayed that moment of recognition even further. It didn't matter: his rebellion, in either case, was an empty gesture. I snatched a towel off the rack and wrapped his forearms together. My first desperate intention was to staunch the bleeding as much as possible, buy myself a few crucial moments in which to try and conceive of some more permanent remedy.

"Leave me, dammit!"

"Shut the hell up!" My words came out in spatters—much like his blood— amidst my efforts to get cloth and pressure on those cuts in spite of his feeble struggles. Then, louder, "Maybe I'm just saving your ass so I can have the pleasure of killing you myself later. You ever think of that?"

Somehow that did shut him up, and I used that reprieve to gather my thoughts in the gaps between heartbeats of terror. Robert quit struggling. I was able to ease him back onto the floor, flatten him out on his back. Feeling reassured, for the moment, that he wouldn't try to undo his wrappings, I stood and raced for the medicine cabinet. I remembered that there'd been peroxide in there, and bandages….

He'd cut himself downwards, not crosswise; the slits were each about three inches long and they stubbornly refused to close. Luckily, drunk as he was, he'd done a sloppy job of it. The initial punctures seemed to be the only places where the razor had dug deep. The blade itself had made it to the bath drain; I could tell by the spluttering sound the remaining water made as it pushed past it.

"There's got to be some place other than this," Robert mumbled. His emotional fever rendered him lucid for a moment. "Do you think so, son? That there's someplace we go when we die, someplace better?"

I had the supplies from the cabinet in my right hand and my left steadied me against the side of the mirror. Despite my urgency, I stopped there and closed my eyes. When had he last called me son? When had he ever? Scouring through the vast bitter fields of my memories, I couldn't isolate a single other moment when I'd ever witnessed him this bare and vulnerable.

I let out a slow breath to borrow time. "I think that we can make a heaven or a hell out of this place," I said. "And if that's true—if we have that power—then we're bound to do the same thing anywhere else we might go to." I looked down at him. He'd wet his cheeks with silent tears. The sight almost stopped me. "I know it's not the most comforting thought," I finished, "but it's all I've got."

It took me a few minutes to get him tightly bandaged. Robert tried to grasp my shoulders. His breath, reeking of liquor, came in ragged bouts. His eyes were wide and carried the gleam of frightened fanaticism, as if he'd just witnessed the angel of mercy transformed into something hideous. His hair was grayer, thinner than it'd been even a year ago. And although he was about the same size, he seemed lighter somehow, less substantial.

"Don't," I cautioned, easing his hands back down. "Let them sit. If you flex those muscles it'll just make the cuts open up again."

"I don't really want to die!"

The whole thrust of his fragile life lay behind that declaration. Perhaps he'd needed to go this far in order to finally understand. His abjection enabled me to be the steady one—more focused and capable than I ever would have imagined myself in such a situation as this.

"Well, you're not going to," I said. "Though you probably would have if I'd gotten here even ten minutes later."

We were both shaking. I lit a cigarette, right there in the bathroom, and turned on the electric vent. I would've caught hell for doing that back when I'd lived here. But to hell with his protests. I'd just saved his life.

The turbulence of Robert's inner state made him pant. He stared down at his crimson bandages. "I don't know how in hell you came to be here just now."

That threw me back upon the incomprehensible riddle of this night. "You'd never believe me if I told you. I hardly even know how to make sense of it."

He was too lost in his own inner ruminations to pay much attention. "God, I want the peace of death." His spirit momentarily flared. "The peace! You hear me?" But just as quickly he sagged. "You should've let me die," he drawled on, in a much smaller voice. "It would've been better if you hadn't showed up. I got nothin'. Nothin'."

I gazed down at my father, this contradictory man who just a moment ago had raged, "I don't want to die!" His white tank top and faded jeans, which lay on the floor a few feet from me, would've looked grubby even without the streaks of blood. In the months following his accident on a construction site years ago—one that had virtually ruined his back—he'd amassed a layer of softer flesh thanks to a lifestyle that largely relegated him to a recliner in front of the TV collecting disability. But this had been mostly flensed away now. He was gaunt, most likely due to malnourishment. Most of his calories these days were probably derived from the booze. But this physical change was trivial when weighed alongside the overall emaciation of his spirit.

"What you have," I said, "is an eight-year-old daughter, almost nine now, who's not only the best reader in her third-grade class, but also the one who everyone wants a playdate with because she invents the most imaginative games you've ever heard of. And although she may not live with you anymore, she does live only about two miles away. And I happen to know for a fact that she loves her daddy."

I took another drag in an attempt to settle the flood of my feelings. Robert kept staring at the ceiling. I can't even fathom where his thoughts may have been.

"You have the respect of the guys who worked on your crew," I went on. "Even if you can't lift stone slabs or tall ladders anymore, still you've got all that know-how in your brain somewhere. Hell, with a few years of schooling, you could turn yourself from a builder of houses to a designer of them."

Then my fork-tongued imp of the depths demanded his say.

"And you've got a son who's the most radical madman poet musician that Sadenport has ever seen—maybe the world, for that matter. And even if he'll never forget how many times you smacked him around—even if he'll never let you get away with shit like that again as long as you live—still he'll run down here in the middle of the night to save your ass when you haven't got any hope left!"

Presently I got back up and extinguished my cigarette in the sink. It was time to settle upon the next step, and my mind was in the dark. I remembered the full depth of my distrust of both the medical and the psychological professions. I realized that I was willing to risk infection, other possible physical complications, and even the chance that my father would suffer complete mental collapse rather than call an ambulance.

I squatted down beside him and strove to make my voice sound as reassuring as possible. "Look, we're just gonna have to deal with this ourselves. This isn't, like, an accident. If you go to the hospital, simple stitches ain't gonna be the end of it. There'll be no way to hide that it was a suicide attempt, and then you're dealing with psych evaluations and being put on crisis watch and all that. Personally, I don't think any of that is gonna do you any good. So I'll stay here while you recuperate. We'll get through this together. And, rest assured, if you go near any sharp objects, I will be kicking your ass thoroughly."

Then I found a patch of floor that was neither wet nor stained, and lowered myself down. My dad and I both sat in silence for a while, he on the towel that I'd first used to staunch his wounds. My logical faculties resumed their steady march. In fact, they seemed to be working double time to make up for their previous lull. A throng of hard facts paraded before me. It was actually a miracle, I admitted to myself, that my old man hadn't succeeded in doing himself in long before now. And ultimately, nothing was really resolved by the simple fact that he still lived.

"Let's go get you dressed," I said, thrusting those larger considerations aside and focusing on the dire stains. "Then I'll get this bathroom cleaned up. It's really not good for either of our heads, to be looking at all this."

I raised my voice and strove to pierce the sickly yellow-gray aura that seemed to hover about him like a cloud. "This is now in the past, alright? Henceforth. Tomorrow is a new day."

Then I helped him rise. Robert was silent, but I felt intention and gratitude in his effort to stand and move. Thus reassured, I was able to let him go so he could dress. He flicked some lights on as he went, dispelling some of the house's brooding menace. I went downstairs to fetch the little sponge mop that he kept leaning against the side of the fridge.

I moved mechanically, with simple and deliberate focus, trying to quiet my thoughts as much as possible. First, I pulled down the showerhead and used it to rinse away the lingering traces of sickly crimson. I got the walls of the tub and the tiles above it, sending more nightmare residue plunging down the drain in the process. I ended up emptying half a can of scented sanitizer spray into the air as if I could thereby not only purge the smell of blood but also the lingering spirit of nihilism that dwelt there.

When I found my father again, he was in the living room, dressed in gray striped pajamas that somewhat resembled prison garb. He looked frail to the point of insubstantiality: a sad, reduced, and expended little creature that I could've perched on my shoulder. But he possessed enough courage to face me—with no subterfuge clouding his gaze.

"Thanks for everything, Brandon," he said. He sounded almost sober.

I acknowledged this with a nod and then opted to give him a dose of tough love. "Yeah, well, I can keep you from killing yourself if I happen to be around. But I can't give you one reason to want to live. That's gotta come from you."

His face was enveloped in still and sullen clouds. After wandering for a while, like an amnesiac searching for eternally lost car keys, he finally settled into the recliner that had, over the years, molded itself to his very being.

"Look," I offered, "why don't you get some sleep now. I'm tired too. I don't have to work until Monday, so…" I nodded towards the recliner. "Maybe I could sleep there?"

I realized, in that moment, that this was where I most longed to be in all the world: in his chair. As he got up and started stumbling towards his room, I spoke to his back. "We can talk more about everything in the morning. I know someone who may be able to help you."

OUR SELF-CREATED WORLDS

It'd been a couple of months since I'd last met with Saul. Of course, we'd interact briefly here and there when Edge was rehearsing and he happened to be around. But I'd taken a hiatus from actual therapy sessions. Returning from our seven-week tour the previous summer, I'd felt capable for the first time in my life, really; like my existence was actually something that I could navigate alone. I trusted myself enough to skirt its edges without fear and without blaming the world, in fitful bursts of rage, when I suffered for my own missteps.

But now everything seemed to be spinning out of control again.

Hearing my desperation over the phone—he knew that it had to be pretty severe if it showed through the tough exterior I tried to project—Saul penciled me in for his earliest opening. By now, he had a clientele of some forty people who saw him regularly, either weekly or biweekly. Many of them were men and women who he'd first gotten acquainted with during his tenure as a crisis responder answering the phone for a suicide hotline. Survivors of life scenarios like that needed more than just a reason not to die. They needed renewed purpose, hope, and a sense of direction that held personal significance. Life must be valued, not merely endured. A life devoid of meaning is unlivable. It doesn't matter how much hard-headed stamina and willpower is brought to bear.

So this is what Saul aimed to do, in the long run: connect people with their inner sense of "soul purpose," so that their problems would have meaning for them, first of all, and so that they could then understand how they had created those challenges in the first place. The power of each individual was always stressed—in a way that, insofar as I could see, rarely was anywhere else in our cultural environment.

He'd once made an effort to summarize, for me, his particular philosophy and approach. "I think that it can and should be liberating to know that we're already carrying, inside of us, everything we need for our life's journey. This is ultimately what any kind of expanded consciousness teaches us, because every reality we can perceive, in whatever state we're in, has its source within us. But, as you know, the world can be such a convincing illusion! Without even noticing that we're doing it, we can still slip into thinking that we're at its mercy.

"Many people look to the unconscious, to dreams and surrealism, and talk about symbols. My thinking turns that formula inside out. To me, the objects and motions of the physical world are the symbols; symbols meant to illustrate what's going on at the inner level. If we're really the creators of our own experience, then physical objects have a nonphysical source, and that source lies within.

"This world is thoroughly real to us—while we're in it. But also try to remain aware that it is only a story that your senses tell you: a work of accepted fiction, so dazzling that it's easy for any of us to mistake it for the whole truth. Remember that it's only one station on the radio band. And we're all tuned in to it at the moment, or else I couldn't speak these words and you couldn't hear them. But it's liberating, at the same time, to know that we can tune in to many others.

"And so what happens when we embark upon this journey of self-discovery?" And this was the part I particularly liked, because it was almost an echo of our band's name and concept. "Well, we discover that we are part of the unknown, and also part of the process through which it becomes known. Most importantly, we discover that the unconscious activity that upholds and replenishes the Universe is in no way separate from us. Because we are the creators of our reality, the invisible forces of life await our conscious direction. That's our divine gift, to draw upon this inexhaustible source and use it to paint the picture of our lives in every detail. We exist at the mercy of nothing, save for ourselves."

❖

I'd often carried belligerence with me into Saul's office, but not this night. For one thing, I missed him. And I regretted all the times in the past when I'd sought his help and then fought with him through every step of the therapeutic process. Besides, I'd exhausted all of my own resources. I felt ready to receive anything that he might say. Any way forward had to be preferable to staying where I was.

Saul looked withdrawn; subdued, even. His mustache and thick eyebrows could lend his visage a dour puppy dog aspect at times, but one would be a fool to assume that his sensitivity made him soft. His underlying grit and tenacity was even more formidable than what was suggested by his lean, steely physique and sleek, pantherish stride. Saul was a primal hunter beneath that therapist suit.

He greeted me with a smile, saying at once, "How 'bout we walk, do our session outside tonight?"

I was amenable, as I hoped that moving around might help my jumbled thoughts to disentangle themselves. We started moving in an oblong circuit around Saul's land. This encompassed probably six or seven acres, and touched upon the barn (with Catacombs beneath), an outhouse, and a small pond amidst various piles of rusty engine innards that had been left behind by the previous owner. I began thinking about the astonishing extent to which my whole spiritual life revolved around this yard.

Saul lit his pipe. "So, I want to begin by just acknowledging that I know about what happened with you and Janie. Now, I promise you that things will always be confidential between us, and the same thing applies to her. But I need to tell you that she's been in to see me a couple of times. That's how I got the story."

This revelation made me burn beneath my skin, so fiercely that I couldn't identify the underlying cause. Was I jealous of Saul, he having access to the woman I loved in a way that was lost to me? Was it the thought of her confiding in him, when I had so long been her most trusted confidante? Or was I just not ready to even think of her, to remember, to long for her and ache....

"How'd that happen?" I managed.

"She'd heard about me from you," Saul said, "and so when she found herself in difficulty, I was the one she thought to call. You and she share similar leanings…. She knows, on some level, that her life is her own creation. And she realizes that the average therapist is not going to work with her from that place of understanding."

I sassed him. "So much for confidentiality!"

"I got her permission to say as much as I have," Saul said, affecting a smug smile.

Then he drew a pensive puff off his pipe. Gazing over his pond towards the darkening east, he continued. "Most people look for an outside reference point against which they believe they have to measure themselves. A behaviorist might try to adapt you to the social norm—whatever his or her idea of that is. A more, quote, 'spiritual person' may think that the object is to surrender to God or some similar conception of an all knowing being. It's rare that you'll find anyone who'll tell you that your life is yours, and that you have made it what it is.

"And so that brings us back to you and your predicament." He was facing me now. "You're suffering. You've lost the woman you love—probably the first woman you ever loved. How do you think that happened?"

"I told Janie about the time that I lost control with that guy outside of the Samurai warehouse, that I nearly killed him!" I snapped. "She freaked out and ran!"

"But let's bring it back to yourself," Saul insisted. "I do think that the incident you mentioned is a good place to start, though. What comes into your mind when you think about it?"

"I try not to—ever," I said.

Saul snapped his fingers. "Exactly! You try to bury that part of your experience because you're listening to the voice of guilt."

He gave me a moment to settle, then went on. "Our natural sense of remorse does carry a certain beneficial, teaching quality. Tell me: have you ever acted out that violently, or to that extent, since you had that experience?"

I traced my way along the intervening couple of years in my mind. "Uh...no. I had that fight with my father where I ended up smashing a window. And then the Pumpkin Festival—but I let that guy win, basically, 'cause I just didn't want to kick his ass badly enough."

"That's what I'm talking about," Saul said. "Our natural sense of regret just says, 'That felt horrible. Let's not ever do that again.' And you haven't, see? But I think that there's this other way in which your mind has played upon that memory. It's done some slow, poisonous work. You probably already carried an exaggerated sense of guilt to begin with. But once you nearly lost control, that guilt had a focus, some sort of apparent justification."

His eyes narrowed, bore into my insides. I hadn't expected us to plunge so deep so quick. I'd forgotten, during my time away, all about Saul's tendency to go for the jugular. He was as unmerciful in those moments as the fearsome killer in our dreams who really comes to free us from our mental prison.

"I'm willing to bet that, ever since that day, you've viewed your whole life in terms of 'what is wrong with me?'" he said. "Do you see that? So then it's no longer about an event, but rather seems to touch upon the essence of who you are. 'What kind of a monster must I be, to do that?'

"You didn't want the woman you loved to get close to that monster, did you? I'm guessing that, in a thousand little ways—and probably without even realizing it—you gave her the signal to keep her distance. Sooner or later, she was going to find out just how 'unstable' or 'dangerous' you were, right? And then it would all be over anyway."

It was so often this way, that Saul's pronouncements would sweep the ground out from under me. His insights undermined the very ideas and beliefs that I'd built the foundation of my life upon. Every revelation was a tremor; an earthquake, even. Saul also had the tendency to speak as if my inner conflicts were audible to him.

"Understanding and acknowledging the self-made trap is just the first step, remember. Remind yourself, at every bend in the road, that you painted the picture of your life this way. With that same power, you can paint a new picture—consciously choose a different course.

"See your guilt for what it is: an emotion grown up around your misunderstanding of life and of your own human nature. Ask yourself what kind of Creator would plant us here, beginning our journey in a state of utterly dependent infancy—'cause that's what we believe, right?—and expect that we'd go through our earthly experience with no missteps. And don't split hairs about how 'bad' your deed was compared to someone else's. The man lived. You live. Life and learning continue—and you've learned not to go down that particular road anymore."

The Abyss was howling beneath me now. "Yeah," I rasped, "but she's still gone, Saul!"

"I can't play the referee between the two of you," he said. "I can only tell you that if you created this painful circumstance with a false sense of guilt, then confronting that guilt and releasing it will give you a new lease on life."

I knew that I couldn't pursue this line of discussion any further.

"OK, I got you. But look, I need to talk about something else right now.... I've been trying to convince my father to come and see you."

"I'm surprised he even heard you out," Saul remarked.

"Well, he's pretty broken. In a way that makes me scared for him. But in another way, he's more approachable now, because his belligerence is just sapped."

"He's hit rock bottom," Saul ventured.

"He tried to kill himself. Cut his wrists. I happened to be there in time to stop it. A dream prompted me, actually."

I stopped. Suddenly I missed gazing at the still water of his pond; I realized how much I'd been relying on it to settle me. "What do you make of that, anyway?"

Saul looked thoughtful for a moment. Then he shrugged. "I've tried explaining this before, that it's our senses that weave the story, telling us that there's a world outside of ourselves that's concrete and real." He cast me a compassionate look, perhaps to acknowledge how difficult such a concept was to accept, for any of us. "Matter isn't nearly as solid as we've imagined. And so what keeps us so perfectly poised in our own time and space, amidst this maelstrom of swirling energy? Well, it's my thinking that we're able to achieve this miracle because all of life is aware of every other part. So, we create our world together by managing to arrive at some sort of agreement. Now, if you consider the depth of perception and intelligence that this implies…well, your ability to be aware of your father in his moment of need, miraculous as it is, is yet a small thing when weighed alongside the true capacities of the inner self."

Then his eyes forsook their clear focus and drifted off to somewhere outside of—or beyond—the immediate and tangible world. I stood and waited.

"It's very ironic, what gets labelled 'self-destructive,' 'insane,' or 'delusional' in our society. Now, the technical definition of 'delusional' is the inability to discriminate between reality and illusion. To me, that describes our culture at large. Popular belief puts forth some of the biggest fallacies concerning human nature that have ever been uttered.

"The science teachers I had in grade school insisted that life was an accidental byproduct of atoms colliding. They said that every thought and emotion of ours was produced by chemical and electrical reactions taking place within our brains. Why weren't they labeled delusional?

"We would do well to consider how expansive and life-affirming our beliefs are, and re-train our minds to be less concerned with 'facts'—which, as the saying goes, are often just accepted fictions."

Then, as if this was just the obvious extension of everything else he'd said thus far, Saul added, "You realize that any work I do with your father will only be effective if he comes to me of his own accord, right? You can't coerce him in any way."

"No, I know that," I said. "I think he will. Something has shifted inside of him; I'm sure of it. That night changed him."

As the light cooled and dimmed, Saul and I talked more about my father's despair and my own ambiguous feelings about helping him. Without a doubt, my aggressive stance before the world owed a lot to all the beatings I'd received at home over the years. It would have been easy to blame Robert Chane for everything, even the loss of Janie.

"And so then you back yourself once more into a corner, where it seems like you have no power," Saul reminded me. "I would urge you to open your mind up to the possibility that you may have chosen your home environment—with all of its circumstances—for your own inner purposes."

It certainly had set me upon the path to the Muse, but that was a small consolation at the moment. I'd known the touch of love, at long last, and then had watched it slip beyond reach. And if guilt and self-doubt had wrought that cruel circumstance, then they weren't going to relinquish their grip so easily. After all, perceiving the fallacy and destructiveness of a belief was not the same as disbelief.

"There's something that I want you to remember," Saul said. "Our inner being says 'Yes!'—always. It says yes because it knows. That's what our spiritual work amounts to, basically: we're playing catch-up with that part of us that already knows. There are deeper parts of you that don't believe, for a moment, in any concepts of sinful humanity or guilt. When you refuse to apologize for who you are, you've got your soul and every living cell in your body right there to back you up."

"I'll probably want to meet with you again regularly for a while," I said after a pause. "Maybe every couple of weeks. I'm in the midst of a rough patch, obviously."

My own inner conflicts had consumed my attention throughout the session. Obliquely, though, I had noticed changes in Saul. He'd been unusually taciturn; sad. In fact, he'd carried himself with the unmistakable suggestion of defeat in his gait. Why?

THE GIFT

I spent the next week or so job hunting in my spare time. I was in such a fragile and vulnerable state that it had become really hard to tolerate any kind of employment that involved social interaction. I searched for manual labor, warehouse positions...repetitive and mindless exertions were about all that I felt capable of. I could contain the tremors of my soul throughout the length of a graveyard shift and then pour them out in the music. It seemed a seaworthy plan. Somehow, in the space between those opposing existential extremes, I would endure.

I arrived for rehearsals one night, feeling frazzled by the frenzied, distracted energies that so consume civilization. I was aching to play, to reconnect with that deeper part of myself that I so often had to smother in order to function. But Tommy and Carlos met my arrival with half-suppressed grins. Obviously, they harbored a mutual secret.

Then Tommy waved a bundled paper. I noticed that it was Visionary Chapbook—probably the latest issue, too, because I didn't recognize the cover. "Pat was true to his word," he said. "Obviously he forgave us for the aborted interview, judging from this review that he gave What Casts the Shadow?"

He opened the paper, and Carlos eagerly peered over his shoulder. As Tommy was six foot five, this required our buoyant drummer to stand on his tiptoes.

Tommy, having landed upon the page he sought, cleared his throat dramatically. Then he began his recitation with mock solemnity. "As their name implies, Edge of the Known embody not just a new style of music, not just a different—and particularly relentless—approach to performing it, but also an

223

emerging kind of new consciousness. We all know that the accustomed behaviors of our race have proven shortsighted and destructive. That's not news to anyone. For many of us, though, this realization has inspired little more than jaded cynicism and a sort of smug ennui.

"But it's crucial that we remember that it is the thinking behind our old ways that has truly failed us. And the songs on this album—every damn one of them— insist that the answers are there, inside of us, waiting to be unearthed. You'll find no cowardly copout cynicism here. Our challenges, whether they are personal or worldly, are self-chosen. And hope, belief, heroism, and courage are not mere fanciful notions but rather concrete realities to the mind that has awakened to them—to the soul that has confronted its own darkness and prevailed.

"In conclusion, I have recently discovered that reality is much easier to face when I play this album—preferably very loudly—before I step out of my front door to do battle with the day."

The timbre of Tommy's voice eloquently relayed the underlying respect in Pat's words. I was the newcomer, the one who was hearing this all for the first time, so the other guys were watching for my reaction. At first, I was too choked up to speak.

"That was about the middle third of it," Tommy explained. "He gives a bit of our history in the beginning and then offers a brief song-by-song analysis at the end. 'Sea Breakers' is obviously his favorite, but he seemed to love them all."

"He really got it," I managed at last.

Carlos nodded. "It's amazing, isn't it, bro, when you set out to communicate something and then that's exactly what another person hears? It don't happen often, huh?"

"No, it doesn't." I replied absently. I was lost in calculations. "And Visionary Chapbook has a good-sized circulation, too, for indie press."

"About twenty thousand, is what they say," Tommy said. "And that's where this gets even better, 'cause Chas used this review—along with our record—to convince the owner of Brasserie D'Alchimie to take a chance on us. We're gonna be the house band over there—three nights a week!"

This meant that, within three weeks' time, we'd deliver more performances in Sadenport than we had in the entirety of our career thus far. Most of our gigs had been abroad. This was startling news. It offered the kind of exposure that we'd thus far only dreamed of. And yet I found myself saying, "I wish I felt readier for this."

To which a voice inside me responded: *something's still tying you to a dead world, man.*

"I'm not saying I can't do it. But I'm gonna just come clean about this. A part of me—a big part—doesn't want to come out of my shell right now. I don't want to express, and I don't want to connect."

"So, fuck everything," Tommy said. But he actually wasn't antagonizing me. His voice was as clinical as the intern at Limn County Mental Health who'd once set all my interview responses down on a clipboard. Tommy was just making sure he had the facts straight.

"Heartbreak is not a laughing matter—I know," Carlos put in. "It will take some time."

Thinking just, *to fucking hell with vulnerability and feelings!* I decided to abort the whole discussion. "Well, let's jam," I said. "I'll start us off with the new one."

"Diamond Maelstrom" was the easiest song for me to play because I'd written it in the same state of escalation that I existed in during most of my waking hours these days. I therefore didn't need to make any kind of effort to "get into character" for it. And if I ever forgot what was great about our band, this song could remind me within six minutes. Tommy and Carlos, joined with me by the telepathic bond that we all understood though we could never explain it, responded in kind. I'm surprised the very salt-gray walls of the Catacombs didn't start to heat and steam.

Afterwards, Tommy declared, "I got it!" He stopped right there, swaying before his mic and milking the dramatic pause.

"Well?" I prodded, feeling half amused and half irritated.

"We'll perform at Brasserie D'Alchimie with a light show," he said. "Like those liquid light, slide projector affairs that the psychedelic bands used in the late sixties, particularly in London and San Francisco. We'll have to find someone to run it for us during the gigs, but it'll be perfect. You'll just be this shadowy figure, Brandon, blended right into the psychedelic display. We'll make it darkened. Then you won't feel exposed at all. You can be in your own imaginary world up there."

Well, we had a somewhat psychedelic sounding name anyway—and sonic template to match—so the notion of some accompanying visual phantasmagoria wasn't too far-fetched. "It's a pretty played-out concept, though, isn't it?" I asked.

"Well, so is video," Tommy argued, "and that doesn't stop all these new bands from making 'em. It's not the medium, but the way that we use it that decides whether it comes across as clichéd or not."

That's all that it took to convince me. I strongly ached for anonymity, for the opportunity to merge with the shadows. Once we wrapped up rehearsals, the three of us returned home and hung out in the living room, munching on cold pizza and sipping lemonade while we bounced around ideas.

Oftentimes, the challenge inherent in creating something is due not to the limits imposed upon one's freedom, but rather the overabundance of possible avenues to explore. We were brimming with too many thoughts, and not one of them seemed to possess any inherently greater merit than the others. At least the excitement of brainstorming allowed me to forget my own pain for a while, though.

At last, we settled upon the idea of using a succession of images that would illustrate the progression of human life from infancy to old age. The entire cycle, we figured, should last about as long as our average song—about five or six minutes. We also wanted to somehow convey the sense that this whole cycle represented, on another level, a mere day in the life of the soul.

Chas ended up hiring his dour, humorless cousin Ken—the same tall and lanky guy who'd spray-painted our van with Manhandle designs—to create the actual slides, based upon our sketches. The liquid slides would run over the static images to add a hallucinatory dimension. The majority of the drawings were done by me, as I was actually the most competent of the three of us.

I produced about thirty sketches, and Tommy and Carlos made roughly another twenty between them. Then we experimented with different running orders for the images. For a couple days, we existed in a sort of microcosm of the film industry, playing at pre-production, production, and direction. We found a cheap projector at a thrift store and put Ken's show to the test one night, shining the images on the living room wall and taking turns either engaging in shadow play or dancing in front of it.

I sorely missed Janie that night. She had always been a part of creative ventures such as these, ever since conducting our first photo session. She'd been there for the gestation of such ideas and also for the celebrations that would inevitably follow those bouts of hard work. She loved photography, and would have relished this particular project. Every time I saw our three silhouettes on the cover of our first album—the same image that graced our flyers—I was reminded.

I excused myself early and laid down in the dark, counting my uneven breaths. I told myself that somehow the flow of life continues, sweeping up new joys in its wake. I could scarcely keep from putting my fists through the wall.

From the outside, Brasserie D'Alchimie looked like a giant circus tent made of wood instead of tarp. Its coat of ochre paint was old, and varied with a greener hue around the upper story, which the owners—a middle-aged hippie couple who'd lived in their van for several years before opening the establishment—had taken for their apartment. It had its back to the Matterpike River—one of Sadenport's widest bridges was a block away—and faced the runner's track that belonged to the technical college across the way. I suppose this kept the neighboring apartments at sufficient distance so that no one complained about the noise.

Inside, it smelled like an organic grocery store, the scent of chai most predominant, and there were tapestries all over the place depicting the full sweep of religious iconography. You'd see Buddha, Krishna, or Christ any which way you turned your head.

Our friend Todd Jacobs joined us that first night. He'd agreed to run our slide show. Todd was two years my junior and one of the few congenial souls I'd encountered back in high school. He was that rarity amongst rabid music fans: a free-spirited punk who carried himself with easygoing humility. He had no underlying chip on his shoulder.

Tracy, one of the owners, was bartending that night. She'd been amenable to keeping the back row of lights off for our benefit. We got our gear set up and plugged in. Tommy solemnly intoned, "America must learn to dream new dreams!" in a half-dozen different inflections into both mics, as Todd adjusted the levels. Then, as soon as he got the projector started, we began.

Some are given to relating it to sex, or to certain kinds of drug-induced euphoria, but you really can't compare the indefinable sensation of reaching people with your music to anything else. When it's good, it's the fruition of that pollinating push of spring wonder that already lived, somewhere in the depths of your soul, when first you wrote the song. You already have this idea that somehow, some way, others are going to participate in this phenomenon with you. What you're really creating is the incipient part of a communal experience—an electric bath of rousing, soothing, affirming, and ultimately healing intent. Both you and the audience know when such an exchange happens, and there's no need to try and talk about it.

God, I'd missed performing.

I felt the chords rattling the tables and the wood of the walls and knew that, for these few hours at least, no one would miss the voice from the mountain. And all the while, I felt almost amphibious, bathed as I was in the oceanic flow of light and surreal imagery curling over my body and over all of our instruments. I was safe and secure somewhere in nameless dark depths.

At some point during the gig, I noticed that members of the local band Cryptykulu were seated a couple of tables away from us, off to our left. They were an intimidating bunch, even for someone with the "live by the sword, die by the sword" philosophy that I'd long adhered to. This was partially due to their appearance: rigor mortis pallor; tall, jagged beanpole frames; acres of leather embellished with pointed steel. Then there was the aura that surrounded them. Underground musical folklore of this city abounded with whispered rumors of what intended members had to do in order to be initiated into the "circle" of Cryptykulu. I'd never seen them perform; I only recognized them from a photo that I'd seen in Chapbook. But those in the know all agreed that the extremity of their lyrics, and their overarching creed, was in no way an act. I wasn't sure exactly what that meant, and the mystery somehow made the concept more chilling.

As we finished up for the night and began gathering up our equipment, I watched the members file out. Their singer and bandleader, a gaunt albino as tall as Tommy who went by the name of Saveel, met my gaze. He bowed low, with an air of complete and solemn reverence, and then strode out.

Feeling unnerved by this silent exchange, for reasons that I couldn't identify, I packed hurriedly.

When we returned a couple nights later, Saveel was there again with another member of his band. They sat hunched over one of the tables closest to the stage, talking low and staring at us intently. Their scrutiny made me uncomfortable, and I masked it with irritation verging on anger. Was Saveel looking to recruit one of us into his own band? If so, he was going about it in an obnoxiously blatant way.

But it was my job to create, alongside the two musicians with me, the atmosphere in the club this night—not to let it be dictated by anyone who might walk through the door. I closed my mind off from Saveel—and whatever other lingering earthly concerns I possessed—with the fury of Edge of the Known's music.

There were probably about thirty people there who had returned to see us following our debut performance. This was tremendous affirmation of the path that we were on. The average Sadenport band gigged once a week or less, simply because they didn't have the drawing power to support more frequent appearances. We were becoming local heroes.

I lived very close to this music and so perhaps couldn't view it with the objectivity of an outsider. But it was obvious even to me that our melodic mayhem was as powerful as anything currently pulsing in the Underground, and superior to just about anything one could hear on corporate-owned radio. If every age must have its Prometheus, lest the flame of humanity's collective spirit be snuffed out forever, then our band fulfilled the dictates of that myth more fully than anyone else currently performing.

So maybe Saveel's here 'cause he's pissed. My lips curled into a smile of relish, midway into a song, as this thought streaked through my transcendent flight.

The floor was covered with whirling, cavorting bodies, each lost in personal transport and yet still connected to the ubiquitous Gyre of Pan that spun us all on the ecstatic wheel. Sometimes when I was onstage, I'd feel as though I was presiding over a very ancient ceremony, a rite that's recognized by the breath and the blood, the earth below and the sky overhead, though the mind may never grasp its source.

Saveel's companion approached us as soon as we finished our last number and the back lights were turned back on. He looked young—no older than seventeen, I would have guessed—and scarred. That word leapt into my mind at once. I swallowed hard when he smiled at me. He was wearing a jean jacket (plain, devoid of patches), ripped jeans, and some kind of thick-woven tan sandals.

"I am Ashur," he said. And of course, I immediately thought that this could not be his birth name. His tone was eerily formal, and partially a whisper. "Of Cryptykulu. We've brought a gift with which to honor your great band."

At once, my eyes fell on the long gray knapsack that had laid between them on the table.

"We cannot offer it here," he went on as he followed my gaze. "Will you meet with us?"

By this time, Carlos and Tommy had both joined me. But though they watched Ashur intently, his attention remained fixed on me.

"You choose the place," he pronounced.

"Saint Christopher's Bridge," I responded at once.

My mind had been racing through frantic calculations. It seemed potentially dangerous to refuse an offer made by these people. At the same time, I didn't trust the entire scenario, and I knew that it would be futile, trying to pry more information out of Saveel's acolyte. The bridge was close to home; and it was familiar. It was also out in the open, more exposed than most of the streets.

"We will follow you," he said, with the same walk-of-the-dead inflection. Then he bowed low to the three of us, just as Saveel had done the previous night.

As soon as Carlos, Tommy, and I were in the van, I aired my underlying unease. "The thing I don't get is, why they're so interested in us in the first place. This is bizarre. I mean, they were right there at the first gig we played, as if they were waiting for us."

Tommy was driving. He shrugged. "It could be the record—What Casts the Shadow? It seems to have been making its way around the city, both tape trading and via the Internet."

"None of which is helping to feed us," I muttered.

"I hear that!" Carlos concurred from the back.

"Well," Tommy offered, "it does seem to be spreading the word about our band, anyway."

By now it was well past midnight. The streets saw few vehicles and the homes were predominantly dark. Tommy took a winding shortcut to the bridge.

"And these guys are, like…I don't know if they're a satanic band, necessarily, but they're definitely occult through and through," I said. "What the hell's their interest in us?"

"When you write songs that are deliberately oblique, metaphorical…" Tommy let that thought dissipate. "You and I are both guilty of that," he told me. "Not that it's something negative. I personally think that the best songs are the ones you can never plumb the depths of. But it does leave it open for people to interpret it however they want, and to draw their own conclusions—even twisted ones."

There was a grassy pull-off not far from the south side of the bridge where people often parked so that they could take the little footpath down to the water.

Tommy stopped there. "I said meet at the bridge, so that's where we'll be," I grated. "If they choose to be insulted because we didn't greet them at the parking space, then they can explain why they're in such a goddamn hurry, riding our asses like that all the way over here."

The two members of Cryptykulu had pulled up in a bus that could've been twenty years old. But it sported a much more recent paint job—as much as I could descry it in the dark—composed of spidery and serpentine etchings in black that covered the entire metal surface in sinuous darkness. It seemed intended to ensnare the eyes, though, so I didn't stare for long.

We moved swiftly and kept our eyes fixed forward. No one spoke. I wasn't frightened for our safety. There were three of us and two of them, and we were all well worth our salt in a tussle. Before leaving the van, I'd also retrieved my hunting knife, with its four-inch sharpened blade, from the glove compartment and tucked it into my boot. Hey, we'd spent weeks sleeping in that vehicle; you can't begrudge me a few precautionary measures. So, unless those guys were packing handguns...

I didn't stop until we'd reached what I judged to be roughly the halfway point of the bridge. A subtle power play was being enacted here, and I didn't want to begin the proceedings with any show of compromise. I deliberately turned at that point to watch the two of them approach.

Sure enough, Ashur was hauling the knapsack. Saveel strode a few paces in front of him. He stopped about ten feet away from us. Once more, he bowed. Somehow his solemnity conveyed more incipient menace than any overt show of aggression would have.

"Cryptykulu greet you, great minstrels!" His lilt was surprisingly high-pitched. I'd been expecting a harsh growl. He waited until Ashur caught up with him before continuing. "Have you all heard the legend of Damien Pratt, who was a resident of these parts until his death some fifty years ago?"

I shook my head; and I sensed, rather than saw, Carlos doing the same. Tommy muttered, noncommittally, "The name sounds familiar...."

Saveel looked pleased to have the opportunity to enlighten us. "He was a great sorcerer of his time. His long—some would say, unnaturally long—lifespan attests to it. His forays into deeper mysteries of the Craft were as exhaustive as Crowley's, Levi's…."

Then he nodded in Ashur's direction. Saveel's acolyte dutifully unzipped the pack he was holding and began rummaging through it.

"It is believed," Saveel went on, "that he even mastered the transubstantiation of the flesh, allowing him to assume other forms—wolf, crow, bat." Ashur withdrew a head of sullied ivory, a bit larger than a softball, and proffered it in our direction. Tommy stiffened and retreated a step.

"Looks like a human enough skull to me!"

I absorbed the stark fact of it as soon as he uttered the words. This was no carving. All the signs of organic nature, of something that had once served as a vessel for life, were writ upon it in a script that my deeper senses could somehow decipher at a glance.

"You dug that up?"

In a matter of heartbeats, I stooped and snatched my hunting knife. I bared the blade to their sight. "Stay. The fuck. Away from us." I held it with both hands— its wooden pommel was long—about a foot in front of my chest. If Saveel wanted to be ceremonial…well, I could play. "Don't come to our performances! Don't tell other people that we're affiliated with you, or that somehow we've been an influence. Nothing! This is your travesty. We've got no part in it!"

Saveel's eyes smoldered. I'd caught a glimpse of them in the club, earlier, beneath much stronger light. Glacial blue, man—iciest eyes you'd ever see. He let out a slow breath of disappointment but didn't move. "I had hoped to honor the potency and dark majesty of your music," he pronounced, "and to recognize our brotherhood. Alas!"

He nodded towards Ashur and the skull that he held. Ashur, intuiting the gesture, shuddered. "Are you certain?" he asked.

Saveel frowned. "The gift was offered and spurned. It has no value to anyone, now."

Ashur deliberated a moment longer. Then he hurled the grim ivory relic so that it arced over the twelve-foot-high railing and sped down to the deep, tranquil waters of the Matterpike below.

"That was really Damien Pratt's skull, huh?" Tommy mused. "I have to admit, I'm impressed."

"It seems I misjudged you all!" Saveel spat. Then he turned on his heels and strode away, Ashur following after like a dependent cur.

The silence that followed, nearly devoid of breeze or thought, was finally broken when Carlos quipped, "Damn, bro...I'd just been thinking 'bout how we had a perfect space for that up on the mantel!"

We all burst into laughter, abetted no doubt by our need to relieve tension. I didn't lower my knife, though, until Ashur and Saveel were a good fifty yards away from us. Those two never looked back.

"We've gotta do something to ensure that shit like this doesn't happen again, that people don't take our words and just go off the deep end with them."

Tommy had been peering over the side of the bridge at the spot where the skull had finally made its splash, as if he was debating whether some means might be contrived to fish it out again. "What's that?" he muttered, distractedly, as he turned around. "We can't, Brandon. That's the thing. Once we create it and put it out into the world, then the world can react towards it however it will. That part is forever out of our hands."

And I had to content myself with that, because, despite the molten heat of my frustration, I knew that it was nothing but the bare truth. I was so unnerved that I ended up calling Saul and requesting an "emergency" session.

I met with him the following day, in the early evening. The air was misty and the ground damp from the rainy first half of the day, but the parting rays of the sun reached over and dispersed the clouds as I made my way over to his house. It seemed like the only thought that sustained me through my days was that of landing on my session with Saul.

When we greeted each other, I again received the impression that he was making an effort to smile at me through a haze of pain. And once more, I assumed that it wasn't my place to intrude and inquire about it. Instead, I offered him an abridged version of our encounter with the members of Cryptykulu.

"Wow. Those guys are pretty fanatical, huh?" Saul mused. "You could go to jail for a long time for digging up a body."

"I guess we'll have to come up with a new descriptive angle for our band," I joked. "It seems that 'extreme' is already spoken for."

Saul chuckled, but also took advantage of the opening. "If you could just steer clear of labels altogether—at least, as much as possible—then it could really limit this sort of thing. Once you symbolize something specific in people's minds, then the things they project upon you become a lot harder to shake."

I lit a cigarette, craving not only the tobacco but also the added moment to gather my thoughts and courage. "Yeah," I said, exhaling my first drag, "that's what I was wanting to talk to you about. Why are we attracting these sorts of reactions? It's not the kind of attention I was looking for. And it goes against the grain of everything that we're saying in our songs, too."

Saul was quiet for a long time. And this is part of the reason I'm given to describing him like a shaman or medicine man: He gets this faraway look, as if he's engaged in silent conversation with forces or entities that the rest of us can't see. Then his eyes return to the familiar world, and there's a light of recognition that seems to emanate from him.

"What it boils down to is a basic misunderstanding of the very nature of creativity itself," he said finally. "So many people carry the belief that the deeper forces of life are locked away somewhere; that they're inaccessible. So then it seems necessary, following from that belief, to have all these elaborate rituals and procedures to help us access the psychic places that we think we're so separate from. And it doesn't matter if we're talking on the small scale—this band that you encountered being one example—or on the larger scale of major religions and whatnot. All of it is acting out of the deep conviction that we're just these little disconnected egos that have to go to drastic measures to feel like a part of Creation. And of course, religions will explain to us why we're supposedly so separate to begin with—Original Sin and all that."

Then he smiled at me. "I'm willing to bet that if you were to scratch the surface with the guys in that band, then you'd find some scared young men who really worry about their own significance in the scheme of things."

I shivered, recalling how Ashur's aura had screamed to me like a raw wound. Saveel, on the other hand, certainly hadn't seemed like a man who possessed any fear whatsoever.

"But of course," Saul said with a gleam in his eye, "we don't want to get too caught up in the general state of the world, because you and I know that the real work is done inside. And so this leaves us with two possible avenues to explore, insofar as your personal work goes. First, we can talk about how this sort of 'I am a tainted stepchild of the universe' idea may be working within you. And then from there, we might better understand why you attract these kinds of shady characters into your life. In other words, how do they mirror you?"

I didn't particularly relish the thought of pursuing either of these avenues. "Damn, Saul, I'm in enough goddamn pain as it is! Do we really have to dive into more 'brutal truths' today? How 'bout we get one place bandaged up before we start worrying about other injuries?"

Saul waited for me to simmer down before he spoke. "So you know why the idea of self-exploration feels threatening? Because you don't see the value of it. Because you still don't believe that your life is mirroring your own inner condition. So examining your own thoughts and feelings seems beside the point. But it is, in fact, the whole point.

"Alright—so maybe you don't want to look at your possible connection with these cult members because you still don't understand why your girlfriend left you. But what if I could show you that there's a clear relationship between those two circumstances?"

I straightened but didn't say anything.

"The woman you love turns away from you," Saul iterated, "and then some strangers give you the kind of attention that you don't want, based on some perception of you that isn't true. Do you see? Neither side affirms you, which leads me to believe that there's some way in which you don't affirm yourself."

236

I shook my head, feeling my morale—what little had been left to me—plummet. "So I don't feel worthy. And I guess that's where it fucking ends, Saul."

"Where it ends is where you uncover the reasons why you're so convinced of your basic unworthiness," Saul retorted. "And then, when you see through those beliefs, when you see that they're erroneous, you discard them and find yourself living in a different world. But right now, for you, it's all coming back to guilt again."

Having no clue where he was heading with this, I just stared back. Saul seemed to be waiting for comprehension to crystallize within me. Then he sighed. "This was a band that's heavily influenced by black magic—the aura and imagery surrounding it, at least," he said. "Now, you've done your own experimenting with the occult arts, right?"

"That was a while back," I protested. "And for a very brief period of time. I don't see—"

"People only ever pursue those kinds of avenues when they're convinced that they have no real power to begin with," Saul interjected. "So here's my pitch: I would suggest that you disown your power because the voice of guilt has convinced you that, if you had power, you'd misuse it. And that same denial of self is what makes you hold love at bay. There's the connection."

"Well, I didn't hold love at bay this time," I muttered, a bit petulantly. "Janie ran."

Saul stared at me somberly. "Do we really need to rehash this argument?"

I waved a hand. "No. I hear you. Somehow I initiated the whole thing, even if I wasn't conscious of doing so."

"Somehow? I've told you exactly how. The voice of guilt, Brandon. Examine it. Learn to recognize the distorted picture that it paints. 'Don't give me power over my own life 'cause I'll abuse it.' 'Don't bring a lover into my life 'cause I'll endanger her. I can't be trusted.'"

I tore my gaze away from Saul. I felt myself immersed in a battle that I had no chance of winning. "If we dispensed with guilt, Saul," I argued, "then what would be left to keep us in line?"

"You see? You see how willing you are to accept the idea that human nature can't be trusted?"

I glared at him. "Maybe it was guilt that restrained me that night at the Samurai. Maybe that's what held me back, kept me from assaulting Saveel."

"Maybe it was your heart."

That was no easier to hear. "My heart is chock-full of pain. I'd almost rather have the guilt."

"Sure," Saul said, "until you actually step back and take a look at what it's done to your life. Natural regret just says, 'don't ever do this again.' It's a preventative measure. Guilt says we should be punished again and again for the rest of our lives for ever having done it. I want you to do something for me. Take a moment, here and there throughout your days, to tell the voice of guilt to go to hell. Then remind yourself that you trust yourself and can navigate your life just fine without it."

SISTER/SATYR

I'd made plans with the Friedmans to take Rachel out the following afternoon, a Saturday. This in itself was typically an unpleasant process. My Aunt Gail treated me like a peripheral part of the family at best. Apparently, the fact that I had essentially raised my little sister since Mom died, and that the two of us had developed a powerful bond during that time, had completely escaped her notice. Instead of acknowledging it with any word or gesture, she instead spun her own variations of my father's favorite derogatory question: "What are you ever gonna do with your life?"

But, whereas it was easy to deflect my father's challenge back at him—because what in the hell was he accomplishing?—the Friedmans had a cozy, solvent, and insular reality to feed their sense of smug superiority. They drove new cars, inhabited a lavish home, were deeply entrenched in high-paying careers, and all in all exhibited the trappings of success. The fact that I had no desire to succeed in their particular world, or even participate in it, was not something that their minds could ever compute.

But they never made it difficult for me to see Rachel, so long as I asked in all humility. And Ernie, at least, was able to hide whatever judgments he harbored about me beneath a veneer of surface friendliness.

It was hard for me not to feel like a derelict whenever I drove up their sleek-paved circular driveway. My car seemed worth about as much as their front door knocker. Ernie was a jeweler and Gail an accountant…but I don't know when—if ever—they found the time to actually enjoy all the wealth that they were so busy amassing.

I'd never had the chance to see how Rachel existed in her new home, what her room looked like, where she ate, because I always waited at the door for her. The suggestion to do so was never overt but rather subliminal, and yet it screamed to the senses of one as sensitive to the jarring flail of rejection as I was.

Because I didn't see her as often nowadays as in years past, the changes manifesting in her were more obvious each time. Her countenance was a bit more somber, unsure. She often paused a moment and reflected before speaking, whereas her younger self had oftentimes been spinning too fast for introspection. Now, there was the hint of underlying questions behind much of what she said, behind even the most innocent-seeming expression. I wished that I had even one answer to offer for the riddle of her life.

"Can we go to Iris Park?" she said at once.

Well, some things apparently hadn't changed at all. She nearly always made this request; and I laughed, now, as I questioned why we even went through this ritual of asking each time. "Can crows carry French fry trays?" I responded.

We'd once seen a crow do this very thing. It'd been eating out of a paper dish of tater fingers that had fallen in the middle of the road. I'd watched it devour as much as it could before the oncoming traffic arrived. Finally, at the last possible moment, it got one edge of the tray in its maw, lifted it evenly, and flew off without dropping a single one of the remaining fries. References to this incident had become a running joke for us ever since.

"Well, we know one that can!" Rachel gushed as she opened the passenger door.

It was now a longer drive than it once had been from the old house. I had time to ask her about school. She was nearly wrapping up the third grade.

"The only subject I like a lot is history," Rachel said. "But it makes me sad, too. Everything goes away after a while so that something else can come along. You learn about dinosaurs but then don't get to go see them. You learn about Indians and then find out that a lot of them are gone, too."

"Maybe they all still exist somewhere," I suggested. "Someplace we just can't see or go to right now. You think?"

Rachel flashed me a sly smile. "My teachers do not think like you do. They'd tell you to get your head out of the clouds, Brandon Chane!"

She giggled. That sound had not changed, either. It was still high and contagious as ever.

"Well, Rachel Amber Chane," I responded, "I have heard it said that only those of us who believe in magic have any hope of finding it, so I guess maybe I feel sorry for your teachers 'cause they're missin' out!"

She just giggled some more. "You're funny!"

Me lecturing her about magic. Ah, the irony....

We were favored with a fair day: a bit balmy, the grass still wet from the previous night's brief rains. Rachel may have visibly matured before my eyes—she was going to turn nine come mid-summer—but she still wanted to play all the same games that we'd indulged in for years. This involved monkey bars, chase, the merry-go-round, followed by more chase. Our routine typically involved running, in one form or another, until we were too exhausted to continue.

Then we lay on the grass talking about animals, boys, girls, school, God, whatever. Rachel was dressed for the occasion in an old pair of overalls, well-worn sneakers, and a sturdy gray woolen shirt. Ernie and Gail weren't about to risk any of her "good" clothes on an outing with me.

A few minutes later, I glanced to my right and caught a glimpse of the cruelest sight my eyes had been afflicted with in an age of the world. There was a sidewalk across the way, beyond the swing set and slide and the tall maples that bordered the park. Janie was walking there...with a man. She was listening, head slightly lowered: receptive. He was talking. His cheeks were colored in a way that bespoke nervousness or excitement, probably both. The intimacy of the scene was palpable. In one hand, they each held paper cups of coffee, most likely. Their other hands were entwined.

Mind and body aflame, I could scarcely breathe. Rachel followed the line of my sight.

There was this distinct air of a first or second date. Their body language was tentative, exploratory. He was probably asking a lot of gentlemanly questions.

They were apparently taking things slower than Janie and I had. And I can hardly recall what he looked like because in that moment I was completely consumed by the fantasy of grabbing him by the hair and yanking so hard that it divorced his head from his neck.

I do remember—one of the keenest torments of this vision—that Janie was wearing the same light-tan fringed blouse that she'd had on when I'd met her in the Albuquerque airport. In another lifetime, when I'd swept her up in my arms and felt appeased to the depths of my soul. That quaint detail was nearly potent enough to unhinge me.

"Is that Janie?" Rachel asked. She sounded confused.

"Rachel...just don't."

The only thing that could have made my abjection any more complete would have been for Janie to see me, to witness my state of horrified paralysis. And that's precisely what happened. She chanced to meet my eyes—and hers widened. She turned away, then, and quickened her pace. Once more, the only answer she was able to latch onto was that of flight.

"Why is she holding that guy's hand?"

The two of them were disappearing. Reality was unravelling.

"Doesn't she love you still? Is she not your girlfriend anymore?"

"Look, shut the fuck up!"

I yelled that loud enough to startle a woman nearby who was pushing a stroller. Rachel recoiled...and before she drew her next breath, the full horror of what'd just happened rebounded on me like a storm wave hitting a ship's prow.

Bastard! After all she's gone through, all the ways she's been hurt...now, to get screamed at by the one person left who she thought she could depend on without question. I held my hands out, but an agonized moment passed before I could muster any words. "Honey, come here! Please. Oh, God, I'm sorry!"

Rachel approached slowly. Once she made up her mind, though, her caution morphed into eagerness. Love is always ready to rebound. It is far wiser, and more farseeing, than doubt, forgetfulness, and fear.

I leaned against a bench and cradled her on my lap. "That will never happen again," I whispered. "I'm sorry."

"That's OK." She was quivering like a rabbit; but her voice, though it was low as mine, was steady. "I'm sorry you're upset." She risked a glance up at my face. My cheeks were already wet. "I wish she still loved you," Rachel offered.

I made a clumsy swipe at my tears. "I'm sure she does. It's more complicated than that…but I just can't talk about it right now."

Something odd happened to me then, at this critical threshold of my anguish. The world receded; or perhaps my mind relinquished its hold on its surroundings. Nothing existed except for Rachel and I, and the love that passed between us as simply and undeniably as the breath of skies. The sensation was divorced from all notions of time. This was a single moment that always had been and always would be.

My feelings bubbled up from their molten core, lightening and quickening as they rose. They mustered vibrations in my throat. Sounds demanded expression, so I opened my mouth wide. The notes slowly joined hands and formed a melody. Words sprang out of it like foam from the denser flesh of a wave. I sang without even stopping to consider what I was actually saying.

And thus, I serenaded Rachel with what would grow to become the song "Sister/Satyr." Fortunately, I repeated it enough times to commit it to memory.

> You're the wild imp, the Fountain Sprite
> Giggling as you're kicking your tin can
> Chasing me down those long, lost alleys
> All those days we blindly ran
>
> But now my joints, they need some oiling
> They could use some of your Elfish grease
> Your laughter moves me past the train wreck
> Your smile brings me dreams of peace

Satyr of my soul
Resuscitate my heart and ripen my mind
I'll trade this entire world of "facts"
for whatever precious trinkets you find

Take this vagabond by his hand
Fill his pockets with your magic sand
Teach him the words when the moment's ripe

Build your pagoda out of his spare parts
Remind him of your ancient arts
and pull his head out of the world's stovepipe

Satyr of my soul
The universe, it melts inside my brain
But I'll let it go without a pang of doubt
For love of you, little Rachel Chane

It ended up being the closest I'd felt to her in a long time, so I guess this was the hidden gift of that awful moment of my reaction, the reciprocal swing of the pendulum. After I dropped her off, I drove around aimlessly for a few hours. The sun went down and no answers emerged.

When I stepped inside the house, Carlos came out at once to meet me in the kitchen. He raised his hands in a slow shrug as if to say, "I'm just the messenger, bro," and then told me that Janie had called a couple of times. I didn't understand this at first, until I fished for my cellphone and realized that it wasn't in my pocket. I must've left it in my room. I felt a surge of wild, unreasoning hope—and then chastised myself for it. What the hell was I thinking? That, fresh from her date, she was gonna say, "Oh, Brandon, I've reconsidered. I love you. I've never stopped."

"How long ago was that?" I asked.

Carlos gave me a wry smile. "She said she'd wait up 'til you got in, however long it takes. 'I know he's not gonna sleep otherwise,' were her words."

I nodded, trying to somehow will my gratitude to show through my turmoil. Then I shut myself in my room. I didn't even bother to turn on the lamp. I put on some ambient music to muffle the sound and to help steady my psyche. Janie's number wasn't saved anymore—I hadn't been able to bear seeing her name on my device—but I still knew it by twisted, limping heart. I could practically hear a deep bell tolling with each key I punched.

She answered at once. The sound of her voice, its earnest presence, stirred up the voice of betraying hope inside me again. My efforts to strangle it almost made me snarl. "I heard you called."

"Well, yeah, of course. I didn't want to just leave things like that." Her tone was a strange admixture of compassion and rectitude. "Look, just because I can't be your lover doesn't mean that I don't still really care about you and want to continue being your friend. And I definitely don't want to hurt you, like I'm sure it did hurt, seeing what you did today."

My mental environment swayed as if, somewhere in its depths, tectonic shifts were deciding the fate of continents. I clung to the darkness. Nothing sapped the fight in me so quickly as someone refusing to react. And Janie had adopted that strategy a long time ago.

"I don't even really know what to say about it," she said. "It's not a serious relationship. We've gone out a few times…I guess what I'm feeling is that I just don't want you to go away with the idea like you're so easily replaced in my life. What we had was not something that I took lightly. And I don't in any way want to trivialize it, like 'Whee! I'm back on the horse again! Life is great!'" She paused for a tension-laden huff. "I've been testing the waters, taking little steps."

I sat on the edge of my bed and wondered whether a quick skewer might not be preferable to this sort of slow flagellation. For all of her compassion and honesty, Janie was essentially just prolonging my agony. "Am I supposed to congratulate you?" I burst out. "Christ, Janie! I don't care what it is, how serious you say it is or isn't. I'm still fucking in love with you, alright?"

She sighed, as if conceding that all her explanations had accomplished nothing. "I love you too, you know. Might be hard for you to believe right now, but—"

"But now you've found a safe guy to give your heart to, someone who'll never scare you!"

"That's not it at all!" Janie was moving at my speed now, her temper rising to the same pitch. "You're like this spinning gyroscope. I can't keep up with it. Sometimes I just feel dim next to you, lackluster…I don't know what-all."

"Sorry, Janie, but I'm not buying it. You were frightened, plain and simple. I'm not saying you're cowardly, alright? But just don't throw me all these red herrings."

"There was probably some fear in there, too, yeah," Janie admitted, so low it was almost a whisper.

While I shook my head, realizing that winning this concession had gained me nothing at all, she plunged on. "Maybe I did the wrong thing in calling you. I feel like it's just made things worse for you."

I bit off a mirthless laugh. "Worse? If you really knew where I've been at, you wouldn't worry. It can get to a point, you know, where it just isn't possible to fall any farther."

Her voice was now hollow and broken. "I'm sorry."

I was scared to trust any of the words I might speak. One way or another, they were bound to reach out and claw her. I gritted my teeth, clenched my free fist, and let the last wisps of that foolish hope burn away.

"I'd still very much like to be friends," Janie said. "I don't want to disappear completely from your life."

It took every bit of strength I possessed to respond without bitterness. "Yeah—I want to keep in touch too."

"OK, then."

"OK."

So the conversation ended there. And how was it that the walls around me refused to crumble, that the world withheld its last dying convulsions?

❖

The following Monday, we were scheduled to do a makeup interview with Visionary Chapbook's Pat Stavons. I was looking forward to it for a couple of reasons: For one thing, I was grateful for his review of our record. Not only had it been sympathetic, but it had also indicated to me that at least one person out there could actually hear what we were trying to convey through our songs. And aside from everything else, I wanted to make things up to Pat, Tommy, and Carlos for having squandered our previous opportunity.

Pat certainly didn't seem to bear any grievances. He held the door and waved us in, got us some refreshments (coffee for Tommy, tea for Carlos, and ginger ale for me), and made us feel right at home in his little office.

Once his tape was rolling, he began. "How 'bout we start by talking about the genesis of the band. We already know that you went on tour before you'd even played out a whole lot in your hometown. That in itself gives you a bit of an air of mystery."

"As far as the real origins go," Tommy started first, "you'd have to trace it back to two misfits in high school—Brandon and me—who bonded over our mutual love of underground music."

"And that was a lot an expression of the desperation and isolation we were feeling at the time," I put in. "People—young people, particularly—can get so marginalized by society that lots of times they'll gravitate to music that gives voice to the frustration, and even the hopelessness, that they're feeling. It's a mistake to try and suppress those feelings—any feelings, really. Like, if you're in pain, then this in itself indicates that you have the capacity to care. If you didn't care, then you wouldn't hurt. So, pain is really an aspect of love. Any feeling is as essential to love as shadow is to light. That was our main motivation, in the beginning: to give voice to everything inside us. No repression, no rules, just let it all out."

"It comes across as threatening to a lot of people at first, that sort of thing," Carlos came in with. "But if you give it a chance, then you might recognize yourself in it. It's like the music is giving you permission to just fully be yourself. That's how I felt when I started playing with these guys. It's a real gift."

Pat was already grinning, clearly enjoying this. "So there's a way in which it's all therapeutic, is that it?"

Carlos was on a roll. "Deep inside, people really want that honest expression, even if they usually don't want to admit it, you know? It reminds me of back when I was drinking heavily and using drugs, all those tiresome party scenes. They seem to promise fulfillment—to the point where you just about catch a glimpse of it, around the corner. One more drink, one more smoke, and maybe, finally, the door will open. Feelings will gel with that guy you're trying to connect with, that girl you're hoping to make it with. Magic words will be spoken. You keep tellin' yourself that 'til the room's spinning, bro, and tomorrow you're paying for it.

"But what is everyone hoping that next drink, or snort, or smoke, is gonna do? Well, you hope it will open you up, get you to show your real self. If anyone was just brave in that moment and said, like, 'I really want to connect with you and I just don't know how, I can't find the words,' then it'd cut through all that. Everyone else could lower their defenses and be genuine and human too. They wouldn't have to wait in the hopes that getting fucked up would lend them the courage to expose themselves. And that's what good music does. When it's real, it gives you that permission to be real—with yourself and with other people. It exposes so many things that we're all thinking and feeling, on the inside, even if people so rarely come out and say those things."

"And yet the artists who express themselves so openly, who let everything out, are so often the misfits, the outsiders," Pat observed.

"Exactly," Tommy concurred. "In order for society to evolve, it must always have its misfits. And they'll create their own artistic productions, which society typically frowns upon, and feels threatened by, until it finds some way to assimilate them."

"Is being outside of society something that's integral to the identity of your band?" Pat asked.

"It's essential for any kind of real art," I said.

248

"Truly," Tommy agreed. "If you're completely bought-in to the status quo, then you're not going to have any contribution to make, no new vision."

"You're just repeating the ideas that the culture at large already lives by," Pat suggested.

"Exactly," Tommy said. "Whereas, if you exist on the margins of society, then this obliges you to search for your own kind of personally resonant truth. And that truth, in turn, can become a gift to the society. That's where you find the irony of our cultural response to rock stars: they're outcasts, and yet they're idolized."

"And so now that you three have joined forces," Pat said, "and you've made one record and honed your chops out on the road, what's next? What are your plans?"

"We have too many," Tommy deadpanned.

"Yeah, I guess we do have some prioritizing to do," I said. "I'm to blame for some of that, too, man. I can be temperamental. I either feel passionate about something, or else I just can't even approach it at all."

"It's the Dionysian thing," Tommy explained. "He's Dionysus and I'm Apollo. If you ever saw one of our rehearsals or listened in on some of our band discussions, then you'd see how this plays out. You should definitely put that in your write-up. Journalists just love to run with that kind of stuff.

"But getting back to your question…there are ideas being bounced around for getting back in the studio. We've got five or six new songs written at this point. And we may be doing a tour of the East Coast sometime—New England, particularly. Chas is a transplanted New Yorker, so he's still got contacts back east. How we'll get ourselves and our equipment over there is another matter…."

At this point, all three of us simultaneously eased back in our seats and sipped at our drinks. The interview was complete: you could palpably feel this in the room. What more could we say? Upon the occasion of our very first appearance in print, we'd already distilled our essential philosophy and delivered our mission statement.

"OK," Pat said, with a brisk and satisfied air. He clicked off his recorder. Then he looked at me. "Now, I'd still like to use some parts of our first interview, but I'll only do so if you feel comfortable with it. I just think that there are some real human moments there that readers, your fans, and potential fans, might appreciate."

I thought this over for a moment and then shrugged. "Sure. Why not? It wasn't the most coherent interview, for sure. But then again, it was real."

"That it was," Pat said with a smile. "And therefore very much befitting for your band. It's been a real honor, guys!"

In the face of all his magnanimous support, we expressed our gratitude to Pat as best we could as we shook hands and said our goodbyes.

❖

For the second time since we'd resumed our unique kind of student-teacher relationship, Saul suggested that the two of us take a walk.

This time, we left his property and followed the bike trail that snaked alongside Townes Street for a while before it cut through several acres of heather strewn with litter. Traffic was sporadic. The entire city of Sadenport—half of which was visible off to the left from our high vantage—felt subdued. Maybe Saul's somber mood was affecting my senses.

He was quiet for a long time, and I didn't feel like it was my place to initiate conversation. Finally, Saul said, "I won't be charging you for today." He was distracted, his eyes cast vaguely over the yellow grassland towards no point in particular. "So let's just get that out of the way and not worry about it." Then he glanced my way and allowed me to see his pain. "I'm sorry that it's taking me a while to get myself together today."

"Look, it's no problem. And I got the session. Hell, there's been times when I've gotten everything I needed from you inside of ten minutes. I'm not gonna split hairs now."

"Yeah, well, I'm not counting it," Saul insisted.

We started making our way across the field. The sounds of human bustle receded even farther. "I'm probably going to have to pull back on my practice for a while anyway," he continued. "June needs me. That's where I feel like I have to devote my energies now. She's not well."

For a moment I was stunned, fixed in place as if I was buffeted by winds hitting my soul on both sides with equal force. I was frightened for Saul's sake, and by the thought of how such a strong man could be brought to this place where he appeared so frail, almost defeated. Also, I realized how attached I'd grown to him. In my wounded and thwarted human need, I'd turned him into something other than human, a being absolved of ordinary hang-ups and sufferings. I felt it sorely as this illusion was rent from me.

"What's wrong with her?"

Saul scowled. This was the angriest I'd ever seen him. He spat the litany of June's woes as if each sentence was a curse hurled at the Creator. "She shivers and aches. Her whole body…it's wracked with pain and fever. I sleep next to her at night sometimes and, goddamn it, it's like her living flesh is a furnace. She sweats through clothes, bedding, changes everything three or four times a day. Not that she's hardly got the strength left even for that task."

He looked at me and hugged his shoulders, mastered his outburst. The rage receded and the pain returned. "God, and she looks so frail. Like a reed—like a stiff wind could just break her."

Something in his attitude, in the implied defiance in his eyes, alerted me. "She hasn't been diagnosed, has she?"

"Diagnosed by who, Brandon? Some doctor who'll turn her into a guinea pig for the drug companies? Or put her through chemotherapy that could kill her quicker than cancer? Just what do you think it actually means, to live outside of convention?"

"So you've decided to work through this on your own, you and her."

Saul looked distant—and not the communing-with-spirits kind of distant that I was used to. "Yeah," he said, as if the word was a latch intended to lock in impending tears. "And there really isn't much that I can do except be there, be her support. It's all up to June. We actually did seek some medical help in the beginning. But her condition has been stubbornly unresponsive to treatments and

251

antibiotics. And then we tried the natural methods: A complete overhaul of her living habits. A transition into a largely raw food diet. No good. June has tried acupuncture and Chinese herbs, Ayurveda and Yoga. Nothing makes a difference; at least, not for long.

"Nowadays she has to force herself to eat at all, because the very thought of it makes her nauseous. She hardly has the stamina left to appreciate the little joys of life. All she really wants is the blankness of sleep."

I wished that I'd known June better, had shared more with her during those times when our paths had crossed, as if this could have enabled me to be of help somehow.

"But let's talk about what you're working through now," Saul said, clapping his hands together and mustering his self-control. "And let me just say it, and get it out of the way: I know that you had a painful experience involving Janie lately, and that you and she talked since then. I know that it's unprofessional of me, blah blah blah—it's not my place to say, but I'm glad you two have communicated on that level finally. That feels a lot more real to me than the place where things were left at before."

I didn't know how to tell Saul that the mere mention of Janie's name stirred up in me a kind of senseless, betraying hope. I grimaced at the turn of my own thoughts. Before long, though, our talk drifted away from my personal life and back to June and her difficulties. And I didn't mind, because I realized that there were lessons for me in all of it. Saul's love for his wife was evident in the way he spoke of her. There was also a note—the merest suggestion—of fatality. The idea of death had a way of reminding me of what was really important in life. It was the sheerest form of catharsis, really.

"It's been a learning experience for her," Saul said, "in the sense that her crisis training and work never prepared her to be needy and dependent herself." He grinned. It was the first time I'd seen him do so that day. "Her pride is taking a blow. We just spend a lot of time sipping tea together and waxing nostalgic. We talk about the year that we lived in a bus while we saved up the money to buy this house. We were different people back then. We were poor and uncertain, but somehow the moments of our days had been full...."

I didn't know how to respond to any of it. I did make one plea to Saul about halfway through the session, though. "Please, can you just find some time to keep working with my dad?" Then I was bit by the old bitterness. I shook my head. "I don't even know why I give a shit, really. But I do. Somehow, I still do. Besides, he's Rachel's father, too, and I know that she'd love to see her daddy get better."

Robert had already come to see Saul a couple of times. I knew that much, although Saul had stuck to his personal resolution to keep things confidential. It would be up to my father to discuss what he was working through or not. And I didn't expect him to share much at this point in time, anyway. No doubt it was all very new and raw.

Saul nodded. "There's several people who I'm keeping on during this period. He can be one of them, if he chooses to come."

"He needs it," I said. "I mean, I don't know if he'll ever be able to face his life, but...I'd say you're the best chance he's got."

"Making that first appointment was a good step for him; a strong symbolic gesture," Saul said. "He took the initiative, at least. But of course you know that I'm only the messenger. The real healing's gonna have to come from him." Then he took a moment to delve into me. I bore his scrutiny as best I could. "What about you?" he asked.

"I'll be fine," I assured him, although I didn't know how much I meant what I was saying. "You know how it sometimes takes me months before I really start to understand and live by the things you tell me, anyway."

Saul suddenly smiled; and in the expression I saw glimmerings of his old impish self. "You know, I had a therapist once," he said.

"Oh yeah?" I was genuinely intrigued by this.

He met my eyes and offered me another glimpse into the turmoil and doubt inside him. "It wasn't easy for me to believe that I existed within a world of my own making. I battled that one for a long time."

"And now this crisis with June has brought it all up again," I blurted, almost without thinking.

Caught by surprised, delighted, his eyes wide and aflame, Saul burst out laughing. "Did I not tell you that we're here to learn from each other?"

But I could only partially participate in his momentary good humor. My most recent insight had led me on to another. "That's why you don't want to take clients," I said, even as it occurred to me. "It's not that you don't have the energy, but that you feel like—"

"A hypocrite," Saul finished. He was somber once more. "Yes. How can I teach people something that I'm reluctant to place my own full faith in?"

I responded much like a child would, one who was in need of a strong father. "Well, you need to find that belief again, Saul! Seriously!"

Unguarded and vulnerable, he regarded me for maybe half a minute. Then he said, "In all the time we've worked together—coming up on two years now—we've never hugged. And I know you can feel uneasy about that sort of thing. But I could sure use one now."

I entered his embrace as soon as he opened his arms. My own feelings were pretty raw and insistent too.

FOOL'S GOLD

When I got home that evening, I learned that Carlos had gone out. Tommy was hanging out in the living room practicing finger exercises on his four-string. Occasionally, he would stop and scribble a line or two in a notebook that was laid open on the coffee table. I watched him at work for a while. He seemed to be in the midst of yet another killer song. Damn, did this guy ever get writer's block?

Then he looked over and asked me a question that he never had before, in all the time that I'd been seeing Saul. "How'd your session go?"

I stopped—I'd been halfway en route to the bathroom—and groped for an answer. "Well, I found out that Saul is just as human as the rest of us, which was probably good for me." Then the deeper reservoir of sadness rose up and engulfed me. "His wife's not doing so well. June. She's real sick."

In a stumbling manner, I described what I knew of her symptoms. And I explained that Saul and June had decided, after a few half-hearted forays into conventional medicine, to move through this crisis on their own.

"Jesus!" Tommy leaned his bass against the table. "It sounds like cancer, man. And they're not seeking help? I don't know…odds are she ain't gonna make it."

"That's basically the same thing I was thinking, at first…." I trailed off, feeling unsure of what I believed anymore.

Suddenly I was crying. The reservoir rose over the dam. I felt like my face bore trails of blood from twin wounds. When Tommy slung his arm over my shoulders I began blabbing, spluttering. "Do you ever wonder, man…the music, the inspiration—is it even enough? I mean, I love it. It's the reason I live. You know that's how I feel about it. But it isn't the sum of life."

A minute or two later, I calmed down enough to catch my breath and try and proceed more coherently. "I guess it's like I was saying that night at Toad's in Albuquerque, when I talked the crowd's ears off. I just realized that it wasn't the answer to everything. I don't just want to be this mad, inspired poet and musician. I want to have a happy and healthy life, too. God, I don't think I really realized that until Janie left."

Tommy rose to meet me in my place of groping need. "I gotta tell you...I haven't been there for you to the extent that I really could have, lately. I've seen what you've been going through. I see how heavy it all is. And yet I've had this attitude, like, 'Well, alright, but we still have things we've got to accomplish.' I guess what I'm saying is, if you need to take a break from all this, put the band on the back burner—"

"No!"

❖

A few days later, Edge of the Known met with Chas to discuss the band and our future. At thirty-one, Chas was still lean and driven: as high-rev a personality as you're ever bound to encounter without uppers figuring into the equation. It was hard, at times, for me to work with him in any state of vulnerability, because he was such a believer in action over introspection. But on this particular afternoon, I felt focused. Even though we only had enough new material written to fill about half a record, I suggested that we spend some time laying down tracks in the studio.

"I think it would just give us a sense of momentum at this point," I said. "We don't want to get too comfortable, you know, just playing at being local heroes over at Brasserie D'Alchimie."

"How big do you hope for your band to become?" Chas asked—rather pointedly.

This left me thoroughly nonplussed. I'd never really thought about it in those terms before. In the naiveté of our original vision—mine and Tommy's, some five years before in high school—"success" in the abstract sense had meant salvation. I suppose we'd hoped to find ourselves surrounded by congenial minds, kindred souls; that we'd never again have to exist within the system that alienated us, if only we "made it." For a moment, I gaped at the shortsightedness of this vision.

"Big enough to eat," Carlos offered. "And to pay the rent and not have to hold day jobs."

"Unfortunately, it's such a feast-or-famine industry," Tommy added.

Chas looked thoughtful. He ran a hand through his short hair. "It's interesting to me, though, how well you guys went over with people when you did that last tour. There seems to be something about you that average people can really latch on to. I mean, you seem to appeal to those who aren't even metalheads, punks, or even music lovers in general."

"The honesty of it?" Carlos suggested.

"There really isn't a hell of a lot of competition out there," Tommy opined.

"Well," I said, "whatever the secret to our magic may be, I have a feeling that we'll spoil it if it becomes too self-conscious a thing. We gotta just keep trusting our instincts and not try to analyze the whole thing."

"Yes," Chas muttered. But he was still following his own mental loop to its culmination. I could see it, when the resolution came, because the focus of his whole being returned in a swoop. "I think I may be able to get you guys into a showcase gig in a few months," he announced. "You know, there'll be a couple of big-draw bands on the bill alongside you, and hopefully some A & R guys—who've been specially invited to the thing—in the audience. There's this event being planned in New York. I know the promoters. Between the power of your record and the rave review in Chapbook…well, I'll call in every favor I can think of, on top of that, and hopefully get you guys in there."

There followed a half minute of silence as we all absorbed this. Then we tumbled over one another in our eagerness to express our interest in the idea and our gratitude to Chas. Then my thoughts hit a disconcerting snag, as another dimension of this idea revealed itself to me.

"But wait a minute, Chas," I said. "'A & R people.' That means possible major label interest. Why are you doing this? I mean, if we sign to a big label, then you'll lose us."

Chas met me squarely. "That's why I was asking you guys how big you want to become. My resources are limited, obviously. Manhandle is for bands that otherwise wouldn't be heard at all. I think your music deserves to reach as many people as humanly possible. If someone can give you that wider exposure, better than I can…"

His generosity caught me off guard. I was speechless. Tommy came through for all of us. "In the event that that happens, I'm telling you, Manhandle's getting a mention somehow on every record that ships out!"

Chas acknowledged this with a humble nod. Then he clapped his hands together, his mind already embarked upon the next venture. "So now let's talk about the new record. If you guys are anywhere near as inspired as you were last time…"

Then, suddenly, the bottom fell out of my fleeting sense of happiness. "Not a record, man," I said. "An EP. I can handle an EP."

When Tommy and Carlos turned towards me, their eyes and body language conveyed a kind of quiet sympathy. It told me that they weren't actually so surprised, that they guessed at the underlying reasons. But I kept my awareness fixed on the compass point of Chas' face.

"I've been through too much upheaval in my personal life lately," I explained. "It's hard for me to concentrate on anything for very long. The couple of new songs that I have written both just leapt out without much conscious effort. I did get blocked, during the last recording, but I had Saul to help me work through it. And he's just not available now. He's got his hands full with his own nightmare. Then I had another dry spell for a few months after we got back from the tour. It seems to all come in fits and starts for me. I'm sorry, Chas. I really don't think that I've got any other songs in me right now."

Tommy stepped up to support my flank. "And in that case, it wouldn't be right for me to pick up the slack and fill the record with my own material, even if

I was able to. We've always had this kind of unspoken pact, that we'd divide everything up more or less evenly. Edge of the Known is a lot about the balance that we've found, the middle ground between our voices and visions. We've got some differing tendencies, both lyrically and musically, and it's oftentimes the tension there that really makes the band interesting."

We were both much more earnest than our producer was. Chas just nodded in acknowledgement. No skin off his back. "An EP it is, then," he said. "So what length are we talking? How many songs?"

"Five songs, one of them being an instrumental," Tommy said. "We've got about a half hour's worth of music ready to record."

"When do you feel like starting?" Chas asked.

"As soon as possible!" I suddenly envisioned those hours in the studio as refuge, escape, forward motion. I needed to feel useful and effective again.

"Soon as possible" turned out to be the very next night. I decided to visit Rachel and soak up some of her faerie magic for the venture. That was tricky. She had school and I had work, which left a window of just a few hours in the early evening. I also hadn't planned this in advance, which meant that I showed up at the Friedmans' door and knocked, unexpectedly. I'd never done that before.

Their reaction surprised me. Ernie stood in the doorway and—quite humbly—told me that it was fine with him. When Gail sidled alongside him, in her utilitarian khaki pants and plain button blouse, he passed the question on to her. She deliberated a bit longer than he had, frowning in concentration, but was just as amenable in the end.

"Rachel!" she called. "Your brother's here! He wants to take you out, if you want to go."

I heard her squeal with delight from her bedroom upstairs. It was the most delightful sound imaginable. And I wondered, in that moment, if it was her love for me that was slowly softening the manner in which the Friedmans responded to me, in spite of their inability to relate to either my physical circumstances or my mental world.

Rachel appeared in pink overalls, brown sandals, and a white longsleeved shirt. Her long auburn hair (most of the red having faded with maturity) was tied in two tight braids. She was quiet and demure as we walked to my car; reflective. I felt suddenly unsure of how to initiate conversation. Then inspiration hit me.

"Hey," I said, pausing at the door on my side, "do you want to go visit Dad?"

Rachel lit up at once, and nodded.

While she buckled up, I said, "So, I haven't talked to him about this beforehand. I actually got the idea just now. So we'll be dropping in and surprising him. Hopefully he'll be OK with it. And if Ernie and Gail get upset about this, then they're going to take it out on me, not you, alright? So just don't even worry about it."

"I don't want to get you in trouble, though," Rachel said.

"Hey, it's not like they're my parents," I responded—and then immediately regretted having done so.

"They're not mine, either," Rachel shot back, with an intensity that surprised me.

I let out a long breath as I began backing the car around. "If they make it difficult for me to come and visit you, then that'll be unfortunate," I said. "But I don't think it'll come to that. And kiddo…you do have a loving home, at least. Not everyone does."

You didn't before, I wanted to add.

"I know," she said, sounding more at ease. "But it's different from how it was when I didn't live there, and they were still just Aunt Gail and Uncle Ernie."

"How so?"

"Well, they want everything to be perfect all the time, for one thing! Nice clothes. Perfect grades. They even sometimes say things like, I should be friends with this person but not that person. It's so stupid! I can make up my own mind! And what do I need good grades for, anyway? They're not gonna help me be a good rock singer, like you. And that's what I want."

I nearly steered us into a rut off the right shoulder of the road. "Since when?"

Little sis giggled. "Marla told me that Rachel Chane sounds like a rock star's name. I think so too."

I recovered from my shock and glanced over, smiled. "Well...yeah...I suppose it does."

After that, I drove in silence for a while, marveling at this new perspective that she'd given me. I was so accustomed to thinking of my own life path as something that I pursued for lack of any other recourse. That it should have romantic implications in someone else's mind was startling.

"Hey, you've never heard me play—I mean, like, with a full band," I said as it occurred to me. "You should come to one of our rehearsals sometime, if you want to."

"That'd be cool."

Oh, how many changes was I going to have to race to catch up with?! "And since when do you say things are 'cool,' rock star Rachel Chane?"

She laughed again—and that was her only reply.

It was unfortunate, at least in terms of my own emotional preparedness, that our banter made time speed by, because before I knew it, I was pulling into the cul-de-sac where our father's house sat. "Here we are."

The walk from the curb to the door transpired inside a dream. I pulled open the screen door and then rapped on the wooden one. A minute later, Robert opened it and met our gazes with the expression of a man who'd lost the capacity for any kind of expectation. He blinked like he suspected we were phantoms.

I was spared the burden of having to break the ice. Rachel beat me to it. With humility and innocence the likes of which I'd scarcely witnessed in the entirety of my life, she stepped forward and said, "Hi Daddy."

That such soft, quiet words could wield such power. They literally brought him to his knees. Robert knelt, and his moist eyes burned towards her. Then, with obvious effort, he offered his open arms. Rachel entered his clasp with a kind of eagerness that I'd often been on the receiving end of myself—and indescribably grateful for, every time.

"Oh, I love you," he wheezed, nearly hoarse.

"I love you, Daddy," she returned, much more evenly.

It was a fairly stiff display, on his part. But it was also, to my knowledge, the first time those words had passed between the two of them in their lives. They bridged chasms, sealed rifts, opened views onto wide skies never before glimpsed.

As they disengaged, I looked at each of them in turn. "I think I'll just let you two hang out for a bit, OK? I'll go take a walk, maybe to the bridge and back. See you in a few."

❖

Of course, following this outing with Rachel, the song that I most wanted to record was the one that I'd written for her. Tommy, Carlos, and I had been woodshedding it over the last couple weeks and had solidified an arrangement that was somehow edgy and dynamic without ever overwhelming the delicate melody—which was, all in all, the quality of the song most dear to me.

I used a distortion pedal while recording my guitar part so that it could ring clear and twangy during the verses—just like how you hear it on a lot of vintage sixties garage band records—and crunchy through the chorus. Classic grunge trick, I know; and I typically disliked processing my sound with anything other than the distortion that my amp on high volume could produce. But it was difficult, in this case, to convey the alternately escalating and subsiding states of emotion without resorting to a bit of technical aid.

Feeling reluctant to commit my sister's full name to a recording, as it existed in the original lyrics, I ended the last line with the innocuous "Sparkle Lane" instead, just so I could preserve the rhyme.

Then, following an obscure impulse (as I was wont to do when the tapes were rolling—or when I was onstage, for that matter) I recited a snatch of poetry over the spacious, psychedelic outro that we'd composed to finish the song. The poem had been an offshoot of the original lyrics anyway, written a couple of days later, so it seemed to be finally settling into its intended spiritual home.

I'll trade this whole
world of facts for
your comic collection and
trusty sea pets

If you could just help me to
wade
beyond the jellyfish
Then—no doubt—
once my head's below water it'll be like
that time in winter when
my reasoned construct of the
universe melted and
I found myself thinking
clearly for the first time in
my life

I was so excited by the result of this experiment that I suggested we wed
another poem of mine to the instrumental we'd composed. Again we were blessed
with a miraculous marriage of words and sonic landscape. And so, "Instrumental
No. 1" was transformed into "Stage Props," utilizing the last two verses of the
original poem.

Logic, standing anxious on its
patch of ever-shifting ground, seeks
the comfort of finality

May it be eased into
recognizing its own source in
the grinding mill of mortality, which
disguises Eternal Nature behind

the stage props of

all who have loved and

lost

Though our intended disc was still unnamed, we finished recording the songs inside of three sessions. Then we treated our next performance at Brasserie D'Alchimie as our celebration.

We'd begun to notice regulars: people who went there to see us nearly every time we played. By now, they'd become familiar with the tunes that would soon surface on our new record, too. We were all bursting with too much enthusiasm to keep our compositions a secret for long. The spoken sections, however, were new to everyone on this night. We'd also abandoned the slideshow. It just didn't fit in with our overall ethic of being transparent within the music.

"We've got the best fucking fans in the world!" I shouted as we finished "Sister/Satyr." The audience, some fifty or sixty strong, responded with cries of tribal, blood-deep assent that rolled like pristine waves onto the stage.

All the energy that we'd poured out rebounded upon us from the crowd in pelts of adoration. I'd scarcely unslung my guitar when the cocktail server, Kayla, came right up and grasped me in an urgent hug. She was there on most of the nights we played, so I'd chatted with her on and off on previous occasions. She had honey-colored hair that ran to her shoulders in mild ringlets, and usually (as was the case tonight) wore high heels and a single-piece dress of deep blue that showcased her shapely thighs and hips. Hoop earrings dangled from both her ears. She also displayed a tasteful arc of golden eyeshadow over each eye; and this last detail threw my otherwise sweet indulgence in the spectacle of her into pained disarray, as it reminded me of Janie.

"God, Brandon!" she gushed. "That was incredible!"

I could tell at once that this went beyond a simple compliment about the music. Undeniable sexual warmth oozed through both the words and her smile. And I was filled with such a sense of plentitude, following that cathartic apotheosis onstage, that I was able to smile back.

"Thanks, Kayla," I said, as humbly as I could manage.

"Can I buy you a drink?"

"Hey, I'm not broke! I can cover myself."

"No, seriously, let me. I get 'em discounted." Her eager pursuit was making me hot all over. "So what'll you have?"

I shrugged. "Just a beer. Any kind…something stout!" I amended.

"Be right back," she replied, with a merry twinkle—and an implied promise.

Tommy had just returned from packing his bass amp in the van. His cool nod somehow acknowledged that he was privy to what was in the air. "Looks like maybe it'd be worth your while to hang out here for a bit. I don't mind a walk home, and I'm sure Carlos doesn't either. You could drive the van back later."

Kayla returned then with a pint of dark ale for me, and Tommy retreated to give us space. After a moment he left, probably to find Carlos. "It's such a trip to actually know someone who can write and perform like that!" Kayla said. "It's one thing to hear a record—you know?—and just sort of admire this musician who you know you're never gonna meet."

I waved a hand. "There's nothing too special about it, really. Everyone has their own different gifts. Hey, you can navigate this place in half darkness, weaving around all the people who're jerking back and forth, a tray of drinks balanced on your shoulder and not spilling a drop. That's something I could never manage."

She sparkled again. "Oh, it is an art form, isn't it? And speaking of which, I'd better get back to it." She cast me a look that was part gauging and part insinuating. "You wanna hang out until I get off, or…? It'll just be, like, another hour."

"Sure," I said, aware of all that I was acceding to. One part of me was already sampling her wares, sating the places that were so starved for touch, closeness, release. When Kayla left, I sat on the edge of the stage and nursed my beer. Now and then, someone would come by and compliment me on the performance. It had been a righteous outburst of Pan's madness. Tommy had managed to announce the imminent release of our mini album in the midst of it, too. None of this touched me like I longed for it to, though. Kayla, and my own want of her, posed an essential dilemma that I had no answer for.

She returned a while later with her purse slung over her shoulder and her server's apron all folded up and clutched in one hand. "I know it's late," she said, "and they're doing last call now, but…you wanna do something tonight?"

The underlying suggestion could hardly have been more blatant. And I realized that I had either already lost this fight or else I just didn't understand the battleground to begin with—nor which side represented what. "The other guys walked back, and I've got the van," I said. With a subtle lilt, I made the word "van" sound like "conveniently close love nest."

Kayla stepped right up then, took me securely by the belt loops beside both my hips, pulled herself closer, and then tilted her head up (she was half a foot shorter than me) to kiss me. "Just thought I'd get it out of the way," she explained as we parted from this sharing of flesh and breath. I soaked up the scent of her, and the loosening of my own feelings and inhibitions, and leaned in for more. We flowed and swayed together, through the bar, out the door, and to the van. Kayla's whole body was taut with eagerness, and it drove a fire straight to my brain.

A stash of condoms was always kept in the van, in the event that situations like this ever occurred. Not that they very often did. After all, we three guys typically occupied the van at the same time; and at this point in time, none of us had steady girlfriends. Kayla slid back into a space between the equipment, hugging her knees and quietly acquiescing to my intent, as I rummaged for my protection.

She had her dress pulled down by the time I returned. Her arms stretched out, she alternately curled and extended her fingers to give me a "come hither" command. I tore off my shirt. Then, kneeling on all fours, I suddenly froze.

"Jesus, Kayla!" I breathed. "I gotta tell you. You gotta know. I'm still real attached to someone. I mean, there's someone who I still love, even though it's over."

This hardly even slowed her down. "Well, it sounds like you're not with her now, so…there's nothing stopping us." She started wrestling with my jeans.

"No, I mean…" I had to pull a deep breath in order to settle enough to continue, "I don't know that I can give myself to you, like, fully. My feelings are still over there, with someone else. Well, a part of me is still there, anyway."

My discomfort just seemed to create a challenge that she was delighted to be confronted with. "Will you relax? I'm not asking you to marry me, you know."

She leaned forward and kissed me, real soft, on the neck. That loosened me enough so that I stopped forestalling her hands, which had paused right at my zipper. My nipples were the next to receive her lips. Her fingers were deft. Somehow, by the end of this brief foreplay, I was entirely naked.

By now, my lower brain was doing the lion's share of the decision-making. Well, I could dispense with guilt, anyway. Kayla had been warned. Besides, she seemed the far less vulnerable one, between the two of us.

"You get hornier after a night of playing like that?" she asked—half tease, half challenge.

And then the time for talk was past. Her lips smothered me. I cupped the back of her head and the small of her back simultaneously, and went in like a dog straining at the uttermost limits of its leash.

Neither of us apparently had any interest in pacing ourselves. I felt like I was panting my lungs' last hoarse reserves, every time. When I came, I almost couldn't comprehend what was happening. A train gone off the rails had finally collided with an unmovable obstacle. My spate of wild flight was over; and no one—nothing—had been saved.

A few minutes later, we were lying on our backs, facing the shadowed roof and indulging in the honored movie cliché of sharing a cigarette.

"Please tell me," I said, "that you didn't just fuck me because I'm in a band."

She elbowed my ribs. "If you weren't in a band, a band that happens to play in the bar that I work at, then I probably wouldn't have even met you." She seemed immune to all intimate insecurities. "But I slept with you because I like you and I'm attracted. The passion you have up onstage is part of that, yeah. I won't lie."

Her candor eased me slightly. I reached over and massaged her head with my fingertips. "I don't know if there can be another time, Kayla." The force of my voice was nearly neutered by the trepidation I felt.

She turned on her side. "You sure? It was really nice, wasn't it?"

"It was beautiful. Don't know if that's even the right word for it, really. It was pretty animal!" Might as well acknowledge it: my body was still quivering. "I'm just fucked up around intimacy in general. I tried to tell you…."

"You did tell me," she said. She searched my face for clues in the darkness. Then, "She must be pretty special to have you all hung up like this."

"We're all special," I responded at once. *Thank you, Saul, for teaching me that. God I need you!*

"Well, I won't act like I'm not disappointed," Kayla said. "If you change your mind, you know where to find me."

"Yeah." I leaned forward and gave her lips all the tenderness that I was capable of, leaving it up to her whether or not to consider it a kiss goodbye—though I knew the truth.

"Come on. I'll walk you to your car."

❖

When I got home, I pulled my phone out and dialed as soon as I'd closed the bedroom door behind me. And I lit into my father the moment I heard his voice on the other end of the line.

"Look, I'm glad that your near brush with death has apparently made you see things with new eyes, made you maybe see the worth of living in a way that you never could before. I really am. But don't think that any of this makes me forget one single time that you ever smacked me around just because you couldn't find any other answer to the goddamn helplessness that you felt inside.

"And let me tell you this, too: It will not ever be happening in the future. You put a hand on me again and I will lay you out on the motherfucking floor! You got that?"

He was quiet so long that I wondered if he was just going to hang up. Had my vehemence provoked a heart attack? Then his voice, possessing a kind of dignity in its honest resignation, reached me.

"Fair enough."

Then I hung up.

CRAB SHELL AND CRYSTAL

No doubt, you've heard some psychologist or other—teachers, even—talk about how we humans supposedly lean towards one of three possible responses to trauma, pain, and fear: fight, flight, or freeze. And I'm sure, by now, you can guess easily enough what my default position had long been. But my heart was sickened by all the fighting—had been for a while. Saul was no longer available to help me find another option. In lieu of his guidance, I naturally began to fantasize about movement.

The road, as it had during another period of time not so far in the past, held out my only hope of salvation. In my mind, it was getting time to go. "If you can just spot us a couple grand for the gas," I told Chas, "we'll take the van. We'll just bomb right out there and be on the East Coast within a week."

I'd dropped by to "hang out" (peer over his shoulder and perk my ears at every note that moved through the soundboard) while he was mixing our new EP. "We've saved up enough money to ensure that we can eat and survive during the time away," I went on. "Just help us to get there, is all."

He finally looked up from the mixing board. If he felt any irritation, he hid it well. "Getting you there doesn't do you much good if I don't line up a bunch of gigs to begin with," he pointed out.

"Send them the record," I urged. "Look, 'Shadow' convinced twenty-three club owners to give us a chance up on their stage, even though they'd never met or even heard of us before. And now we've got Patrick's review—and pretty soon, the interview in Chapbook—that'll give us even more clout."

Chas acknowledged this quietly. He was that rarest of creatures: artist and businessman in equal measure. "That's a fair bit of change you're asking for, though," he said. "How can you expect to recoup that?"

"Look, Chas, if I'd ever stopped to worry about what I could recoup, about what possible assurances I had, then I never would've picked up a goddamn guitar in the first place. You can't separate that out of the music that we make, man. The desperation and the power are wedded together. We write songs like we do, and perform like we do, mainly because this band is all we've got!"

He turned back to the console, tweaking a few knobs and letting the current song run its course before responding. "OK, so obviously I can't protest too much since I'm the one who planted this idea in your head in the first place. I just was never clear about how we'd actually accomplish it, what with the travel and whatnot. Maybe your idea is really the way to go. Maybe it's the only way. I'm gonna draw upon the profits from future record sales to make back what I invest in this trip, you understand?"

"Oh, definitely."

"And I think it's time you guys got a proper manager, too," Chas said.

An unfamiliar sensation stirred when I heard that word: manager. Now, you might suppose given my turbulent history with authority figures—which began within my own home—that I'd rebel against the notion of someone else coming in and trying to chart my band's course. I would've expected such a reaction from myself. But instead I seemed to settle inside; it was a strange premonition of peace, of protection. As Chas continued to speak, I just stood in silence, nodding occasionally and marveling at this foreign feeling, using my mind's fingers to sort of delicately probe its edges.

"I've got someone in mind. A lady who's actually very interested, having heard your record. But of course, it's up to you guys."

Hearing that the person was female seemed to articulate my hope more clearly, clarify it. Yes, I know—how convenient, a mother substitute for a guy who hadn't had one since his early teens. But I was also momentarily brought up short by the speed at which everything seemed suddenly to be developing. Management suggested that we were—or were fast becoming—"professionals."

"Uh...who is she?"

For the first time since this conversation had begun, Chas looked pleased. His smile put me at ease. "Maureen Connelly. She lives in Boston, so what I would do is arrange for you guys to meet once you arrived out there. She's in this game because she's a music lover, Brandon. That's rarer in the industry than you might realize.

"I think you might like her. This is her trick of the trade, because I've seen it in action before: When she believes in something, then she has a way of making everyone around her fully aware of her enthusiasm. After a while they're just like, 'Alright—I'll give it a listen!' almost with an attitude of capitulation. And—" his smile widened, "she happens to think that Edge of the Known exhibits signs of, I quote, 'true and rare greatness.'"

For the second time in the course of our careers thus far, we were about to forsake our fragile links to our livelihood—our homes and jobs—and let our fates be determined by the waiting audiences of the world. There may have been an element of courage in this; but then, risks are more eagerly undertaken by those who have little to lose.

"Chas could have the record pressed in a few weeks, and shows lined up not too long after that," I told Tommy and Carlos during rehearsals that night. "There is the big gig in New York. Chas seems pretty confident that he can get us on the bill. And there's supposed to be industry people there...."

"That's all we need," Tommy said. "Our music speaks for itself. Everyone who hears it knows how far it can go. It's at least as good as anything else out there, and a hell of a lot better than most of it. It just needs to reach people!"

There really wasn't much to consider. We were three young men utterly sidelined by the American Dream. Change was our one holy and unassailable god.

The way things stood was the enemy. Following from this line of logic—and filled out by our quite potent imaginations—upheaval, disruption, and recklessness were all welcome prospects so long as they had any hope of breaking through the dead-pale china casings of where we were.

Edge of the Known was ready to unleash our mayhem upon the world once more.

❖

Of course, I couldn't embark upon another road trip without seeing Rachel again. And I hadn't spoken to the Friedmans since making the executive decision to bring her to Robert's house for a visit. I wondered if perhaps I'd burned that bridge permanently.

In my doubt and trepidation, I deliberated over making that phone call for a full week. Then, one Saturday morning, I awoke with the distinct feeling that I was tired of guilt, tired of berating myself for all of my perceived "mistakes"—which had all, in fact, constituted necessary learnings—and I was tired of feeling like a second-class citizen every time I talked to my sister's foster parents. The very vulnerability that had seemed to sap my courage before now cut through, like a bright sword aflame, the din of negative self-talk that had so long cluttered my mind.

I rolled out of bed and scrambled around for my phone. I dialed while the impulse was still fresh, giving myself no pause within which to reconsider what I was doing. *Trust yourself, dammit! There's no Janie, no Saul, no God in Heaven. You're all you've got. Sink or swim, right now!*

Gail's voice sounded tentative, probing. Maybe she was unused to receiving calls at that time of morning. I launched right in. "Hi. It's Brandon. Look…yeah, I took Rachel to see Robert. And I didn't ask you guys beforehand because I'd made up my mind that it was a good idea, that it needed doing, and I didn't want to risk your saying no. So, if you're pissed at me, I understand."

"But I want to point this out, too, that I'm not about to take sides in this thing. Look, I've had my issues with Dad—more than you or anyone else have, truth be told. I didn't create any conflicts when the custody battle was happening and I'm not going to now. I just want to see my sister without having to jump through hoops all the time."

Then I had to settle down onto the edge of my bed, alternately pushed and pulled as I was by internal winds. Part of me waited for judgment to be spoken like a guillotine blade descending on my neck.

But Gail sounded measured and calm. In fact, her voice evinced a quality of softness that I'd never heard before. "I never intended that Rachel should not see her father," she said. "I questioned his ability to raise her, and I think I was right in that. But what you did was fine. Yes, I was a little upset that you didn't ask beforehand. But I also recognize your right to make your own decisions with her. And believe it or not, Brandon, I completely trust you with her."

This was such a novel concept to me that I was rendered speechless for the moment.

"I don't disapprove of who you are," Gail said. "I just don't always understand your choices. And I'm a woman who speaks her mind, typically."

There was a hint of humor and self-conscious irony there that made me chuckle. It loosened me up enough to voice the revelation that hit me. "You've changed towards me. I can't put my finger on what it is, but—"

"I've come to a different understanding," Gail conceded at once.

"Well, *I* don't understand."

I heard reluctance in her sigh. And I guessed its source. Persisting in her present course would oblige Gail to admit that she'd been mistaken, something that she loathed doing. "Rachel has been telling us things. Little bits here and there, but enough so Ernie and I can piece together a story," she said. "We hear about how you'd come home late and yet still be up in the morning before her, have a plate of eggs and toast ready for her when she came downstairs. You'd have her school lunch all packed. Stuff like that. And apparently, this had been going on for years, from what I can gather."

Gail laughed then. It was a sound that I do not believe my ears had ever before received. "She explained to us—" this was broken up by even more laughter, "that the reason why she has so many pajamas is because you give her a new pair for Christmas every year. And the stuffed animals—they're in the garage now, she's outgrown them—but a lot of them came from you, too. And all the books you read to her. Oh, I could go on and on. She's told us so much. And she adores you."

My personal universe began to tilt around the hub of my stunned mind as I realized that Gail—stoic, unsmiling, all-business Gail—had worked herself up nearly to the point of tears.

"Oh, you have to understand, Brandon…when I see someone wearing a skull necklace, and a T-shirt covered with fire and demons and blood, someone wearing a belt and bracelets that look more like weapons than functional clothing…well, I just don't think of that kind of nurturing instinct. It all just looks like violence and hate to me. I think—" she nearly stumbled, "I think I've been a little afraid of you, for quite a few years now."

I felt that her confession deserved a little reverential silence. I allowed the space for it. Then, for the second time during the course of this conversation, spirit moved me to speak before I'd mentally rehearsed the words. "I might be to blame for some of that, too. Maybe part of the reason why I've dressed like that is 'cause I wanted to scare people a bit."

This prompted another revelation from Gail. "We've heard other things from Rachel, too. I know that Robert has been abusive with you, especially when he was drinking."

At this point, I brushed her off. I didn't want to be brusque, especially during this moment when she was showing me her vulnerable side for the first time ever. But I didn't want the shadows of my past home life to become anyone else's affair to either explain or mitigate. It was my reality, and I would define its pitfalls and consequences for myself.

"Yeah, well, that's in the past now," I said. Then I rushed on. "Anyway, I'm going to be heading out on the road with my band again, soon. I don't know how long it will be this time. Maybe a couple of months. I'd really like to take Rachel out again, for some kind of day-long outing maybe, if I could."

"Yes, of course."

"And Gail…it's been real nice to talk to you like this."

She was reserved once more; I could almost hear the sluice gates rise up within her, closing off the free flow of emotion that had so recently frothed over her high stone walls—the walls that (presumably) had protected her for so long. But I didn't begrudge her that. Maybe we'd gone as far as I'd dared, too. And anyway, the truth—once heard—can't be unspoken.

Rachel and I ended up taking a drive out to the coast the following Saturday. Spring's soft air had heated up in the onset of June, but many of her blooms endured; and Rachel drew my attention to every flourishing lilac that she could espy off to the side of the road. She loved all things of a violet hue.

I was still feeling spring's renewal, too; but it was a remote spark, tiny and undaunted, resolute. It was that diminutive voice that wields inexplicable might. It will not give up at the last, no matter how the world might rear its shadows, because it knows the underlying truth of life—the truth that refutes those shadows.

This led to deeper ponderings than I wanted to indulge in at the moment, though. I tried to latch onto something more earthy and concrete, and took something from our last conversation as my cue. "So you know, if you really want to be a singer, then you'll have to do this a lot—travel around, play in different places, sleep in hotels. You think you can manage that?"

"I guess so," she said, simply and noncommittally. There obviously wasn't any imminent decision that needed to be made about the matter now. Then her brow furrowed with reflection. "I thought you said you already had a place to play a lot of nights. Why do you have to go off to other places, then?"

I grinned, while at the same time acknowledging the underlying love in her that was essentially asking, "Why can't you just stay here where you're close to me?"

"If you just stay in one place, then the best you can hope for is to become what they call a 'local hero.' That means that you may have a lot of fans near you, people who love your music, but then what you're doing can't grow any bigger because you keep playing to those who already know about it. The rest of the world never gets to hear it.

"You know, it's not just rock stars who live like this, either. This sort of thing has been going on for a long time. Centuries. Like, troubadours used to travel constantly. They'd even perform for kings. Towns would celebrate when a minstrel came along."

Rachel's eyes widened. "Really?"

"Well, yeah, because that was the only way they got to hear music. Unless there was someone in town who really knew how to play—a local hero." I winked. "They didn't have stereos and digital players. The only way you could hear a song is if someone right in front of you performed it. It was the same with books, too. They were a lot rarer back then. It's more likely that you'd hear tales of the outside world from a storyteller than that you'd read about them for yourself."

"Sounds like it was hard to live in those times," Rachel opined. "I'm glad I'm not there."

I considered this for a moment. "Yeah, but imagine how magical a song or story would sound to you if you'd waited all winter for the warm weather to come so that the minstrel could visit your village."

Rachel stared out the window for a while and then mused, with keen curiosity, "I wonder what they sang about?"

My mind was stumbling through associations, and fragmented connections, so I answered distractedly at first. "Probably places and happenings that most people didn't know anything about. The world was a lot less known back then."

But the insight that I'd stumbled upon was this: The world was no more truly known in our own time. Its surface had been explored, sure. We knew its skin, for the most part. But all that we were really familiar with was our own perceptions, our own stories about it—and oftentimes we were only half-conscious of those.

"That's the same thing that musicians should be doing nowadays," I finished, at the same time thinking, *that's why we're Edge of the Known.*

We arrived at our destination in the late afternoon. The high waves of the full tide, churning up a white froth, were visibly cold even from a distance. The breeze blew right off the water, carrying the tang of salt, sea life, and sailors' longings. Couples skirted along the beach's edges here and there; but it was still early in the season, and few dared swim or surf.

"I have something for you!" Rachel announced suddenly. "It's a going-away present."

Today she was dressed in overalls, of a sort of light periwinkle color, and brown sandals. She'd pulled her hands behind her back. And the smile she gave me made my heart melt and run like heated wax in my chest.

"You do?"

She nodded fervently. "Yup! But you've got to find something for me, to give in trade."

"Well yeah, of course."

It was an odd time for us to be exchanging gifts. My twenty-second birthday had occurred a couple months earlier. And Rachel's ninth, which landed near the middle of July, was more than a month away. But then, I figured it was always a good time for the two of us to give and receive.

Shaking my head in wonderment, I began scouting around for washed-up treasures. Eventually I found the prize: a perfectly-preserved shell of a blue crab, just a tiny hole at the top of its head where a gull had probably poked in order to suck its insides like a salty, gooey cocktail.

Yes! Rachel was a Cancer. I cupped it in my hand and proffered it. "Will this do?" I wasn't too worried about disappointing her. Tomboy that she was, she would no doubt be more interested in this particular find than she would have been with a more elegant conch shell, for instance.

"Sure!"

Then her hands reemerged, and she opened the left one to reveal a sight that tugged at old memories: a translucent, milky-white stone with orange in its heart, much like a tiny apricot sealed within a sanctuary of quartz.

"I brought this home from the playground one day after I saw you, and been keeping it," she explained. "When I told the other kids that you'd made a wish on it, they let me keep it and didn't argue."

I shook my head, trying to dispel my sudden stunned bewilderment. "I know. I remember," I stammered. Was it possible that she actually understood its significance to me? "Do you have any idea how amazing you are?"

She just laughed briefly, and blushed.

So we traded presents then, Rachel cupping her crab in both hands like it was a precious relic. I don't think it'd been dead long, as the shell and limbs were still somewhat moist and supple. I put my new agate in the pocket of my jeans and promised myself that I'd keep it forever.

We stole it from the trolls…. It grants wishes.

Saul had taught me that the trolls were all in my mind. I was beginning to believe him.

❖

So this was the night when Rachel finally got to sit in at one of our rehearsals. I was still struggling to comprehend how Gail Friedman had actually been amenable to this….

Sis was quiet as I walked her down into the Catacombs, soaking up the sight and the damp, musty scents as if it was a dungeon from antiquity. "The guy who built this," I whispered, "had the idea that he could come down here and survive in the aftermath of a nuclear war or some such catastrophe like that."

Carlos and Tommy were already set up and laying down some grooves together. A joyous meeting ensued. Carlos, in particular, was always especially animate on the few occasions when he'd hung out with Rachel.

So there they were, many of the people I loved most, gathered into a shadowed and claustrophobic space that we routinely transformed into our vessel of exploration, a submarine of the astral, with our music. My heart swelled with plentitude and the urge to play.

But before we began, I needed to address the other guys. I was nearly grinning from ear to ear as I showed them the stone Rachel had given me. Carlos leaned over his drum kit, alight at both the spectacle and his recollection of the story behind it. Tommy deliberated for a moment and then suddenly proclaimed, "That's gotta go on our album cover somewhere!"

Although she couldn't possibly have grasped the implications of all that was taking place around her, Rachel was, nonetheless, obviously enjoying her place in the spotlight. She smiled and twisted from side to side with delight.

"Well then, the title ought to relate to it somehow—eh, brothers?" Carlos said.

From there, we launched into a debate about possible symbolism, metaphor, and allusion. Rachel got to witness Edge of the Known's mental gears in motion.

The agate had originally evoked, for me, such phrases as The Light That Can't Be Extinguished and The Light That Never Left You. But we all felt that these were somehow overly lofty phrases to bestow upon an album containing a mere five songs. So we simplified things and settled, at first, upon The Essence. Same essential (pardon the inevitable pun) significance, in fewer words.

Carlos, meanwhile, had been intermittently glancing over at Rachel, who was still cupping the crab mummy that I'd salvaged for her. With the look of inspiration grown to fruition, he suddenly rose and approached her. "Hey, can I see that for a minute?"

Rachel gladly obliged.

"Come here, guys," Carlos bid us. "Brandon, bring that stone. Let's have a look at this!"

So we all crowded around Carlos as he first took the crab and positioned it in the center of one of his floor toms. Then he asked for my agate. This he situated between the crab's claws, nudging them closer so that they seemed to clutch or guard it.

"What do you think?" he asked, with a smile of satisfaction.

The montage was rife with implications. I again thought of Rachel's astrological sign, Cancer, and its associated domesticity. Home. Within the context that we were exploring, "home" and "essence" and "the undying light" all conveyed similar references to our spiritual origins. Then, of course, there was the symbolism of the shell itself—what is visible to the eyes of the world—"guarding" the precious treasure that lies within it. And the agate had a "coat" surrounding its colorful core. Layers within layers....

As Tommy and I nodded in joint eagerness—and Rachel gushed, "Oh! Cool!"—Carlos dug his phone out of his pocket. "Let me see if I can get a good picture of this!"

Tommy pulled one of the lamps closer and kept experimenting with different positions until Carlos got what he felt was his ideal light. He snapped four times.

Turns out, one of the crab's legs had gotten separated from its body during all of this creative abandon. But we were nonetheless all ecstatic when we saw the resulting images. "That's it!" Tommy said. "Edge of the Known—The Essence— with that for a visual."

"Cover image inspired by Rachel Chane!" Carlos added, winking at her.

We were all so exuberant, so enraptured by the free flowing of new ideas, that we had to take some time to make small talk and ground ourselves before we were even able to play. Then Rachel took a seat on my amp (only to leap up again about twenty minutes later when it started getting hot) and we began. My little sister was, of course, thrilled to learn that a song about her was going to be on our new EP.

Throughout the drive home, the winds of mourning wailed in some deep caverns of my mind. The tour that Chas was putting together felt essentially different from our self-made excursion of the previous year. I couldn't shake the odd certainty that we would not, in any way, be returning to the life that we'd hitherto known. The notion carried notes of hope—glimmers of wild ecstasy, even—alongside loss. But I was beginning to realize that my oft-repeated assertion that I had "nothing to lose" was just an artifice intended to hold fear at bay, to engender courage through illusion.

TRUST IN THE UNSEEN

Well, all the shared enthusiasm that'd been stirred up at the rehearsal spilled over into new conversations, which eventually resulted in a final title change for our mini album. Tommy initiated the process, speculating about all the coincidences in our lives that are really too uncanny to even be called coincidences. Then I voiced an idea that Saul had put forth to me, one that I'd now struggled for a couple of years to try and accept: Our experiences don't actually come to us from the world at all, but are really woven from within us. Consciousness comes first, in all things. The world as it is perceived is a mirror for the inner state of the perceiver.

There was actually much more that I wanted to share about this, thoughts that had been provoked by recent experiences, but it all seemed too delicate a matter, perhaps unfit for the rapid-fire style of our band discussions. Anyhow, we phoned Chas at the end of all this and informed him that we had finally settled upon a name: Trust in the Unseen.

The clearest digital image that'd been captured on Carlos' phone still seemed to us an utterly appropriate one. When you think about it, any picture would be suitable for a title like that because the image that you see is, at the same time, dependent upon all that is not seen. Everything exists in relation. There are no isolated worlds or realities. A camera simply freezes one moment of the kaleidoscopic display in flux and then leaves you to speculate about past and future shadows that may be cast by that moment. Every picture not only tells a story, but also evokes countless others—if you let it.

You might just be standing there in the photo with your blue graduation gown on, but that captured instant is, at the same time, poised in a reality within which it affects everything else. We tend to see ourselves as sitting, standing, or lying at the very hub of the universe. And if what Saul says is correct, that we are the authors of this dream, then this sensation speaks truly. We are always at the hub of perception, the choice point from which our world is determined.

Chas informed us that he'd booked thirteen solid dates for us on the East Coast, including a spot at the coveted showcase at Broomstick Belladonna's in New York. This was a scant number of gigs compared to our foray of the year before, but they were (for the most part) more prestigious. We were actually being advertised as a band that was generating a bit of a buzz in the west. There was a sense of curiosity, and anticipation, whereas before we'd simply shown up to play as complete unknowns.

"It begins mid-July, in Boston," Chas said, "and it's gonna take you several days to get out there. So basically you've got less than a month to settle your affairs."

He said that, and I felt the instinctive lash of mortal fright clawing at my insides. I just breathed and let it wash over and through me. It's called a leap of faith precisely because you can offer reason and logic nothing in the way of assurances beforehand. And "faith" was a word that religion had soured inside me, but Saul had helped me arrive at a more expansive, truer definition. Belief in ourselves is the prerequisite for belief in anything else. We were, after all, Edge of the Known. It was time that we returned to our proper place on that potentially perilous frontier, peering forth into the unmapped Beyond.

"These gigs are our affairs, Chas," Tommy told him. "The rest of reality can attend to itself, as it always has."

Chas laughed in appreciation of our collective bravado. He was the veteran and visionary behind a punk band that had defied all the conventions of a movement that was supposed to be devoid of conventions. He knew that we were not making idle boasts. Hell, this was a major reason why he'd signed us in the first place. "If you manage anything like what I've seen you do at Brasserie

D'Alchimie," he said, "then you'll conquer them down to the last man, woman, and child."

We all gave our employers our notice the following day, and told our landlady Megan that we'd pay through July but be vacating the premises even earlier. This was our demonstration of belief in the new paradigm that we were struggling to create. We were convinced that security of any sort would only entice us to grasp at what we were trying to transcend, and to wax nostalgic about what rightfully belonged in the past.

We carried the gesture further by holding a weekend lawn sale, during which time we shifted obsolete equipment, records, books, furniture, clothing, posters, and memorabilia to a throng of Sadenport bargain seekers. The entire time, we felt as avid to shed weight as we did to amass cash.

In the aftermath, we were left with about a week's worth of clothing apiece, our gear, maybe enough books between us to fill one shelf of a case, and a milk crate's worth of personal mementos. By the time July rolled around, my existence was austere even by my standards.

Adolescence is a time, for many of us, when something cracks open inside and our senses suddenly awaken to the perception of new worlds. My sense of the spiritual life—and I mean this as something distinctly separate from any religious concepts that I grew up with—really began there. Maybe that's why it was such a hard era to truly let go of. I missed the intensity of those times, and the prevailing sense that everything was in motion and nothing was certain. I guess the unpredictability of the road was the closest I could come to recapturing that sensation in my adult life.

And so, at long last, we three were staring at a packed van and pondering our course. The house was bare and cleaned. I'd always thought of it as a transitional space, never a home. Perhaps, like Saul insisted, "home" was a place that I carried with me and not an eventual destination at all....

Carlos, with his newly reinstated license, took the wheel and got us onto I-80 E. We hoped to stay on this route for most of our journey east. Evening brought rain. I watched, from my shotgun position, as the sweep of the windshield wipers constantly enacted the erection and demolition of all my dreams.

By about nine o'clock, we'd crossed over into Idaho. The skies had cleared, and we stopped at the nearest gas station to fuel the van and stock up on road rations. The parking lot, in the lambency of the streetlights, looked recently paved. As soon as I stepped out, my phone started vibrating in my pocket. What the hell? Nobody ever called me....

Janie's name on the caller ID smote me to the very pit of my gut. I wasn't ready; I couldn't get ready. There was nothing to do but to answer without allowing myself time to consider what I was doing. Sapped by the old wound, my voice came out hollow and unsure. "Hello?"

"Hey. It's me. I just...I ran into Tommy the other day at the health food store...."

"Oh. He didn't tell me."

The conversation, such as it was thus far, was so jagged and disjointed (no doubt due to our shared trepidation) that it couldn't get off the ground. But Janie pressed on like a trouper. "Well, yeah, he just told me that you guys were going out on the road, playing some shows around Boston and New York, and I wanted to wish you luck."

The high point of our first tour, for me, had been reuniting with her for a brief time in New Mexico. Her presence had inspired me to expose myself to the audience in Albuquerque in a way that I'd never managed before. I paced around the van for a minute, feeling immersed in the warmth that her voice often awoke inside my body. Then I decided to drown this sensation by having a smoke. I fished a cigarette out of my jean jacket pocket. A hard lump had formed in my throat, one that I couldn't speak past.

"So good luck," Janie said, in a voice brimming—almost to the point of spilling over—with all that lay unsaid between us. "When do you get back?"

"Uh, in like five or six weeks," I managed. "But I'm not sure where 'back' will be, exactly. We let go of the house we were living in. We're really just throwing our fates to the wind with this."

"You always were brave."

She gave that word peculiar emphasis, as if it was one that she'd been spending a lot of time thinking about of late. It seemed to have layers of significance: one meaning for her and an entirely different one for me.

"Or desperate!" I returned, and I almost chuckled despite the deep tremors of anguish.

"I think it's courage," she said, even more intently now. Then, after a pause, "Well, if you don't end up back in Sadenport, then I do hope you call and let me know. I don't want to lose touch with you completely, alright?"

"Deal," I said. I was now anticipating the end of this conversation, and torn between the impulse to grasp for her and the longing for some reprieve from the unbearable tension.

"Alright, then. Go bring your gospel to those thirsty souls."

"Thank you, Janie." Even my own ears heard the echo of my heart's former warmth for her.

"You're welcome. Bye for now."

I was grateful that Carlos came out almost immediately and joined me. I craved any distraction. He was clutching a tall bottle of lemon iced tea. He nodded towards the store.

"Tommy's got the rest of the stuff. They've actually got a great selection of metal magazines in there. Rare thing to find these days, bro. He's checkin' 'em out right now."

I latched on to his presence to help me detach my mind from the conversation I'd just had. I took another drag. Then inspiration hit me, the memory of something that I'd wanted to bring up at our last rehearsal. I broached it now. "I had this pretty uncanny phone conversation with Aunt Gail—Rachel's guardian—the other day." I groped for the essence of my puzzlement. "She sounded sympathetic, in a way that she never had before with me."

"Were you being nicer than usual with her?" Carlos suggested.

I smiled. "Actually, yeah. But I feel like there was more to it than that. See, I've just been feeling so tired of having this animosity between myself and others.

Saul told me, over and over again, that I perceive the world as my enemy. I really want to let that go. And I guess my way of doing that lately has been to insist on seeing everyone as a human being rather than as an obstacle in my path."

He pursed his lips in thought. While so many other people just itched for their chance to speak, Carlos really heard you out. This quality made him one of my favorite people to talk to. It suddenly occurred to me that he and Tommy were both unusually good listeners. How lucky was I? "Well, people can feel your attitude towards them, bro. And react to it. They'll hear it in your voice—"

I nodded in acknowledgment, but cut in nonetheless. "I'm thinking something even deeper than that."

Carlos cast me a look that seemed to say that he half guessed what I was getting at, but wanted to give me the space to articulate it for myself.

"Saul says that we're the authors of our lives," I elaborated. "You and I have both heard that a thousand times from him. And I've always found it hard to accept. Also, I've played this sort of mental game where I think that the rule applies to certain circumstances but not to others.

"But is it possible, Carlos, that if I hold to a different image of Gail in my mind, to a different feeling of her, that she becomes, like, a different person? That who she is actually changes, in my experience? Does it happen so literally like that? Because I swear, I felt like that's what was going on."

He took a drink and then screwed his face into an exaggerated "who the hell knows?" expression. "Like you say, it's hard to accept. But I do think that Saul means it literally. People have a lot of faces, you know? The one they show you will depend upon your attitudes and beliefs. I think that's what he would say."

"Right," I acknowledged. "And then, no one is in our lives by accident in the first place. We've attracted everyone to us, for our own inner reasons."

Tommy came out then holding a tall, stuffed paper bag in both hands. On the occasion of our first night out on the road, he was dressed in gray leather pants, tall, pointy black boots, and a long white shirt with fat buttons that reminded me of Celtic nobility. And, of course, even in this heat he still had on the trench coat (albeit unbuttoned) and leather cap.

"Reality is our own creation," I remarked when he reached us. "We've just decided."

Tommy accepted this with characteristic nonchalance. "Can I create a reality, then, wherein I ride shotgun now?"

I was amenable. "I'll drive for a bit—get us into Wyoming, at least."

We'd never actually been through Wyoming before. We'd done a gig in Salt Lake City, on our last tour, and followed it up with a performance in Denver a few days later. But we'd taken a "scenic" route back then, driving south to the town of Salina and then cutting across on I-70 E.

We traveled mostly at night, we three nocturnal, right-brained madmen. But from what I could descry through the general darkness, this was a rugged land, with its mountains of high chiseled grooves filled, in places, with snows that endured even the summers. We rolled down our windows and inhaled the kind of air that one associates with lofty and lonely heights. Then there were low hills, dreaming of peace beneath their blankets of heather, and flats that allowed for miles-long views of the moonlit straight road ahead of us. I quite forgot that we were embarked upon a tour, after a while, and let my reveries carry me to a mythical land somewhere out there beyond the final boundary of stark rock, where nature reigned in her own inviolate harmony.

There is always that war within the heart of the traveler, between the allure of the longed-for destination and the beauty of the myriad places in between—all of which, when you think about it, serve as the object of someone else's most cherished dream in this vast world.

My solution to this particular paradox, as with so many others, was always the same: keep moving. Many leagues now lay between me and my troubled father; and the lost, desperate young people who projected onto me their need for clarity and solace in this confused world; and the woman who I had lost, but who somehow still held my heart clenched in her fist.

Some part of me felt strongly pulled back towards Oregon, where so much was unresolved. Maybe that was my problem—the belief that there had to be resolution.

"Is that part of the Dionysian thing that you talk about?" I asked Tommy. By this time he was across from me at the wheel. "You allow that there will always be the element of chaos in life? You don't try to control it?"

He smiled slowly. If my question had caught him off guard, he didn't show it. "Yeah, don't waste either your physical or your mental energy in trying to put the universe in order. It already is. Just give yourself over to the ecstasy and madness of the moment." He glanced over at me. "But you don't need me to tell you. You take that even more in stride than I do.

"You've learned to translate the inner understanding that's been growing in you, through your work with Saul, into your songs. But you aren't offering our audience any answers, per se. Pretty much, from day one, we've conceived our music as Dionysian. From the Dionysian perspective, life isn't a riddle to be solved. It's an eternal mystery, and—at least insofar as our human experience is concerned—suffering is always a part of it. We learn to cherish things because of loss, because of our awareness of mortality.

"So our overriding goal has been to create a state of rapture—capture it on record and generate it onstage—so the boundaries that normally separate everyone can dissolve. We can escape for a while the state of consciousness that dominates the world and is hell-bent on destroying myth and replacing it with 'fact.'

"Us and the audience, we travel together to reach the innermost source of life, which constantly replenishes the world even amidst all this death and sorrow. So it's not our intent to offer solutions to what Dionysus accepts and bears and rejoices in as part of the rapture of living. Safety or non-safety—Dionysus doesn't care one way or the other! This life that we know, that we identify with now, could be obliterated at any moment. So let's live in the ecstasy of this time, however we find it. That's the principle. 'Be drunken ceaselessly,' as Baudelaire put it."

And with that sermon in tow, I slowly began to give myself over to the intoxication of the road as the sore patches upon this earth retreated behind. There would always be the music within which to dissolve myself and my troubles.

Another couple of hours saw us crossing over into Iowa, with a fair bit of sunlight still holding overhead. Traffic was languid, the road smooth, and the other guys' spirits running high. "Maybe Maureen can put us up for a day so we can catch up on sleep and get showers," Carlos said.

"I just hope that she's cool and that it works out," I said. "I really do. Then we can just concentrate on the music and let someone else make the deals. That's the way it should be anyway. Nobody asks their plumbers if they've produced any transcendental poetry lately, and yet somehow we artists are supposed to master this whole separate world of business on top of our art."

Tommy and I switched, and I proceeded to hammer the pedal for a solid nine hours (minus bathroom breaks) after that. I saw us through Pennsylvania, a patch of New Jersey, and then all the way to Milford, Connecticut.

We arrived there at a magical hour, as the sun was just beginning to stretch her fingers over the Atlantic Ocean, creating sparkles like the dance of a troupe of pixies over the waves. We rolled slowly over a freshly paved street that ran parallel to the beach, and breathed in the sight. I'd seldom beheld sweeter azure than within that arc of sky that leaned protectively over the sea, and her brood of white sailboats.

Aching for a stretch, we parked and got out. An old man, apparently dressed for a day out on a golf course, brown leather cap on his head that somewhat resembled Tommy's, sat on a green bench by the stairs, looking out. He gazed at us with open curiosity.

"Three days on the road!" I said. "We need to move these legs!"

He grinned and then turned back towards the wide ocean, pointing. "Tide's still going out. Will be at its peak low in about an hour or so. Perfect timing. You can take the path all the way to that island there and have plenty of time to get back, if you leave now."

"You're kidding me!"

I conferred with the other guys but we were, of course, of one mind on the matter. "Thanks for the tip!" I called out as we made our way down the stone steps until we reached the sand, pebbles, dry seaweed, and salty air of the beach at low tide.

Soon, I was immersed in the low sloshing of waves rolling over fudge-colored sandbars, the peel of gulls overhead—seeing them scatter before us only to quickly find nearby beachheads where they could regroup. The rocky path, momentarily unveiled by the ebbing waters, was wide enough for maybe six people to walk abreast. The island itself beckoned like a half-recalled sanctuary sprung out of my childhood dreams.

We made some brief exclamations of our wonder and joy. But aside from that, we scarcely talked. We felt the tremendous marshalled power of nature—here in her mightiest bastion, the ocean—to both sides of us, and were utterly humbled.

When we attained the edges of the island, we picked our way amongst the veritable reefs of washed up shells, sponges, and seaweed. Further inland, bushy trees waved in the warm breeze. I turned and surveyed the mainland that we'd left behind.

My reaction was compulsory—a commanding joy. With such eagerness that my hands fumbled at the laces, I undid my boots and removed them, and took one in each hand. "The sea, she demands a sacrifice!" I cried. And with that, I hurled each boot in turn so that it arced up and out, to be swallowed by the beatific and wild waters that cradled the shores of our newfound oasis.

MAUREEN

Afterwards, back on the mainland, we hung out by the stairs as Tommy made some phone calls. First, he got Chas on the line and repeated the directions to Maureen's house out loud so that I could take them down in my notebook. Carlos and I then took a walk while Tommy phoned Maureen, so I missed the minutiae of that particular conversation. When we got back, though, he was shaking his head in semi-amazement.

"Well, I tell you what," he marveled. "She loves us. I almost felt like I was talking to a groupie rather than a potential manager."

My mind warmed and bounced to that revelation. But I stowed the reaction away in order to pursue a more practical point. "Can we stay with her?"

"Well, she's got space," Tommy said, "and she's thrilled to have us. But we'll be sleeping on the floor—or, you know, fighting over the one couch."

"So, business as usual," I said. Carlos nodded in agreement. "And Boston's not too far from here, right?" he said. "We can probably be there early evening? I'll drive the last leg."

I was feeling eager, now, for a place to land. And the fact that Maureen might prove to be an empathetic soul helped me to unwind. The drive was grueling due to our poor timing, hitting rush hour traffic outside of Hartford at about four thirty. In this way, we ended up paying for our excursion out to the island. But the trip was just a little over four hours for all that; nothing compared to my marathon of the night before. Carlos was, perhaps, not the ideal candidate to navigate Boston on account of his becoming newly reacquainted with driving. The city's grid, if one could be content in calling it that, had obviously been made up as they went along. Either that, or it was a deliberately diabolical labyrinth designed to torment visitors. And if you missed any crucial turn—like we did, twice—God knows when you'd find an opportunity to get back on course again.

"To hell with this!" I grated—my way of expressing some sympathy to Carlos. "If I lived here, I'd just sell my car and take the transit everywhere." My vehicle, incidentally, was at that moment sitting alongside Tommy's on Saul's lawn, kept company by rusted engine debris of yesteryear.

"I wonder if it might not come to that," Tommy mused from the back. "If we end up with a manager who lives here, and signed to a label that's based somewhere in the vicinity, then it may well be time for us to relocate."

And this brought us back around to the looming shadow of our uncertain future. I let the fear wash over me, refusing to either fight it or try to explain it away. No thoughts arose to offer comfort or resolution. Was "do or die" the only possible answer to the riddle of my existence, at every juncture? From whence did security come? Victory? Peace?

No matter. I had my Muse, and she would travel with me to any corner of this Earth.

"I'm itchin' to plug in so bad," I said. "It's been too long."

"Two days!" Tommy said. "We're booked at The Hangman night after tomorrow."

"It's a known venue for metal, I guess," Carlos added. "So who knows; we may find an appreciative crowd there."

Maureen lived in an apartment in Jamaica Plain. When we got there, she was standing in her driveway, her whole being spilling eagerness. I guessed that she was about forty, a brunette with the energy and freshness of a young lady just entering college. Maureen was dressed in faded jeans and a black sweater, and her thick curled hair was bound back in a green scarf, lending her a gypsy air.

She jogged alongside and began talking even as we were still rolling up to park. "You guys find me OK?"

Tommy leaned forward to speak out the front passenger window. "Oh, yeah. I figure Boston's gotta be befuddling to anyone who doesn't know it—maybe even for a lot of people who do—but your directions were great."

"Well, I've got chicken kabobs on the grill!" she announced. I could see them smoking on the small red deck that extended from the side door of her building. Apparently, this was a duplex. It had no upper floor.

"That sounds great!" Carlos enthused.

"Yeah, I figured you guys would be sick of road food by now."

And this was as far as we got by way of making formal introductions. Maureen just took it for granted that we knew who she was, and she got to know our names sporadically as we ate and talked. As versed as she was in our recording, this didn't take much doing. It was a simple matter of taking names she already knew and attaching them to the right faces.

I'd consumed very little in the way of vegetables for almost a week, so the grilled green peppers, onions, and mushrooms, all cut thick, were delicious.

Afterwards, as twilight descended and the hiss of traffic formed a lulling backdrop to our conversation, Maureen fetched four glasses from inside and opened up a bottle of champagne. After toasting and taking her first sip, she finally got around to discussing the topic that obviously burned relentlessly in her: our music.

"So, I've listened to your CD, like, a couple dozen times!" she gushed. "And I've been dying to hear the EP. Chas wouldn't send it to me; he said I had to be patient until you guys showed up. Please tell me you've brought copies!"

Tommy answered. "We have."

Carlos quickly added, "Let me go get one right now!"

And then, suddenly, I felt alone with Maureen, as Tommy drifted to the other end of the deck.

Maureen, carried on by her own inner rapture, continued as if there'd been no shift at all in the personal dynamics. "So, I've seen and heard a lot of bands that were reacting to something. You know, they rail against politics, or corporations, the rape of the Earth, whatever. And I definitely see the value in that, don't get me wrong. There's got to be people out there—preferably really loudmouthed people—who are a thorn in authority's side. But what you're doing...it isn't reactionary in that way. And yet it's not escapism either. These songs of yours...it's like you're not so much offering answers as you're trying to get people to ask different questions."

I took a sip of champagne to purchase myself a moment in which to think. Her observation was both astute and thoroughly unexpected. "Huh. I never thought of it in that way. But yeah, I can see it now that you mention it. I guess I always felt like I was asking questions that no one else was. It's easy to find yourself frustrated with what is. Finding a new vision of how things could be, that takes more effort."

"That's real art," Maureen put in.

Her enthusiasm somewhat embarrassed me. "So yeah, thank you," I muttered.

She waved a hand. "Don't thank me—I'm not saying it out of charity. There's seriously maybe a handful of bands that have ever rocked my world like you guys have. What Casts the Shadow? blew my mind."

Carlos had returned by this point, and he and Tommy flanked me, facing Maureen, as if they sensed that she was reaching a crucial pitch. And apparently she was. "I'd really like to manage you guys, if you'll have me. I won't make a bit of money off of it until you do. I just want to help expose your music to the widest audience possible."

I finished my glass. Here's the thing, man: I was a slow burner. Passionate, yes; but I liked to stir it up to a steady flame first. Maureen was forcing me to move at an unaccustomed speed. "God...I knew it was coming, but I didn't expect you to pose the question so quick."

Maureen held her ground. "It's my way to be forthright. I hate to sound trite, but life is short. Besides, I'd be kicking myself for a long time to come if somebody else snatched you guys up first."

"You've managed bands before?" Carlos asked, coming to my rescue with a practical question.

"Two," she said. "Well, one band and one solo performer. And not to toot my own horn here, but I was the one to score you guys the gig at Broomstick Belladonna's in New York. I've got as good an ear for the street buzz as any music fan out there. And then, if you ever attract label interest, I can think like a lawyer on your behalf."

Tommy had been quiet this whole time, no doubt maneuvering through a stream of inner calculations that couldn't be verbalized until he hit pay dirt. Me, I resorted to the only thing that I knew how to do when faced with unknown variables: I followed my gut.

"You believe in us," I said. "That means a hell of a lot to me."

Maureen smiled. "That's the main part of what I do. I won't take on a band that I don't like. And if I pass on one that goes on to sell a million records, I still won't regret my decision. I'm in this for the music. And you guys have the music! I'll go open another bottle while you guys think about it." And with that, she pushed the screen door aside and disappeared.

We conferred at once. "What about going into it on a trial basis?" Carlos offered. "We let her act as manager to the extent that she wants to—say, for the duration of our tour out here—and we just don't sign anything for the time being, no formal contract."

When Maureen returned, we all took a moment to toast and drink. Then we proposed our open trial period idea to her. She was almost laughing in her eagerness. "Look," she said, "that's all I'm asking for anyway. Just give me a chance. We don't have to sign anything. Just take some time and see what I can do for you before you consider somebody else, is all I ask."

"We don't actually know any other managers," Tommy acknowledged.

"If I have my way, then that's the way it'll stay," Maureen said, with a merry twinkle. "You guys ought to know this business by now. It doesn't always attract the most upstanding types of people with the noblest of motives."

"No, it doesn't," I muttered.

For some reason, my gaze wandered down to my feet then, and I saw the bits of sand from Charles Island still clutching at the spaces between my bare toes. I thought about my old boots, past their prime of life anyway, sunk into a deep saltwater drop-off where the shifting tides probably had them half-submerged into the ocean floor by now.

Maureen, following the line of my sight, cracked a grin. "Perhaps my first order of business should be to find you some serviceable footwear?"

❖

I won the coin toss for the couch, and I slept beneath the slow breath and peaceful emanations of two jade plants and one spider plant. I'd spent some time beforehand idly wondering why someone as attractive and vivacious as Maureen was without a man in her life, but I suppose she filled the void with floral companions. Each of the windows on the opposite end of the room were kept company by a trio of plants as well.

I awoke with the vague sense that I had dreamed of being a chameleon that crawled in and out of the various pots in search of insects. "I" the lizard had ended up having to settle for some droplets of water.

Maureen continued to woo us with good food that morning: giant mushroom, pepper, and cheese omelets with heaps of hash browns.

"Let's pretend to be undecided, so she keeps cooking for us!" Carlos chided, loud enough so she could hear from the kitchen. Maureen giggled.

About twenty minutes later, as we were finishing our plates, she said, "So you probably ought to set up in the living room and rehearse for a while today, don't you think? So you don't go out to the gig totally cold tomorrow?"

We were, of course, amenable, especially as she seemed confident that it wouldn't aggravate her neighbors so long as we did it in the afternoon. Maureen ended up watching almost the entire rehearsal, and she was laughing with delight and bouncing in response to every number.

"Oh!" she gushed at one point. "There is this truly great thing that rock 'n' roll can be, but we so rarely get to experience it. This indescribable magic…we must respect and honor it when it comes. And it's here! You guys have it!"

This was also the occasion upon which we discovered that our prospective manager loved to smoke grass. She confessed that she oftentimes would suck down a joint before she even got around to coffee or breakfast. I was tempted, at first, to attribute her lofty and oft-times elliptical praise to this very fact. But as you get to know Maureen, you realize that her manner of speaking never changes much one way or the other, intoxicated or sober—although she did settle into a calmer and more free-floating state of mind when she was high.

And she, for her part, was astounded that none of us cared to indulge. "Oh, God!" She actually blushed. "I just assumed, from the sound of your music— particularly some of the spacey moments—and the surrealistic kinds of lyrics you write…"

"That's a natural thing," I told her, striving to smile to put her at ease. "I get high from the music. Or, you know, I can slip into a different state of mind at other times, just naturally, too."

"There's all kinds of routes one can take," Tommy elaborated. "But basically people get involved in various different methods of trying to get at something that's already alive inside them. But that doesn't mean that we—" he swept his arm to indicate each of us, "harbor any kind of judgments about it. I mean, if smoking gets you there, then that's all good with us."

Maureen smiled. She still looked slightly abashed. "OK, cool." She pointed to each of us in turn. "And just know that it will not affect my bookkeeping skills!" She was so good-natured and forthright. Seeing her discomfort made me ill at ease. I glanced at my bandmates.

"Look," I said, "how 'bout we get past this thing right now, alright? We all know that we like Maureen and feel comfortable with everything that's happening here. I think it'd even be safe for me to say that our meeting wasn't an accident, that we can all sense that…let's just say that we're partners, alright? We're in this together now. Like, what other kind of sign are we waiting for?"

Carlos and Tommy just kinda pursed their lips and nodded, accepting this casually; and in that moment, I think we all realized that our minds had been made up, that this was all inevitable, but we'd just been trying to exercise some sort of "professional" aloofness until this point.

"Alright, Maureen," I said, turning to her, "you are now the manager of Edge of the Known, hands-down the craziest band on Earth. How does it feel?"

She literally quivered with delight. "Like all my years in this nasty business have finally come to fruition!" She waved to us and simultaneously retreated backwards. "Alright. You guys get back to playing. My head's swimming with so many ideas now, I gotta go write them down!"

We'd practically played our entire repertoire by this point. Before starting in again, we all shared a look, a communal exchange that communicated our collective satisfaction with this turn of events.

Tommy summed it up: "Even if we found someone with twice the business sense…seeing as there's no way they'd possibly match that kind of enthusiasm, I'd still say let's stick with her."

❖

Many of us go through a good portion of our lives feeling like our identity ends at our skin, the boundaries of the flesh. There's times when I'd be sitting in my room—particularly when in a bleak mood—and it'd seem like those walls comprised the uttermost limits of my personal world.

And yet, there is a deeper part of us that is never separate at all, not from one iota of Creation anywhere. Even if you wanted to be entirely pragmatic about this, you'd have to admit that our physical being is composed of the stuff of the earth; that we share the same essential air and water again and again; that we all dip down into the same wellspring of dream.

When I played music, that was when those artificial mental barriers were most likely to dissolve. That's how the miracle oftentimes unfolded at the Catacombs: First, I'd tune into this sort of cascading flow of mind and spirit that emanated from Tommy and Carlos. It swept me along to a certain juncture, an existential crossroads that was like a meeting place of souls. We don't often think about it consciously; but deeper down, we know. We came here to fulfill certain purposes, both individually and in the sense of a vast cooperative adventure. All of us who're alive in this time are passengers on the same cosmic ship.

And this is where Edge of the Known truly found its groove. Sometimes, my awareness spread out to encompass everything around. I became sensitized to the memories of trees and the feeling sensations of shadows. I felt the warm inner intent of Saul's work; there was a light that emanated from his house, and I knew it was created, in part, by all those others who perceived it as an oasis, an abode of spiritual solace. The grassy yard supported this bastion, gave it a place to be. It knew and loved those who lived upon it. The trees on the outer edges were more than sentinels: they were caretakers; guardians, even. Although they might follow their own unfolding thoughts over the sap-movement of decades, they still radiated compassion for those of us whose lives are more fitful and transient.

Under the influence of rhythm and beat and poetry, I could feel the vast undercurrent of love and cooperation that upholds the world. When we played The Hangman, I descended into this level of awareness.

I remember that it was one of the most diverse crowds we ever played for. Peering into the dancing pit I'd see a middle-aged man in a suit, a young woman in all black (right down to her lipstick and eyeshadow), and a fresh-faced kid in a college jersey and new jeans with a pint sloshing in his upraised hand, all weaving around one another. The onslaught of the music conveyed the essence of the journey we were proposing; and the audience, with their bodies and voices and minds, conveyed their eager assent to it.

Older songs assumed new significances for me that night. The image of The Hanged Man from the Tarot—upside down, mostly naked, his old and gnarled limbs demarcating the number four—ran along the dark wood ceiling in white. The lighting in the bar was subdued, perfect for our twilight shamanic tendencies. And I got the feeling that a good portion of the crowd was there to hear music.

I can scarcely describe how I'd ached, throughout all those restless hours on the road, for volume, electricity, release, clamor, and the feeling of the stage beneath my feet. And those feet, by the way, were bare. Maureen had loaned me a pair of her sandals, but I left them off for the performance.

And this is how the three of us had learned to weather the storms of life with our own brand of sanity intact. Reality intensified to a keen edge, like the tip of a welding iron, when I played and sang. That white-hot tip performed the act of alchemy. Pain was churned to ecstasy; fear to exaltedness; loss could spark the flames of victory. As I had often roamed amongst the trees alongside Saul's property while rehearsing in the Catacombs, I now communed with every human being within The Hangman. Most of them stayed in the club and worked through to their own personal catharsis and recognition before the end. I've never discovered the proper word for what we did, for what Edge of the Known's art really was. I probably never will. But we applied it with a fine brush that night in Boston.

The exclamations and praise that was hurled our way created a din almost comparable to the musical ferocity—and how does one respond to that? I packed up my guitar, left it on the stage for the moment, and stumbled off like a drunken man. People tried to engage me. I nodded, smiled as best I could, and kept walking. I'd never relished that aspect of being a performing musician. It's not that I longed to get away, necessarily. I'd just already expressed everything that was within me. What could I add to the conversation now?

To my right, a maze of tables cluttered the space between me and the Old West-style swinging doors that led to the restrooms. Every table was full, and easily half of those eyes were on me. To my left, and up ahead, was about three car-lengths of bar. All those seats, too, were occupied. Whatever the owners were planning on paying us, we'd no doubt earned it from them.

I squeezed into a spot, ignoring the glances to both sides of me, and ordered a scotch and water. About five minutes later I moved on to beer—and secured a seat that a young blonde smilingly offered me on her way out.

Maureen found me there a while later and began showering me with ebullient praise. The drink was working in me by then, mingling with the sweet simmer of post-performance adrenaline.

With my characteristic lack of tact, I skipped preliminary explanations and dove right into trying to describe the feelings that her presence provoked in me. "I lost my mom when I was a teenager. My dad was hardly a father to me, and I ended up raising my little sister like she was my own kid. I'm just saying…if you start acting motherly with me, then there's a chance I'll get carried away in return. Just warnin' ya."

She'd frowned in sympathy while I was talking. But she grinned once I finished, and spoke with the most affected politesse. "I promise to always behave with the proper professional detachment, Brandon!" Then she gave me a quick peck on the cheek and wiggled my ear. Withdrawing, she screwed her face into a mock-scandalized expression. "Well, most of the time!" she amended.

TO HAVE CHOSEN THIS TIME AND PLACE

So my spirits were lifted for a brief time, thanks to the audience's reception at The Hangman and Maureen's loyalty. Before long, though, the inherent conundrum of touring started leering at me. No matter how well we went over with our audiences, in the end—once the dates were done—I would have to return to my old familiar nightmare. Was this creativity's sole efficacy, then…that it could simply stave off one's awareness of the Abyss for fleeting instants? Was I just sculpting sandcastles before an oncoming tide every time I wrote a song, or climbed onstage to sing?

Back home, Maureen declared her intention to tag along for the rest of the tour. "I'm there for everything to do with band business from here on. I'm Edge of the Known's nanny. That big black beast of yours isn't going anywhere now without being stalked by my little yellow buggie!"

She apologized for having created a lot of extra driving for us on account of how the itinerary was arranged. What she was referring to was the fact that, having first fulfilled our rendezvous with her, we now had to backtrack to honor a date in New Haven, Connecticut and another in Hartford before returning to Massachusetts, rather than hitting the cities in their logical order. I assured her that I really didn't care. Bringing music to the people isn't a linear quest to begin with. No map can tell the real tale of it.

At any rate, we figured that we could get to New Haven in well under three hours.

"And a good thing, too," Maureen said, smiling, "because we're gonna have to get up at the crack of dawn tomorrow—at least by your standards!"

307

"What do you mean?" Tommy demanded, his eyes sharpening in the way they often did when he was confronted with something that he didn't already know.

"Oh, surprise, surprise," Maureen said. She knocked her pipe on her palm, examined the debris and, finding nothing to salvage amidst the ash, blew it off. "This date that I lined up for you isn't in a club. It's actually an open-air festival in the park. Two other bands are on the bill; you'll play in the middle. This happens in the late afternoon—four-ish, I think. I'll have to check my book. But the event is pretty popular. This could end up being the biggest audience that you've played for so far."

A change of scenery felt welcome. We wondered how well our sound would carry outdoors, though. We'd only done something like this once before, at the Pumpkin Festival in Jennes where I'd first met Janie. Back then, our repertoire had still been dominated by loud, abrasive, and primitive metal—with Tim Peralta, not Carlos, providing the propulsion. It was difficult to envision how the subtler musical dynamics that we'd developed since then would translate in an open-air environment.

"You do realize that we're more used to staying up 'til dawn than waking up then, right?" I said.

She cast us all an impish glance. "Sure you guys don't wanna puff? It'll help you sleep…"

The weather was gorgeous, both for the drive and for the festival itself. They'd set up stands with carnival-type viands along the broad mowed field. Scents of fish, fried dough, onions, and peppers mingled in the hot afternoon air. People of all ages and stripes were meandering, tight-knit families to poor, lonely-looking drifters.

The stage had a tall black satin backdrop proclaiming the local promoter of the event. After creating our backline of equipment, we milled about, sampling the food (it's detrimental to stuff yourself before a performance), and talking.

I can't recall the name of the band that played before us, and I didn't care for them. They were too polished and professional: total anathema to my ethic of putting honesty and passion before virtuosity. What does it matter if you hit and hold all the right notes, if your sound is designed to be nothing more than crowd-pleasing and your moves are obviously scripted for video? Their front man, with his fashionably long hair and black leather lending him an air of harmless rebellion, even made a self-conscious spectacle of himself by hopping off the stage during one instrumental break and dancing with some of the little kids in front.

I almost felt sorry about having to obliterate this safe and tidy musical universe that they were trying to construct. My impatience and irritation roughened the opening of our set—to its benefit. To test the mic, I wretched from a dry hollow in the pit of my solar plexus, loud as I could. Then I punctuated this tortured sound by hammering on a raw, distorted E chord. Back and forth it went. Then Carlos began a ponderous roll, Tommy insinuated his deep pulse into the mayhem, and Edge of the Known unleashed itself upon New Haven.

Sometimes, music carried me past the borders of civilization and into the perilous wilderness....

After about an hour of this sort of audible catharsis, though, my deeper world-weariness and sorrow rose up to claim me. I could literally see this mood ripening to fruition, much as a landscape is shadowed by thunderheads rolling in on a cold front. Although the volume soothed and relieved, some deeper disturbance still lay unresolved.

I finished singing "Breath of the Deep," a number from our first record, and wavered. The audience was in black and white. My inner sea change had washed away all color. I pounded on a single power chord as fast and hard as I could and then stopped dead. I repeated this; and yet again.

Machine-gun, rapid-fire riffing finally released me from enough rage that I could actually speak. "I could blame my mom for dying! I could blame my father for the beatings! I could blame my school for trying to shove me through the mental meat grinder! Or all those people who seem hell bent on destroying this good earth and making sure that we're all stripped of every kind of hope and comfort before that end comes!"

The audience, easily a hundred strong, was predominantly quiet by now, milling and confused. And yet they were still waiting. I suddenly remembered that I was talking to real people, human beings with struggles and sufferings as real as my own. My voice settled into a more natural cadence.

"I could do that—and, you know, I'd find a million reasons to back it up and feel justified for saying it. It's all true, right? And yet, if I repeat that mantra, cling to it as my truth, it ain't gonna do anything but perpetuate that hell forever. Because I'm gonna keep creating the very thing that I'm trying to be rid of!"

I tried to let the murmurs, the scattered admonition here or there to "just sing another song, man!" all wash over me. Then, *screw it*, I thought. I told those couple of hecklers, "Hey, just because I'm being paid to play this gig doesn't make me a human fucking jukebox!" That steadied me.

"There's only one thing for it," I went on. "One way out. One escape path. I have to just say it, admit it—that I chose all this. I wanted to be an outsider, see. I wanted to be denied all those tried-and-true roads that society loves, because then I'd be obliged to find my own answers. I wanted to ask the questions that no one else seemed to be asking so I could create the art that no one else was making.

"So, no, I don't attribute my breakthroughs and victories to God, and I don't blame demons—or whatever other label you may want to use for dark forces—I don't blame them for my suffering. My life is my own creation."

I knew in that moment that I'd chosen my circumstances—not consciously, of course, but on some deeper level—because I wanted to use them as an impetus for my soul journey. I might not have had the motivation to undertake that journey, otherwise. At some time—perhaps "before" time—all of us decided upon the paths that we would take in this life. If we can look back over the course of our lives and say, "Yeah, I chose all those events as a backdrop against which I could hopefully grow and fulfill myself," then we can lay claim to what is really ours already: the power to create our own reality.

"And so then, what you get out of it is this!" I forewarned the audience.

And from there, my friends crashed in behind me and we delivered what was probably our most impassioned rendition of "Sea Breakers" ever. Because this was our last song, we milked its tail end with improvisation that included even a languid bass solo from Tommy that made my throat clench with the force of all my suppressed weeping. We wove soundscapes of feedback. Eventually, this settled into a quiet, steady groove, initiated first by Carlos. It felt natural for me to begin scat-singing a bit of doggerel that I'd scribbled down on the dashboard of the van (whilst somewhere in Iowa, I believe).

Guilt speaks in a voice from your past
Says, "No plea-bargain for you
I'll give you back your natural grace
just as soon as your whole life's through"

There were a couple other verses like that, and I repeated them all several times. This quieted by increments…until, finally, our show was over.

It was scarcely eloquent; but then again, it was one of the most incendiary performances we'd ever delivered. And I noted, with some satisfaction, that the applause was a lot louder for us than it'd been for the previous, video-prepped band.

❖

The pendulum's backswing occurred at Gladys Pub in Hartford. We made the mistake of showing up early. The owner, a man in his mid-fifties named Elmer who looked and dressed like a cab driver and chewed a cigar, insisted that we go on right away. There were scarcely half a dozen people in the bar and the sun was still shining.

"What the hell for?" we collectively asked.

He wouldn't budge. So we did a sound check, launched into a number, and he immediately stalked over to the stage waving his beefy arms over his head. Too loud. Christ, we ended up turning down twice in order to please that turd. By the time the gig was properly underway, too much of my passion had been sapped by this unnecessary aggravation. I ended up hammered that night, sitting in the front seat of the van with my forehead against the dash, crying for June, Janie, Saul, Rachel, even Kayla from Brasserie D'Alchimie, who'd used me at least as much as I had her, while everyone in my entourage took turns trying to console me.

I nursed my hangover as we drove out for our second engagement in Boston, at a place called Grim Reaper Penthouse where virtually every punter was dressed in black from head to foot. Maureen had told the owner that we were the heaviest band on Earth, and so he'd just booked us at once out of curiosity. None of us were feeling particularly high-spirited, but we managed to be professional and deliver the goods regardless. Besides, our collective unease and simmering frustration was probably more of an asset than a detriment when we were faced with an audience that was hungry for extremity.

Poor Carlos had to play both of our dates in Springfield with a fever. He refused to sit them out, but soldiered through with a clench to his jaw that suggested that his face might crack if he released it. Fat beads of sweat rolled into his eyes as he drummed, and he cast them off with furious shakes. *Hell with it*, I thought. *If he goes down, we all go down—that's how this band works.* As it turned out, though, he was the only one in the group to get sick. We did opt to splurge on hotels, though, giving Carlos his own single-bed unit as a way of quarantining him. Although, by this point, we had some gig money to throw into the pot, this particular gesture left us in Maureen's debt.

By the time we arrived in Provincetown, Rhode Island, our drummer was rallying his strength. I noticed that the poetry-heavy numbers from "Trust in the Unseen" drew particularly favorable responses. That inspired me to stay up late and write more poetry. We'd played our best set (in a packed bar by the name of Turkish Delights) since the festival in New Haven.

312

From there, we shot over to Manchester, New Hampshire, serenading the long, gray hall of a VFW bar and its small constituency that was largely twice our age. Feeling restless with the repetition of our established songs, I requested that we take a couple of our "open-ended" improvisational pieces and really stretch them—to the extent that they constituted our entire set.

This spontaneous approach opened up so many enticing avenues that we were inspired to try it again in Concord. At Taylor's Bar, we were spurred on by a rowdy audience that was there to drink and dance on a Friday night. And we abetted them by holding to a chugging rhythm rife with attitude, occasionally working up to crescendos that would inevitably crash and collapse into dissonance and the wailing of amplifiers.

There were certain songs that we would never declare finished anyway. If the universe ever ceased to move and change, then it would die. An element of unpredictability must always be preserved.

We'd been finding wooded and secluded areas where we could park the van and sleep through the late night and morning hours while we were in New Hampshire. Following the performance at Taylor's, we shelled out a bit of money for a camping space so that Maureen could pitch her little orange tent and avoid having to pay for a hotel room again.

"So what are we doing after this, anyway?" Tommy asked, over the gentle crackle of the small fire that he and Carlos had just started. "I forgot. I know I've got the itinerary stashed in the van somewhere, but…"

"Two gigs in Portland, Maine," Maureen said, rubbing her hands a few feet above the flames. She looked even younger in the truculent yellow glow. "Then, Chas and I figured you guys could mellow out in the glorious Vermont summer before you go do your big showcase. The shows are small, but it's worth visiting the state, seriously. We lined up three appearances: Burlington, Montpelier, and Stowe."

It was hard for me to believe that we'd already completed half of our dates, and in little over two weeks' time. Maybe it was my own inner turmoil that had made the days and performances and the onrush of new faces and landscapes all swirl and merge. Aside from this, I didn't want the tour to end. I didn't want to go back to my life of before.

I suppose a spell was cast on me by the fire, the baroque shadows, the quiet vigil of the ash trees, and the clear stars above them. Somehow, the flames summoned to my consciousness yet another memory of Saul and his words. I'd once asked him what he thought about humankind's "chances."

The darkness that humanity is experiencing at this juncture can, at times, seem insurmountable, I know. But it only appears so to the extent to which we deny ourselves. After all, it's our own creative power that has woven the tale of this age in the first place. The soul does not manifest where all is hopeless, and the inner self never sets us up to fail. These are myths spun from the mind, and supported by the same limiting and erroneous beliefs that keep so many of us from trusting and speaking our own truth....

"I don't want to save the world so much as I just want a goddamn happy life," I mused aloud.

I started pacing from one side of the fire to the other. "I'm not looking for any kind of response to that," I said, striking a hand down in response to a protest that hadn't even been uttered. I was just frustrated, and needing to move it through my body. I was caught in a war between my need and the part of me that judged that need as a sign of weakness. "I'm just sick of fucking riddles without answers!"

"I think your creativity rises up out of that very tension," Tommy said, in a tone that seemed to add, *Dude, you just gotta live with it.* "If you ever 'answered the riddle,' then you'd stop asking those very questions that lead to your poems and songs."

"That makes a lot of sense," Maureen said. She looked and sounded unusually somber. "You probably don't want to go too far in either direction. If you totally make peace with the world and adapt to it, then you'd lose that unique vision that you have and would not have nearly so much to say. But then, if you give yourself over totally to the vision—and this is what I think is the bigger temptation, for you—if you did that then you'd forget to share it with the rest of us. And what would be the point of even having it, then?"

I was grateful for my friends' input. I really was. But I was wound up inside and I kept pacing. Thoughts exploded, and their shrapnel fragments sped off in all directions at once. I tried to sift through the remnants of inane fears and the fossils of old, bankrupt beliefs.

"But all this pain and sacrifice for what?" I ranted. "I'm just this fucked-up guy in a world populated by billions. And everything else is so goddamn big. Governments, banks, corporations, religions…"

It always circled back to that, for me: the futility of individual action in the face of massive systems and institutions. They had claimed everything. They were ubiquitous and invincible. And not only was I insignificant, I was also too busy battling myself to be a threat to anything else in the world.

"Remember what you and me have been learning about, though," Carlos said. "What you're saying seems true only if you're looking on the surface and not trying to go any deeper. Think about it. There's another source. Like, a government doesn't really create wars. It's the unresolved aggressions and pent-up frustrations inside us that lead to wars. And it's our feeling, our belief that we're separate from nature, that puts her in jeopardy. It's the fear of our own power that creates whatever kinds of oppression we might experience. The power structures in the world, these things you're talking about, they just mirror that internal battlefield."

I nodded, but answered noncommittally, in an exhausted monotone. "The answers are inside us. They're not out there in the world." Then I met his eyes. "I probably remind myself of that twenty times a day. Somehow it never sticks, man!"

He lifted his hands in a gesture of supplication. "We're working against a whole lifetime of believing the exact opposite."

Maureen was sitting on a short log that she'd dragged out of the woods. She lit and began puffing pensively on her glass pipe. "Well, I don't know about all that," she said through a long exhalation. "But I do know that the great artists really do change the world. Don't think for a moment that they don't."

"You just can't even start questioning the worth of yourself and what you're doing," Tommy put in. "It's challenging enough to make it in the world, on your own terms, when you *have* belief."

"And as far as making a difference goes," Maureen said, her voice a little high-pitched and disjointed from the smoke, "I think there's a lot to be said for seeing a guy wrestling his demons and working his issues out onstage. A lot more people struggle with these sorts of questions than you probably know. Your perspective isn't nearly as crazy as you think. And," the fire was getting hot now, so she rose off her stump and retreated a few steps, "I guarantee you there's still people in Boston talking about your performance."

Then, for a while, there was just the crackling of the fire, the light, the trees overhead, and the breeze. Carlos took a long time mustering his courage to address me again. "But just the issue of belief doesn't solve it all, does it?" His voice was low, tentatively probing. "Because if you see life as your creation, then you gotta think that you somehow fractured a relationship you had with a woman you loved, right? And that your poverty, and the lack of recognition for your work, is somehow a reflection of your own feelings of worth. And even your family life... It hurts, having to see it that way, huh?"

"You think?" I said, in a voice so high it nearly cracked. It was one part wry humor and one part near-hysteria. I decided to move on, right then—force the pain down and enjoy the night as best I could. "Hey, let's toast those hot dogs!"

SHATTERED REMNANTS

The night that we camped outside of Concord really cemented the feeling that we were a family unit now—us three guys and our new manager. I carried this comforting familial sense with me when we played in Portland, Maine. Thanks to road construction, and our own lazy attitudes beforehand, we barely made it there in time to honor our first engagement.

This was at an all-ages space, a converted warehouse that reminded me very much of the one adjacent to The Samurai in Sadenport where Edge of the Known had played our first-ever gig. I always relished the chance to play for younger people, many of whom I figured could relate better to the turbulent and confused emotions that I reflected in my songs.

We sold nearly fifty records at that show: a personal record for us. We insisted that Maureen accept a good chunk of the resulting money as but one token of our appreciation for all that she'd done for us. Though we didn't say so aloud, we all knew that she needed it, that her efforts on our behalf were slowly draining her slim resources. She, in turn, insisted that part of the money was going towards proper footwear for me. I wound up with some durable leather sandals.

We spent the rest of the intervening day at the beach, witnessing the most frenzied waves that I'd seen since leaving the West Coast. After exhausting ourselves on Portland's friendly streets, we returned to the beach that night to pass a whiskey bottle around until we finally sank down, one by one, to sleep.

The following night, we lugged our gear into Creeping Vines of Wine, one of my favorite clubs of all we ever visited. It was pretty nondescript by surface appearances, and dark. But the stage was high, carpeted, and prominent. And it was there, no doubt, that all the offbeat, eccentric, radical minds of Portland had made a tacit agreement to meet and celebrate their collective oddity with the kind of Dionysian revelry that befitted the venue's name.

You could feel intellectual fecundity in the air, the kind that questions, sifts, and discards everything in its restless quest for a more expansive description of the world. It wafted over me as soon as I walked through the door.

"We're gonna do a song that I wrote one day in the park for my sister. She was sitting on my lap the whole time. And I wish she was here so I could tell her how much she means to me. I know she knows it anyway, but I never get tired of saying it."

This was the first, almost consciously-recognized warning sign that I was racing towards my breaking point. I could hear it in the way my voice cracked. I rolled into the gentle intro of "Sister/Satyr," Tommy and Carlos joining me just before I reached the first verse, and the cold, dark waves slowly rolled back. But that didn't last long. Thinking of that day in the park also brought Janie vividly to mind: hand in hand with another man, ostensibly moving on from what we'd known and shared and hoped for. My voice came out raw as a dying soldier's. The audience whooped in response to every elongated high note. How often does it happen that one man's torment is a spectator's entertainment?

In Burlington, the following night, I let myself get talked into swallowing a chunk of hash that looked like the bit-off tip of a brown crayon. We'd set up early at Lester's; and then some hippies, who'd been slowly nursing pints at the bar, started chatting me up. Eventually they invited me to go for a walk. Maybe I was fed up with my psychic civil war and longing for any kind of alteration of my mental state. For whatever reason, I got excited when the drug was proffered.

It hit me about a half hour later, as we were making our way back up the hill. I began questioning things that I normally took for granted. I couldn't converse at all, because I'd travel through four tangents that branched off from whatever had originally been said. Then I'd reply, and it would bear no relevance in any kind of context. I was completely in my own world, man. Those guys didn't care, but I was growing paranoid. I couldn't do or say a damn thing without judging myself for it the next moment.

❖

Maureen caught up with us about two blocks from the club. "Oh, OK," she said as she espied me. "You guys aren't expected on quite yet, but I was worried 'cause I couldn't find you."

Being a seasoned stoner, she of course immediately marked my reddened eyes, and the other telltale signs, and smirked.

I managed to introduce my friends. "Ernie. Jake. This is Maureen. She manages us. She's great."

They began making amiable greetings, which I cut into by announcing, "I can't sing tonight."

"What? Why?"

"I can't do it like this. I'm too high. Hell, I feel too exposed even talking. I got no armor, you know?"

"Shit—I'm sorry, man!" Jake said. He sounded genuinely remorseful.

"Nah, it's not your fault," I said. "I react differently from most people I know. I know my limits, and I should've just spoken up. But you gotta relax and let go in order to sing good, you know? And right now I'm just analyzing everything in the world at light speed and I don't know how to get loose."

The four of us walked back to the club together, the others trying to cheer me up as if I was battling depression rather than drowning in the mad sea waves of my frothing unconscious. I always lived too close to those waters for comfort as it was. I didn't need to be chemically exploding the last few buoys that were left there to keep my sense of identity afloat.

When I found Tommy, I explained my predicament as best I could. Luckily, he knew me well enough to fill in the gaps. He was probably the only one there with the necessary experience. "Well, we only have two choices, then," he declared. "Either we stick to my songs, and stretch them out as much as possible with instrumentation, or else I sing yours, too."

"Could you?"

"Sure, why not? I know the words by heart. And none of it's out of my range."

No doubt, he knew that there was much more involved with it, though he didn't say so. My songs had all arisen from a very personal and vulnerable place: hence my fear of the moment. Once again—for easily the thousandth time in the course of my life—I was profoundly touched by Tommy's loyalty.

"I think that way feels best," I decided.

The more things veered towards crisis, the more pragmatic Tommy became. "Alright, then. We'll stick to the same set list and I'll just handle the vocals tonight. I'll go tell Carlos."

While I waited, some old words of Saul's drifted up from the barren grottoes of my mind.

Fear never tells us the truth. It's like that desert lizard that puffs itself and fans out its headdress in order to look twice as big and ferocious and scare off predators. Fear is just fighting for its own existence. And it's got an infinite arsenal at its disposal. Think of all the opportunities for tragedy that our world holds out. Think of all the ways that you could die. But the truth is that you and I will die when and how we choose to. And so what is the basis for our fear?

I was convinced that the gig was a disaster—until we got about ten minutes into actually playing it. Then the music conveyed a much different story, one that contradicted both guilt and fear. The vibe was powerful and righteously upbeat. The crowd—there must've been forty or fifty bouncing around—were wildly appreciative. And above all, I was profoundly moved by the sincerity in Tommy's voice.

He sang all the songs like they were his own, and I doubt that anyone there could've guessed that these words had originated in two different minds. He did me a deep honor that night. His vocals opened up a window through which I could glimpse what these words and melodies had really meant to him throughout all those months—years, now—of rehearsing.

How could you really tell, with a guy like that? He'd always just sort of nod his head at the end of a run-through, indicating approval but not much else. Tommy was erudite and loquacious when dealing with concepts, but reticent around open displays of feeling. And I never judged him for that, because I knew that those feelings were there. They just found their outlet through other channels, like his music.

So Tommy was our band's front man that night, and I enjoyed letting him have the spotlight. I poured my aching, longing, too-full heart into my guitar, all the while thinking about the incomprehensible journey that had finally brought us to this stage in this time.

This was enough to help me rally myself for some backing vocals…and then, finally, I claimed my own mic for "Sensations of Spring Grass." This served, tonight, as our showstopper.

I rolled up my guitar cord with a smile on my face. A gig that averted meltdown and snatched triumph from the jaws of catastrophe was even better than a gig that went full fury straight out of the gate. I realized that I loved every place that we'd played. Well, the pub in Hartford still stuck like a thorn. But, hell, the miseries make the joys sweeter; that's just the way of it. And the arms of Dionysus, which sweep us out of this world's woes and into those Elysian Fields that we've been convinced of ever since childhood, embrace it all unequivocally.

I'm sure it must be obvious by now that me, Tommy, and Carlos spent a hell of lot of time together: in our shared house, at rehearsals, in the van…. When duty relaxed her grip, we were all often eager to fly down the nearest open alley. We could hardly be blamed for that. But on this night, we moved as a unit. It had something to do with our having weathered a potential crisis in our own inimitable style. It called for a shared drink or two.

"So am I gonna have to sing all the songs when we get to Montpelier, then?" I chided.

"Maybe I should start learning them all, so that we have a plan C!" Carlos suggested.

Then, finishing our second round of drinks, we piled into the van and followed Maureen to the capitol of Vermont. In the aftermath of our previous epic excursion between the West Coast and here, this trip passed like a flickering intermission. I soon espied the gold plated capitol building, with proud and unassailable Ceres atop it all bathed in moonlight, as we pulled off the highway.

Our gig at Ulysses' Bar and Grill marked the final demise of my black spray-painted Telecaster, the guitar that had been with me from the beginning, since the days of my first awkward chords and feeble attempts at composition. I remember that, for a while afterwards, I felt bereft as if from an amputation. Even though its splintered fragments lay in a damp green dumpster behind the club, I still seemed to carry it around with me at times like a phantom limb.

The destruction was difficult to comprehend, or even believe. It was ironic, too, that it should occur at the culmination of a great performance. We'd had a rowdy audience that relished our heaviness and reckless delivery. Our set was particularly aggressive. But see, it was often those exultant moments that would then trigger feelings that were most difficult for me to cope with.

As that last resounding chord was still ringing in my ears, and reverberating in the club…as Carlos' symbols hissed like snakes in a skillet and a whoop of affirmation hit us like a jubilant wind from the crowd…I realized that none of this changed a goddamn thing. The recognition of the fact, and my physical reaction, came almost simultaneously. I lifted my guitar high with both hands and then brought it down on the stage like the last chop of the ax that felled Rome.

But I destroyed nothing except something very dear to me, resolved nothing. I merely fulfilled my own self-uttered prophecy of alienation and failure. *Right on, you rock 'n' roll cliché!* It was neither shamanic nor rebellious. There was nothing for it but to complete the desecration, beat that body and neck into fragments. Of course, if I'd been more lucid, I would've realized that the original damage could have perhaps been mended. Now it was too late. It no doubt looked exactly like what it was: a lost young man's futile meltdown.

Of course, a lot of people clapped and hollered anyway, because a destructive spectacle—much like a man's agony—can serve as entertainment. Perhaps I could've immolated myself for an encore. The owner, Kristin, a slim middle-aged redhead who looked like she'd been settling barroom brawls since she was a teenager, was furious. Fortunately, she discovered that no real damage had been done to the (admittedly ramshackle, anyway) stage. My guitar had capitulated much more readily than the floorboards had.

"What the fuck?" she demanded anyway.

I was still trembling and staring at the wreckage in incomprehension. "Do I look like I've got an answer? Christ, it's my guitar! I slept with the fucking thing!" Then I glared at my bandmates, as if they'd confronted me too. "Have I ever claimed to be sane? Huh?" My face wet with tears, my words as fractured as my beloved instrument, I gathered the pieces and stalked off.

The steel bin was nearly empty. It clanged, hollowly, when the fragments hit, and then was silent again. I stared at the gnarled jungle of pain, guilt, confusion, and resolve that had been my adolescence. I gripped the top of the dumpster with both hands and shook as I wept some more. I was sure that some part of me knew what I was grieving for, but I couldn't consciously name it.

No one bothered me out there. In fact, I started hearing music again: Tommy and Carlos were improvising a bass and drum groove. I managed to smile. I guessed that they were doing it to support me, to keep the people in there entertained so that I could have some privacy and peace. They meandered into a series of riffs that we'd experimented with in rehearsals but never managed to evolve into proper songs.

Just then, my phone started vibrating in my pocket.

Not now!

I probably would not have answered it if it'd been anyone else in the world. But I checked the number and recognized it. Saul.

I drew three slow breaths to settle myself. Him calling me here, now…it could not bode well. My thumb seemed to depress the green answer button on its own accord. Then I risked casting a word into the Void. "Hello?"

"Hi there. It's me, Saul." His voice was so steady, with the underlying grit of sand, that it betrayed nothing, no hint of intent or of what was to come.

"Hi Saul," I stammered. Then I went for broke. "I just smashed my guitar, my dear sweet guitar, to bits. How are things?"

"I'm sorry to hear that." Somehow, he did not sound surprised. Then, with a breath saturated with controlled emotion, he went on. "Listen, I'm taking a turn right now being the one who needs, the one who hasn't got the answers for everyone else. OK? So, since you asked how I am...well, I could really use a friend."

To this, my soul in response cast aside all my personal woes for the moment and insisted, *nothing in the world matters now but this!*

"I'm here," I said.

Saul chuckled—more an expression of embarrassment than humor, it sounded. "I guess what I'm saying is that I'd really love to see you here, if that's at all possible."

"What? Like, immediately?"

It was here that my mental feet tread over empty space and slid into a chasm. The sense of dread lurking within me since he'd first rung was finally articulated. There could be only one explanation. Saul understood full well where I was, what I was doing, what was at stake. He knew the significance as thoroughly as my own bandmates did. Therefore, only a single circumstance could've possibly pushed him into such a state of desperation that he would actually make this request of me.

I swallowed hard. "I'm sorry, man. I'm here for you. I'll do what I can."

I glanced down at the remains of my guitar once more. It looked like the ruins of my whole life. But perhaps even that did not compare.... Then, with a wrench of my insides, I realized that the wreckage of my instrument signified the end of the dream, at least for now. No New York. *Hell with that!* I berated myself. *What is that, alongside his loss?*

"I gotta tell you though, Saul, that what I can do may not be anything. I'm on the other side of the goddamn country, broke—"

"I'll pay for it," he said at once. "If I get you the ticket, will you come?"

Still I wavered, much as I loved Saul. I couldn't stop thinking about the imagined culmination that my band and I had worked so hard toward—that we deserved, goddamn it!

"I've got the loft tidied up for you," he persisted. "I can pick you up at the airport and I can send you back out that way if that's what you want. It'd just mean a lot to me…if you could be here for a time."

God. June!

"Ah, hell—what's that matter, anyway?" I was trying to combat the void with a brusque outburst. "Didn't you hear me say that my guitar's in shambles anyway? The tour's over. We're done. At least for now. So yeah, just get the ticket. Burlington's the closest airport to me right now. Just tell me where to be, and when, and I'll do it."

"Thanks so much, Brandon. I fully realized what I would be asking of you when I called. Don't think I take this lightly, OK?"

I hung up with Saul just as Maureen, Tommy, and Carlos were making their way across the parking lot to meet me. The street facing the club was noisier now with the bustle of drivers who'd been cast adrift by last call. Saul's bedtime in Oregon equaled a late night for us in the east.

I pocketed my phone. They came to a standstill a few paces from me, and I could hardly meet their eyes. "I have to go," I muttered.

Then I forced myself to look up at Maureen, the one person there who I feared might have a difficult time comprehending. Her eyes were wet. What a dear soul, I suddenly realized. We were so lucky; many bands would kill for a manager who actually cared like she did, who invested so much of herself.

"I so badly wish I could've given you something more substantial in return for your faith," I told her.

She shook her head, strove to deny the self-condemnation beneath my words. "I'm sorry," she said. "No judgment, just…so sorry." She swiped her eyes. "This is just a setback. There are going to be other opportunities."

This was also her way of saying that she would've purchased me another guitar on the spot if she'd had the means.

"Where are you going?" Tommy asked. There was an edge of bitterness in his voice.

"To see Saul. He's flying me back for a few days. He needs my support right now."

"Now?" Tommy took a step forward, as if to grab me and give me a shake, and then—mastering himself visibly—retreated. "Don't you think this may be a good time for us to show solidarity as a band, stick together and process what's happened and plan our next moves? This can't wait at least a couple days?"

"Jesus, Tommy!" I fumed. "The man saved my fucking life, alright? If he needs something from me then he's got it, no questions asked. He called before he even knew about the incident tonight. Knowing what we're here for and how important it is, he still made this request. Now what in the hell do you suppose that means?"

Tommy nodded slowly, casting his gaze to the dirt by his boots. "June," he acknowledged quietly.

Swept on by fierce and contradictory emotions, I bent my tirade around to strike at myself again. "I fucked this up! And it's done. This is what I do, man! Every joy that tries to spring up in the desert of my life, I strangle it before it can bloom."

"Oh, to hell with that, Brandon!" Tommy retorted. "This band wouldn't even exist if not for you. I couldn't have done it alone, and I doubt I could've ever done it with anyone else."

Hot tears raced down my cheeks. Goddamn it, I was sick of futility, of doubt—sick of the darkness always winning. Grief bore me down until I was steadying myself on my bent knees. June! Oh, Saul!

Someone's arm was laid across my back. Carlos' forehead touched mine. I felt Tommy's hard shoulder. I'd trusted it, relied upon it, since way back in high school…. Gradually, I realized that the four of us were caught in a football-style huddle—swaying, breathing as one.

"You're chasing after a ray of light that never left you, dude," quoted Tommy. That provoked in me a quick, sharp burst of laughter in spite of everything.

But I became aware that there was another thread within this convoluted emotional entanglement, one that had escaped my notice whilst I'd been consumed by my own private pain. I lifted my head and met Carlos' steady eyes. I needed clarity, and retreated from our communal huddle. "Did you know about this?"

I sensed several different—and perhaps even contradictory—replies stirring in him. But for all of this internal tumult, Carlos didn't waver. "Saul and I have talked, yeah," he said.

Perplexed, I shook my head. "I don't get it, though. I mean, it's none of my business—and excuse me if I'm trespassing here—but you've been seeing him almost as long as I have, and more consistently, too. I know there's a lot of love between the two of you. How come he didn't ask you to go?"

Carlos was normally real transparent. Thoughts, words, and facial expressions were so often perfectly aligned. I wasn't used to this from him, these long reflective pauses and measured responses. "Look, bro…I think this is something that maybe you need as much as Saul does."

And with that, I had to be content.

They all accompanied me to the airport: Tommy driving, Carlos riding shotgun, and Maureen in the way back. She'd insisted that I take the seat, so now she was kneeling, steadying herself against the occasional bumps with one hand on Tommy's amplifier. She flashed me commiserating looks so often that I finally had to smile back at her.

"Well, there were some triumphant moments," I allowed. "New Haven, Creeping Vines, both Boston gigs…" The van rumbled on, perhaps reflecting on how the greater part of its duty was now accomplished.

Saul had booked me a flight on a Friday morning—ten a.m.—which meant that we'd had to rouse ourselves at even a normal person's crack of dawn. You can't ask for a clearer declaration of loyalty and love from your friends than this. I'd opted to forgo coffee. Instead, I sipped a beer on the ride, intending to drink another once I was in the air, and then hopefully nap through the five-and-a-half-hour main flight—the one from Boston to Sadenport.

Not a word was uttered about the showcase or my guitar. No one wanted to rub salt in the wounds.

My joy had fled along with my hope, for the most part, but I was not altogether unhappy. After all, I was flying from one oasis of love to another. I was aware of that. Disappointment made me see it more clearly, somehow. Despite the overall penury of what I'd thus far called my life, I'd always been fortunate with friends. In that sphere of endeavor, I was uncommonly wealthy. I'd not have gotten far, otherwise. Maybe this would be enough, in time, to renew the dream—or to paint a new one.

Tommy made for the parking garage. He ended up finding a space on the third floor. "Despite the ungodly hour," Maureen said, "at least you're flying out of one of the smallest and mellowest airports anywhere."

I nodded, too overcome with sudden emotion to speak. Then we all got out. I stood by the van. "We might as well say goodbye for now, right here, guys," I said. "I'm pretty useless for conversation at the moment."

Tommy leaned in and clutched my shoulder, catching me completely off guard. "So it makes the most sense if we wait for you in Boston? We're agreed on that?"

I nodded. "Saul already got the ticket. This is a quick trip. I'll be flying there tomorrow night." I tried to fathom the logic behind this, and shrugged. "Maybe he's worried that I'll be overwhelmed if I stay too long. Or maybe he figures he'll want space to himself by then. I don't know."

We'd all thrown our fates to the wind, trusting in the unknown—in the Unseen, like our EP so proudly proclaimed—and that leap had thus far landed us in a place where we couldn't even grope our way forward in the dark anymore.

It was surreal to the extreme, walking into an airport alone and preparing to board a plane that would take me back west. I lumbered through those broad halls, the great existential junctures of greetings and farewells, like a phantom. The last time I'd been in an airport I'd raced to sweep Janie up in my arms. The memory made my insides feel like a monstrous cavern of ice. I deliberately opted for stairs over escalators in an effort to exhaust myself. But I only had to pass two wings to reach my terminal. I tried to swallow my scowl as I was searched at the gate. I knew that those uniformed guys with their flashing and beeping wands weren't to blame for my world of woe.

I was grateful to be seated next to an old woman from a world fundamentally removed from my own. She made pleasant small talk for a few minutes and then resumed reading her Victorian drama. Sometime later, I got my ridiculously overpriced beer and downed it fast. This drew her attention again.

"Does flying make you nervous?" she asked. Pretty intently, too. Her blue eyes were windows into a sharp intelligence that I had underestimated.

"No, it's not that." I broke eye contact, aimed my words at the seat in front of me. "There's just been a lot going on. Thought I'd sleep through my long flight to escape it. I won't bore you with details."

Her chuckle snatched my gaze back to her. "I've probably got four good friends left in this world of an original twenty," she said, wrinkling her nose sassily. "But you apparently think I wouldn't understand someone having a rough day!"

I laughed nervously. "I guess I'm just not used to people caring." I let out a long breath that was laden with tension and suppressed tears. "Ah, hell. I was here with my band. We had a gig coming up—it could've been our big break. And I smashed my guitar. I was just upset about a lot of things. Losing this girl who I love, most of all. And now I'm leaving everything behind because a friend needs me."

She laid a pale and wrinkled hand on mine. Her skin was cool, but her presence was warm. "If you're going there for that reason," she said, "to be there for a friend who needs you, then you won't go wrong in the end. God takes note of things like that."

"Ah, man, don't even tell me about God," I groaned. "I'm tired of even hearing that word." I turned away again.

She squeezed my hand. "Then don't use it. What's it matter? We've got all kinds of different words for the love of the universe. And then, of course, 'love' itself is a word." She leaned towards my ear to whisper. "Doesn't matter what you call it. What matters is that you trust it."

I stared off for a moment, reeling with a symphony of inner echoes. "Christ," I breathed at last, "you're an angel!"

When I turned to her, groping for more to say, she just nodded in a way that told me, *don't knock yourself out trying to explain the unexplainable, kid.* She reminded me of this exchange about twenty minutes later, as we touched down in the Boston airport and I stepped out into the aisle. "Find your own word for it!" she called.

"I think I already have," I returned with a smile. "The Unseen Source."

"Ah, poetic!"

❖

I had another beer at a pub inside the terminal and then, thankfully, was able to catnap during my flight westwards. In fact, I awoke as the captain was announcing our final descent into Sadenport. That approach took fifteen minutes, just long enough for me to waken fully. The sun told me that it was early afternoon in Oregon.

I bought a sandwich and orange juice in the food court and sat down at a table for a while, watching the people pass back and forth and not thinking of much in particular. I wasn't feeling ready to see Saul. He'd once told me that we can only see as deeply into others as we've dared to peer into ourselves. What that meant to me, in that moment, was that my inability to grieve was a liability. Saul was grieving, and I didn't know how to meet him in that place.

I'd spent years—my adolescent years, prior to knowing him—damming up the channels of pain inside me. I'd cried a few times over the course of a week when Mom died. Then I'd set upon a quest to drown my anguish with volume, aggression, and screams. Hell, in a way I felt like my father had died back then, too. But I'd tried to disown that part of me, too—the part that mourned the loss of him. It was only since I'd begun working with Saul—going on two years by this time—that I'd begun to recapture, reawaken, my own capacity to feel pain.

He deserved my empathy.

Probably two hours passed, in that purgatorial terminal where it felt like the same people surged and receded like a shifting human tide, before I finally phoned him. As before, Saul sounded like a man with a white-knuckled grip on the wheel of his emotional vessel. "Do you want me to pick you up?" he asked at one point.

"You know, I don't think so. If that's alright, I mean. I could actually use the exercise. And I know I can make it to your house within an hour or two from here." I was still stalling. "Thanks, though."

Saul seemed eager to accommodate my wish. "We'll plan on about two hours, then?" And in hindsight, I can hear the peculiar emphasis he gave to the word 'plan.' "I understand. I get the itch to move after sitting that long, particularly on cramped plane seats."

"Two hours it is, Saul." Finally, I mustered the courage to expose some of the truth. "I need some time to get my head together." I couldn't help but laugh, a bit sheepishly, at the absurdity of calling attention to my own personal struggle in the face of his tremendous loss.

But Saul just said, "I understand. I'll see you soon, then," and hung up.

❖

My route from the airport to his place mainly involved cutting across the eastern outskirts of the city, which meant that I didn't pass by any familiar landmarks: no Brasserie D'Alchimie, Samurai, Pioneer or Robert Chane's house. I was grateful for this. I wanted to step lightly across Sadenport's verges, not get pulled into the emotional complexities of my life there. I'd only come for Saul, this time.

I began pondering whether he'd extended his invitation to anyone else. Surely, I wasn't his one true friend, the only person he could turn to in his time of need. At the same time, he knew about my aversion to crowds, particularly large groups of strangers. He'd remember, right?

No doubt there'd be a gathering for the funeral. I suddenly realized that I'd forgotten to ask when that would be. Maybe I'd thought of it and had just been unable to utter the word.

I turned onto Glassbrook Road, a long two-lane strip with yellow heather flats stretching out from both sides. I saw maybe one car every five minutes. I smoked to pass the time. June had followed a healthy regimen, and look where it'd gotten her. My momentary callousness made me tear up.

The road joined up with Townes Street, and I could see Saul's brown shanty—at least, the roof and chimney through the trees—as soon as I made that right. It wasn't far, now. As I drew closer, though, I was drawn into even deeper perplexity than before.

My father's dirty tan truck was parked in the driveway. And he was standing by it, hands driven in his pockets, waiting for me.

What in the hell?

My face must have framed the question, nearly screamed it, but he didn't answer until I was about ten feet away. "Hey there. Saul told me you'd be coming. He scheduled a session with me this evening. Be 'bout ten minutes or so, we're gonna start."

I pushed down the throng of questions—and my utter befuddlement—and forced myself to look at Robert. He was a bit leaner, his face more defined, as if privation—or confronting some bitter truths—had flensed the opulence from his cheeks. They had some color, too; color proper to sun and life. And he regarded me warily. I wasn't used to that. His brain had typically been too inebriated for that degree of self-consciousness in the past. With an inward start, I realized his expression and body language, his whole being, expressed utter sobriety.

Spurred by unnameable regrets and longings, I began. "Look, about that last phone call…"

He waved away my guilt, dispelled it with the look in his eyes. "You've got every right to be angry, and to vent your anger the way you did. A man's got no business treating his son the way I've treated you these last few years. And I've beat myself up for it, too. But that don't get me off the hook. And it don't undo it, either."

For a minute or two, I was too strung out on adrenaline—the backlog of adolescent outrage and denied fury—to speak. "There's a part of me that would just love to…" That's as far as I could get. But no doubt the way that I alternately clenched and opened both fists conveyed my essential intent.

"Yeah. I know." His voice was a curious admixture of petulance and stubborn resolve: his old and new selves, battling it out. The newly-emerging part won out momentarily. "Look, I can't wipe away what's done. I know that. All I can do is try harder, strive to be better, from here on."

I realized that my indignation wasn't going away because it was a rightful part of me. I allowed it to live and breathe. "Well, if you still want contact with me, then I guess I have to say that I won't settle for less than that. I've been fighting hard to build a new life for myself, and there's nothing that says you necessarily have to be a part of it."

He just acknowledged this with a nod. I tried to soften my glower. Then Robert Chane glanced at his watch—a new acquisition, I noticed. He'd had it cupped in his hand, as the cuffs of his shirt were pulled up high—presumably to hide his razor scars.

"Welp…it's about that time."

By quiet consent, we made for the front door side by side. Both the air and the light had cooled. The yard was quiet, and the crickets were distant. Saul's house looked peaceful and beatific, as if it was oblivious to loss. I stomped up the three steps, opened the screen, and rapped on the wooden door behind.

When it was pulled back, some ten seconds later, I saw June standing there.

I remember that I gulped when I witnessed the vitality, the raw health and presence, manifested in her. Then Saul's head appeared over her right shoulder.

That sonofabitch, he couldn't even conceal the mischievous gleam in his eye! Probably he didn't try. But he adopted a mask of professional solicitude.

"Robert," he said, "you wanna come in?"

My father slowly moved past me.

"Have a good session, Dad."

Why shouldn't I say that? What the hell was real anyway? I glanced up again. There was no buttress now between my eyes and the impossible, effervescent fact of June. She moved down a step and let the door close behind her. The two steps that remained put her only a bit higher than me, as I'd retreated back to the ground.

"It looks like they'll be busy for the next hour or so," she observed, in a voice like the soft essence of spring. "Shall we take a walk?"

JUNE

We began making the same circle around the property that Saul and I had once traversed. It occurred to me that I'd first heard about June's illness during one of my walks with Saul. Neither she nor I said a word for the first ten minutes or so. June was dressed as if to work out in the garden: worn blue jeans and a sturdy brown flannel shirt rolled up to her elbows. Her nearly-white hair was tied in a ponytail. Try as I might, I couldn't in any way account for her presence there beside me.

I finally gathered enough stray strands of consciousness together to voice the obvious. "I thought I was coming here to your funeral." This, in turn, opened the floodgates to an irrational surge of anger. "Alright: I don't know what the hell is going on! If Saul lied to me, if this was all a goddamn game from the beginning...!"

"Oh dear," she said. "You mean about my sickness? No, no. Oh, Brandon, we would never do such a thing—not to you or anyone else."

Then she bit off a laugh. Her eyes sparkled like a pixie's in a flight of wild fancy. "My husband does have a bit of the trickster in him, as I'm sure you've noticed. But no...the pain, the danger, all of that was very real. Often, I'd wished that it would just kill me. There was a fire in my tissues that made my corner of the universe feel like Hell on earth."

She glanced at me then, in a way that allowed me to see the agony that she referred to. "I tried to escape it in sleep," she went on, "and would wake up to pools of sweat that had collected right where my back met the sheets. It got to the point where Saul would constantly have to clean it up, because I had no energy anymore. No, Brandon, nothing that he told you was any exaggeration at all. I was truly on death's door."

The ground was damp, almost spongy. Sadenport must have been doused while I'd been away. We stopped a short distance from the Mason's pond, where Saul had once revealed to me the true source of power and knowledge: myself.

"Obviously this has been profound for the both of us," June said. "My recovery, I mean. It was a path of learning that was outright harrowing at times. But as much as I feel the urge to apologize in the face of your shock, I have to say that I agreed with my husband about this. He felt that there could be a powerful lesson for you here, and that it might have its greatest impact if you were not told before you came."

Then she spread her arms wide and smiled, in case I'd failed to notice the way that her very being offered an ebullient cry of "Yes!" to all of Creation. I shook my head, as if in an attempt to awaken from a dream that I couldn't rationalize. "You healed yourself!" I stammered.

June nodded. "I risked everything these last several months. I let go of all of my supports and went inward, searching for the true source of that illness. Assuming that the cancer—I didn't even want to label it, see?—but assuming that it was my creation, then what convictions and imaginings and fears of mine had given birth to it? That was my question.

"My body ailed because my spirit did not reassure it. I did not tell it, 'This is your place to be,' and so it found no reprieve. I no longer chose life. And my body was going to continue to suffer, eventually giving up the fight entirely, until I committed to either being here or there, so to speak."

Her somber moment of reflection granted me another glimpse into the grim struggle that she was describing. "But I won't beat myself up for all of that anymore," she said. "I think the pain was probably necessary. The mind must at times be shaken free of what it expects, so that there's room for the unforeseen solutions to emerge; and also so that they're not discarded."

No words were adequate to convey my amazement. "Without chemo, drugs, surgery…" In silent acquiescence, we resumed our walk.

Although June was a head shorter than me, I felt daunted by her new stature. She exuded a kind of quiet surety and strength that surpassed any of my previous conceptions of personal power. "I have been very afraid, Brandon," she confessed, as if contradicting my assessment. "The truth is that I was so scared to be here...that some part of me preferred the slow capitulation of terminal illness to all other possible fates. So that was the work that needed to be done, the place that needed to be confronted. But I didn't only have to uncover the reasons for my fear, see. I had to make a decision, to commit to physical life in the first place. I had to find it within myself to affirm the beauty and value of it."

She glanced over at me and I saw that, although the spritely sparkles were still there, they were mingled now with fleeting reflections of rue. "There were many moments when it seemed easier to just surrender to the beckoning of death," she admitted.

I nodded. "I do understand that part. There's been times when I felt like it was only my love for Rachel, or maybe Tommy and Carlos, that kept me here."

"You've suffered a lot, and have had little support in your life for any of it," June acknowledged. "I know a bit about that, just from what my husband has shared with me. I think he sees himself in your struggles, at times. And in my case...what I was really fantasizing about, of course, was a world I could go to where my fear couldn't follow. But what if my unfinished work pulled me back here to face it all over again?" She laughed. "Oh, that thought was a motivation at times!"

I swallowed hard. I wasn't ready to explore the implications of this idea, and I knew it. "I get what you're saying," I told her after some hesitation. "And I don't mean to in any way minimize what you've gone through and overcome. But...cancer. God. I mean, it's cell growth run rampant. It takes over the other cells and literally, like, devours your body."

It took my mother away! I know what it does!

I stopped moving then. I literally couldn't nurture my perplexity and navigate my course at the same time. I pushed both hands through my hair, and rubbed my war-torn head. "I just don't see how you can combat something like that with your thoughts, or by confronting your fear, or embracing life, or—"

Grinning like an impish child, June leaned over and pinched my left arm. "Don't you believe Saul when he tells you that what we are in this world is our own idea of ourselves?"

"Well, he's never used those particular words, but—"

She pinched me again, harder this time. I gasped, and flinched, before I could even catch myself. "Even many physicists are learning that this 'matter' here is not nearly so solid as it appears," she said. "Someday they will have to acknowledge that it follows the dictates of thought and belief, that consciousness comes first in all things. Now, if this applies to our 'oh too solid flesh,' then surely it applies to germs, viruses, and cancers? It was not so much that I combatted the disease, Brandon, as that I learned to stop creating it in the first place. Now, do you feel the difference? I had to change paths. That old way, the way of fear, was already dead for me—had been for a long time."

I tried to breathe it all in, to let it settle within me. Something was digging its way beneath the very roots of my world. I felt my intimate foundations tilting, shifting. "Wow. I guess, well, I never really took what Saul said so literally." Then I forced myself to look at June, to focus on her and accept the physical proof, there before me, of everything that she was telling me. "So you're no longer afraid?"

She pursed her lips as she considered her reply. "I know that my life is mine. It is not given me by the world, or society, or fate." We started walking again; and as we did so, I could literally see her sink down into a deeper level of personal truth. "It may be that there will always be some fear in me, so long as I remain in this physical world—with all the thorns of life!" She giggled. "But another part of me also knows now, without question, that fear does not reflect reality. I exist in a safe universe."

I realized, in that moment, how nearly everything I'd ever heard since early childhood had, in one way or another, essentially argued for the opposite view.

"My illness had accomplished precisely that," June went on. "A precious gift had laid wrapped within all those layers of pain. And once the prize had been snatched, the accompanying pain was no longer necessary."

By this time, we'd reached the front steps once again. Telepathic exchanges still deciding our joint course, we sat side by side on the second step. There, the full emotional realization of what had occurred here finally swept over me. I turned and impulsively offered an embrace that Saul's wife accepted and eagerly returned.

"Oh, June! You did it! It's a miracle!"

One of her hands worked at the knots of tension in my back. "It really is," she whispered. "*We* are a miracle."

A few minutes later, the door swung open and Saul and my father emerged. The sun was beginning to dip below the level of the trees and the light was a mournful kind of cool. I stood up and met the eyes of my mentor, the man who'd taught me to steer my life away from the Abyss.

"I hope you've enjoyed all this!"

"Enjoyed?" Saul grinned. "Why speakest thou in the past tense? The evening is yet young!"

June moved up the steps to embrace her husband sidewise, as Robert came down. Saul took a moment to acknowledge his wife, a brief glance that nonetheless seemed to encompass all that they'd suffered and transcended during the course of this, their most trying year together. Then he looked back at me. "You probably ought to get going," he said. "I have a feeling that June isn't the only one who wants to talk to you today."

I felt my eyes narrow with suspicion. "What, you aren't done with surprises and secrets yet?"

Saul affected a look of mock surprise. "Me? Oh, I assure you that I had only the most peripheral involvement in this one."

I couldn't sustain my questions. My aching heart was too loud; logical concerns couldn't compete with that level of volume. I felt my eyes itch and moisten. Then the wet warmth began sliding down my cheeks. All of this was overwhelming.

June! Somehow, she'd claimed final authority over her own life and death. And goddamn it, I was crying while my old man was watching me. But who the hell cared? My throat was so clenched with emotion that my words took twice as long to emerge as they normally would have. "I have a feeling that, somehow, this changes the whole world for me."

Saul lifted an open hand as if in salute. "And you've got the rest of your life to figure out exactly how." Then he gestured towards his barn. "You're all set up in there with bedding and some food in the cooler, by the way. Make yourself at home, like you did way back when." Then he ended with an echo of his previous ambiguity. "That is, assuming you end up still wanting to sleep there."

Then he and June said goodnight to my father and me and disappeared inside. I walked with Dad back to his car. He looked raw in the way that I'd often felt, coming out of a session with Saul. This kind of work could dredge up poltergeists or nuggets of gold, depending on where you were along the path.

He stopped, with one hand on the door handle, and finally met my eyes. "Damn," he said. "That guy has a way of making you see your whole life in a different light."

"Yeah," I muttered. "So does his wife."

As if on cue, my phone started vibrating in my pocket as soon as I got inside Saul's newly-refurbished barn. Come to find out that there were electric lights in there now; but as I was clueless about it at the time, I didn't search for switches. The glow of the phone would have to suffice. I fished it out, opened it, and then trembled when I saw the number.

Janie.

Christ! How rubbed raw was I going to be before this day was done? I gave myself no time to think, lashed my will into motion, and answered. She plunged right in as soon as she heard my voice. "OK, you were right! I got scared. I made choices out of fear. You don't have to rub it in my face anymore because I'll just admit it to you! You told me a really heavy thing, alright?"

I veered. My dizzied mind required that my body find a place to land. She wasn't just sobbing; she sounded nearly on the edge of hysteria. I couldn't find a chair anywhere, and so settled for propping myself against the iron woodstove. "Whoa…take a breath, Janie. Easy. What's going on?"

"What's going on? I turned my back on something beautiful in my life, the first man I probably ever really loved, because of fucking fear! And I hurt you! God, I know—"

"Shhhh…" This was the second conversation of the day that I somehow couldn't believe was even happening. "Don't beat yourself up, alright? If there's one thing that I've learned over this past year, it's that guilt is a useless emotion. You don't spare anyone pain by punishing yourself. And besides, like you said, I did tell you something pretty disturbing. And you had no way of knowing that I'm not really that kind of person."

"But I do know; that's just the thing." Her very words were wet. "I believed in you. I believe in you now. But I didn't follow it, act on it. I let the things I was scared of turn me away."

In a strange way, her emotional extremity enabled me to forget all about my own bereavement. I set aside my wounded ego. I only wanted to be there for her. "Well, I forgive you, if that's what you're asking. I'm able to do that because I can forgive myself. Seriously—my whole life shouldn't be judged by one of my worst acts, during a very unclear and fucked-up moment. When you think about it, that kind of self-condemnation ends up doing even more damage than the original offense. But anyway, enough about me and what's in the past. I never stopped caring for you, you know."

"I never stopped caring for you. I never stopped loving you."

That brought me up short. What little there remained of my "ordered universe" was now obliterated. "I love you," I stammered. Then, suddenly, I felt compelled to come clean with her, to continue this conversation with total transparency. "I tried to have something with someone else—you know, a sexual relationship. It didn't work out at all."

"Yeah, and I slept with David, the guy you saw me with that day," she said, hurriedly.

This was like the clean slash of a finely-sharpened blade, one of those cuts that you look at and think this is gonna hurt like hell later; but for the moment, it's as if your nerves haven't figured out what's happened yet. I quickly stowed my reactions away. *Bleed over it some other time, man!*

Janie seemed equally intent on moving forward. "So what do you think?" she ventured, in a small voice.

Ah, another question without an answer. Whoever believed that the gods lacked a sense of humor had obviously never witnessed the bizarre twists and turns of my life. "I think I've got until tomorrow afternoon before I fly back east."

"What? You're here?"

This time I chuckled aloud. God, I'd missed her fire. "I came because Saul asked me to. I thought it was because June had died. Turns out she's very much alive...more so than most people are, probably."

"Yeah," Janie said, almost in a whisper. "Seeing her, watching her transformation...that's what set me to reconsidering everything, weighing what's really important in life. How I don't want to let fear decide my courses anymore."

If working with Saul helped you to come to those realizations, I thought, *then I owe him my life twice over, for real.* "So then, what do you think, Janie McCabe?"

In her sigh, I heard the full weight of all the disappointments, regrets, and wounds that she'd nurtured throughout that "lost time" during which we hadn't communicated much—the time during which I could only guess at the turmoil that might have been churning about within the heart and soul of the woman I loved. "I think," she enunciated, "that I am not going to make the same idiot mistake with you twice in this life, Brandon Chane. You get your ass over here, OK?"

PAINT A NEW PICTURE

Those of you who've experienced it won't need me to describe the keen joys of makeup sex. When heart and desire get chugging at full throttle together, all while you're moving in harmony with one another, it's a sensation that can whisk you clear off the face of whatever world you'd previously been rooted to.

Janie wasted no time at all. Her mouth found mine before I'd even made it through the doorway. I guess we both figured there'd be time enough to talk and play catch-up later. Her eyes were full of promises and apologies. I imagine mine were too. But we both knew that we were forgiven anyway, come what may.

Love scares us all because of its ferocious power. Maybe Janie had run in response to both of our fears, me just being silently complicit and therefore appearing like the victim of the whole thing. Saul always insisted that it takes two. If there are no accidents, then this means that, in the wider scheme of things, there really are no victims.

We didn't talk for a long time afterwards, though our eyes communicated much. Janie was still in the same apartment that the hippie couple had painted in sunburst colors and vibrant slogans. Her bed was low, scarcely raised above the ground, 'cause that's how she liked it. Close to the Earth this woman, in all ways.

"Does it just feel like we travel someplace else when we're together like this," she whispered, into the pristine silence of pre-dawn, "or do we really go?"

I smiled. It was a pure lover's moment, you know? Only she would ever have asked me a question like that, and only I could have ever known what she meant. "Paint a new picture on the inside," quoth I, "and you step right out of one world and into another. That's what Saul says."

She hugged me hard. "I'm so grateful that he helped me to see, to know, that I was listening to the wrong voice."

"Me too," I breathed, giving her ear a little nibble for emphasis.

❖

I got to experience my blissful epiphany twice, as it turned out. Somehow, during my brief period of sleep, I forgot where I was, and about trials overcome and barriers dissolved. I hadn't intended to sleep in the first place, honestly. I didn't want to miss one moment of Janie's breathing, of her warmth, her hair, her scent, her skin. But contentment wields a powerful pull over a weary body and soul. And so it was that I awoke not knowing where I was—not recalling, at first, that my heart's long grief had been annealed.

Then I heard Janie's voice coming from the kitchen. "Pleeease, Krystal! I just patched things up with Brandon after a really painful time apart and he leaves again tonight! What? No, of course it's not your fault. I'm just sayin'… Oh, thank you! Thank you! Anything you want covered, morning or afternoon shift…I will make this up to you!"

She came back into the room dressed only in a long white T-shirt with some kind of pretty "tree of life" design emblazoned across the chest. She looked relieved. "Called in to work?" I asked with a grin.

"I found somebody to cover for me, yeah. Otherwise I would've had to leave, like, now."

"You didn't have to do that, you know."

"Yes, I did." She walked over and knelt on the edge of the bed. She swiped my forehead gently with the back of her hand like a nurse from olden times checking my temperature.

"We need this day," she declared, in a voice that almost dared me to contradict her. "Now, tell me about your tour. I want to hear everything." She wagged a finger at me. "No leaving things out because of your false modesty. I want to know about all the awesomeness."

I knew that her interest was sincere, but also that this served as a means of steering away from the subject of her and how she'd filled her life in the time that we'd been apart. I didn't want that specter casting a shadow over us. I decided to confront it. "Tell me this first: do you have to break things off with David, now?"

Janie, true to her new commitment not to shrink in the face of fear, answered at once. "It ended about a month ago, actually. He knew that I had feelings for you, that all my talk of moving forward was just a brave charade. I have to give him credit for that."

"Pretty chivalrous, really, to be so understanding," I marveled.

"OK," Janie said, rising. "Now that that's over with, I'll go make coffee. Then, in return, you give me the whole odyssey."

The wafting scent of the strong brew somehow reminded me that this was all real. *Wake up and smell the coffee*, indeed. For once, I was awake in a sweet dream rather than asleep in one. Gratefully, I accepted her mug—white, with a picture of an orange cat and a funny caption—and smiled.

Even though the story came to such a lackluster conclusion, I discovered that I was filled with such plentitude that I didn't mind relating it. I delivered the details, beginning with Chas and all his plans for us. I described our two interviews and our race across America. Like many periods of trial and travail in my life, it all seemed more heroic—and less arduous—in the telling. Hindsight has a way of highlighting the secret luminosity behind events, the unnameable quality that lends nostalgia its keen ache.

I even tried recalling everything that I'd said onstage at the gigs, because I knew Janie enjoyed hearing that kind of stuff. I got on such a roll that by the time I finished my narrative I realized I'd hardly touched my coffee. When I tasted it, it was lukewarm.

"Well," Janie surmised, "we're obviously gonna have to get you a new guitar."

I pulled her down beside me, wrestled her into a bear hug while she pretended to struggle and then surrender. "What do you mean, hon? I'm completely broke. And you should see Maureen. She looks after us like a mother hen to her chicks. If there was even the remote possibility that she could've afforded it, she would've offered right away. And Chas already parted with all the petty cash he had on hand to send us cross country."

"I have it," Janie whispered. "I've been saving practically the whole time I've been at the jewelry shop. Nearly three years now. And if it's used, or a decent copy, I can swing it no problem."

My smile dissolved. "Oh, I can't let you do that!"

She wiggled around to face me, and I was treated to the tigress smile of hers that I'd so sorely missed. "Excuse me? You are my lover, Mister Chane. You are not my master!"

"It's a lot of money...you should use it for something really important, for yourself."

"And maybe helping the man I love to pursue his dream," she said, "and not only that, but to fulfill the thing that this world needs for him to do, too, is the most important thing that I can think of at the moment.... Besides, I seem to recall you shelling a few hundred out on a plane ticket for me, once."

I finally found what I thought was a potent protest. "I owed you that, as far as I'm concerned."

Janie's eyes had flecks of sorrow dancing amidst the resolve, now. "I think I owe you one, this time."

I discovered a Les Paul copy at a local pawnshop. Janie tried to talk me into shopping around before settling upon anything, but I fell in love with this guitar as soon as I pulled it down from its peg and started playing. It had a real solid, dependable feel against my hip—easy action. I even liked its curves and blood-orange swirl. A more jagged flying-V might have better served the original incarnation of Edge of the Known.... But much had changed since then.

"I am paying you back for this," I told Janie as we approached the counter.

She didn't answer, but instead just insisted that we get a case for it as well. This all comes along with one getting involved with a spirited lass. Recognizing this fact, I swallowed my protests.

"So you think she'll do you justice for the big showcase?" Janie asked, as we stepped out onto the afternoon's sunlit sidewalk.

I just stared back at her, momentarily shoved out of the seat of reason.

Janie made a ludicrous face when she realized how caught off guard I really was. "You did realize that this was half the reason we were making the trip out here today, right?"

"Ah, hell…I told you, we had to cancel that along with the other gig, the one in Vermont."

"But it hasn't passed yet, right?" Janie argued. "You said it was early next week. Maybe Maureen can still get you guys on the bill."

I smiled, trying to convey my appreciation for all her support, but I imagine that it probably came out all askew. "It's not just the gig itself," I explained. "She and Chas had also convinced artist and repertoire people from two different record labels to come see it—specifically, to see us. That's why we've been calling it the 'Showcase.' God, Janie…it really doesn't matter. I told you once already, how I realized that if I could just feed myself and pay rent off of this band then I'd be happy. I don't need to be on a big label."

"I understand that you're probably not motivated by the money you could make," she acknowledged. "But think of all the people you could reach."

I hesitated. Perhaps I'd never explored my own feelings in that area to the extent that I could take a stance one way or the other.

"Call her!" Janie insisted, glancing down at my pocket where my phone was sheltered. "There might still be time."

I couldn't repress my grin. I shook my head. "So is this 'have your way day?'"

Janie matched me sass for sass. "You do this one little thing for me, and then we go back to the apartment and you can have your way!"

"Imp, imp, imp!"

"Who knows," she persisted. "It could end up being a repeat of last night."

"Alright, I'm calling!" And I made a dramatic display of fishing that phone out as frantically as I could.

I caught Maureen just as she was sitting down for coffee, in her home in Boston, with Tommy and Carlos. She probed me delicately at first. "How are you?"

"Oh, I'm good."

"Really?"

I suddenly realized that we inhabited fundamentally different universes. I wasn't sure how to bridge that gulf—leastways, not in brief. "Umm…yeah, I'll have to explain it all to you later. But June is alive and very well, and I'm standing here with Janie and with a new guitar in my hand."

"O…K…" For a moment, Maureen sounded like she was questioning my sanity. But, being an empathetic soul with a business head, she was capable of navigating the most unexpected waters. "I can't wait to hear it. Sounds like one hell of a story. So, you're booked to come back late tonight, right?"

"Yeah. But listen—" Now that the moment had come, I wasn't sure how to broach things. *Just stumble through and don't think about it.* "Uh…is there any possible way we could still do the gig in New York? That we could get the same people to come out to it?"

"You know…" Maureen laughed in a way that told me she was embarrassed. "OK, I actually never told anybody that you guys weren't coming. Oh, God— you're gonna think I'm such a flake! I get these little nudges inside, and I've learned to trust them. Crazy as this sounds, Brandon, I just had the feeling that, despite everything that's gone wrong, somehow you'd still end up playing there. And Carlos seconded the notion." She laughed again, but it sounded much lighter—less laden with self-doubt—this time. "I've actually been waiting for a call from you with, like, bated breath."

"God, Maureen, you're a genius!" From the way that Janie started grinning beside me, I assumed that she'd grasped the essence of this exchange. "I could hug you. That little voice knows more than the brain could ever compute in a hundred years. You're wise to trust it."

"Oh, alright!" Maureen sounded relieved. "I thought maybe you'd call me crazy! Yay! We're doing the gig! Unless, of course…I've got you on speaker phone, Brandon, if you want to put it to a vote with your bandmates," she finished, teasingly.

"Speaker phone, eh? Hey Carlos!"

A moment later I heard him. "Right here, bro."

"You're busted! You knew about it. You knew what I was flying back to discover." I hoped that my essential good humor would carry over the line.

His reply set me at ease. "You were strugglin' to believe. You had been for a while. When Saul asked me what I thought about it, I just said that the best thing for you would be to see June with your own eyes."

"You're like a brother to me!" I called over. "You too, Tommy! I'll see you guys tonight!"

❖

Under other circumstances, parting with Janie like this—even while the sweet scent of our reconciliation still lingered—would have strained my heart to the bursting point. But I had walked with June and witnessed her resurrection. A love-borne state of quiet ecstasy was stealthily awakening in me. There were "rules" that had once banished the realm of the miraculous, of the magical, from my mental and spiritual domain. Now those rules had been crucially undermined. Oh, yes, the possibilities were truly unfathomable. We're fools to ever think otherwise. My brain lacked the fingers to grasp it all, but my heart had resolved its last lingering doubts.

Life was sacred. No longer was this conjecture, or poetic fancy, or empirical deduction. I felt it with the kind of certainty that held me aloft with such buoyancy. It was as if my body sought its soul-marriage in the kingdom of high winds. Every glance and kiss and breeze and bereavement was sacred. The other place existed as verily as this one; perhaps it was "more real." And that fact sustained me.

In the midst of all these buffeting winds, Janie and I decided that we would be together. If it was my destiny not to return, then she would rejoin me in Boston. Our love was not going to conform to the dictates of the world. Rather, those other circumstances would have to adapt to our shared journey.

She saw me off at the gate that night, dressed all in earthy browns. Janie had a light amber complexion, so the color suited her. Her loose-fitting leggings were made from a kind of material that I couldn't identify. But it looked so silky-furry that I imagined it'd be much like petting a deer, running my hands across it. I regretted that this was neither the time nor the place to try the experiment. A strip of yellow twine served as a belt. Over her skirt she wore a shawl of light-colored leather, with fringe that splayed over her breasts and shoulders. My indigenous princess. My heart throbbed like a stubbed toe. Sensing my tangled emotions, Janie leaned in to kiss me.

"I'm sorry I can't be there for the big gig," she said. Then, acting on sudden impulse, she began undoing her makeshift belt. "These stay up just fine without it," she remarked. Once she had the twine loose, she started wrapping it around my right arm, over the bicep. Finally, she fastened it tight. "There. Now you can be like one of those knights of old who'd ride into a joust or battle in full armor, bearing a lady's brooch."

Her smile, and the unabashed affection in her eyes, nearly made me weep. "I love you with everything in me, Janie. You will be there."

It was scarcely a whisper. And she didn't answer, probably because the lack of any need to respond was the truest testament to what lay between us. I had to go. The stage was calling me back, for one more round—the final campaign in this war. And there was nothing more to say. I hugged her quick and hard.

Every life seems to have its definitive beginning and ending points. That's how we learn to frame it all in our minds. Most children are a lot looser in this regard, though. You can hear some of them talk about the world that they came from, not so long ago. They'll play at being orphans in order to grapple with a deeper sense of inarticulate loss. And when they pretend to be parents, or elderly people, it isn't mere imitation. Perhaps their knowledge is culled as much from the future as it is from the past? For they understand, and take for granted, the elasticity of time.

June had, in many ways, reminded me of this child's view. My life suddenly appeared open-ended again; no longer was it a fixed narrative with "birth" and "death" as its bookends.

"The trick is to be awake for the moment," Saul had once told me. "When you do that, you step into an ocean that touches upon every shore on every world."

When I met Carlos, Tommy, and Maureen during the surreally late-night hour at the Boston airport, beneath the garish and artificial white glow, I tried to somehow convey this state of "silent knowing" that I'd stumbled upon. Fortunately for me, the two guys were already accustomed to my occasional blazes of right-brained madness. And Maureen was learning fast. They took turns filtering my elliptical epiphanies and translating them into their own personal brand of philosophy or metaphysics. It just made me acutely aware of my deep love for each one of them. Realizations of this sort are highly personal: they should never be proclaimed as The Truth, with a capital "T," for all.

"Wow. She beat cancer," Maureen marveled. Then she looked at Carlos. "And you knew about this?"

"Saul called me right before we played in Montpelier, the night Brandon destroyed his other guitar," he said.

I just drifted along, my mind in a free-floating space. My thoughts could not attach themselves to facts, certainties, or expectations. I learned to just appreciate my questions without demanding that they produce answers. And I came to discover that the deeper region of knowing carries its own form of certainty. It just isn't arrived at through deduction.

I suppose you could compare it to the phenomenon that sportsmen remark about sometimes: just knowing that you're going to sink a basket, or bowl a strike, before the ball even leaves your hand. It's as if the essential thing, the miracle, has already manifested. It just needs to play itself out in the field of time.

That's how it was when we played Broomstick Belladonna's a couple days later.

A month or so earlier, I'd been nervous about this gig. So much hung upon it. But my brief interaction with Saul's wife, the woman who had reversed her own self-created death sentence, had granted me a glimpse of what lies on the other side of this life. And from that place…

There was nothing to fear.

There is never anything to fear.

And I saw how fear had always lain beneath my anger, my perceived need to prove myself, my violent outbursts. Releasing fear—at least for the moment—I simultaneously relinquished the thoughts and emotions that had always upheld it.

For the first time in my life, I climbed onstage and played for nothing other than my sheer love of it.

The World is Our Mirror

"New York!" Tommy intoned. "Let us now create a space wherein our souls may breathe!"

And so it began: an extreme band like ours, with one front man with a penchant for openers like that. I suppose playing in Edge of the Known was similar to being a professional comedian in that regard. There were times when I thought half of Tommy's job involved just being able to keep a straight face.

When we finished rousing the club with the sheer bombast of his "Stone Soul Etchings," we segued into a newer thing of mine. I had, in fact, just written it since returning to the East Coast, in the wake of what some people may refer to as a spiritual awakening. This night marked the third time that we'd ever played it together as a band.

I'd just been trying to arrive at the essence, the thing that I somehow knew I hadn't understood before, the inner recognition and awakening that made life lighter and yet infinitely more precious, both at once.

I called the piece "The Jaws of Time."

Life's infancy, and the echo,
through our weary days remains
But you were well worth a
lifetime's quest to reclaim

My guitar parts in this song never resolved themselves into any recognizable riffs or progressions. I'd shown Tommy a baseline: probably not the most exciting thing in the world for him to play, as it was simple, repetitive, and hypnotic. But sometimes the simple part is the right part. I wanted the song to rol-l-l-llll like a waterfall, endlessly. Over the languid groove that Tommy and Carlos laid, I painted with aural color—a shimmering minor chord here, some ghostly arpeggios there, sometimes just a single haunted note bent and sustained to the point of fraying.

> Like hounds, we hunt only
> after a sniff of your meat
> Or else, blind fools, we race
> up and down illusory streets

> Relishing what rapture we can
> snatch from the jaws of time
> All is born from our minds: both the cliff and
> the thrill of the climb

It was almost jazzy in its unexpected deployment, its lack of identifiable structure…something dredged up from the deep swamps where the reptiles croak melodies as old as Earth itself and the birds overhead respond with calls that are the promises of Eternity.

> Like hounds, we hunt only
> after a sniff of your meat
> Or else, blind fools, we race
> up and down illusory streets

> Womb of the soul that
> can't be taught to kneel
> Remind us of what the child knew:
> The faith that makes illusion real

That was the crucial paradox. The world was, in some sense, illusion, and yet it was utterly real and dear to me. June had brought herself back from the brink of death, and yet June could never really die. And I looked out, once the last chords of the song resolved in evanescence. I beheld this gathering of souls, at our agreed upon meeting place of illusion and truth: Broomstick Belladonna's.

It had a high stage, one that was level with my chest when I stood on the stone floor. That floor was bulging now with bodies and perspiration and collective need. What little breathing room there'd been had been consumed halfway through our first song. The darkness was apt for the journey we were embarking upon. And our high vantage lent us the kind of remote mystique that we'd once sought—misguidedly, perhaps—behind our liquid light show.

I'd enjoyed the previous band, Sendaline, and had made a mental note to meet the guys after the performance. Maybe they were somewhere out there in that milling mass. Supposedly an A & R guy from Phantom Hordes was there, as well as another from Widowed Soul Records. I could scarcely see the bar, off on the left-hand side. The overhead televisions in that anteroom area had been turned off, as no one was paying attention to them.

It's almost as if I thought that I owed the audience an explanation for the song, even though music should never be explained. But I figured that the story of June Mason was something that the world should know, because it was essentially everyone's story.

My voice ventured out into that dense and expectant darkness. "I used to have these fears, man, that someday someone would find out about the things that were living inside my head and then that'd be it: a cell somewhere, maybe a padded one, to the end of my days."

There were some cheers in response to this. Maybe they thought it was a planned part of the "evening's entertainment." But hell, even I didn't know where I was going with this. I'd just passed through experiences that had shaken my existential certainty to its foundations.

"Thing is, I'd made my own life a kind of prison—and so what did it matter whether or not there were actual physical bars there in front of me? I'd accepted the cell already. It was home. I thought it was the full tale of the world."

Then, just as I was faltering, Carlos produced some heavy punctuation behind me as if to say, *Keep going, bro! Let it out!* I grinned, then masked it and soldiered on. "I just flew out here for this gig a couple of days ago. There wasn't nothin' to do on the six-hour flight but read the paper. That's not something I normally do, and while some people will say, 'Dude, you gotta stay aware of what's happening in the world,' I always figured that if you spend too much time making yourself aware of horrible things, things you feel you have no power over, then you're bound to drive yourself fucking insane sooner or later.

"So basically, I'm kind of a dim bulb when it comes to world events. And for that reason, I probably can't give you a lot of accurate details about what I read. Maybe it's all old news to you anyway. But I think I can summarize it pretty well. Many thousands of people were gunned down or otherwise killed. And many times, that many starved, or died from illnesses that could've been prevented. It's always the same with me, man. I read stuff like that and I immediately wonder what the significance of my own life is. I'm one out of several billion, you know? What do my thoughts, feelings, and choices matter, one way or the other?"

More musical encouragement arose, this time from Tommy: an echo of the hypnotic thrum of "Jaws of Time." I silently thanked and blessed my bandmates.

I started following the cadences of this impromptu music. "See, but I'd just gotten back from visiting a woman who we were all sure wasn't gonna make it. She had an illness that, supposedly, you don't recover from. But she did recover. And it wasn't because of any drug or miracle of modern science, either. It was because she understood that her life was hers, that it's her creation. The power was hers, hers to choose: illness or health, life or death. And if not for her, I wouldn't be standing here telling you all this. It's all connected, see. We're all connected. And there really isn't a world that exists outside yourself to begin with. Think about that the next time you question your own worthiness for life. 'You were born into the time and place where your voice would be needed,' as my friend Saul says. Everything you experience is your mirror. The whole goddamn world depends on who you are!"

Carlos started pounding out a beat then, responding to something that the three of us up on that stage all knew: it was now time to rock hard. We did so without apology or restraint.

The finale, which came maybe a half hour later, took the form of several minutes of frenzied inspiration. I couldn't help but grin as I heard the manic propulsion issuing from behind me. Carlos had no doubt weathered his own death and rebirth over these last few months, a process that I, sadly, had been too embroiled in my own personal struggles to fully notice or respond to.

I tried to make it up to him in the groove. He was like a wide receiver who, having caught the long pass and sailed past the goal line, proceeds to run up the bleachers, hurl himself from the top of the stadium walls and then land in a somersault to sprint off into the sunset. At this point, his cymbals sizzled, faded away, and we were left with no doubts that he'd said the absolute last word on the matter.

Afterwards, I relinquished myself to one of my favorite places on any stage: the shadow of Tommy's tall amplifier. I'd first met Janie in a comparable position. The gods could ask no more of me, or anyone. I was exhausted and sated in equal measure. I grazed my hand across Janie's strip of twine and mused, "What did you think of that, sweetheart?"

As if by way of delivering the Universe's reply, Maureen stopped a few feet in front of me. I recognized her shoes. I looked up to meet the beaming—and tear-wet—face of a proud mother. "Tommy and Carlos are now caught having to schmooze," she said. "I tried my best to draw the attention. You probably made a wise choice, hiding out here." Then her eyes smoldered. "Look, I have no real control over what happens from this point forward, as you know," she said. "But I will make you this promise: if that performance you just gave didn't earn you guys a contract, I will quit this goddamn business!"

I regarded this woman, who had done everything she could to succor and encourage me through one of the most trying months of my life, for a moment longer. Then I realized that I'd absolutely had enough intensity for one day. This thing had to be diffused.

"Maureen...you're stoned!"

❖

Sometime later, after Mike Makand and Nobody's Business began tearing up the club with their brand of heavy blues, I was able to pull away from the social circle of "industry insiders," musicians and patrons who continually offered us drinks and lofty praise. I stood on the sidewalk outside as the daunting skyscrapers hovered overhead, reminding me of my mortality. And yet my world was as vast— and some parts of it seemed still as remote—as the one that surrounded me. I fought the sweeping sense of insignificance by reminding myself of my own earlier "sermon" onstage.

On impulse, I retrieved my cellphone and dialed the Friedmans' number. I was hoping the change in time zones would save me. It wasn't quite nine p.m. where Rachel was....

Gail answered at once, catching me off guard. I said hello in stumbling fashion and, as humbly as I could manage without sounding phony, asked if I could talk to my little sis.

"It is her bath time," Gail said, "but I guess it's OK."

There was that undercurrent of affection in her voice, of respect, that had but newly grown up in the spaces between us. I felt so grateful for old animosities dissolved, for this newly emerging human warmth, that I tilted my head up towards the light-obscured sky and mouthed a prayer of thanks. Not that I believed in "somebody up there," per se, but...I guess some mental habits are tenacious.

"Hello?" Rachel was always informed of who was calling, and yet she consistently answered as if she had no idea.

"Hey kiddo!"

"Brandon! Where are you?"

"We just played our last show of this tour," I said. "I'm in New York City. It's way huger even than Sadenport. Anyway, it went really well. Afterwards, we met some guys from two different record labels. They wanna wine and dine us. You know, take us out to dinner and talk business."

I could hear her tasting the foreign word. "What are labels?"

I laughed for the sheer joy of connecting with her. "Oh, that's a word for a record company. I guess 'cause their label goes on every CD that they print up. Kinda like it is with cereal boxes."

Rachel's mind leapt from there straight to the gold. "So does that mean that you and Tommy and Carlos are gonna be famous?"

My smile was a little bittersweet this time. Perhaps I caught a glimpse then of what lay ahead, the twists and turns that were to dwarf all of my previous conceptions of craziness. And as naïve as Rachel may have sounded, I had to admit that my own thinking had not been so far removed from that, not so long ago.

"It may not mean much at all," I said. "But what ideally happens is that a record company gets your music out to all the people out there who really want to hear it. It helps the music to reach them. Doesn't always work out that way, but that's what you hope for. We'll have to do our part and put in a lot of work, too."

Following a period of silence, I risked a piece of myself in the space. "I'm actually a little nervous."

"How come?"

"Well…geez, how do I even describe it? If you make it big, then there's that risk that a lot of people will think that they love you, and for a lot of the wrong reasons."

I was still growing accustomed to her new tendency towards thoughtfulness—towards taking a moment, before speaking, for reflection. "But you don't have to change how you are for them," she said. "If people think of us a certain way, it doesn't mean we owe it to them to be the way they think. And besides, there's people who love you for real."

That nearly provoked tears. "I know." I gulped hard. "I've been really lucky with that. And I love you." Then I offered, "Hey, why don't you ask Gail and Ernie if I can tell you a goodnight story, like we used to do?"

"OK!" Her answer was brisk; and by the sound of things, she must've run right off immediately to do what I suggested. She returned mere minutes later.

"It's alright! I didn't play outside today because it was raining, so they said I could skip my bath."

"Alright, then," I said, over the hiss of traffic and the plod of pedestrians and the distant sirens. "I'll tell you about the girl who woke up one day to realize that she'd woven the whole world out of her dreams...."

❖

This was the story that I was always struggling to believe. There's times when I still do, I'll admit. Maybe I will—at least to some extent—to the end of my days. It may be that we really "graduate" from this schoolroom that we call life the moment we fully realize, without any lingering voices of doubt, that we were the authors of this dream all along.

In the meantime it seems that, ironically, both our joys and our sorrows stem directly from our forgetfulness, our ignorance of this crucial fact. And the tension between them—the longing for the one and the fear of the other—creates the adventures that we call our lives. Without a doubt, that first kiss with Janie was a lot sweeter, after months of believing that I'd lost her forever, than it would have been without that sense of loss. And no doubt I wouldn't have felt such a fierce, piercing joy in beholding June if I hadn't mourned her beforehand.

It's the thing that I tried to express in song. It's the Divine Bait. We humans are like hounds of the hunt, in that respect. We'd never run if we weren't first offered that quick sniff of the celestial meat before it was all, seemingly, taken away.

CPSIA information can be obtained
at www.ICGtesting.com
Printed in the USA
BVHW080941221220
596004BV00001B/2